HEDGEROWS

HEDGEROWS

Their History and Wildlife

Richard and Nina Muir

Michael Joseph
London

First published in Great Britain by Michael Joseph Ltd
27 Wrights Lane, London W8 5TZ

British Library Cataloguing in Publication Data

Muir, Richard, *1943*–
   Hedgerows: their history and wildlife.
   1. Windbreaks, shelterbelts, etc.——
   Great Britain
   I. Title   II. Muir, Nina
   574.5′2643   SD409.5

ISBN 0-7181-2835-4

Printed in Great Britain by
Butler & Tanner Ltd, Frome and London

CONTENTS

To the memory of the late Captain Swing

INTRODUCTION

We should like to have written a celebration of hedgerows, but fear that this may be an epitaph. Each region of England and Wales has its own characteristic landscapes, and in a few of them, like the Fens or High Pennines, hedgerows are not a prominent feature of the scene. But if we explore the perception of England that is held by most members of the nation then we encounter visions of a gently rolling landscape, punctuated by cottage clusters, dappled with little woods and bound all around by hedgerows – a landscape seemingly caught in the leafy green mesh of a net cast by some celestial fisherman. This is a powerful vision, exploited by nationalists, advertisers, publishers and propagandists alike. Yet now, for reasons which are seldom convincing and sometimes corrupt, the fabric of good countryside is being unravelled. If we lose our setting we may lose ourselves – and develop a new, meaner, colourless personality, rooted only in concrete, plastic and the sterile soil of prairie fields.

In this book, Nina has explored the wildlife of the hedgerow while I have written about the history and taken the photographs. Hedgerows are a feature of the man-made landscape, but they have been colonised by a galaxy of plants and wildlife, most of which would find their natural homes in woods and woodland margins. Meanwhile, the hedgebanks and verges often exist as the last refuge of herbs and creatures evicted from the adjacent fields by changes in farming practices. While mentioning the traditional uses of some hedgerow resources, we have not written about the culinary aspects of the hedgerow. Frankly, we find the notion of well-brought-up ladies in Laura Ashley dresses rummaging around in hedges in search of food for free rather comical – and anyway the nuts, fungi and berries are best left for the wild creatures that really need them. There is a long chapter which refutes the concept of hedgerow-dating, and, because it breaks some new ground and might seem controversial, a system of academic referencing is used here, and here alone. We have tapped a wide spectrum of published material, much of it of a specialised nature, and so a bibliography is provided at the end of the book.

I owe a special debt to Dr Tom Williamson of the University of East Anglia. When I lived in Cambridgeshire, Tom and I gave joint lectures on landscape history and devoted the hours of travel to long, animated conversations about the more mysterious aspects of our subject, with fields and hedgerows featuring prominently. Somewhere between Potton and Epping we may have solved the riddles – or perhaps we simply found that we agreed about almost everything. In any event, I know that some of the ideas expounded here were his, and have referenced them accordingly. Some are mine, but there are others of which the originator escapes my memory. But, since neither of us are territorial where ideas are concerned, this will not matter very much. We should also like to express our gratitude to John Herrington, Mac Cook, Andy Stokes of the Conservation Volunteers, Christopher Taylor and Dominic Powsland for the various kinds of help they have given.

Richard Muir
Nidderdale
September 1986

·1·

THE OLDEST HEDGEROWS

Farming in Britain has a history which extends back through time for up to seven thousand years, and we can be sure that fields of one kind or another must have a similarly impressive antiquity. But how old are hedgerows? Until recently such a question would have seemed unanswerable, but during the 1980s morsels of evidence have come to light which push the proven antiquity of hedgerows back into Roman times and beyond. We have not been alone in imagining that many Iron Age countrysides were patterned by a criss-cross tracery of hedges. At the same time, such a perception of ancient landscapes seemed virtually incapable of proof.

If we look at existing countrysides – or at least those that are still largely unspoilt – we see that in most lowland areas, where the rocks tend to be soft clays, sandstones or chalk or where the older geological strata are masked by thick sediments or glacial boulder clay, hedgerows are favoured as field boundaries. In the uplands, in contrast, tougher rocks are usually easily obtained, while exposure, thin soils or waterlogging militate against the vigorous growth of suitable trees and shrubs; in such places drystone walls are favoured. Even allowing for the factors of climatic change it is fairly safe to assume that similar distinctions between the hedged fields of the lowlands and the walled enclosures of the uplands existed in ancient times, even though most surviving field walls in Yorkshire and Northumberland and, perhaps, elsewhere, seem to be post-medieval in age.

Prehistoric field walls can be recognised at numerous places in the British Isles. The oldest so far discovered date right back to the New Stone Age or Neolithic period and were exposed by peat-stripping near the north coast of Co. Mayo. Dating from around 3000 BC, the network of drystone walls forms field patterns which do not strike the eye as being exceptionally archaic or unusual. Bronze Age field systems are quite numerous. On Dartmoor extensive networks of fields defined by stone walls or 'reaves' have been mapped, and field and paddock walls and the footings of circular stone-walled dwellings pattern the flanks of Rough Tor in Cornwall; near Land's End are banked Bronze Age fields which are still in use. The Dartmoor reaves are tumbled banks of rubble and stone which span vast areas of the moor and clearly reveal the organised patterns of land division and field boundaries which were created around 1600 BC. The investigation of the fascinating reaves network has been spearheaded by the archaeologist Andrew Fleming. In the 1985 edition of *Devon Archaeology* he writes: 'despite the dense packing of stones within reaves, recent observation of modern land boundaries in North Wales has convinced me that they could have carried hedges in the standard English sense of that word.' Walled fields of Iron Age or Romano-British date are displayed in a variety of upland settings, like Grassington and Malham in the Yorkshire Dales.

However, there is a crucial archaeological distinction between ancient field walls and ditches on the one hand and hedgerows on the other. Unless subjected to a drastic and deliberate campaign of removal or unusually active conditions of erosion or sedimentation, both walls and ditches will endure as detectable archaeological features. Hedges, as assemblages of living plants, are different. It is very likely that in a few localities prehistoric hedgerows still endure. But how can we recognise one? We do not know what such a hedgerow would look like. Would it be packed with different trees and shrubs or would one species have established its ascendancy over all competitors? Were we to search for long enough we would be able to find a hedge growing on an Iron Age field bank. But how could we tell that the bank had always been hedged? The hedge concerned might have grown or been planted on ground which had lost its original hedgerow or have existed as an unhedged bank for an indeterminable number of centuries. When a hedge dies its branches decay and eventually its roots will rot and disintegrate. With this in mind, it would have been reasonable to suppose that the riddle of the ancient hedgerows was archaeologically insoluble and, owing to the non-existence of any written records, a mystery for all time.

The first fields to be created in most British localities were clearings hacked out of the primeval wildwood. Such woods contained various animals, like red and roe deer and boar, which would seriously threaten the growing crops. And so it seems reasonable to suppose that efforts must have been made to secure the boundaries of cultivation against depredation by such robust herbivores. One theory, which is often presented but which seems to us to be highly improbable, suggests that during the removal of forest (either in ancient or historical times), rows of trees would be left unfelled and would be trained and managed as hedgerows during the cultivation of the land on either side. We do not know exactly what wildwood looked like, but it was probably a mixture of native deciduous trees – lime, oak, elm, ash, hazel and so on – of all sizes, conditions and ages. There would have been mature trees of massive girth, weedy seedlings and saplings and dead or decaying trees. Go into a wood which fits this description and you will see that size and spacing of the trees presents no credible opportunities so far as the making of hedge-lines is concerned.

So how did the pioneer lowland farmer of the Neolithic and Bronze Age periods defend his fields? The most effective solution would involve the construction of huge earthbank-and-ditch complexes similar to those which enclosed medieval deer parks – but such earthworks would probably have been too costly in the resources of time and labour to have been countenanced. The most likely device would have been a dead hedge. Most of the felled timber

ABOVE Hedgerows are a feature of lowland rather than upland Britain. In the Lake District they can occasionally be seen in sheltered valleys, like the Newlands Valley below Causey Pike (where the hedges are rich in blackthorn). BELOW On the northern flanks of the Brecon Beacons the climate is warmer than in the Lake District and the rich old hedgerows can flourish on higher ground.

would have been burned to enrich the modestly fertile woodland soil, but saplings and branches could have been saved and woven around earthfast posts to produce a tolerably effective though perishable perimeter.

Prehistoric farming was of the mixed type, and most good excavated sites reveal bones of cattle, sheep and pigs, remains of a wide variety of game and evidence of cultivated cereals like emmer wheat and eincorn. Stock would have browsed and foraged in the surviving woods, thus accelerating their destruction, but manure from grazing stock would also have been essential to fertilise the fallowing fields. In any system of mixed farming it is essential to exclude livestock from the growing crops, and as cultivation expanded the clearings would have been superseded by permanent networks of fields. It seems most credible that at this time, too, dead hedges would have been supplanted by living hedgerows. Dead hedges soon decay and are wasteful of material and labour, while the retreat of the wildwood and the demands on timber for construction and fuel would have urged a greater emphasis on the conservation of timber supplies. A living hedge, formed of young trees dug up in the forest, would need to be planted and then protected for a while against browsing – presumably by a dead hedge or a post-and-rail fence. But in return for the original effort it offered a permanent barrier plus the bonus of the crop of poles and brushwood which could be harvested every few years during hedgerow maintenance.

The making and laying of hedges does not demand a sophisticated tool kit. Antler picks would have been adequate for any digging work, axes of flint or bronze perfectly ample for the cutting and slashing tasks and the making of a hammer or 'mell' would have been easily accomplished. It is quite reasonable to suppose that prehistoric hedges were laid and would have resembled the few properly maintained hedges of today. Laying demands a large supply of living or dead posts (see Ch. 8) and the hedge itself can supply these. Trackways of poles and brushwood – alder, ash, oak and birch – were built across the sodden expanses of the Somerset Levels from Neolithic to Iron Age times and consumed prodigious amounts of pegs, poles and brushwood bundles. Managed coppices – and, perhaps, hedgerows – must have contributed the massive quantities of light timber required. Work on one of these tracks, the 6,000-year-old Sweet Track, led by Professor John Coles, suggests that most of the timber for the 1¼ mile (2 km) track was cut in one year and, amazingly, put in place in a single day.

The choice of field boundary defences was quite a wide one, for as well as walls or hedges the farmer might have considered earthbanks, ditches, fences or hurdles of woven branches. Even if an earthbank was not crowned by a planted hedgerow (the roots of which would help to bind the bank while the foliage would reduce erosion by heavy rain), it would soon acquire a 'spontaneous' hedge as seeds germinated and flourished atop the bank. Given that deciduous woodland is the natural vegetation of most of Britain, almost any ribbon of land that is not given over to ploughing and grazing will develop a hedgerow. In the rolling countrysides of Wessex and elsewhere, fossilised 'Celtic fields' of various (uncertain) Iron Age, Roman or even Bronze Age dates were familiar features of the scene until the modern blight of subsidies resulted in the

The relics of a Bronze Age 'reave' on Dartmoor, the tumbled wall (or hedgebank) running from the bottom to the top of the picture.

ploughing-up of the old downlands and heaths. Such fields are bounded by 'lynchets', step-like features produced by ploughing adjacent fields and the associated soil creep (downslope drift of surface soil) from the bare field. After several centuries of prehistoric ploughing the step up from the field below to the one just above could be several feet in height. We do not know whether the lynchets carried hedgerows, though hedges would certainly have helped to stabilise the soils and would have reduced the steady encroachment of upper fields onto lower fields.

On Overton Down in Wiltshire the excavation of a prehistoric field boundary revealed that posts had been placed at intervals of 4 ft (1.25 m). These post holes were not too widely spaced to rule out the possibility of posts inserted during hedge laying; the posts could have carried a rail fence, but there is also the possibility that they supported hurdles. Hurdles, made of cleft ash or hazel, or of withies or hazel woven into a framework of ash or hazel poles, are still made today, often for use as attractive garden fencing. In the medieval period hurdles were popular because they provided movable pens or fences, useful for controlling grazing on fallowing open ploughland. Hurdles have the advantage of portability but are not as durable as hedges and are much more costly to create.

The most impressive networks of prehistoric fields are not really visible from the ground but emerge as 'crop-marks' in aerial photographs. Where the geology is favourable and where later ploughing has not scraped away the last traces of ancient endeavour – as on the Bunter Sandstone of the Midlands and many other places – we can recognise that the networks of fields stretched unchecked for mile after mile. The lay-outs vary, but generally the fields were small and rectangular, forming chequerboard or brickwork patterns which were sometimes traversed by long parallel lanes, drifts or droves. We can still see these fields from above because the silts which accumulated in their boundary

ditches now support stronger crop growth, allowing the taller plants to cast discernible shadows on their neighbours. Field ditches are still common today, and apart from low, flat, ill-drained plains the ditch is usually flanked by a hedgerow. It seems far more likely than not that the ancient ditched fields would have been similarly hedged. Moreover, the air photographs frequently show that the ditch boundary patterns will suddenly come to an end for no obvious reason. What can be more likely than that in these voids the field patterns were defined by hedges alone, drainage ditches being deemed unnecessary on the land concerned?

One unsolved riddle posed by excavations and air photographs concerns 'pit alignments': chains of ancient pits of various quite early prehistoric dates which run across country for considerable distances and seem to mark boundaries. These rows of sizable holes might seem to be a rather bizarre and demanding way of marking out a boundary, and there is not a great deal of archaeological support for the notion that these pits were dug to accommodate lines of trees. But we would not yet wish to rule this out completely.

Thus far we have been dealing with probabilities and suppositions to advance our argument that prehistoric lowland countrysides were densely hedged. Had we been writing in 1980 rather than 1986, the story could have progressed no further. But the West Heslerton project, an archaeological programme aimed at the total analysis of an area in the Yorkshire Wolds, has revealed much of interest, including a prehistoric field ditch of the Iron Age; and the archaeologist Dominic Powsland has described how the remains of snails which frequent woods and hedgerows have been discovered along just one side of this ditch. The implication is obvious: that on this side of the ditch there ran a hedge.

As we have described, the problem of prehistoric hedgerows seemed to founder on the fact that, like most other organic materials, hedges will die and decay and eventually earthworm activity will disperse any chemical traces of the

LEFT AND BELOW One can only wonder whether these ancient Cornish fieldscapes, seen from the ramparts of Trencrom Iron Age hillfort, were not in existence when the fort was occupied.

former existence of roots. However, under very special peaty, waterlogged conditions fragile organic materials will survive – as demonstrated by the recovery of Iron Age corpses from peat bogs in Britain (one) and Europe (many), or the recovery of fragile Roman household materials from Vindolanda, beside Hadrian's Wall. In the early 1980s excavation was in progress at the Roman fort at Bar Hill on the Antonine Wall in Scotland. Work on building this fort began around AD 142 and a pre-existing system of ditches had to be filled in. This was accomplished using large turves and armfuls of brushwood, which were preserved and revealed by the excavators. The brushwood consisted of hawthorn branches which were two to six years old and were scarred and bent. While it might be argued that this damage had been caused by browsing, this is highly unlikely. The twigs had all the characteristics of brushwood from a cut and managed hedgerow. It is quite improbable that the hedge concerned was of a Roman-influenced origin; it was probably a small component in a native hedged countryside of the Scottish Iron Age where hedge management practices were well established.

Pollen grains are protected by very tough coats and will survive for thousands of years in damp, acidic conditions. (At Bar Hill the pollen evidence from the turves suggested a late Iron Age local landscape of scattered alder and hazel

These field patterns near Christow in Devon have not been dated, but we suspect that many countrysides in Devon looked much like this in the Iron Age.

woods which had retreated under the pressure of grazing, then with the expansion of heather as grazing became less intense.) Iron Age and Roman riverside settlements at Farmoor in Oxfordshire were explored by the archaeologists G. Lambrick and M. Robinson in the 1970s, and here the fossil plant and insect evidence seemed to describe a Roman countryside of fields surrounded by thorny hawthorn, briar and blackthorn hedges. Unfortunately these most popular hedging shrubs are insect pollinated and do not produce the clouds of pollen which might easily be detected in general excavations, while wind-blown pollen from other trees might tend to over-represent woodland in reconstructions of past landscapes. Excavations of various Roman villa or palace sites, like Fishbourne in West Sussex, have produced evidence of box, though of course the box was grown in formal garden hedges and not around fields.

For the first recorded mention of a hedgerow in the general vicinity of Britain we must go to Julius Caesar's description of *The Battle for Gaul*. In 57 BC Caesar was engaged in a battle with the Nervii in the territory of the Belgae, which spanned the modern Franco-Belgian borderlands. Although his narrative is largely concerned with military deeds, tactics and diplomacy, he provides a description of hedges which seems identical to the few well-laid ones seen in modern times: having hardly any cavalry of their own, the Nervii

> had to find a way of thwarting the cavalry forces of neighbouring tribes when they made plundering raids on them. They had succeeded in making hedges that were almost like walls, by cutting into saplings, bending them over, and intertwining thorns and brambles among the dense side branches that grew out. These hedges provided such protection that it was impossible to see through them, let alone penetrate them.

Caesar had clearly got himself in a difficult position, similar to that which the Allies faced in the bocage country of Normandy in 1944. The fact that he provides such a lucid description of the Belgic hedges might suggest that his Roman audience would be unfamiliar with the appearance of a 'bullock hedge'. But this is unlikely, since writers Columella and Palladius Rutilius, for example, described a complicated hedging method, and hedges *(vepres)* were common in Italy. Columella wrote in the first century BC that berries from sharp thorns, briars, holly and wild eglantine should be collected for sowing later in trenches. The seeds were mingled with meal and put on an old wet rope, which was dried and laid in a prepared furrow. The hedge must have had a long existence in the Classical lands before Columella's time, for he wrote of how the 'ancient authors' preferred living hedges to built fences because they were cheaper and more permanent. The Roman writer Cato advised the farmer to hedge his boundaries and roadsides with elm and poplar, producing leafy browse and timber. Pliny favoured elm, as did Varro, who also recommended tree lines of pine and cypresses; he quoted Scrota, who wrote of enclosure by hedging with living brush or thorn. The implication that such hedges were built to frustrate hostile cavalry is probably hearsay or intended to bolster Caesar's military reputation – his legions had probably only encountered some well-maintained farm hedges. Around the time when Caesar was writing, and for a century or two before, members of the Belgae were settling in southern and eastern England – and doubtless they applied their hedging skills there.

There is little evidence to suggest that Romans introduced the practice of 'centuriation' to Britain, though in other parts of the empire vast geometrical networks of fields were created. The most credible systems of Roman hedges are found running across almost all the non-marshland areas of the Dengie Peninsula and also in the countryside around Thurrock in Essex. The Dengie fields are rectangular and grouped in great blocks of commonly aligned fields and superficially resemble the Parliamentary Enclosure fieldscapes of the eighteenth and nineteenth centuries. Their straight boundaries show that the fields were a product of large-scale reorganisation and surveying, but very slight kinks occur where the surveyor encountered 'dead ground' which cut their field of vision. Archaeology is thus far unable to date the fields, but excavations at Asheldham church suggest that the fields are older than the late Saxon period, when the churchyard expanded across existing field boundaries. Interestingly, the Dengie field hedges are composed almost entirely of elm, although this does not prove that the peasants of Roman Essex planted elm hedges, for during the many centuries which followed elm could easily have invaded and displaced the other hedgerow shrubs.

The first conceivable known mention of a hedge in Britain occurs in *The Anglo-Saxon Chronicle* entry for AD 547 which mentions how Ida of Northumbria built Bamburgh. The original enclosure of Bamburgh, soon superseded by a rampart, could be translated as a hedge, a stockade or some other sort of barrier. In fact the distinction is probably insignificant since at this time the country was doubtless much more thickly hedged than today. As the historical record becomes progressively less skimpy, so the documented mentions of hedges increase.

Had we suggested just five years ago that it might be possible for a reader to reach out and pluck twigs and blossom from a prehistoric hedge, and had we written that the grandparents of thousands of East Anglians would have lived and worked amongst mile upon mile of prehistoric hedgerow, then all concerned would have reasonably concluded that the authors were off their trolleys. Dr Tom Williamson of the University of East Anglia is developing a technique of 'landscape stratigraphy'. As we all know, landscapes acquire different features at different times, so that, unless they fall into the grips of the barley barons, countrysides will display facets inherited from various different periods of the past. Many of these features can be dated, so that as one progressively strips away the younger elements it may be possible to recognise the historical foundations of scenery. Sometimes the antiquity of a particular component is uncertain, but can be determined by studying its relationship with other features. Imagine, for example, that the government should decide to direct a motorway straight through your town, or one nearby. In years to come

An enlargement of a Luftwaffe WW2 photograph of a small part of the surviving Roman hedged-field network on the Dengie Peninsula, Essex. (National Archives and Records Administration, Washington. Records of the Defence Intelligence Agency (RG 373) Photo no. GX 10358 SD 011.)

people will know that the town was there before the motorway, because the thoroughfare will slice straight across the alignments of the pre-existing streets.

Similarly, if a new road is superimposed upon an existing pattern of fields it will sit uneasily upon them. Field boundaries will be seen to be cut by the road and awkwardly shaped little enclosures will be stranded on either side of the highway. The reader can check this out by looking at maps of datable roads, like some new turnpikes of the eighteenth century. If a Roman road slices across a field network in this way, then the principle is still valid: the fields must be older than the road which cuts them. The archaeologists P. J. Drury and W. Rodwell found that this could be recognised in parts of Essex and other instances of this occurring were discovered by Dr Tom Williamson in the course of research on rural East Anglia. Despite the scourge of hedgerow removal, numerous fragments of the pre-Roman fieldscape survive in East Anglia, as at Yaxley in Suffolk, where a Roman road clearly cuts through four older square fields. Here the original fields had side lengths of around 655 ft (200 m) and are, or were until recently, hedged.

However, the most remarkable discovery so far involves the Tivershall and Scole area of south Norfolk, where the fields cut by a younger Roman road fill a vast area of around 15 square miles (40 sq. km). The pre-Roman fields were organised on a north-south alignment and divided into blocks by straightish, roughly parallel lanes or drifts which followed the grain of the field boundaries and ran approximately north-south: only a few features run continuously for

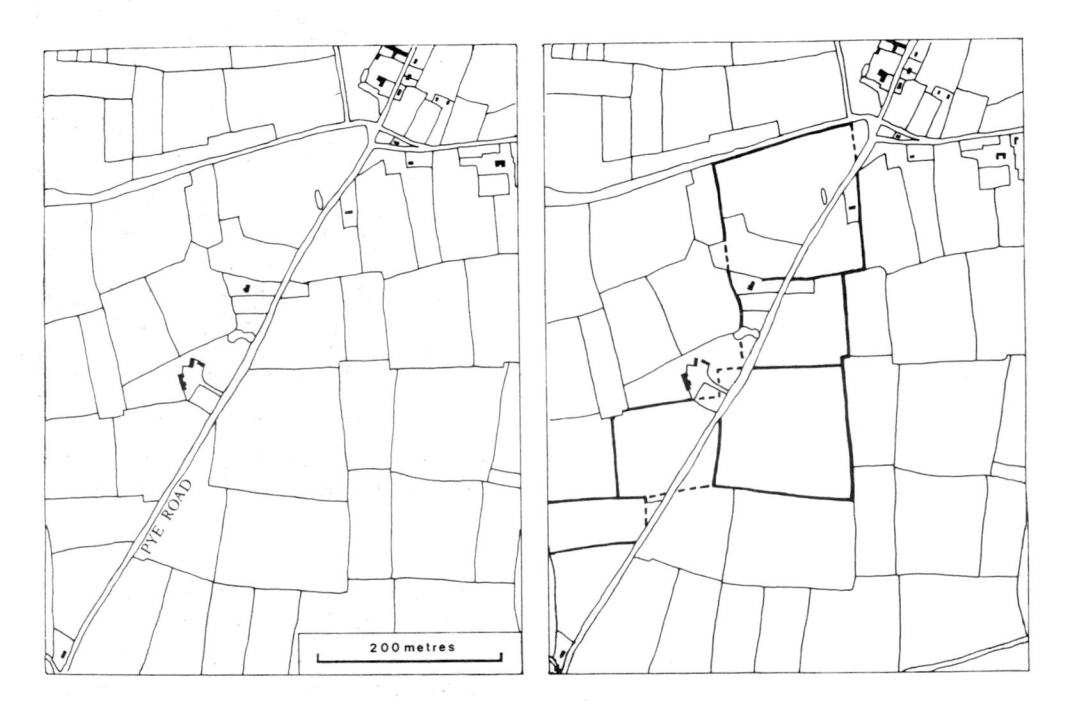

The Pye Road, a Roman road, superimposed on a pattern of older hedged fields at Yaxley, Suffolk. The fields were mapped on the Tithe Award map of 1839. (Tom Williamson, *Journal of Historical Geography, 12,* 3.)

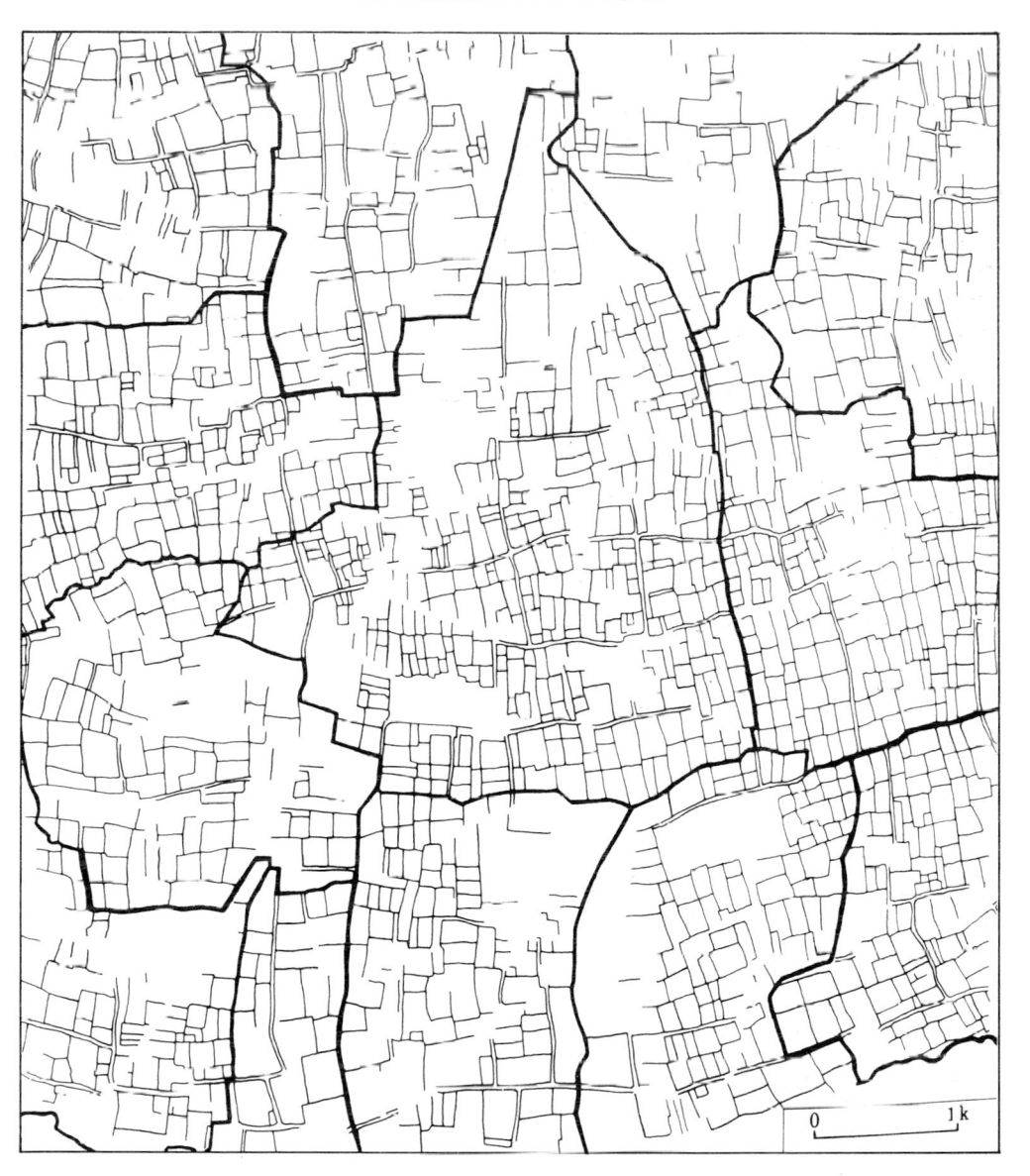

Ancient field patterns in south Norfolk. Note how the fields share the same alignment and seem to be set out in blocks divided by lanes or 'drifts'. Parish boundaries are shown in heavier lines. (T. Williamson, *Journal of Historical Geography, 12,* 3.)

any great distance east to west (the Roman Road itself runs NNE–SSW). The whole field mosaic might have been created long ago by someone as a great planned entity and inscribed on the countryside with considerable surveying skills. Since Roman roads were largely an early creation, built soon after the invasion, initially to facilitate the movement of troops, and were provided before the resources of native agriculture were efficiently martialled, there is no reason to suppose that the fields concerned have an early Roman date. They were a living part of the native farming landscape and quite likely of Iron Age date (though they do have uncanny affinities with fossil field systems dated to the Bronze Age, and this possibility is currently being explored).

Meanwhile, at Long Stratton in Norfolk, for example, Dr Williamson has recognised networks of hedge fields which take their alignment from a pre-existing Roman road. Also, in the Ilketshalls and South Elmham parishes in North Suffolk, others, notably Professor W. G. Hoskins, have noticed a 14-square-mile (35 sq. km) gridwork of fields which must have been planned and set out as a coherent whole. And, since land ownership here became fragmented during the Dark Ages, these hedged fields are probably of a Roman vintage.

The ancient fields of East Anglia do not provide much support for the hedgerow-dating theory, which is discussed at length in Ch. 5. The Norfolk examples passed through a long episode of open-field strip cultivation, most surviving with their boundaries intact, although one cannot know the extent of any hedgerow removal during this phase of their long life. The hedges of the planned Roman field networks which have been recognised in the Dengie Peninsula of Essex contain mixed species, but they are heavily affected by elm invasion which will drastically reduce the count of shrub species in the sections concerned.

These ancient East Anglian field systems survived the passing millennia virtually intact as a vast gridwork of hedged enclosures, and they were recorded on relatively recent maps. Many of the fields still endure within their hedgerows; some fell victims to the modern campaign of hedgerow destruction. When they removed their hedges many of the farmers here must have been aware of vandalising the countryside, but nobody can have known that a magnificent and gigantic prehistoric monument was being torn apart. Yet even had the knowledge existed one must doubt that the hedges would have been saved, the Ministry of Agriculture serving as little more than an annexe of the National Farmers' Union during the years of hedgerow destruction. It remains to be seen whether hedged prehistoric fields endure as living entities in places beyond the bounds of East Anglia, where the prospects for their survival might only be better. The Long Stratton and South Elmham field systems have recently been badly smashed up, though the best place to see impressive fragments of a pre-Roman field network is near Diss, in the Billingford area.

·2·

COUNTRYSIDES IN
THE MAKING

First, from the Trent where the thieves hang in the middle of barley ford meadow straight on to a spot five field strips before the stockade of Burton, from the strip to the stream, up the ridge to the boundary thorn, then to a ploughland then along a hedge to a brook, along the brook to a dyke . . .

This Saxon charter describes the boundaries of the grant, by King Aethelred II, of one and a half hides of land at Wetmore in Staffordshire to Abbot Wulfgeat of Burton Abbey in 1012. Such charters sometimes include similar descriptions of the boundaries of the lands involved, and the very frequent mentions of hedgerows indicate that lowland England was heavily hedged in Saxon times. The woodland historian, Oliver Rackham, has counted 372 mentions of hedges and 48 places named after hedges, and has estimated that hedges constitute 2.6 per cent of features mentioned in Saxon boundary descriptions.

The followers of hedgerow-dating (see Ch. 5) have tended to imply that the mention of a hedge in these charters constitutes a date for the *planting* of the hedge concerned. Such an idea is quite insupportable, tantamount to assuming that the hedges that one might see from a train were all planted yesterday. Indeed, occasionally the boundary narration actually draws attention to the antiquity of a hedge. Professor W. G. Hoskins has mentioned the case of a holloway flanked by hedgebanks in mid-Devon which was described as 'the old trench (or embankment)' in a charter of 976, and another 'old hedge' at North Wootton in Somerset was mentioned in 816. Unless they are deliberately removed, countryside features will persist, and may become more ancient than we ever imagine. For example, the meadow where the thieves hung near Burton in Saxon times is still known as Gallows Flat and some of the other landmarks mentioned in the charter are still recognisable.

The charter references to hedges are usually identified by one of two words: *haeg*, *hege* or *gehaeg*, an enclosure, and *haga*, a hedge or hedged enclosure. *Haeg* and *hege* give us our modern word 'hedge', and *haga* could just be a

southern dialect version: while 'hedgerow' was *hegeraewe*, with *raewe* alone sometimes denoting a hedge. The use of *haeg* may not always be sufficiently specific, so that the enclosure concerned may or may not have been hedged. For example, another of Aethelred's charters to Abbot Wulfgaet, of 1008, mentions bounds: 'from the great thorn [probably a hawthorn tree] to the *haeg stowe* . . . from the middle grove to the *scid haege* . . . to Wulfstan's *haege* and along *haeges* . . . to Leofnad's *dic haege* . . . from the [steep little?] hill to the *haeg stowe* to the deep pit . . .' The *haeg stowe* or 'hedge place' mentions could refer

This photograph, of an area near Luppitt in Devon, epitomises ancient countryside, with rich, winding hedgerows, hollowed lanes, small woods and scattered farmsteads.

to sheep enclosures or pens which might have been fenced; the *scid haege* seems to be an enclosure of split branches, perhaps hurdles or fencing; the *dic haege* is surrounded by a dyke, either a ditch or a bank; while the other *haeg* references probably relate to hedged fields.

Hedges quite commonly feature in place-names, like Thornhaugh ('thorn hedge'), formerly in Huntingdonshire, and some hedge place-names that once existed have been lost. In the thirteenth century, Marden in Herefordshire was known as Hendre Aghes, probably meaning 'old homestead hedged enclosure' and combining the Welsh *hendref* and the Old English *haga*.

With their references to features like badger setts, the place where the carts laden with barley would cross a stream, the great red oak and *witena leage* or the wood of the counsellors, such charters paint an enchanting picture of the Saxon countryside. And yet they do not deliberately attempt to inform us about the management and history of the landscape; they are legal documents and their authors doubtless assumed that any reader would be conversant with all the nuts and bolts of existing farming practice.

For too long and for no compelling reason the Saxon settlers were regarded as the architects of the countryside. In fact they seem to have arrived in dribs and drabs and were relatively unsophisticated in comparison to the native British. The countryside which they inherited – or rather, the countryside which inherited the language of this minority – was already an ancient one, and most of its fields, groves and hedges are likely to have been venerable when they were recorded in the Saxon documents. Some of the fields in Norfolk which are mentioned in the previous chapter must have been *at least* 1,900 years old when they were marked on maps in the nineteenth century, and they could have been much older still. And so it is not unreasonable to suppose that many of the fields farmed by Old English-speaking countryfolk were bounded by hedges planted in Roman, Iron Age and Bronze Age times (a hedge planted in the Later Bronze Age, say around 1000 BC, would only have been about 1,500 years old at the time of the Saxon settlement, and around 2,000 years old by the time of the Norman Conquest).

During the nineteenth century, when the English countryside had reached its glorious maturity and was still unsullied by hedge destruction and other blights, one could have walked through many passages of scenery, with deep, hedged lanes and small, hedged pastures, which would have looked very much as they did in Saxon, Roman and even Iron Age times. Sooner or later, however, one would have set foot in another type of scene, still an attractive one, but quite different in its ethos: here the neat young hedgerows trace out a geometrical pattern of rectangles and a plump village is never far away.

How did we come to inherit the two different types of countryside? Some of the answers can be gleaned from the works of Oliver Rackham and Tom Williamson, and some of what follows is based, to a certain degree, on a simplification of their ideas and research.

The Roman decision to invade and occupy Britain must have been influenced by the productivity of native British agriculture, particularly the bountiful grain harvest. The lowland countrysides were perhaps less wooded than today and covered with a patchwork of small, hedged fields, in many respects like those shown on the Norfolk map (on page 15). During the Roman occupation some new networks of rectangular hedged fields were created, but in general native agriculture, buoyed up by an insatiable demand for farm produce, was not generally transformed. Towards the end of the Roman period the excessive pressure to produce had resulted in extreme deforestation, soil exhaustion and severe erosion of the croplands. Following the collapse of Roman power there came a period of doom and gloom marked by environmental problems, political instability, economic collapse and sporadic warfare. These ills alone may not explain the severe decline in population which occurred; it is very possible that a sequence of terrible plagues erupted.

With the mortalities and the loss of incentives for commercial farm production the frontiers of agriculture must have contracted, as weeds, thorns and then woodland reclaimed many of the former fields. Hedges would gradually have merged into the young woodlands which appeared in many areas. (Incidentally, it is possible to recognise more recent examples of hedges engulfed by woodland in a number of places today. In the Weald, in Devon and in the Chilterns, where the woodland margins have tended to fluctuate or where hilltops have been afforested to provide game cover, this writer has recognised woodland holloways representing old lanes which are flanked by trees that are taller and older than those of the surrounding wood, and which have grown up from the hedgerows lining the old lanes; or, in Devon, beech hedgebanks fossilised within the woods.)

Hedgerows can be fossilised inside later woods. Here, on the Black Down Hills south of Taunton, a beech-planted hedgebank has been incorporated into a wood and the hedgerow beech have developed into large trees, which appear to be about 150 to 200 years old.

Very gradually a recovery set in, which was probably evident by about the eighth century, but not complete till about the thirteenth century. The Iron Age countryside had been divided into great estates, and new estates, with Romanised or Roman owners, would have been forged during the Roman occupation. In the course of the Dark Age troubles these estates became fragmented. Sometimes the disintegration progressed to produce numerous landholdings no bigger than a farm, though in other places fragments the size of a parish or larger survived.

Sometime around the ninth century a new system of open-field farming emerged, which was quite different from preceding patterns of farming. It involved the pooling of ploughland to create two, three or more huge open (i.e. hedge-free) fields, where each tenant had a number of widely scattered strips or 'lands' and rights to graze beasts on whichever field was lying fallow. Meadowland was also shared out among peasant-tenanted meadow strips or 'doles'. New, nucleated villages gradually coalesced at the heart of the ploughlands, although beyond the margins of arable farming old fields may have endured as hedged pastures, while an outlying expanse of common or waste usually completed the pattern.

The greater English (or Danish) landowners must have been very influential in advocating and enforcing the introduction of the new arrangement, but it might have been possible to implement such a scheme only if an estate was large enough to accommodate a set of open fields, a village-sized population, some meadow, pasture and waste. If the disintegration of estates had gone too far, then the old countryside would survive.

This sort of scenario may explain the distinction between 'ancient' or 'woodland' countryside on the one hand and 'planned' or 'champion' countryside on the other. In woodland countryside it was not possible to impose the great amalgamation and redistribution of tenant land which was needed to produce a fully fledged open-field system, the ownership of land having become too fragmented. Here, instead, old and ancient hedged fields survived. Land was held 'in severalty' with the numerous owners and tenants not moving into new, compact villages, but remaining dispersed among scattered hamlets and farmsteads, many of them standing on ancient settlement sites. Patches of woodland dappled the landscape, and though a few open-strip fields were created, these were small and shared between only a handful of households. The distinction between ancient or woodland and planned or champion country was recognised by sixteenth-century writers, like Thomas Tusser, but although woodland countryside contains small woods it really takes its name from the woodland products of its many old hedgerows. Tusser, an East Anglian, used the labels 'champion' – from the Latin *campus*, 'a field' – and 'severall', to distinguish between open-field country and other places where land was held in severalty, dispersed between many holders. Later the split personality of the rural scene may have been overlooked, though in 1955 Professor Hoskins recognised the contrasts between what he then termed 'ancient' and 'planned' countryside. In fact earlier generations had been well aware of the long-standing rural schizophrenia, and in Warwickshire peasants talked of the 'arden' (woodland) and 'fielden' (champion) countrysides.

ABOVE A characteristic expanse of planned countryside near Newland on Exmoor, in this case created by moorland enclosure using beech hedges. BELOW Several countrysides, like the Vale of York, consist of a complicated mixture of 'planned' and 'ancient' elements, each component recognisable by its straight-sided or irregular fields.

Ancient countryside can be found quite close to London, as in this locality near Saffron Walden, with deep, crooked hedge-girt lanes.

Woodland countryside endures in a number of parts of England and Wales, and where it is well preserved it is quite enchanting and redolent of antiquity. Winding lanes run in deeply hollowed troughs between high, shaggy hedgerows. Fields are small and defined by rich, curving hedges. Villages of any size are few, but there are plenty of hamlets, as well as the farmsteads, which often preserve the name of a medieval or pre-medieval occupant. There often were open-strip fields in woodland countryside, but they were small and scattered – a parish could contain up to twenty of them, dotted around amongst the woods and 'private' enclosures. Often they were fairly short-lived and then surrendered into the spreading hedgerow net. Such landscapes can be discovered on London's doorstep in parts of counties like Kent and Essex, in the Welsh Marches and Welsh lowlands, in the Chilterns and in parts of Devon and Norfolk.

In the English Midlands, however, planned or champion countrysides predominate. Here the extensive open fields might have been enclosed piecemeal before the eighteenth century, but frequently it was the Parliamentary Enclosures of the eighteenth and nineteenth centuries which partitioned the commons and the vast, unhedged common ploughlands to produce a neat gridwork of straight thorn hedges which were planned by the Enclosure surveyors. Here we have countrysides which focused on villages with Saxon or Norman pedigrees. Often the twentieth century has witnessed the ruthless removal of the hedges, but where planned countryside survives, the hedgerows, spinneys and shelterbelts provide havens to wildlife; and though the scenery lacks the natural curves and secretive aura of the ancient fieldscapes, it can still be most appealing.

If almost all the lowland English landscapes existed as ancient or woodland countryside until around the ninth century AD, the creation of open-field champion countrysides in the period between then and about the thirteenth century must have involved a massive onslaught of hedgerow and woodland removal. It has been argued that some pre-existing hedged fields may have endured in a new guise, becoming the 'furlong' or 'shott' divisions of the open fields (strips generally being grouped together in blocks or bundles to form the furlong divisions). In some places this may have happened, though recent evidence, mainly from East Yorkshire, suggests that the initial stage in the creation of 'text-book' open-field countryside involved the creation of peculiar 'long furlongs' and 'long strips', amazingly attenuated units, which could be hundreds of yards in length, and which would subsequently be subdivided to form the conventional strip and furlong patterns. But whatever the origins of medieval open-field farming, it can only have been established at the cost of countless thousands of miles of already ancient hedgerow. These changes will have favoured the birds and beasts of the field – the lark, corncrake, stone curlew, lapwing and hare – at the expense of the woodland songbirds and shy, furtive creatures of the wood and hedgerow. In the course of the medieval period, rising population and shortages of farmland intensified the assaults on woodland which had spread across the old Roman fieldscape, so that in woodland and champion areas alike, new hedged fields or 'assarts' were formed around the retreating woodland margins.

Although much is still to be learnt about the formation of our countrysides, it does seem clear that lowland England embraces two types of man-made scenery: the woodland, with its small fields and rich old hedges, and the planned, where the thorny gridwork of Parliamentary Enclosure is so often superimposed upon the former expanses of open ploughland. Both types of countryside were heavily hedged in times long ago. Dr Rackham's survey of Saxon charter boundaries show that hedges constituted 3.4 per cent of named features in what he terms ancient countryside and 1.8 per cent of features in his planned countryside. This variation could reflect the fact that the removal of hedgerows to create open fields was taking place at the time when Saxon charters were being granted, although the figures should not be taken too literally as no hedges are mentioned in Cornwall – which could have been so heavily hedged that charter mentions of hedgerows would only cause confusion.

·3·

THE MEDIEVAL HEDGEROWS

British agriculture has supported a public relations machine which most political parties should envy and which honest opponents of the destruction of the countryside have had good reason to fear. Anybody who believes that public relations is entirely about the dissemination of truth will soon end up with a house packed with junk and will vote for the party of the latest slick spokesman to appear on television. Since school-children are taught very little about the history of the countryside, organised misinformation can be very effective. Faced with mounting criticism of the removal of hedgerows, the story was put about that our hedgerows only date from the period of Parliamentary Enclosure, roughly 1750–1850. Nobody, it was argued, should therefore be too concerned about the removal of hedges, since they were a relatively modern feature of the landscape. Either the people who promulgated such stories knew them to be false or else they were so ignorant of landscape history as to be unworthy of a hearing.

In any event, a bird or animal living in the shelter of a hedge would not much care whether that hedge was 200 or 2,000 years old, but it would care very much when the bulldozer evicted it from its home.

Although perhaps around 200,000 miles of hedgerows were planted during the century or so of Enclosure, it was calculated by E. C. K. Gonner as long ago as 1911 that the Enclosure Acts affected and changed less than one fifth of the area of England. In this chapter we look at medieval hedges; if the public relations spokespersons of agri-business are correct then it will be an exceedingly short chapter, the subject-matter being virtually non-existent.

In both the woodland and the champion areas, field and and hedgerow patterns evolved during the Middle Ages. Woodland parishes and townships had inherited an old field-and-hedgerow pattern, with fields of a small size of around 4 acres (1.6 ha) being very common. The details of the pattern could evolve, with, for example, the planting of new hedges if inheritance or sale resulted in the division of a field. Meanwhile, the assaults on the woodland, mounting as population swelled in the decades preceding the arrival of the Black Death in 1348, resulted in the appearance of new hedged 'assarts' around the edges of the old farmed area: enclosed fields created mainly in the medieval period largely through the felling of woodland and enclosure of 'waste'.

Hedged assarts were also common in the champion areas, where ploughland and pasture could only be extended at the expense of woodland or heath. Generally such assarts were held privately rather than communally. However, in the open fields, the multitudes of strips were originally unhedged. Hedgerows usually followed the perimeters of the great open fields, securing them against animals which would graze on the growing crops, and also lining the roadsides wherever the routes across the fields were used for the movement of livestock. Old maps show that, at least by the seventeenth and eighteenth centuries, some furlongs were also hedged, while each village tended to become enmeshed by a cluster of small, hedged, privately held fields and paddocks. In the case of southern and Midland villages these were generally little, roughly rectangular 'closes', though the planned villages of the north, most of them apparently of Norman creation, had ribbon-like 'tofts' running back from the dwellings. Probably sooner rather than later, many of these acquired hedged boundaries. South Zeal on the northern edge of Dartmoor was a medieval borough founded in 1299 and it still preserves its hedged, 'toft-like' burgage plots. Thus we can picture the 'typical' hedge patterns of the champion parishes: long hedgerows bounding the vast open-strip fields, small hedged fields representing the peripheral assarts and a detailed mosaic of hedged paddocks and closes enmeshing the village. In the champion countrysides change could be more marked than in the conservative woodland regions. The early breakdown of communal farming might see the fragmentation of open-field land into a multitude of hedged fields; or the forced removal of village communities, which became an epidemic in Tudor times, could result in the appearance of large hedged sheep pastures.

There is no reason to doubt that most hedges were living hedges, though only very rarely do the authors of the old documents actually bother to point this out, as with the live hedge or *cwichege* mentioned in the very early charter of the eighth century of Beasfield in Kent. Dead hedges might be favoured as temporary barriers or to protect the vulnerable young saplings in a newly planted hedgerow from browsing. The most famous dead hedge is the 'Penny' or penance hedge which is still symbolically built at Whitby on the Eve of Ascension. Legend tells that in 1315 three noblemen pursued a wounded boar into the hermitage of a monk of Whitby Abbey. The monk tried to save the beast, but the huntsmen beat him with their spears. He forgave his assailants and his Abbot decreed that they and their successors should, as pain of forfeiture, yearly cut posts and rods in Strayhead Wood in Eskdale and build a dead hedge on the foreshore at Whitby, the hedge being strong enough to survive three tides. A dead hedge built in the Whitby manner would resemble a newly laid living hedge, with the cut rods being woven between earthfast posts, like living 'pleachers'. Such dead hedging can still be used today during the laying of gappy old hedges, the sections of dead hedge filling the gaps and protecting new plantings of hawthorn.

In his book *Hedgerow*, John T. White claims that Saxon hedges were dead hedges: 'Every year the hedge needs renewing. Pigs and cattle blunder into it, sheep tangle in it, the winter storms tear holes in it.' We find it hard to believe that the farmers of the Dark Ages had time and timber to waste restoring mile after mile of dead hedges each year when living ones offered a more practical and economic alternative. Even in the later and much more fully documented rural affairs of the Middle Ages unambiguous mentions of dead hedges are hard to find. E. Pollard, M. D. Hooper and N. W. Moore mention four possible cases of the repair or construction of dead hedges, but it is not clear whether the timber being taken and the work concerned was involved in dead hedging or the establishment or repair of living hedges. Perhaps the best of the examples concerns repairing two and a half perches of hedge on a Bedfordshire manor with cut thorns carried from a wood: had the hedge concerned been living it might have yielded its own thorns. Thus, in 1272: 'The Abbot and Convent [at Colchester] shall, at their own expense, cause a hedge to be planted lengthwise from the first gate up to the second, so that the place shall become a lane between the two gates . . . taking branches from the trees growing in the said hedge to maintain the hedge.' Dead hedging seems to have remained a current but secondary craft through into modern times, while in his *Book of Husbandry*, of 1523, John Fitzherbert advised his readers to protect a newly planted living hedge from browsing with cut thorns.

We are indebted for new information to the Surrey local historian, Philip Brooks, whose researches into Farnham Castle have revealed the use of dead hedging to form a defensive stockade around the fortress. Such hedging also appears to have provided an animal-proof barrier around the medieval new town of Farnham, which was set out around 1200. The contemporary accounts reveal the following uses of large quantities of cut thorn, which probably arrived by cart in bundles lashed with brambles:

1231 For enclosing 99½ perches round the castle by order of the Bishop 4s 0¾d.
      For 64 cart loads bringing in the enclosing material 32d.
1235 For 38 perches of thorns enclosing the bailey of the castle 19d.
1245 Thorns brought from the Park to make a *haya* from the new grange to the well and around the new garden in the bailey towards the inner bridge of the castle 14d. Carriage of thorns 2s 0d.
1246 72 perches enclosing around the bailey of the castle 7s 6d.
1252 For 66 perches of thorns put in front of the *jannia* of the castle 4s 9d.
      For 64 perches of thorns against the castle 5s 4d.
      Repair to the thorns against the inner bailey ditch of the castle 2s 4d.
1254 87 perches of hedge made against the ditch of the castle 5s 5d.

[The standard perch measures 16.5 feet (5.03 m) though the unit will have been more variable in medieval times]

Clearly the thorn stockades of Farnham Castle devoured prodigious amounts of thorn, time and expense.

Such military applications for dead hedges apart, living medieval hedges had a number of uses, some obvious and still current, but others of a former importance. They demarcated property boundaries; they divided the country-side into convenient field packages, adjusting stock to pasture and excluding them from crops; they provided animals with shelter from the wind, and they

Away from the areas of open-field farming, many medieval countrysides would have looked like this locality, near Honiton in Devon, with small, roughly rectangular hedged fields and with timber-yielding trees growing as standards or pollards above the hedgerows.

also provided copious supplies of useful timber, fruit and nuts, while valuable herbs could be gathered in the verges and the protected zone 'twixt hedge and ditch. The hedges thus provided fuel, light timber for hurdles, wattle, poles and many other uses, nutritious food and herbs for flavouring or medicinal uses. In champion countrysides, where hedgerows were fewer than in the woodland areas, damage to crops by wandering beasts was a constant headache – one which continued long after the Middle Ages in the unenclosed areas. Thus at Great Linford in Buckinghamshire it was recorded in 1658 that 'many spoils, trespasses and destructions have daily happened by escapes of cattle into corn and grass whereby many actions, suits and trialles have been raised and more are likely daily to arise if the fields and land there should still be kept open and continued in common as heretofore'.

The hedge was plainly a valuable component of any holding, and anyone robbing or damaging a hedge could expect to pay a penalty. Oliver Rackham has quoted the following examples, from the manor court rolls of Newton Longville (Buckinghamshire) and Hatfield Broad Oak (Essex), respectively: 1283: 'Ralph Cheseman cut down and took away thorns growing in the (Plaintiff's) hedge to the value of ½ mark'; 1443: 'James Mede complains that

John Palmer senior in the month of March cut down to the ground, took and carried away divers Trees . . . viz oak, ash, Maples, white thorn and black, lately growing in a certain hedge . . . between heighfeld and hegfeld, and had been repeating this trespass from time to time for 7 years (previously) . . . by which the said James . . . has suffered damage to the value of 20s'. He also quotes from the by-laws of Saffron Walden of 1561: 'Every hedgebreaker taken in breaching of hedges and carrying of suchlike wood shall pay . . . 16d. and 3 hours punishment in the stocks . . . 4d. to the lord, to the owners of such wood 4d. . . . to the bailiff 4d., and to him that shall take an offender 4d.' To these cases we can add one from numerous northern examples: John son of Beatrice being fined 2s. at Wakefield manor court in 1316 for encroaching on and removing the hedge of an assart on the lord's waste. These fines seem trivial in terms of modern values, but it is worth remembering that in the thirteenth century a skilled craftsman might earn 3d. a day and in the fifteenth century he would do well to earn 6d. a day.

The only disadvantage of the living hedge was its permanence, and in open-field country movable barriers were useful to control livestock grazing in the communal ploughlands and meadow components of the manors. In the meadow, as in the open fields, land was held in strips or 'doles', each villager holding strips of meadow commensurate with his share in the arable fields. Here temporary fences could be used to demarcate the doles, but these fences would have to be removed at the locally prescribed date following the mowing of the last hay crop, so that the meadow could then be thrown open as common grazing for the village livestock. Occasionally a villein would attempt to defy the local custom by erecting a permanent boundary in the form of a ditch and paling fence: Robert Carpenter was convicted at Wakefield in 1316 and forced to remove his obstructions to the operation of customary common rights.

Impermanent barriers were also needed to make pens and folds in areas where sheep were farmed. In the fourteenth century oak hurdles, used for making a fold for lambs or one where ewes could be milked, were sold for around ¾d. each. Not all sheep pens were created in this way; for example, in the early thirteenth century Byland Abbey received a grant of the right to pasture some 360 sheep, along with one to take all that was necessary from the wood for making a sheep enclosure 'and for making a hedge and enclosure round this sheep-cote, so that the sheep may lie where the monks willed'. Hurdles were also used on fallowing open-field land to control the manuring of the ploughsoil, the animals being moved around to ensure a proper distribution of the manure.

Although it is sometimes improbably suggested that lines of trees and shrubs would be left to form hedges when woodland was cleared for agriculture, there is plenty of evidence to show that medieval woods tended to be surrounded by their own hedges, woodbanks and ditches, which were essential to exclude browsing livestock from the soft young coppices. Hedging could be quite an expensive business, and in 1457–8 the cost of hedging about 1,650 yards (about 1,500 m) around Bradley Wood near Huddersfield was some 41s. 8d. In the previous century a hedge was established around a rabbit warren on the manor of Petworth in Sussex and one man was employed, working 24 days to make 3½ furlongs and 18 perches of new hedge on the east and north sides of the enclosure respectively. In 1391 Thomas Sharleston agreed to provide protection for Wakefield Wood, by 'making a certain large ditch (perhaps a deer leap to allow deer in, but prevent their escape) there with a certain hedge above it for enclosing the said wood'. The accounts show that this wood also enjoyed the protection of some kind of paling fence (*palicum*), and palisade (*garillum*), but the use of *haia* shows that a hedge was also involved. Often the medieval documents use the word *sepes*, which could imply a hedge, fence or wall, though it usually refers to a hedge. (In the north of England there is evidence that some medieval hedges on higher ground were subsequently replaced by drystone walls.) Quickthorn hedges can be mentioned specifically as *viva sepes*; in 1413 William Scoley and his wife were granted land in West Yorkshire with the obligation to ditch the northern and western boundary and surround the land with a *viva sepes*, though this denotes a living hedge, not necessarily one of hawthorn. Where boundaries were marked by hedge and ditch it was normal for the legal boundary to follow the externally placed ditch.

As well as there being hedges planted around common features of the medieval countryside, like woods, deer parks and sheep enclosures, the records show that less familiar features, like 'coneygarths' or rabbit-breeding enclosures within warrens, were also hedged.

Thousands of miles of hedgerow were planted in the course of medieval assarting, when enormous acreages of woodland were felled to create new ploughlands and pastures. Most assarting in the post-Norman period was associated with the creation of privately – rather than commonly – held fields, and the movement achieved an intensity of activity in the thirteenth century and in the years preceding the ravages of the Black Death, which arrived in 1348 and put a stop to the population pressure which had fuelled all the assarting. Occasionally a mass of people were involved in an assarting campaign (as in the Drax area of Yorkshire in the reign of King John) and sometimes individuals specialised in the winning of farmland by assarting, but generally it was a rather piecemeal process of clearance and enclosure.

Licences were required for the assarting of forest land, although illegal assarting was common, and there was generally an obligation to hedge the cleared area. In 1356, for example, Roger, son of William de Stanbury, was fined for not enclosing his fields at Stanbury in West Yorkshire with hedges, thus allowing cattle to enter and damage the crops. Enclosure ensured that livestock would be confined and it also allowed the farmer to control the grazing of the new pasture land. In the plague year of 1348 an assart called Edwarderode at Ardsley in West Yorkshire was granted 'as it was enclosed of old time with hedges and ditches'. The name is interesting; the word 'rode' refers to cleared land, and it was probably someone called Edward who had cleared it. Medieval assarts often existed as smallish, somewhat irregular hedged fields often of just one or two acres. Sometimes their names survive to indicate their origins as assarts, in field names like Rode, Ridding, Stubbs, Stocks and Stebbings, which refer either to the 'ridding' of the land of trees or the presence of tree stumps. The word 'intake' can refer either to an assart or to upland grazing taken in from the moor.

While some medieval hedges and field patterns were to persist for centuries, in a few places the arrangements experienced considerable changes during the Middle Ages. A very good example is provided by the study by Andrew Fleming and Nicholas Ralph of Holne Moor on Dartmoor, near the Venford reservoir. Here a pattern of reaves (see Ch. 1) represents the Bronze Age partitioning of the moor, while in Saxon times a set of large rounded 'fields' or 'lobes' was set out around a nucleus. The first of these lobes was subdivided into four fields and the fields were in turn divided into strips, each about an acre in area. The fields within the lobe were divided by hedgebanks and the lobes themselves were divided by hedges standing on banks and block walls built of lines of granite boulders. However, after the Norman Conquest Dartmoor became a Royal Forest, and dead and living hedges which would restrict the movements of deer were outlawed. As a result the hedges were replaced by 'corn ditches'. A ditch backed by a high wall faced towards the open moor, but on the field side there was no obstruction to prevent deer from escaping back to the open ground. In 1239 the Forest Law was lifted from Dartmoor – and as a result hedges were re-established on Holne Moor to supersede the corn ditches. In Tudor times sheep farming gained ascendancy in the area and massive wall banks of earth that were faced in stone and carried hedges on their crests were built to confine the flocks. However, in Elizabethan and Stuart times the area was invaded by tin workers who enjoyed special privileges on the moor. The tinners broke down many wall banks, pillaging their materials to build 'pillow mounds' or artificial rabbit warrens, thus utterly disrupting and destroying cultivation in the locality.

As we have seen, the hedge was a common and useful facet of the medieval countryside; but it could also be an emotive and controversial feature, sym-bolising the clash between private and public interests. This conflict tended to intensify in the post-medieval centuries – and it is still a feature of modern life. It operates at many different levels. At the regional level there have been confrontations like the mass trespasses in the Peak District or the more recent 'fish-ins' in Irish loughs. In such cases moral indignation rather than legal issues have usually fuelled protest, the activists feeling that those who work hard for a living should not be excluded from the countryside by a privileged minority who do not. However, legal issues can sometimes be at stake, as at the time of writing, when the Ramblers' Association is prosecuting Kent County Council for allegedly failing in its obligation to produce an up-to-date map of public rights of way, and it is taking action against two farmers in Gloucestershire and Staffordshire for obstruction. Then, at the national level, there is the perennial clash of public and private interests between those on the left, who believe that society should help its weaker and poorer members, and those on the right, who believe that the more gifted, selfish or cunning should be free to enjoy the fruits of their enterprise or advantage.

In the medieval period the hedgerow was often the focus of clashes between

Medieval England still relied heavily on the Roman road network, though road maintenance was often neglected. Scenes such as this one, near Cambridge, with hedges encroaching towards a Roman road must have been quite common.

public and private interests. It was the symbol of private property, and most disputes centred on claims that the 'privatisation' of land was depriving a community of traditional common rights. Such conflicts did not always pitch the impoverished peasants against a greedy lord or farmer: they could set villager against villager or lord against lord. In the thirteenth century, for example, Gilbert de Gaunt sent his forester and a force of about eighty men to destroy hedges or fences erected by Henry Fitz Ranulf on his sub-manor of Fremington in Swaledale. Gilbert claimed that the hedges were interfering with his hunting rights; Henry said they were needed to protect his corn, and when he sued Gilbert at the Assizes the jury decided that, since the barriers had stood for almost a year, they should remain. Perhaps they too had corn that was threatened by huntsmen or deer.

The offences against hedges that were mentioned earlier in the chapter seem to have concerned just the pilfering of materials, but more serious issues were also involved, for the erection of fences on communally farmed land could disrupt the whole basis of village open-field farming. In 1346, for example, William de Baildon claimed that people from the Haworth area had broken his hedge and ditch at Oxenhope, allowing their cattle into his corn and meadow and causing crop damage to the high cost of £20. Although strips of arable or meadow land were individually tenanted, the most common disputes occurred when the fields were fallowing and thrown open to the village livestock. Thus in 1315 the men of Thornes and Snapethorpe in West Yorkshire complained that enclosures had robbed them of their rights to graze local meadows during 'open time'. Hedges, if not furnished with gates, could be an impediment to access. In 1343 the court at Bradford found that the delightfully named Adam Nutbrown had a hedge which prevented Thomas Harper from reaching his herbs and peas. Of course, anyone who failed to provide proper gates in their hedges was likely to suffer damage when carters decided that the shortest distance between two points was a straight line. Hedges could be a nuisance if they were not properly trimmed, and in 1512 Richard Bunhall was fined at Great Canfield in Essex because he had seven perches of hedge overhanging the King's highway with branches and thorns.

Before open-field farming was very old it began, gradually, to be dismantled. In many places it survived well into the nineteenth century, but the strip fields seldom endured intact and on many manors they had vanished before Parliamentary Enclosure and had been replaced by privately held closes. Sometimes the early enclosure was accomplished by a general agreement, with villagers swapping and selling strips so that each could obtain compacted fields. Often the agreements appealed to a few tenants but not others – and this was when the trouble was likely to begin. But eventually most village lands included at least some hedged closes which had been 'privatised' and taken out of communal control. The amount of genuine agreement involved in the 'enclosures by agreement' varied very much from place to place. In 1611 one tenant at Knossington in Leicestershire complained that the lord of the manor had coerced his tenants, hedged and thus enclosed parts of the tenancies and employed ruffians to prevent the complainant from reaching his lands.

Today we might imagine that medieval enclosure could cause a local shindig,

The gradual dismantling of open-field farming began in many places during the Middle Ages. In this excerpt from a map of Gamlingay, Cambridgeshire, drawn in 1601, we can see how the land on the left-hand margin of the map still lies in open-field strips, but elsewhere strips have been amalgamated and enclosed to produce elongated little privately owned closes. Note how the cartographer has identified owners and acreages and also represented hedgerows with pollard or standard trees growing above them. (Warden and Scholars of Merton College, Oxford.)

but it is hard to appreciate that the anger and hatred could expand to reach a revolutionary level. Kett's Rebellion of 1549 was a case in point. Trouble came to a head in that year with an enclosure riot at Attleborough in Norfolk, where the fences erected by Squire Greene were torn down. Three weeks later, during the annual feast at Wymondham, tempers boiled over again and fences erected illegally on the common by one Flowerdew were destroyed. The insurgents found an unlikely leader in the yeoman, Robert Kett, himself, surprisingly, an encloser. A manifesto was composed, which complained of how:

> The lands which in the memory of our fathers were common, those are ditched and hedged and made several; the pastures are enclosed and we are

shut out... Shall they, as they have brought hedges about common pasture, enclose with their intolerable lusts also all the commodities and pleasure of this life, which Nature, the parent of us all, would have common, and bringeth forth every day, for us, as well as for them?

The rebels should have known that then (as now) the law of England was more concerned with property than causes. Kett's peasant army of 20,000 was defeated by the State's cannons and German mercenaries and was massacred; Robert Kett was captured and hung in chains on the walls of Norwich Castle.

We can begin to understand the hatred directed at enclosures and their hedges when we appreciate that in Tudor times enclosure might not simply have involved the notional illegal alienation of common rights, but often involved the eviction of the entire community as well. A minority of medieval hedgerows defined sheep enclosures which cut across former commons and open-field land and the old villages themselves. Society was polarised on the issue of enclosure. Peasants would sing:

> Commons to close and keep
> Poor folk for bread to cry and weep
> Towns pulled down to pasture sheep
> This is the new guise.

A more economical Tudor expression of the same sentiments ran:

> Horne and Thorne shall make England forlorne

(the horn being sheep and the thorn the enclosure hedge). The advocates of 'progress' duly found an influential spokesman in the sixteenth-century versifier and agriculturalist, Thomas Tusser:

> More mutton and beef
> Corn butter, and cheese of the best
> We find ye (go search any coast)
> Than there where enclosure is most?
and
> Town layeth for turfe and for sedge,
> And hath it with wonderful suit,
> When tother in every hedge
> Hath plentie of fewell and fruit.
> Evils twenty times worser than these,
> Enclosure quickly would ease.

(The first two lines of the dreadful verse refer to the 'suit' or difficulty of obtaining fuel in the unenclosed champion countrysides, while in 'tother' – the other hedgerow-enclosed lands – the hedgerows provided abundant fruit and fuel.) Popular indignation against enclosure continued down the centuries, and duly came to be expressed in the bitter irony of the rhyme:

They hang the man and flog the woman
Who steals the goose from off the common.
But let the greater criminal loose
Who steals the common from the goose.

The most unjust and despised of the enclosures had their origin in the economic circumstances created by the Black Death, and many a landlord decided that, given the shortage of labour and newly born obduracy of the surviving tenants, it was more profitable to raise sheep on an empty estate than to exist on the rents and services of villagers. Some evictors were minor lords or speculators who had no roots in the lands they acquired. But there were also some dynasties, like the Knightleys and the Spencers in the Midlands, who rose to positions of great wealth and influence on the profits of systematic eviction and sheep or cattle farming, and had dozens of dead villages as their trophies. New hedgerow patterns, running across the ridge and furrow corrugations of old open-field land, were the hallmarks of the clearances. For example, after the Spencers had pillaged Wormleighton in Warwickshire in the years around 1499, the erection of fences and the planting of great double hedgerows probably divided the estate into four large blocks, each the territory of a master shepherd, and by the time that the estates were surveyed in 1634, these blocks had become 'charges' or leases, held by different leaseholders. Some of the original double hedgerows were still surviving when this writer was there at the start of this decade. Such controversial transformations were common throughout the realm, and there was no shortage of landowners like William Ashby of Lowesby in Leicestershire, who 'caused the said messuages [three farms] to be destroyed and the said lands [about 120 acres (49 ha) of ploughland] to be enclosed with hedges and converted from tillage into cattle pasture'.

As we explain in the chapters which follow, we do not have much faith in hedgerow-dating as a means of determining the age of a hedge. However, field shapes can often help to provide a rough date for a hedgerow, and field names and documentary evidence can add important support. We have seen that assarts may survive as small, often very small, hedged fields and sometimes a field name such as 'rode', 'sart' or 'stocks' or similar will confirm the origin. Assarts can usually be distinguished from fields enclosed by agreement from old strip fields, for the hedges of the latter will reflect the old strip boundaries. Because medieval ploughs were hauled by a long string of six or eight oxen the ploughman would begin to swing his lead beasts towards the turn well before the end of the plough ridge was reached. In consequence such strips were not straight, but had a reversed 'S'- or 'C'-shaped outline. The hedges enclosing old strips preserve this gently curving form and can easily be recognised. Occasionally strips were enclosed in ones or twos, as reflected in the closely parallel sweeps of hedge existing till very recently at Middleton in North Yorkshire or the similar walls at Chelmorton in Derbyshire. Much more frequently strips were enclosed in larger blocks, but the 'wavy-edged' rule still applies. Only on the rarest occasions will the field-shape principle mislead, although the British Trust for Conservation Volunteers' handbook *Hedging* mentions the case of a reversed 'S' hedge at Crimscote in Warwickshire. Here hawthorn scrub

The village of Middleton, near Pickering, was surrounded by a pattern of (Dark Age?) 'long strips' of an unusual, curving form. As a result of earlier enclosure they escaped Parliamentary Enclosure and this remarkable archaeological monument should have been preserved. When this air photograph was taken in 1984, many hedges had been removed, and the removal appears to be continuing. Note how the road running diagonally across the photograph is a later addition to the landscape, severing the ends of some strips and creating an awkward little triangular field (right centre), much in the manner of the superimposed Roman roads described in Chapter 1. (North Yorkshire County Council, Department of Archaeology.)

spontaneously colonised an old, curving open-field furrow when the land was neglected during the agricultural depression of the 1920s. Sheep enclosure hedges like the Wormleighton examples are harder to recognise, though historical records of village clearance may be discovered. Tudor, Elizabethan and Stuart enclosures could be very large, encompassing hundreds of acres, though in due course experience argued for subdivision. Professor Hoskins has quoted a 281-acre (114-ha) Leicestershire field which was subdivided into ten smaller fields within possibly thirty years of its creation.

The specific cases of medieval hedgerows which we have mentioned in this chapter amount to only a fraction of the examples which we could quote. But they are sufficient to show that hedges were a common, useful and controversial feature in the Middle Ages countryside. Even so, the nature of medieval life ensured that they tended to be recorded only when they were noted in court rolls, in connection with property disputes of one kind or another, or when landowners recorded the costs of hedging on their estates. In areas of woodland countryside many hedgerows were ancient by the dawn of the medieval period, and were then quite likely to survive right through it. In the champion countryside existing hedges would initially be removed to create the open ploughlands and meadows, but new hedgerows would later appear during episodes of enclosure by agreement or sheep clearances. Even if the open fields and commons endured into the eighteenth or nineteenth centuries, Parliamentary Enclosure would eventually bring the re-introduction of hedgerows (or walls). Unless the modern barley barons have been up to their tricks, any patch of lowland countryside should contain some medieval hedgerows, and in many places the medieval hedges are very much in the majority.

·4·

THE GREAT ENCLOSURE

During the long currency of the hedgerow in Britain there have been times when hedgerows have multiplied to enmesh vast expanses in their leafy web, and other times – like the late Saxon and modern periods – when the shrub networks have been grubbed out to create more open countrysides. As we have seen, in Tudor times and the two centuries which followed there was a substantial and somewhat controversial increase in the amount of hedged countryside as a result of the innumerable local bouts of enclosure by agreement. This piecemeal process formed an important prelude to the period of Parliamentary Enclosure, during which the arrangements were more formalised and when the hedging movement reached a crescendo of activity, with the planting of over a billion shrubs and the creation of around 200,000 miles (321,870 km) of new hedgerow. In the period 1750–1850 hedges must have been planted at an average rate of about 2,000 miles (3,220 km) each year.

Even so, we should not over-stress the importance of Parliamentary Enclosure in the shaping of the landscape, remembering E. C. K. Gonner's estimate that the transformation affected only one fifth of the area of England. Rather less than half of the hedgerow mileage is of this Georgian and Victorian vintage. In the 1960s it was guessed that England still contained about 500,000 miles (804,675 km) of hedgerow, and a substantial mileage of Enclosure hedge had already been lost. So perhaps around one-third of all the hedges which existed as the movement drew to the close in the later Victorian times were the products of Parliamentary Enclosure.

Although the arrival of the Enclosure Acts marked a considerable quickening in the pace of enclosure and a change in the procedures involved, it was not as revolutionary a process as one might imagine. The tyrannical sheep enclosures of the Tudor period, which extinguished so many villages and cast thousands of peasant families adrift on the roads, were accompanied and followed by the enclosures by agreement – or disagreement, depending on the local circumstances. These arrangements foreshadowed the formal Acts in a number of ways. For example, in his treatise on 'The Duty of a Steward to His Lord' of 1727, E. Lawrence argued that in seeking to enclose open fields and commons the vigilant steward should first seek to buy out all the freeholders, but if these people could not be persuaded to sell,

> yet at least an Agreement for Inclosing should be push'd forward by the steward, and a scheme laid wherein it may appear, that an exact and proportional share will be allotted to every Proprietor, persuading them first, if possible, to sign a Form of Agreement, and then to chuse Commissioners on both sides.

Parliamentary Enclosure also involved commissioners and the notion of proportional shares – though in reality it favoured the bigger fish in the village pond, and the smaller ones could never be adequately recompensed for their loss of rights to the common fund or resources.

All manner of injustices masquerade in the guise of progress, and if open-field farming had been so inefficient its detractors bore the burden of explaining why it persisted in some places for a thousand years before being dismantled by the Acts. In fact the motives for Enclosure were too complicated to be explained as

This illustration has been reproduced in previous books, but we make no apology for using it again as it provides a unique image of Parliamentary Enclosure surveyors at work. The surveyors, working at Henlow in Bedfordshire, are marking out their allocation; in due course a new hedgerow network will appear. (Bedfordshire County Council.)

the simple pursuit of progress and national interest. There is evidence that in some places Enclosure was followed by rises in grain production, while the ability of the entrepreneurial owner of enclosed fields to respond to changing market prices could give him an advantage over those whose strip holdings were locked into the open-field crop rotations, with their three- or four-yearly fallow.

The simple desire to follow fashion and to leap aboard any passing local bandwagon must also have encouraged many landowers to support Enclosure, though the prospect of exploiting Enclosure as a means of jacking-up rents must have appealed strongly to numerous larger landlords. The smallest farmers could not even afford to pay for the costs of Enclosure and soon left the land, but the bigger men could meet these costs and then reap the higher rents charged for 'improved' tenancies. Thus at Ripley, near Harrogate, in 1778 John Ingilby paid £195 for the Act and £658 for fencing, hedging and walling his 384 acres – but was then able to raise his rental by more than £100 per annum. On the Earl of Scarborough's estate at Winteringham in Lincolnshire, Enclosure came in 1761–2, but rents were not at first raised as high as they might have been, and the reasons for this were explained to the landlord in 1784:

> The cause of Winteringham's being before let at a less value, arose from the Inclosure, and the Tenants being under restrictions respecting the Nourishment and Care of Quicksetts, which was very inefficiently fenced and some parts not fenced at all, so that the Tenants could not occupy their farms to the best Advantage.

Even so, in 1765 the rent roll stood at £809, but by 1777 it was at £1,858.

Since Enclosure was a boon to the rich and a curse on the poor its supporters were normally drawn from the holders of moderate or large areas of land. The leading lights in each parish would petition to obtain the necessary Act of Parliament. After this had been achieved, commissioners were officially ratified to produce the new allocation of land. They were generally named in the petition, being chosen from the ranks of the nobles, notable farmers and churchmen, and frequently a trio of commissioners was involved. A public meeting would be held in the parish concerned, where anti-Enclosure meetings, often of a stormy nature, could be expected to reflect the apprehensions of the poorer and most threatened interests. In due course the commissioners appointed a valuer and a surveyor to assist in producing a seemingly equitable redistribution of lands, with each bona fide claimant receiving a compacted holding which was notionally equivalent to the scattered pre-Enclosure one. For some places both Enclosure and pre-Enclosure maps survive, allowing one to gain a detailed picture of a countryside just before and just after Enclosure.

Sometimes the commissioners offered their services free, but in any event the recipients of the award were faced with a hefty and sometimes crippling bill. Boundary hedges, fences or walls had to be erected around each holding (the hedging or walling of the fields within could be done later), and each farmer had to contribute to the costs of enclosing, paying in proportion to the size of his allocation. (Since the provision of such boundary features was a legal obligation on farmers, it has recently been argued that the removal of Enclosure hedges is illegal – though one cannot imagine the current Conservative government attempting to enforce this particular law.) In addition to the payment of the specialists' fees, the purchase of hedging plants and the costs of planting, there were also legal bills to be paid, as well as the various travelling expenses. The deliberation, organisation, surveying and general to-ing and fro-ing could go on for half a decade or more, with the disruption, disagreement, uncertainty and readjustment all contributing to a period of dislocation of farming life – as reflected in the problems at Winteringham, mentioned above. Often it was found that fields specified in the original allocation were too large for practical farming, and their subdivision added to the hedging costs involved. On larger farms, fields of around 50 acres (20 ha) in area were often subdivided into 5- or 10-acre (2- or 4-ha) units.

As the parish settled down and the quicksets began to flourish, a very different kind of countryside came into being. Previously enclosure by agreement had created 'countrysides of amalgamation', with field strips being grouped together in clusters and bounded by curving and stepped boundaries which preserved many of the older strip outlines. The landscapes of Parliamentary Enclosure were radically different: surveyors' landscapes of straight and simple lines which sliced right across the twists and turns of the old rural lifestyle, with the geometrical gridwork of new fields superimposed upon the dying world of peasant farming. The geometrical aspect was also embodied in many of the new Enclosure roads which were often a component of the award: arrow-straight little routeways spanning just a parish and complementing or replacing the older, curving lanes.

Parliamentary Enclosure did not have an immediate impact upon the appearance of England and Wales. The first village to be affected was Radipole in Dorset in 1604 and a small trickle of Acts confronted Parliament in the reigns of Queen Anne and the first George. The trickle became a stream in the reign of George II (1727–60), during which over 200 Acts were passed. In the following reign, however, which continued until 1820, about 3,200 parishes experienced Parliamentary Enclosure; and a General Enclosure Act was introduced in 1801 to simplify proceedings. Surprisingly, there was a certain amount of destruction of old hedges in the later eighteenth century, and despite the acceleration of the Enclosure movement it was sometimes felt that England was being de-hedged. Most of the areas affected by Enclosure were open ploughlands and commons, where pre-Enclosure hedges would have been few. By 1850 the movement had almost run its course, though new Acts appeared sporadically in the years which followed, with the last Act coming in 1914. Just a few fragments of old England escaped – commons like Oxford's Port Meadow, many but by no means all old village greens and a few strip fields, like those at Laxton in Nottinghamshire or Braunton in Devon. By the end of the Enclosure era there had been 5,265 Acts and 20.9 per cent of the area of England had been affected.

The Parliamentary Enclosure movement was by no means even in its effects upon England, and the historian Michael Turner has described how 2.2 million of the 6.8 million acres (890,328 of the 2,751,922 ha) affected lay in just five counties. In descending order of the acreages affected they were Lincolnshire,

A reasonably well-preserved landscape of rectangular Parliamentary Enclosure fields near Westbury in Wiltshire. However, Dutch elm disease is taking a severe toll of the hedgerow standards here.

West Yorkshire, Norfolk, Northamptonshire and East Yorkshire. Various counties were only lightly affected, and in contrast to the 362 Lincolnshire Acts, Monmouth had only 13, Cornwall 31 and Kent 34. Other counties which largely escaped such legislation were Devon, Dorset, Somerset, Middlesex, Essex and the shires of the Welsh Marches; while others, like those of the north-west, Surrey, Sussex and Hertfordshire, were more influenced by earlier enclosures by agreement. There were also significant differences in the timing of Enclosure: in some counties the process had almost been completed by the 1790s, in others it had not yet got under way. It is also worth noting that Parliamentary Enclosure did not always transform a parish and superimpose a rectilinear hedgerow grid. Fields resulting from earlier enclosure would normally be preserved, and sometimes new, compacted fields would perpetuate the boundaries which surrounded furlongs or small open-strip fields. Langley in Essex is a good example, for here old furlong boundaries were preserved, and though the packages of field strips disappeared, few new hedged boundaries were created. Thus, although the social consequences of Parliamentary Enclosure here would have been quite profound, the flavour of early enclosure was preserved and the appearance of the countryside was deceptive. However, this is a rather unusual example, influenced by the considerable scope of earlier enclosure here and the relatively few landholders involved.

The Parliamentary Enclosure era was more civilised than the modern one in at least one respect: there were no PR people. But had the government been able to hire a firm to market Enclosure then the publicists would not have had to look far for a logo – the hawthorn leaf would have been an instantly recognisable symbol. Although the traditional practice of scouring the woods and wastes for suitable seedlings was still occasionally followed, most of the hedging plants were hawthorns brought from commercial nurseries with hedges of commercially grown Scots pine being used in the Brecklands. Commercial nurseries which could supply hedging materials appeared in the seventeenth century, and in the Enclosure era many more appeared; and much of their prosperity could be attributed to the sustained demand for hawthorn, which was bought in prodigious quantities. Occasionally the records of old nurserymen have survived, so we know, for example, that in 1766 William Pendar of Woolhampton, Berkshire, included 4,000 quicksets at 5s. in his estimate of a monumental order of trees and shrubs for Lord Bruce of Tottenham at Savernake. He added, 'My Lord, the Large Beechs and Plains are to enlarge the Clumps in the Forist which your Lordship ordred – the Elms for the London road.'

The planting of standard timber or ornamental trees at intervals in field and roadside hedges was more a feature of the eighteenth than the nineteenth century. But it was certainly not an innovation of the Enclosure era, for medieval documents and paintings of the seventeenth and eighteenth centuries show that the English hedgerows were packed with valuable pollard and standard trees, which yielded light and heavy timber respectively, oak, ash, elm, willow and poplar being amongst those favoured. In former times the poles cut from hedgerow pollards belonged to the tenant rather than the landlord, but the trees grown in the eighteenth-century Enclosure hedges were usually grown as standards rather than as pollards.

In modern times the lovers of countryside and nature have good reason to bemoan the destruction of the thousands of miles of Parliamentary Enclosure hedgerow – while, we hope, being aware that only a minority of our hedges are of this vintage. At the time of Enclosure, however, several arbiters of taste despised the new landscapes which Enclosure was forging. Plainly, the rolling expanses of herb-rich common and the strip-striped open ploughlands, with their poppies, marigolds, daisies, cornflowers and corn cockles, would have been as different from modern prairie fields as a life-teeming pond is from a polluted mire. Writing of his native Yorkshire Dales in the 1780s, T. D. Whitaker complained that:

enclosures, however convenient for occupation or conducive to improvement, have spoiled the face of the county as an object; the cornfields which

by variegated hues of tillage relieved the uniformity of verdure about them are now no more: and the fine swelling outlines of the pastures, formerly as extensive as large parks, and wanting little but the accompaniment of deer to render them beautiful, are now strapped over with large bandages of stone, and present nothing to the eye but right lined and angular deformity.

Looking at the scene with modern eyes we can appreciate how the Enclosure walls, now mellowed with moss and lichen, are an indispensable part of this landscape.

John Clare was a more celebrated writer and poet of the Enclosure era; he hated the neat and angular new countryside and mourned the passing of the looser, more boisterous ancient scenery. In 1821 he wrote:

> Inclosure, thou'rt curse upon the land
> And tasteless was the wretch who thy existence planned.

Around his native village of Helpston, in Northamptonshire, he witnessed the Enclosure of Emmondsales Heath, and recalled the event with horror in his poem 'Remembrances':

> Inclosure like a Buonaparte let not a thing remain,
> It levelled every bush and tree and levelled every hill,
> And hung the moles for traitors –
>   though the brook is running still
> It runs a naked stream and chill.

Parliamentary Enclosure was much more than a reorganisation of scenery and agriculture: it was a highly controversial and widely despised assault upon rural life and customs. It sentenced a multitude of semi-subsistence peasant farmers to exile and largely completed the erosion of customary rights which had begun with the informal and often equally resented medieval enclosures. It tolled the death knell for the England of the village peasant. The sentiments of the villagers so affected were embodied in the anonymous 'Thornborough Lamentation', the ironically named Buckinghamshire parish of that name having being enclosed in 1798:

> The time alas will soon approach,
> When we must all our pasture yield;
> The wealthy on our rights encroach,
> And will enclose our common field.

Parliamentary Enclosure did not necessarily produce monotonous countrysides, as these photographs of countrysides near Burrington, Avon (TOP), and Killinghall, North Yorkshire (BOTTOM), show. The hawthorn hedges and the oak, ash and elm standards provided invaluable refuges for wildlife.

·5·

HEDGEROW-DATING – MAGIC OR MYTH?

Our understanding of the history of our landscape owes a tremendous debt to the work of a few pioneering scholars: men like O. G. S. Crawford, M. W. Beresford and W. G. Hoskins. The name of Professor Hoskins will be familiar to all who have an interest in the heritage of man-made landscape. He applied a most perceptive form of scholarship to the study of what was then an unfashionable backwater of history, and he broadcast his ideas with a literary talent which one could not easily praise too highly. With the advantage of being able to draw upon more recent scholarship, it is possible to disprove some of Professor Hoskins' ideas, but the value of his contribution is scarcely diminished. In 1967 he wrote:

> It occurred to me . . . [many years ago] knowing no botany whatsoever, that hedgebanks of such antiquity ought to show considerable differences in their vegetation from more modern hedges; that along the edge of a wood, for example, one might find vegetation that was really a hang-over, as it were, from ancient woodland. But I could not pursue this idea for lack of any botanical knowledge.[1]

'However,' he continues, 'in recent years, Dr Max Hooper of the Nature Conservancy hit upon the same idea and was able to pursue it actively, with exciting results.'[2]

As a consequence of published work by Dr Hooper and his associates E. Pollard and N. W. Moore, the 'dating' of hedgerows by the simple technique of counting their constituent species has become an extremely well-known and popular activity.[3] Although it has been widely, though not universally, accepted in the academic world, it has also seemed so easy to accomplish that any country-lover capable of telling an ash from an aspen could attempt it. Scores have.

Let us say at the outset that we do not believe in hedgerow-dating of the type described. In 1981 I wrote that while I was unable to fathom *why* hedgerow-dating should work, the results obtained seemed to provide 'a handy guide to the age of any enclosure'.[4] Now I have changed my mind. Not only is it not possible to see why the method *should* work; there are also various reasons to explain why it *does not* work. (Since some readers may wish to pursue the case through scholarly literature, we have provided references.)

According to Hooper's research[5], the age of a 30-yard section of hedgerow equals

$$(99 \times \text{the number of shrub species}) - 16$$

A correlation of +0.92 and a margin of error of 100 years either way were claimed. Other forms of the formula commonly applied are:

$$\text{Age of hedge (in years)} = (110 \times \text{number of species}) + 30$$

and

$$\text{Age of hedge} = \text{number of species} \times 110.$$

In practice these formulae are often simplified into the form

$$\text{Age of hedge} = \text{number of species per 30 yards} \times 100.$$

This produces the remarkably easy conclusions that a 6-species hedge would be 600 years old, a 9-species hedge would be 900 years old, and so on. Although

The landscape archaeologist, Dr Tom Williamson, leading a species count of old hedges in the Weald.

the authors of the theory recognised and explained some of its vulnerabilities, other exponents have not – and their results are often rooted more in blind faith than in critical exploration.

However, in our experience the theory is so beset by faults of various quite unrelated and serious kinds that it is fundamentally flawed and should not be the key component of research into local landscape history. This is a great shame, since if hedgerow-dating did deliver the goods it would be an invaluable weapon in the local historian's armoury.

The objections to hedgerow-dating can be set out under a series of headings:

LOGISTICAL WEAKNESSES

These faults do not always necessarily invalidate the *theory* of hedgerow-dating, but are quite likely to affect its *practice*, and consequently undermine its results.

To begin with, hedgerow-dating presupposes an ability to identify a spectrum of hedgerow shrubs. There will be very few readers who cannot tell an oak from an elm – but answer honestly: can you tell a gean from a bullace, and would you recognise the rare wild pear if you were lucky enough to find it in a hedge?

Whether the hedgerow-daters are novices or experts in the identification game, a single error might for instance result in a Tudor hedgerow being confused with a Stuart hedgerow. The sorts of mistakes which a dater might make can be exemplified as follows:

> The novice could make elementary mistakes, like confusing the coarse, pinnate leaves of hazel and elm.
> The fairly experienced observer could have difficulties in, for example, separating out the different *Prunus* species.
> The professional botanist, if not a devoted specialist in the study of roses and brambles, could confuse the various wild roses and would only recognise a tiny fraction of the variants on the blackberry theme.

A considerable amount of published and unpublished work on hedgerow-dating has been based on expert-organised student surveys. Students, like other people, come in different kinds. Botany students should be competent identifiers of most hedgerow shrubs. Modern geography students might expound at length about statistical obscurities, like coefficients of circularity or the Chi^2 test, but might be unable to distinguish between pines and poplars, whether climbing up them or falling out of them. Some historians, meanwhile, are unhappy out of doors.

Students vary in other ways. Experience in geographical fieldwork suggests that they divide into the keen and competent; the reticent followers; and those who see the departure of the supervisor as a preliminary to hurling the ranging pole, which is itself a preliminary to fudging the results, and advancing on the nearest pub. In surveys students are divided into small working parties: some

Only the most experienced hedgerow researcher would recognise this real rarity: wild pear. Most would mistake it for something much more common, like wild cherry.

good and some bad, some competent and some less so. Obviously these differences must be reflected in the results.

Species counting is not easy, and experts are quite capable of making mistakes. For example, I was quite recently a member of a hedge-dating group in the Weald, which included one professional ecologist, one professional landscape historian (two counting myself) and three capable students. Being rather bored I created a variation of the game. I would burrow around in the depths of the hedges for additional species which the other members of the group missed. In two out of four hedge sections sampled I was able to produce such extra shrubs, jacking-up the 'age' of the hedge by 100 years in each case.

The logistic problem does not only concern the identification aspect, for different researchers have included different ranges of shrub species in their investigations. Obviously these differences will greatly affect the results. Let us imagine, for example, an imaginary extreme example of a hedge which includes the following plants within a 30-yard length: common and Midland hawthorn and a hybrid hawthorn; dog rose; downy rose; two kinds of bramble and honeysuckle. A dater of a deflationary persuasion might count the hawthorns as one, the roses as one and consider the bramble and honeysuckle as ineligible.

ABOVE Bramble is a thorn in the side of hedgerow-dating. It comes in a multitude of sub-species, which only a handful of botanists might recognise. Some researchers include it in species counts, though some do not; while some distinguish between bramble and dewberry and others do not. LEFT Wild gooseberry. Researchers who find gooseberry in hedges must try to decide if it is a 'natural' wild colonist or an escapee from cultivation.

He therefore has a species count of two and dates the hedge to the eighteenth century. The inflationary dater counts three hawthorns, two roses, two brambles and honeysuckle. He counts eight different members of the hedgerow community and dates the hedge to the Norman period.

In actual practice all sorts of discrepancies emerge. Some daters count bramble and some do not. Some count bramble but not honeysuckle – yet honeysuckle can make thick, robust, woody growth. Some distinguish between bramble (*Rubus fruticosus*) and dewberry (*R. caesius*) and others do not, while others still would not recognise the unridged stem and whitish bloom of the dewberry. Inconsistencies such as these are rife, even in some of the best published literature of hedgerow-dating. For example, in her study of hedgerows in the Norfolk parish of Tasburgh, S. Addington took Hooper's advice and excluded what are called 'trailing plants',[6] though in a study of Otford in Kent, G. Hewlett included both bramble and old man's beard.[7]

Categories that might seem to be straightforward may be less so in practice. In his survey of hedges in Church Broughton parish, Derbyshire, Alan Willmot counted only 'woody species', defined as those whose growth was robust enough to form a hedge on their own without the support of other species.[8] The pedantic critic could argue that this could lead to the inclusion of field rose, but the exclusion of dog rose, which uses its thorns to anchor it to other hedgerow shrubs. He or she could also say that two shrubs either *are* the same or they *are not* – so why does Willmot count each *Prunus* species and *Prunus* sub-species separately, yet lump all *Rosa* sub-species together; recognise three poplar species yet group other poplars together; and count *Salix fragilis* separately and group all the other *Salix* types together? In contrast, Addington lists five willows.[9] In fact, we could go on and on listing contradictions such as these. Plainly the choice of what to count and what not to count, how to subdivide and how to lump together, involves a measure of subjectivity. This would not matter were it not the case that differences in the basic rules of the game will create centuries' worth of difference in the presumed age of a hedge.

Subconscious factors may also somehow exert an effect, for it is noticeable that those who seem predisposed towards the theory tend to find their beliefs confirmed by their fieldwork, while the 'antis' tend to find support for their scepticism. Funny things, hedges.

THE WEAKNESS OF THE HISTORICAL FOUNDATION

The theory of hedgerow-dating was based on counting numbers of species in hedgerows whose age was presumed to be recorded independently in historical sources. However, when we come to look closely at the data we do not find a continuous range of useful dates, but a concentration in two extreme clusters. These clusters represent Parliamentary Enclosure hedges at the young extreme and Saxon charter hedges at the old extreme. There is not very much in between. Parliamentary Enclosure hedges can normally be fairly closely dated to a planting within a few years of the Enclosure Act concerned. Saxon charter hedges are *not* dated by the charter concerned, for as we have seen a hedge could have been hundreds of years old by the time its existence was noted in a charter.

Where the Saxon boundary hedges are concerned, it is all too easy to presume that the hedge mentioned in the charter coincides with a convenient 10-, 11- or 12-species hedge still existing in the vicinity of the area concerned. In some cases one can trace a Saxon boundary across a stretch of modern countryside, but more often than not the landmarks mentioned are vanished or ambiguous. In order for an old hedge to be dated wlth certainty by historical documents one would need to discover a record going something like this: 'In this year 1100 I planted a hedge where none has been before, running between map references 12345678 and 87654321.' Plainly nothing of this kind exists: precise map references based on a national gridwork are a creation of the nineteenth century, and even when one does find a rare medieval record of the planting (rather than use or existence) of a hedge its exact location is almost invariably uncertain.

All too often work on hedgerow-dating has flattered flimsy evidence and given an undeserved aura of certainty to the results. For example, I know that in our own township of Clint, West Yorkshire, a man called Henry Arkel, whose death as the holder of two farms and 28 forest acres was recorded on 29 October 1349, was very active as a leading assarter of the 1340s.[10] I also have an idea of whereabouts in Clint he was based, since a farmstead called Hark Hill Nook may perpetuate his name. How easy then to presume that the hedgerows around the fields at Hark Hill Nook were planted just after Henry had felled the forest. Hedgerow dates have been 'confirmed' by much flimsier evidence than this, but it is quite wrong to base theory on rank uncertainty. In this particular case, for example, Hark Hill Nook could take its name not from Henry Arkel of the fourteenth century, but from Archill who held land close by at Whipley at the time of Domesday. Also, Whipley seems to be a deserted early medieval village whose precise site is still unknown; and could not some of the Hark Hill hedges derive from Whipley's field and lane hedges?

The more that one learns about landscape history the more one becomes aware of the temptations to err, which seem to lurk in every corner of the countryside. There is certainly no substitute for intimate local knowledge. For example, we were recently very surprised to find gooseberry growing in a local hedge, as this is a fairly uncommon hedgerow plant and previously unknown in this particular area. In the adjacent field the farmer was growing gooseberries, and any stranger would surely have felt utterly confident in concluding that the hedgerow gooseberry had spread from the crop growing just yards away. However, we know that the hedgerow gooseberry, being several years old, could not have colonised from the field, where the gooseberries only recently superseded strawberries on land previously cropped for hay and corn and existing as meadowland in medieval times.

Saxon charter hedges could have been as old as Methuselah by the time that they were recorded and can seldom be related directly to living hedges; precisely dated and exactly identifiable medieval hedges are as rare as gold-dust, but Parliamentary Enclosures can be very closely dated. When we look at these Enclosure hedges they tend to be species-poor, typically of hawthorn with a few colonists. Yet even the young Enclosure hedges often defy the tenets of dating theory. In his doctoral thesis, Tom Williamson wrote 'In N.W. Essex, the common adaptation of Hooper's rule of "one species per hundred years", does not work. Hedges dating from the early nineteenth century, for example, commonly have 4 species per 30 yards.'[11] Hedgerow-dating would place these hedges of the early nineteenth century in the sixteenth century, but Williamson does not rule out the idea of a hedgerow succession. Neither do we, but the form of hedgerow-dating described does not work. Even if it did work we would not be able to prove it, since there hardly seems to be a sufficient range of historically dated hedgerows about to allow a proper testing.

HEDGEROW INVASION

The theory of hedgerow-dating assumes an initial single-species planting followed by colonisation of the hedgerow by other shrubs at the rate of one new shrub species per 30-yard length per century. In this way the older a hedge becomes, the more varied its contents. We could take the reader to innumerable stretches of hedgerow which have not become species-rich with age, but species-poor.

In describing one of her hedges, Addington writes: 'It does, though, have two places where the original hedge has been interrupted and an elm hedge has been planted.'[12] This sounds very much like an unwitting encounter with elm invasion. Such elm would not all have been planted but would have spread by suckering, displacing the other hedgerow shrubs as it advanced. In most places one will not need to walk far before discovering similar examples of elm invasion, often spanning 30 yards or more. Of course the elm-invaded section

This is what elm invasion looks like: a long stretch of hedgerow completely dominated by elm.

ABOVE A blackthorn-invaded hedge in full bloom – the extent of blackthorn invasion is most obvious in April when some fields seem to be tied up with white ribbons of blossom. RIGHT This Roman road in Cambridgeshire may have been hedged since it was built, but blackthorn invasion has displaced most competing species along this stretch.

will be the same age as the rest of the hedge, but it will have a species count of just one, falsely implying a very young hedge.

Blackthorn appears in some places to be another invasive species, and it also suckers from the base. Back in 1534 Fitzherbert advised his readers to avoid blackthorn when hedging, since it would grow out to invade the pastures.[13] Running through the Gog Magog hills near Cambridge is a Roman road which may well have been hedged since its creation. Some hedges have been replaced by beech shelterbelts in the nineteenth century, some of the beech apparently having been originally laid in hedgerow fashion. Other stretches are dominated by blackthorn, which forms wide unkempt hedges to give the path a tunnel-like quality. Such stretches of hedge could conceivably be of Roman date, but they are blackthorn-rich and species-poor.

In the gritstone parts of the Yorkshire Dales, holly is evidently invasive, advancing through hawthorn hedges of uncertain date and eventually constituting

long, single-species stretches. It is not clear whether some of the holly was originally planted or whether it has colonised the thorn hedges. On the one hand holly is sometimes (surprisingly) said to have poor stock-proof qualities and it is certainly very slow to grow after planting. On the other hand, as we describe in Chapter 9 it used to provide browse in winter and in medieval times it was specially grown in woods or 'Hollings', and 'Hollings' place-names still endure. It probably spreads through self-layering, and downward-growing branches will readily root in the leaf mould beside the parent tree. In our part of Nidderdale most older roadside hedges are heavily invaded by holly. Our nearest field hedge, however, is quite holly-free. It is probably medieval or a little later, flanked by a deep ditch, and runs across the sandy alluvial soil of an old flood plain and former meadow. Perhaps holly does not like the setting, though it is present on the adjacent river bank. This hedge is one of our richest, with hawthorn, blackthorn, hazel, alder, ash, goat willow, gooseberry, dog rose and bramble. Elsewhere in the locality the hedges are poorer and heavily invaded by holly, which must depress the species counts. Under ideal conditions bird cherry has also been seen to be invasive.

Within any hedge the relationship between the shrubs must be to some extent symbiotic, each member helping to shield its neighbour and maintain the barrier. But the relationship is also extremely competitive. Ash and elder may shade out their neighbours, while at least three of the other shrubs appear to be quite capable of invading and monopolising long stretches of hedgerow – with drastic consequences for their neighbours and for hedgerow-daters.

THE 12-SPECIES MAXIMUM

If the hedgerow-dating formula is accurate then a 30-yard stretch of surviving Roman hedge will contain 15 to 19 different species of shrubs. However, there is only space in a stretch of this length to accommodate about a dozen mature shrubs. Therefore even if hedgerow-dating did work it would be useless as a means of recognising hedges that are older than the late Saxon period. Nonetheless, a complete field-side length of hedgerow can be found to include a large number of different species and 17, 18 or 19 types could occasionally be counted.

ENVIRONMENTAL FACTORS

Although the science of ecology emphasises the delicate relationships between plants and their environments, the hedgerow-dating formula makes no allowance for such crucial matters. Even so, the proponents of hedgerow-dating have advised against sampling from hedges abutting directly onto woodland, owing to the greater ease of colonisation, and Hooper has suggested that a local correlation should be worked out for each area.[14] However, if the formula has

Parliamentary Enclosure hawthorn hedges, particularly those of the eighteenth century, were often punctuated by additional species grown as standards for timber, fruit or ornament. In this hedge, close to our home in Nidderdale, an exotic cherry tree is an unusual but striking inclusion.

to be recalibrated for every single area in which it is applied, what would remain at the end of the day would be all recalibration and no theory. Factors like soil type, climate, exposure, aspect and micro-climate must apply in hedges, as they do everywhere else, to say nothing of the history of human management.

Some hedgerow shrubs are more prolific in some areas than others, while in many places some shrubs are either absent, or else present in such small and localised quantities that they will not find their way into hedgerows in any numbers. Hazel has been found to be much more prolific in the wet west and much less likely to continue colonisation in areas where nut-loving grey squirrels are rampant. Similarly, holly can be the most numerous shrub in many northern hedges, but is relatively poorly represented in the hedges of the East Midlands where the dating theory was evolved. In a nice little example from Chelsham in Surrey, Geoffrey Hewlett mentions a four-species hedge that has oak, hawthorn, sycamore and sweet chestnut where it runs on clay with flints, but hawthorn, holly, privet and whitebeam when the subsoil changes to chalk.[15]

When living in Cambridgeshire we found that one of the few pleasures of the rapidly decaying countryside was the presence still of some species-rich hedges. In such hedges on the chalk or chalky-boulder clay wayfaring tree, dogwood, spindle and field maple were ten a penny and Midland hawthorn, guelder rose and purging buckthorn could often be found. In the sandstone Dales, where we now live, however, field maple is uncommon in hedgerows; the rambler could wear his boots out before finding much hedgerow dogwood, guelder rose, buckthorn or spindle; and he could wear his legs down to his knees and not find any wayfaring tree or Midland hawthorn.

Each hedgerow shrub has its own British distribution and few are common in all areas where hedgerows are grown. Plainly it must follow that if some areas have more potential indigenous hedgerow colonising species than others, then their hedges will be richer in species, irrespective of the age factor. In a large Wealden estate I found that all the hedges except newly planted hawthorn ones were species-rich, averaging 8 or 9 species per 30-yard section. In Nidderdale, where there must also be a good few old hedges, one will do very well to find a 6-species hedgerow. Environmental factors, like climate and soil acidity, significantly reduce the potential number of hedgerow shrubs.

THE PLANTING OF MIXED HEDGES

At the bottom of our garden there is a species-rich hedge. As well as plenty of hawthorn there is hazel and holly, honeysuckle, two kinds of wild rose, dogwood, field maple, gean, wild privet, spindle and jewels like guelder rose and wayfaring tree, with rowan and bird cherry growing as unusual standards. According to hedgerow-dating lore the hedge should be of a Dark Age vintage, but at the time of writing it is four months old. Obviously it was planted as a mixed hedge; the material came from a nursery near Huddersfield which specialises in authentic native plants. But what would we have done if, like most medieval farmers, we had been impoverished and less scrupulous about pillaging hedging materials from the countryside? Beside the house there is a meadow with a fine old oak, and each autumn the rooks and jackdaws strip

Hedges lose species as well as gain them. Where grey squirrels are very active there may be no young hazel to replace the old trees, all the nut resources being pillaged by the squirrels.

away the acorns and try to split them open with their beaks. Many are beaten into the ground, and each summer when the hay is mown a large crop of oak seedlings is cut. The prospective hedger could obtain any amount of material here, supplementing it with the ash seedlings which sprout in the village gardens. Nearby woods and verges offer unlimited supplies of saplings and brambles without there ever being a need to resort to cuttings and seeds.

It would be strange indeed if such bountiful supplies of mixed shrub materials were scorned by the hedgers of old – but of course, if it can be shown that old hedgerows were commonly planted as mixed hedges of several species, then the whole theory of hedgerow-dating is invalidated as a practical technique. In fact such evidence exists in abundance. Many examples have been collected by Wendy Johnson and we have discovered many more: there is too much evidence to be fully itemised here. As Johnson points out, the reaction of the founder of hedgerow-dating to such evidence is inconsistent: in one context Hooper acknowledges the evidence of mixed planting in Shropshire, but doubts that it occurs in more than about one hedge in ten and also even doubts the veracity of the frequent contemporary reports of mixed plantings.[16] However, in the same year Pollard, Hooper and Moore wrote that: 'Very early planted hedges are likely to have several woodland species, as the abundant surrounding woodland would have provided shrubs for planting and a rich seed supply for colonisation.'[17] If one regards 'very early' as continuing up to and sometimes beyond the mid-eighteenth century then the latter statement is acceptable.

The contemporary evidence about the planting of hedges largely divides between two categories: first, the published advice of 'experts', and second, passing documentary mentions of the composition of new hedges. Modern writers, such as Johnson and Rackham, have discovered numerous examples from the former category, several reproduced here, and these show that hedges were propagated in a variety of ways, using seed, cuttings and seedlings or saplings.[18]

Thomas Tusser advocated the use of seed, which should be planted in October:

> Where speedy quickset for fence ye will draw
> To sow in the seed of the bramble and haw.[19]

He also provided a very tantalising reference amongst his advice for February:

> Buy quickset at market, new gather'd and small,
> Buy bushes or willows, to fence it withall.[20]

Plainly quickset for hedging was available at some markets at this time of the year, and it has also been suggested that hedging plants were commercially available as early as 1316.[21] Were the medieval vendors of hedging plants nurserymen or peasants who had dug up the quicksets in their local woods? On balance the latter explanation would seem the more likely. And what about the bushes or willows: were these being used to build a protective dead hedge around the newly planted quicksets? Probably so, for willow can substitute for hazel in the making of the heathering.

One of the advantages of the mixed hedge was that it would yield different types of timber for different uses. Tusser advocated the use of a variety of trees: ash, crab apple, elm, hazel, holly, thorn and sallow. Fitzherbert, who produced a *Boke of Husbandry* in 1534, agreed: 'gette thy quicksettes in the woode countreye and let theym be of whyte thorne and crabtree for they be beste, holye and hasell be good. And if thou dwelle in the playne countrey, then mayste thou gete both ashe, oke and elm, for those wyll encrease moche woode in shorte space.'[22] Somewhat later, in 1614, Barnaby Googe repeated Columella's 'Roman old rope' method of planting a hedge (See Ch. 1), but claimed to have invented a new technique, whereby young thorns were gathered in the woods: 'cutting off their tops, and I set them on the bank of the ditch so that they stand half a foot out of the ground'.[23] He also provided what Johnson believes to be the earliest reference to a nursery for hedgerow plants.

Commercial nurseries producing hedging material seem to have appeared in the seventeenth century; in 1662 the influential spokesman of the tree-planting movement, John Evelyn, wrote of a gentleman 'who has considerably improv'd his Revenue by sowing Haws only, and raising Nurseries of Quicksets which he sells by the hundred far and near'.[24] This marks the late dawning of the single-species hedgerow, and as the Parliamentary Enclosure movement gained strength in the late eighteenth century, nurseries became the main suppliers of hedging material, with hawthorn by far the most popular choice.

However, in the seventeenth century and part, at least, of the eighteenth century mixed plantings of pillaged seedlings and saplings still remained the norm. In 1609 John Norden showed that hedging plants were still hard to come by, provided yet another exposition of the 'old rope trick' and advocated the planting of hawthorn interspersed with oak and ash[25]. Evelyn advocated the use of hawthorn, but with oak, elm, ash or the like planted at equal intervals of 20 to 30 feet, and noted that crab apple was planted in Herefordshire hedges. Even in the Parliamentary Enclosure hedges of the eighteenth century it was common for useful timber, crab apple or more exotic fruits, or even ornamental trees, to be planted at intervals in hedgerows, though this practice seems to have declined in the nineteenth century. During the period of Parliamentary Enclosure the age-old methods of hedgerow planting were not forgotten, for there were still communities with good access to woodland sources and less ability or inclination to patronise a nursery. Michael Aston writes that 'In Somerset there were few nurserymen even in the nineteenth century and so enclosure in Neroche Forest seems to have involved digging up shrubs in the woods – hedges begin with eight to ten species!'[26]

All this is confirmed when we explore the second category of documentary evidence.[27]

In 1338 a furlong or 'culture' of ploughland was leased at Holedenbank in West Yorkshire, the lessee being given permission to exploit the wood for 'branches, brambles and thorns for making hedges for the said culture'.[28] When William Scoley and his wife were granted land in the Hemsworth area of West Yorkshire in 1413, they were obliged to surround it with a quickthorn (i.e. living) hedge 'which they shall dig at their own cost'.[29] In 1376–8, 'pulling plants of thorns and ashes to put along a ditch on the east of the manor house' was recorded at Forncett in Norfolk.[30]

In Chapter 3 we saw how the Spencers depopulated many villages, often replacing the open ploughlands with hedged sheep pastures. In the sixteenth century some of the sheep barons came under pressure to reconvert to tillage and restore the rural populations, but at Wormleighton the owners petitioned against a reconversion order:

> His hedges . . . be now twenty year old which be grown full of all manner of wood, and one of the greatest commodity in the country . . . and if the hedges were thrown down it should cause much variance betwixt the tenants of the lordship and towns adjoining thereinto which have no right of common.[31]

Not only does this tell us that the twenty-year-old hedges were 'grown full of all manner of wood', and must therefore have been planted as mixed hedges; it also underlines the economic attractions of such diverse hedgerows.

Of all the potent arguments which can be ranged against the theory of hedgerow-dating, that of mixed planting is the most damning. Either the numerous medieval and seventeenth-century writers who recorded mixed planting were deluded, blind, drunk or dishonest or else the theory cannot be used as a basis for the study of hedges. Old hedges are species-rich; that is the way that they were planted. Since planting they may have gained or lost species, but in any event species counting will not date a hedge.

THE WOODLAND RELIC THEORY

This is a concept which frequently appears in accounts of hedgerow-dating, although it is not incorporated into the hedgerow-dating formula. One of the problems of the woodland relic concept is that a careful reading of the relevant literature by various authors may leave unanswered questions about what precisely the theory is saying. The idea has been developed by Dr E. Pollard and applied in a range of local hedgerow studies.[32] The essence of the idea seems to be that while some hedges were planted on cultivated farmland, others originated as wood boundaries or were established on land just taken from the forest. Hedges of the latter type could be richer in species because they might retain a range of woodland shrubs and plants and would be closer to the woodland seed banks. These hedges would contain more 'poor colonisers' or 'woodland relics' – shrubs which seem to have difficulty in colonising young hedges, like field maple, hazel and dogwood – and would also contain woodland relic flora, like wood anemone, primrose, herb Paris and dog's mercury.

It is worth noting in passing that although it frequently appears in accounts of hedgerow-dating, in fact the woodland relic theory contradicts the hedgerow-dating theory, which relates the composition of a hedge solely to age and makes no allowance for origin.

We approach the woodland relic theory with a certain amount of scepticism. Dog's mercury, the most frequently cited woodland relic plant, can be found in most ancient woods, but we have also seen it in woods that are not old and have heard of it, for example, as a weed in a Norwich garden. It can also be found in abundance on our local railway embankment, circa 1870. Primroses can be seen growing in walls, as well as hedgerows and carpet cliff tops in Cornwall which have surely been deforested since quite deeply prehistoric times. Equally, while field maple is regarded as a slow coloniser, associated with old, species-rich hedges, one can find long stretches of hedge which largely consist of field maple. Even so, it is obvious that some shrubs, like elder, ash, wild rose and bramble, will colonise Parliamentary Enclosure hedgerows much more readily than will others.

R. A. D. Cameron writes that 'subsequent work in many parts of the country has amply confirmed Pollard's conclusions'.[33] But frequently such studies show that in the regions studied some hedges are rich in woodland relics, and others are not. The relationship between woodland relics and assarting is often not established, and occasionally the results actually appear unwittingly to contradict the favoured thesis. For example, the hedges in Tasburgh which Addington found to be rich in woodland relics are in fact formed by the subsequent enclosure of open-field strips.[34] It is as plain as a pikestaff that their curving and stepped boundaries are preserving the forms of the old selions – which is evidence that time could better be spent in looking at hedgerow *shapes* than in counting *species*. If we assume that the open fields here were formed around AD 1000 and survived until Tudor times then the Tasburgh land experienced half a millennium of ploughing – quite long enough to knock out any woodland survivors. It may be significant that the woodland relics are associated here with

Dog's mercury (ABOVE) and primrose (BELOW) are said to be woodland relic indicators, yet both can easily be found growing in places that have not been wooded since prehistoric times.

the heavier soils in the parish. Perhaps the factors which encourage woodland plants to colonise a hedgerow are those of shelter, aspect and moisture rather than the origin of the hedgerow. Or could it be that, since woodlands tended to be relegated to the poorer soils, juvenile hedgerow plants growing on cleared land suffer less competition from the grasses which flourish in fertile soils?

Each hedgerow is a miniature woodland environment and each side and each little section of a hedgerow is an environment with its own particular conditions. And so it is not surprising that plants associated with woodlands will each succeed in colonising some environments and fail to be established in others. In every case a multitude of different factors must be involved in the interplay which produced 'favourable' or 'unfavourable' environments for particular plants; research by D. R. Helliwell in Shropshire reveals a small degree of correlation between the presence of woodland relic plants and the proximity of their hedgerow to woodland, just as one might expect.[35]

THE HISTORY OF MANAGEMENT

Hedgerows are features of the man-made landscape and the history of human management or neglect is the most important factor governing the condition and longevity of a hedge. The planters of hedges chose which shrubs to include and which to leave out, and the hedge layers decided which shrub to revitalise by laying and which to dig out. Hedges can be embanked or ditched, or both, or neither. Modern hedge layers often choose to dig out elder, and although little laying is done nowadays, in the past this practice must at least to some extent explain the frequent presence of elder in younger rather than older

The history of human management will affect the composition of a hedge. Here a conservation volunteer is removing elder in the course of hedge-laying.

THE HEDGED LANDSCAPE

Hedgerow patterns in the Vale of York seen from Sutton Bank.

ABOVE Hedged fields around Llanddewi Brefi, Dyfed. BELOW Old hedged fields in the view looking towards Moretonhampstead and Dartmoor. TOP RIGHT Parliamentary Enclosure hedgerows in the view looking north from Dolebury Warren hillfort, Avon. The fields nearest the camera date from 1797. BOTTOM RIGHT Field patterns on the flanks of Hembury hillfort, Devon. Old hedgerows are recognisable to ramblers in the hilltop woods, but otherwise this scene may not have changed greatly since the Iron Age.

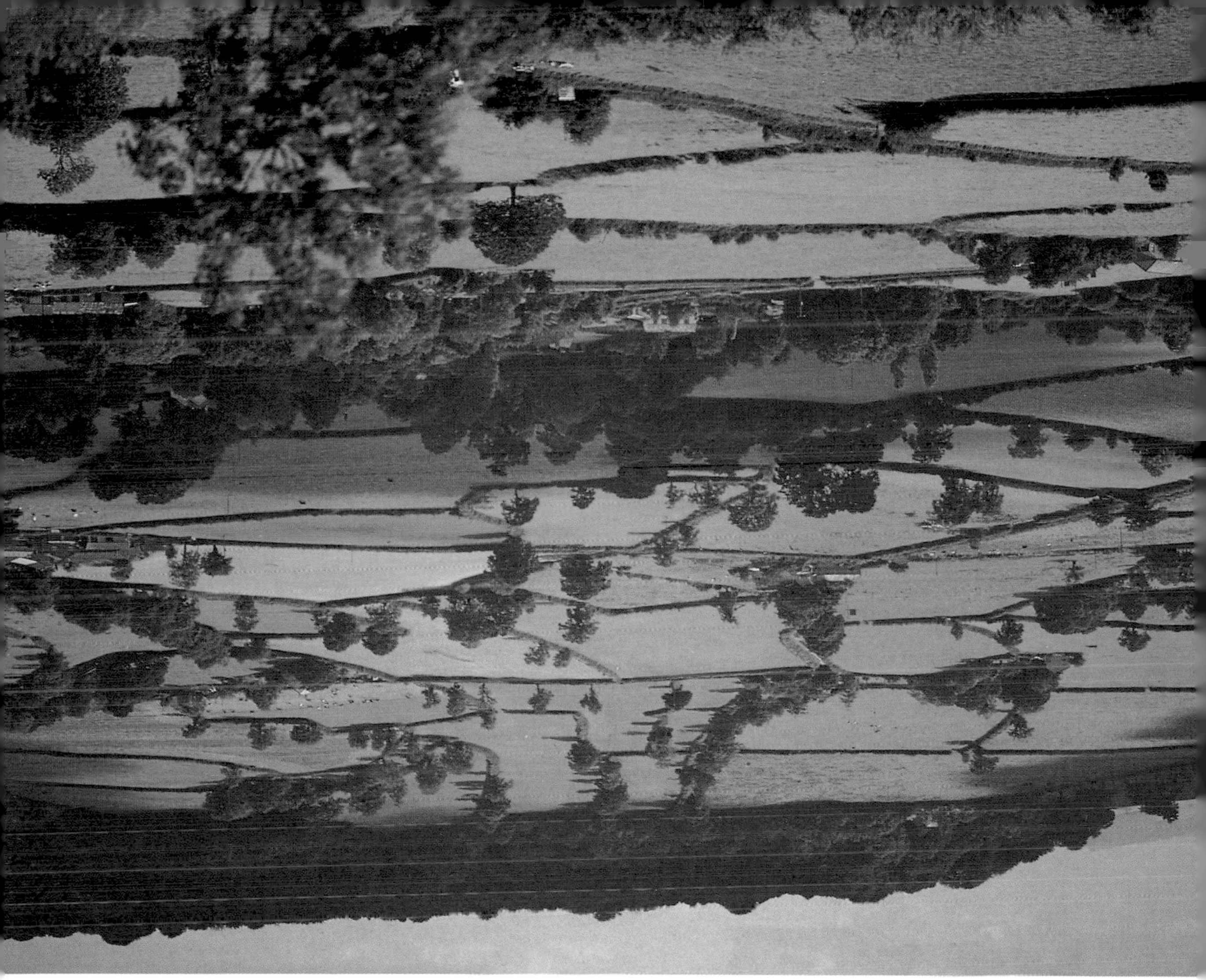
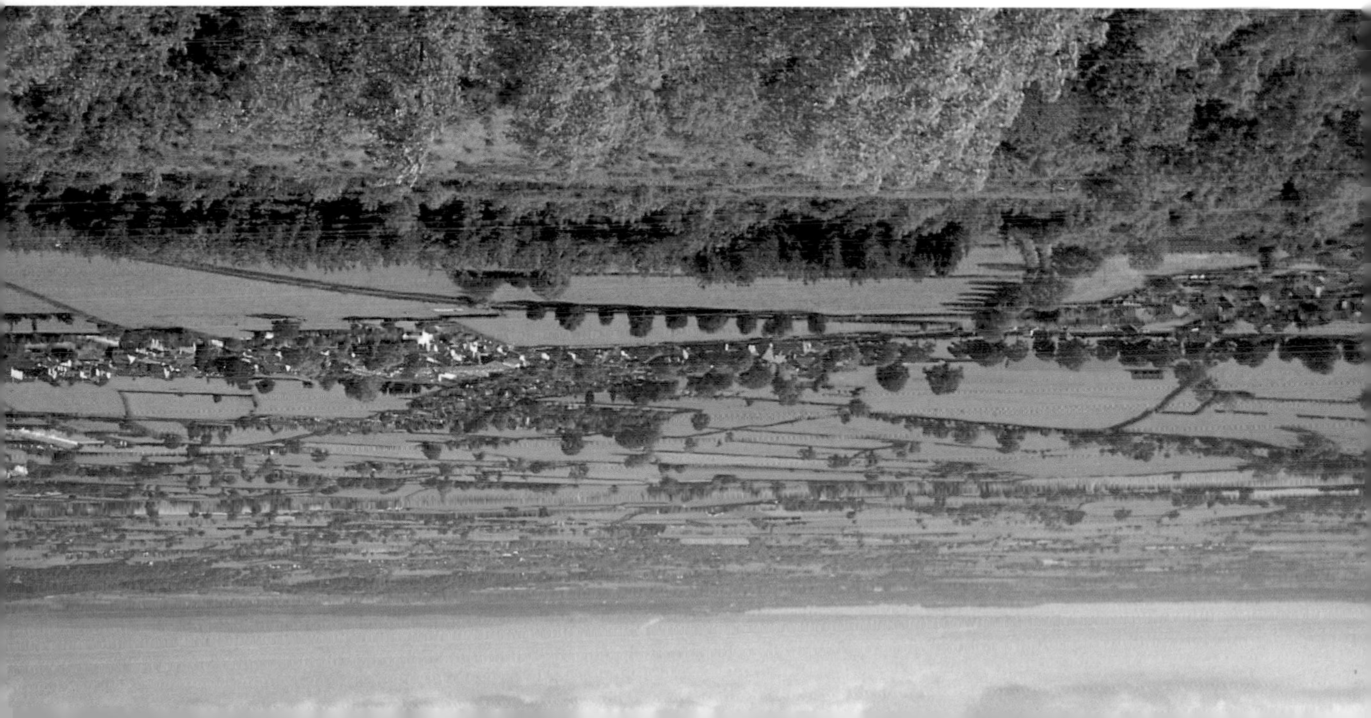

ABOVE Part of the Nidderdale hedgerows explored in Chapter 14. BELOW A Kentish hedge photographed two years after it was laid by a county hedge-laying champion.

hedges. However, there were no hard and fast rules about hedge management. Different regional types exist, ranging from the Cornish hedges, which are walls sometimes crowned with a tuft of hedgerow, and the dense double hedges seen in some other parts. The Midland stockman wanted a strong, bullock-proof barrier and the Yorkshire sheep farmer a lower but denser hedgerow. Experts past and present disagree on the merits of certain shrubs, and depending on whom you read you will find both 'good' and 'bad' labels attached to shrubs like holly and blackthorn.

The history of its management must affect the composition of any hedgerow. Some plants must be more invigorated by laying than others and some must be better able to survive the competition and afflictions in a neglected hedge. Today some will surely survive the battering and twig-shredding inflicted by mechanical trimming better than will others. However, there is no allowance for all this in the hedgerow-dating formula. Moreover, regular trimming will reduce the hedge to a height of somewhere around 5 feet (1.5 m) but the neglect of trimming must favour the more vigorous shrubs at the expense of others. In this way ash, elm, field maple and hazel would shade out spindle, wayfaring tree, buckthorn and dogwood and thus reduce any species count.

STATISTICAL ANALYSIS

The statistician possesses highly specialised skills and in an ideal world these could be applied to confirm or refute hedgerow-dating theory. However, a statistical technique is only as good as the raw data to which it is applied. One needs a large population of independently dated hedgerows and complete accuracy in the counting of their species. In a study of hedges at Otford in Kent, Geoffrey Hewlett wrote that: 'In all, 250 hedges were examined, and results suggest that Dr Hooper's figures are substantially correct.'[36] This seems a rather ambitious conclusion, since only nine of these hedges appeared to be dated by historical sources with any degree of certainty.

The data used in hedgerow-dating are normally organised in the form of a 'scattergram' with the age of the hedge forming the vertical axis and the species count forming the horizontal axis. If hedgerow-dating worked perfectly and the independent dating data were adequate, then the plots of each hedge sampled would lie along a 'regression line' which expressed the relationship between hedgerow age and species. However, available historical information usually results in the appearance of two clusters of plots, one cluster representing dated Parliamentary Enclosure hedgerows, and the other hedges which are not actually dated, but mentioned in Saxon charters.

If hedgerow-dating worked tolerably well but not perfectly then the individual hedge plots would not all lie exactly along the regression line, but would be scattered around it. Sidestepping some more complicated statistical concepts, the degree of scattering and the probability that hedge dates predicted by hedgerow-dating will be reliable can be expressed by a 'correlation coefficient'. As we have seen, Hooper claimed a very high correlation between the age of a hedge and the number of species contained, but C. J. Johnson has shown, using an unsophisticated regression technique, a margin of error of 100 years on either

When allowed to grow quite freely an old hedge may look like this example (from the western margins of the Vale of York). It contains a selection of species; hawthorn is not particularly prominent, though ash and elm are plentiful.

side of the predicted date, rather than the *statistically more acceptable* margin of 200 years on either side of the date.[37] As Williamson has pointed out, 'there would be a 95 per cent chance that a hedge containing four species per 30 yards was planted between circa 1380 and circa 1780'.[38] Readers will be aware that the four centuries spanned by these margins of error amount to rather a lot of time; while confidence in hedgerow-dating is not increased by Williamson's discovery mentioned above, that, in the part of north-west Essex that he studied, early nineteenth-century hedges commonly contain four species per 30-yard length contradicting the 'one species per hundred years' rule.[39]

Statistical techniques could have an important role to play in the study of hedgerows. If there is some sort of botanical succession which affects the ways in which shrubs enter a hedgerow, it might be useful to explore how one shrub might pave the way for colonisation by another, and also to attempt an analysis of nearest neighbours in the hedgerows community, in order to explore the ecological aspects of co-existence. However, the last word in this section can be left to Johnson: 'To those who would contend that statistics is no concern of the historian, the only possible reply is that hedge-dating is a statistical game, and must therefore be played by the statistician's rules.'[40]

CONCLUSION

The number of shrub species contained in a hedgerow does not represent a reliable guide to the age of the hedge concerned. During recent years enthusiasts have spent countless hours in such shrub counts, despite the great shortage of historical information available to test the validity of the technique. We are sure that the time involved would have been spent more productively in efforts to record and preserve field names and to relate hedges to fields with distinctive and loosely datable shapes, like the shapes produced by the early enclosure of open-strip fields.

Even so, hedgerow-dating has greatly increased the general awareness of hedges and their importance in the rural landscape, and if it serves as a stepping-stone towards a better understanding of hedgerows it can only be a positive contribution.

Although we do not believe that the theory reveals the ages of hedges there is an underlying truth. Young hedges do tend to be species-poor, normally containing hawthorn and a few colonists, like elder, wild rose and bramble. Old hedges, in contrast, often prove to be species-rich. This may largely be due to the fact of their original planting as mixed hedges, but colonisation probably has a role to play. Some shrubs seem to be associated with older hedges, while elder

Colonisation in progress: this sycamore seedling may succeed in exploiting a hedgerow gap.

seems to flourish in younger, gappy ones. Williamson found elder to be present in 80 per cent of 3-species hedges but only 40 per cent of 12-species hedges, and bramble showed a fairly similar pattern. In contrast, field maple, hazel, dogwood and ash showed a marked preference for species-rich hedgerows, as did oak; while purging buckthorn, wayfaring tree and spindle were not found in hedges with less than six shrubs and became more numerous as the hedges became richer.[41]

General conclusions are hard to find, but on the evidence available we would suggest that hedges with four or fewer shrubs are likely to date between circa 1750 to circa 1850, the period of Parliamentary Enclosure, while those with more are likely to be older. Field maple, hazel, dogwood, oak, buckthorn, wayfaring tree, guelder rose and spindle seem to be associated with the older sorts of hedges.

REFERENCES TO CHAPTER 5

1 Hoskins, W. G., *Fieldwork in Local History*, Faber & Faber, 1967, 1982 edn, 118.
2 *ibid.*
3 Pollard, E., Hooper, M. D. and Moore, N. W., *Hedges*, Collins, 1974.
4 Muir, R., *The Shell Guide to Reading the Landscape*, Michael Joseph, 1981, 109
5 See Hoskins, 1967, Hooper, 1971 and Pollard, Hooper and Moore, *op. cit.*
6 Addington, S., 'The Hedgerows of Tasburgh', *Norfolk Archaeology*, 1977, 70–83
7 Hewlett, G., Reconstructing an Historical Landscape from Field and Documentary Evidence; Otford in Kent, *Agr. Hist. Rev XXI*, 95, 1973, 94–110.
8 Willmot, A., 'The Woody Species of Hedges with Special Reference to Age in Church Broughton Parish, Derbyshire,' *Journal of Ecology, 68*, 1980, 249–285.
9 Addington, S., *op. cit.* 72.
10 The first entry in the Honour court of the Forest of Knaresborough held in Knaresborough Castle, 29 October 1349.
11 Williamson, T., unpublished University of Cambridge doctoral thesis, 100.
12 Addington, S., *op cit*, 71.
13 Fitzherbert, *The Boke of Husbandry*, 1534.
14 Pollard, E., Hooper, M. R. and Moore, N. W., *op cit.* 80.
15 Hewlett, G., 'Stages in the Settlement of a Downland Parish: a Study of the Hedges of Chelsham', *Survey Archaeology Collections, 82*, 1980, 93.
16 Johnson, W., 'Hedges – a Review of Some Early Literature', *The Local Historian*, 1978, 195–204.
17 Pollard, E., Hooper, M. D. and Moore, N. W., *op cit*, 104.
18 Johnson, W. *op cit* and Rackham, O., *Ancient Woodland: Its History, Vegetation and Uses in England*, Edward Arnold, 1980.
19 Tusser, Thomas, *Five Hundred Points of Good Husbandry*, 1573.
20 Tusser, *op cit*.
21 Rackham, O. in Woodell, S. R. J. (ed.), *The English Landscape, Past, Present and Future*, Oxford, 1985, 93, quoting Thorold Rogers, 1866, Vol 2, 594.
22 Fitzherbert, *op cit*.
23 Googe, Barnaby (1614), *The Whole Art of Husbandry Contained in Four Books*.
24 Evelyn, John, *Sylva* (1662).
25 Norden, John, *The Surveyor's Dialogue* (1609).
26 Aston, M., *Interpreting the Landscape*, Batsford, 1985.
27 Rackham, O., *op cit*, 93.
28 Clay, C. T. (ed) 'Yorkshire Deeds VII', *Yorkshire Archaeol. Soc. Rec. Ser. 83*, 1932, 37, No. 98.
29 Price, M. J. S. (ed), 'Yorkshire Deeds X', *Yorkshire Archaeol. Soc. Rec. Ser. 120*, 1955, 110, No. 306.
30 Davenport, F. G., *The Economic Development of a Norfolk Manor 1086–1565*, 1967, London.
31 Fisher, F. J. *EcH.R.* X, 105, quoted in Beresford, M. W. (1954), *The Lost Villages of England*, 1954, Lutterworth, 215–6.
32 Pollard, E., 'Hedges VII: Woodland Relic Hedges in Huntingdon and Peterborough', *Journal of Ecology, 61*, 1973, 343–352.
33 Cameron, R. A. D., 'The Biology and History of Hedges: Explaining the Connection', *Biologist, 31*, 1984, No. 4, 204.
34 Addington, S., *op cit*, 75.
35 Helliwell, D. R., 'The Distribution of Woodland Plant Species in Some Shropshire Hedgerows', *Biol Conservation 7* (1975), 61–72.
36 Hewlett, G., *op cit.* 1973, 95.
37 Johnson, C. J. 'The Statistical Limitations of Hedge Dating', *Local Historian*, Feb. 1980, 29–33.
38 Williamson, T., *op cit*, 99.
39 Williamson, T., *op cit*, 100.
40 Johnson, W., *op cit*, 33.
41 Williamson, T., *op cit*, 101–104.

·6·

HOW CAN YOU DATE A HEDGE?

Hedges can be dated – or at least some of them can. As we have seen, species counting will not provide the answers, so instead one must turn to the methodical and time-consuming techniques of the local historian. Only a small proportion of older hedgerows can now be dated to within a few decades of their being planted, but one can often locate the age of a hedge within certain time brackets. Essentially the method is one of moving backwards through time and using whatever documentary evidence one can find to allocate dates to the particular features of a countryside. In this chapter we bring together evidence from other chapters that can be used by the reader in a local hedgerow survey.

If the hedges in the area concerned form straight, rectilinear patterns, then the odds are stacked heavily in favour of a Parliamentary Enclosure date, which will almost certainly fall in the period 1750–1850 and more likely towards the middle than the margins of this time bracket. Bear in mind, though, that hedgerow patterns like those in the Dengie Peninsula loosely resemble the Parliamentary Enclosure patterns and were also set out by surveyors, but are Roman in age. Enquiries at the country record office will easily produce a date for the Parliamentary Enclosure of the parish concerned and may also produce the original Enclosure map – perhaps too a complimentary pre-Enclosure map drawn at the same time and revealing a detailed picture of the parish on the eve of Enclosure. The field boundaries determined by the Enclosure commissioners had to be marked by hedges (or walls) within a year of the allocation. However, often the new fields were large and owners might soon choose to subdivide them. Successive editions of large-scale Ordnance Survey maps chart the emergence of such internal hedgerows and allow them to be dated fairly closely. (OS maps at 25-inch scale are 130–150 years old, depending on the area concerned.) In the Midlands, Parliamentary Enclosure mainly affected arable lands, but towards the upland margins – in the Pennines, Devon and Cornwall – commons and wastes were affected, with walls generally being built in the north and hedgebanks in the south-west.

A hedge like this one (on the outskirts of Burton Leonard, North Yorkshire) must be at least as old as its oldest standard trees, which are at least a century old. But to find out more you must study its shape (straight, curving, reversed-'S' and so on) and explore the evidence of old maps and other documents.

A substantial number of Enclosure Award maps have been lost and scores of parishes were completely untouched by the Enclosure movement. In such parishes, however, the Tithe Award map can provide a superior source of information. These maps date mainly from the years 1836–44 and were compiled following the Tithe Commutation Act of 1836. Where a parish had experienced Parliamentary Enclosure, tithes were normally extinguished at this time, so the Tithe maps form a complimentary distribution. They tend to be available for only a minority of parishes in the Midlands Enclosure counties, but in counties like Kent, Shropshire and Cornwall the coverage is almost complete. The parish may still possess its Tithe map, but in any event the local record office will have a copy. Not only are the current field boundaries depicted, but also the acreages, owners and field names are given.

As we go beyond the Victorian and Georgian eras, the map coverage becomes more patchy and varied, though privately commissioned estate maps of the post-medieval period are quite numerous and can provide a detailed and dated picture of field and hedge patterns.

The older the hedge, the more fieldwork and careful observation of the countryside gain importance. Piecemeal enclosure by agreement in Tudor or later times would be sure to preserve some of the outlines of medieval open-field farming in the newly hedged networks. Sometimes the old records describe a large-scale bout of enclosure by agreement in a parish or estate, but generally such enclosure was gradual and piecemeal. Hedges with a 'reversed-"S"' shape tell of the enclosure of field strips, and, since church land was difficult to alienate under such agreements, the hedge-bounded strips of the vicar's or rector's glebe may still endure. Field names, often gleaned today from the Tithe map, may record old enclosures by agreement in names like Adlands or Hades, referring to fields composed of former headlands (the part of the old field where the ploughs turned): Furlong or Shott, Severals, or, in East Anglia, Wongs. Deer parks proliferated in the earlier medieval centuries and were then disparked in large numbers in the centuries which followed. Sometimes the field pattern which still exists today or which is recorded on a Tithe or Enclosure map will show the oval or oblong form of a deer park with the internal hedgerows, often outlining a fairly regular pattern of divisions, revealing a network of hedges planted when disparking occurred.

Medieval assarts, mainly dating from the couple of centuries before the arrival of the Black Death, tend to form smallish, irregular fields, and the Tithe map or other map with field names is likely to record the diagnostic assart names: 'Stocks', 'Stocking', 'Stubbing', 'Riddens', 'Riddings', 'Sart', 'Stubbs' and 'Rode'. Small crofts or closes around the houses in a village might be as old as the village itself, but could also have appeared as the village expanded. Others were created in the sixteenth and seventeenth centuries, when there was a rising demand for pastures and paddocks. Often a manor or country seat will be seen to be surrounded by little hedged fields with diagnostic names like 'Orchard Close', 'Kitchen Field', 'Oasthouse Field' or 'Dovecot Close'. These enclosures, each playing a special role in the household economy, could be as old as the house, or they could be older fields which gained their special role when, or after, the mansion was built.

While the 'Stocks' and 'Stubbing' assart names tend to predate 1250, at this point the evidence really peters out, for the Saxon charter description of perambulations and the spatially imprecise medieval documentary sources only give information on a small minority of hedges. All that one can now do is look at the relationship between old fields and datable man-made features – like Roman roads. If the roads cut across the grain of the fields to leave oddly shaped cut-offs then the fields – though not necessarily their hedges – are likely to be pre-Roman. Finally it is worth mentioning that recently emerging evidence suggests that pre-Roman countrysides tended to consist of large blocks of smallish, squarish fields, all the components of a block sharing a common axis, while fairly straight parallel lanes, 'drifts' or 'droves' formed the boundaries of the blocks. Find such a pattern of 'co-axial' fields which is cut across by a younger Roman road and you may have made a most useful discovery.

·7·

HEDGEROWS OF DIFFERENT KINDS

Hedgerows come in a wide spectrum of forms. A range of factors, like origin, function, management, local farming tradition, age, soil and climate, can each play a part in determining the character of a hedge. While it would be easy to stretch the importance of regional farming tradition too far, it is fair to say that several regions of the country do tend to have their own type of hedge. While a Parliamentary Enclosure hawthorn hedge in, say, Suffolk may not seem greatly different from a comparable one in, say, Avon, there are strikingly obvious differences between a Yorkshire sheep hedge, the shrub-tufted wall of a Cornish 'hedge' and the verdant curtain of a Scilly Isles daffodil field hedge.

We have already described how environmental factors will influence the composition of a hedgerow. Some shrubs, most notably hawthorn, combine excellent hedging qualities with their presence and their ability to flourish in virtually every situation where a hedge might be planted; while others, such as wayfaring tree or purging buckthorn, are seldom encountered in hedges planted beyond the main range of the rather fastidious shrubs concerned. Often environmental factors, which determine what will prosper in the competitive world of the hedgerow and which species are available to the local hedge planter, can be seen to exert a considerable influence within a relatively small area. In 1976, hedges in the former East Riding of Yorkshire were surveyed and a range of local characteristics emerged, even though it was not always possible to separate out the influences of environment, history and management. D. J. Boatman reported that the lime-loving wayfaring tree and dogwood were respectively beyond and close to their northern limits, and while dogwood could be found in a minority of the hedges on the chalk Wolds and Holderness, wayfaring tree was absent. The distribution of field maple was uneven, the shrub appearing in 80 per cent of Holderness hedges, but only 35 per cent of those in the Wolds and only 17 per cent of those in the Vale of York. Wild privet, a lime-loving shrub, was absent in the Vale, rare in Holderness, but found in 10 per cent of hedges in the Wolds; guelder rose was also absent in the Vale but found in around 15 per cent of hedgerows in the other two regions; while crab apple was found in almost half the hedges of the Vale but made infrequent appearances elsewhere. The local traditions of management must play some part in explaining the variations, with oak being trimmed in the Vale, where it is widespread, but grown as hedgerow standards in the Wolds and Holderness, where it is less frequent. While the gardener will have little difficulty in growing a shrub like guelder rose throughout most of northern Britain, the cut and thrust of hedgerow life makes no concession to shrubs that are poorly attuned to the local environment.

The origin of a hedge will be reflected in its appearance, although in time management and factors like invasion and colonisation will, increasingly, modify its form. 'Spontaneous hedges' have not been deliberately planted, but once established they have been either tolerated or encouraged by man. Were we and our grazing animals to disappear from these islands, most parts of Britain would swiftly revert to scrub and then broadleafed woodland. And so it follows that any ground which is protected from grazing and ploughing will soon acquire a community of shrubs and climbers. Most old hedges were deliberately planted, but a portion will have had spontaneous origins. This could occur as shrubs became established in the protective shelter of decaying fences or dead hedges, or colonised the verge between a trackway and such barriers.

This 'spontaneous hedge', on the edge of the North York Moors, has successfully colonised the top of an older wall. It is rich in ash, hawthorn and honeysuckle. The overgrown relics of field walls can sometimes be found in the bottoms of north country hedgerows.

It is not easy to devise criteria which will differentiate between the hedgerow and the zone of shrubs which will colonise a ribbon of protected land. In former times country roads could exist as trench-like holloways, engraved into the landscape by the regular passage of wheels, hoofs and shoes. But they often existed as broad, rutted green 'drifts' or 'droves', the width of the thoroughfare providing grazing for beasts in transit and allowing alternative lines to be exploited in winter when the main track was churned into mud. With the advent of the sheep-and-cattle lorry and the metalling of an economical strip of roadway, broad verges can be left, and if they are not managed by the road authorities then 'hedges' will appear. While on the subject of roadside hedges it is worth noting that a few studies have found that roadside hedges tend to be slightly richer in species than those around adjacent fields. In the Weald, for example, we have looked at areas with field hedges of around eight shrub species abutting roadside hedges with nine or ten species. The reason for this is not known. Could it be that the roads have served as busy corridors for the dispersal of seeds, somewhat in the way that trains dispersed Oxford ragwort along our rail arteries? Alternatively, it can be argued that roadside hedges were much more likely to be damaged than others: jostling cattle, overturning carts, waggons trying to pass in restricted spaces and travellers breaking through to avoid a swampy track would all open gaps in the hedge, providing spaces which new colonisers could exploit.

In the north of England drystone walls were sometimes built to supersede existing hedgerows in the post-medieval period, but many of these walls have in turn surrendered to spontaneous hedges. In the Yorkshire Dales and North York Moors one will often find that old wall stones lie hidden and entwined by shrubs at the foot of the hedge. In such cases it is plain that a neglected wall has provided just sufficient protection to allow shrubs to root and grow in its crevices. More recently, the arrival of the diesel and electric trains has removed the threat of fires started by stray sparks from the firebox of a passing engine, so that the coppicing and controlled burning of railway cuttings and embankments is less important than before. In the course of a century or so bare earthen railway banks and cuttings have often become diverse and almost impenetrable ribbons of woodland. Beside Hayley Wood in Cambridgeshire is the abandoned track of a railway dating from 1862. Railway workers were unable to reach the base of the boundary fence with their scythes, and in the course of a century or so an 8-species hedges (including woodland relic field maple) developed, it now being preserved and managed like a conventional hedge. While this may depress the advocates of hedgerow-dating, it does show the ability of the spontaneous hedge to cash in on every opportunity that man allows. Since a spontaneous hedge that has become the subject of trimming or laying will take on an appearance that could be indistinguishable from that of an old planted hedge, it is impossible to know how many of our hedges have spontaneous origins. Oliver Rackham guesses that perhaps one quarter of English hedges 'have arisen naturally along fences and boundaries, chiefly at time of recession and neglect'. This strikes us as a considerable over-statement of the case, and we would be rather surprised if even one-eighth of our hedges could be shown to be spontaneous.

When the few surviving hawthorn plants die this scarp of stabilised earth will be the last relic of an old hedgerow. The field above the scarp was ridge-and-furrow ploughland in the Middle Ages and the 'evolved hedgebank' could be largely composed of soil which was trapped then by the hedge. A similar 'lynchet' can just be discerned on the left-hand section of the skyline.

In most parts of the country one will find some hedges which stand on hedgebanks, and in a few regions really imposing hedgebanks are the norm. Hedgebanks are sometimes associated with old territorial boundaries, though whether particular boundaries of this kind date from Saxon, Roman or earlier times may be very difficult to know. It is even more difficult to discover whether the boundary banks concerned were hedged from the outset. However, since a hedge could only enhance the quality and visibility of the barrier one would expect that hedges of either the planted or the spontaneous kind would soon be acquired. Boundary banks can be single, double, or double with a hollowed trackway occupying the central space. From the Bronze Age through to Norman times some boundary banks were massive and existed as political rather than proprietorial frontier works. Offa's Dyke on the old Anglo-Welsh border, Grimsdyke in Wessex and Devil's Dyke in Cambridgeshire are the best known examples, but there are many more. Whether these great ditch-fronted earthworks were originally hedged, palisaded or bare-topped is not known. In the twelfth, thirteenth and fourteenth centuries substantial banks, hedgebanks and ditches were erected around deer parks.

As we shall see, hedgebanks commonly surround fields in Wales and in the south-west of England, but on sloping ground in all parts of the country scarp-like 'evolved' hedgebanks will gradually form, particularly if adjacent fields are periodically ploughed. The exposure of soil by ploughing enormously increases the erosive power of slope-wash, so that particles of soil are carried downslope

by the surface run-off of rainwater or snow-melt. A hedge running across the slope will act as an effective 'dam', with the eroded silts accumulating at its foot. However, this hedge can do nothing to arrest the erosion of material on its downslope side, although this material may be trapped and stabilised by a hedgerow lying further down the slope. Over time, the hillslope hedge will acquire a position running along the crest of a downhill-facing escarpment, and if the hillside hedges are removed, then the hill will be seen to have a step-like profile, each step or scarp formed by drifting silts which were stabilised by the hedges. Smaller steps may also be found in association with hedges running downslope or diagonally to the angle of slope, reflecting differences in the cultivation of adjacent fields (ploughed and intermittently ploughed fields eroding far more rapidly than the rate of soil creep in permanent pasture), as well as localised patterns of slope and run-off. Over time such hedge scarps can become impressive features, and one can find examples where the land on the upslope side of a hedge is ten feet (about 3 m) higher than that on the downslope side. In Otford parish in Kent, Geoffrey Hewlett has described 4-ft (1.2 m) evolved banks which have formed on slopes of only two degrees. The size of an evolved bank cannot be used to date a hedge – too many variables are involved – but any hedge associated with a sizable evolved bank, scarp or 'lynchet' is likely to be pretty old.

There are two fundamental types of managed hedge, the Midlands type and the banked forms of Wales and the south-west, but within these main categories there are numerous regional variants. An example of the former is the Midlands bullock hedge or standard hedge which can be seen southwards from Co. Durham, through the Midlands and westwards to the Welsh Marches. This type of hedge is not planted on an earthbank, although of course it can acquire an evolved bank or become banked if it is used as a repository for mud scraped up during a scouring of an adjacent ditch. A ditch is generally present, often assisting in the drainage of heavy land, but also protecting one side of the hedge against browsing by livestock. When such a hedge is laid, the pleachers (see Ch. 8) are slanted away from the ditch to protect the young growth rising from the foot of the hedge against browsing from the unditched side.

This is a tall and robust type of hedge, capable of confining powerful bullocks, though regional variations can be found. In parts of Yorkshire, where sheep have traditionally been more important than cattle, hedgers have aimed to produce hedges which are lower but denser than the Midlands stereotype; while in the East Midlands, where the emphasis has swung towards arable farming, the pleachers are aligned with the hedge and new growth rises through the old, and so there is less incursion on the adjacent crops. The Leicestershire 'bullfinch' (presumably meaning 'bull fence') seems to have been a common type of hedge in this county in the nineteenth century, existing as an unusually

The landscape detective can read much of the history of this beech shelterbelt in Cambridgeshire. The beech must have replaced an older (blackthorn?) hedge beside this Roman road about a century ago. Originally it was laid in the style of a Midland hedge – as the 'elbows' at the base of the multiple trunks show – but subsequently the beech was allowed to grow tall in the manner of the shelterbelt rather than the hedge.

tall and bulky ditched hawthorn hedge. Its daunting proportions made it unpopular with the fox-hunting gentlemen of the time (and let us hope that it brought a number of them to their doom).

Changes in farming practice are reflected in changes in the management of hedges. Often this simply involves the removal or neglect of hedgerows. In East Anglia and parts of the eastern counties, where the harvesting of EEC grain subsidies has become the main preoccupation, hedges that might once have been laid are now coppiced, all growth being cut down to the 'stools' at the base of the shrubs. This invigorates the hedgerow, encourages a rapid regrowth and provides shelter for partridge, but it does not produce a stock-proof barrier. Coppicing seems to have been practised in the east for many decades, but when livestock were still kept the adjacent fields were cropped for several years after coppicing until the barrier was strong enough to withstand grazing. Close to our home in Yorkshire an expanse of riverside land which was medieval meadow and then periodically ploughed pasture has been exploited for fruit and vegetable farming. The greater need for shelter has resulted in the planting of a poplar shelterbelt close to the lines of a quite recently grubbed-up hedgerow, while a formerly nondescript surviving hedge has been allowed to grow as a magnificent 10-ft (3.9-m) tall wind barrier.

In a few widely scattered parts of Britain tall hedgerows have been exploited as protection for specialised crops rather than as stock-proof barriers. In Kent, Sussex, Herefordshire and Worcestershire, for example, one may find curtains of hawthorn and other species sheltering the remaining hop fields. Now, as the British hop industry contracts with the growth of lager drinking and the importation of continental hops, these fine hedges must be threatened. In the Scilly Isles and parts of Cornwall the development of early daffodil farming during the last century has led to the appearance of networks of tiny, rectangular fields enmeshed in massive twenty-foot hedges which afford protection from the fierce, salt-laden Atlantic gales. Alien shrubs like *Escallonia* and *Pittosporum crassifolium* have been favoured. In some parts of Kent, like the Chingley Wood area, 'walls' of lofty but closely spaced poplars were planted to shelter the orchards. Hedges such as these are a halfway house between the conventional hedgerow and the shelter-belt, which are represented by the wonderful Scots pine alignments of the Norfolk Brecklands, the characteristic woodland strips or 'shaws' of the Weald, or the incongruous rows of poplars seen in various parts of the English lowlands. However, it is worth noting that some of the rows of Scots pine planted during the enclosure of the dry, sandy expanses of the Norfolk Brecklands were originally managed as hedgerows. Generally the attempts to control the intractable pines were soon abandoned, so that shelterbelts resulted.

The hedgerows of Wales and south-western England display much more diversity than the Midlands type. These hedges, which may or may not be embanked, are mainly constructed as sheep fences and are low and dense, incorporating dead wood which is placed in the heart of the hedge after laying to preserve a sheep-proof barrier. In the border counties, hedges which combine features of the Welsh and Midlands types can be seen. In Welsh hedges the pleachers may be layed 'single-brush', like those of the Midlands hedge, or

ABOVE Robust beech hedgebanks are a characteristic legacy of the enclosure of a large part of Exmoor by the Knight dynasty in the early nineteenth century. This is a typical countryside near Simonsbath. Planted beech makes a good, windproof barrier, though beech is seldom seen as a colonist of hedgerows. BELOW An unusual combination of hedgerows and double Scots Pine shelterbelts on an exposed plateau near Hemyock in Devon.

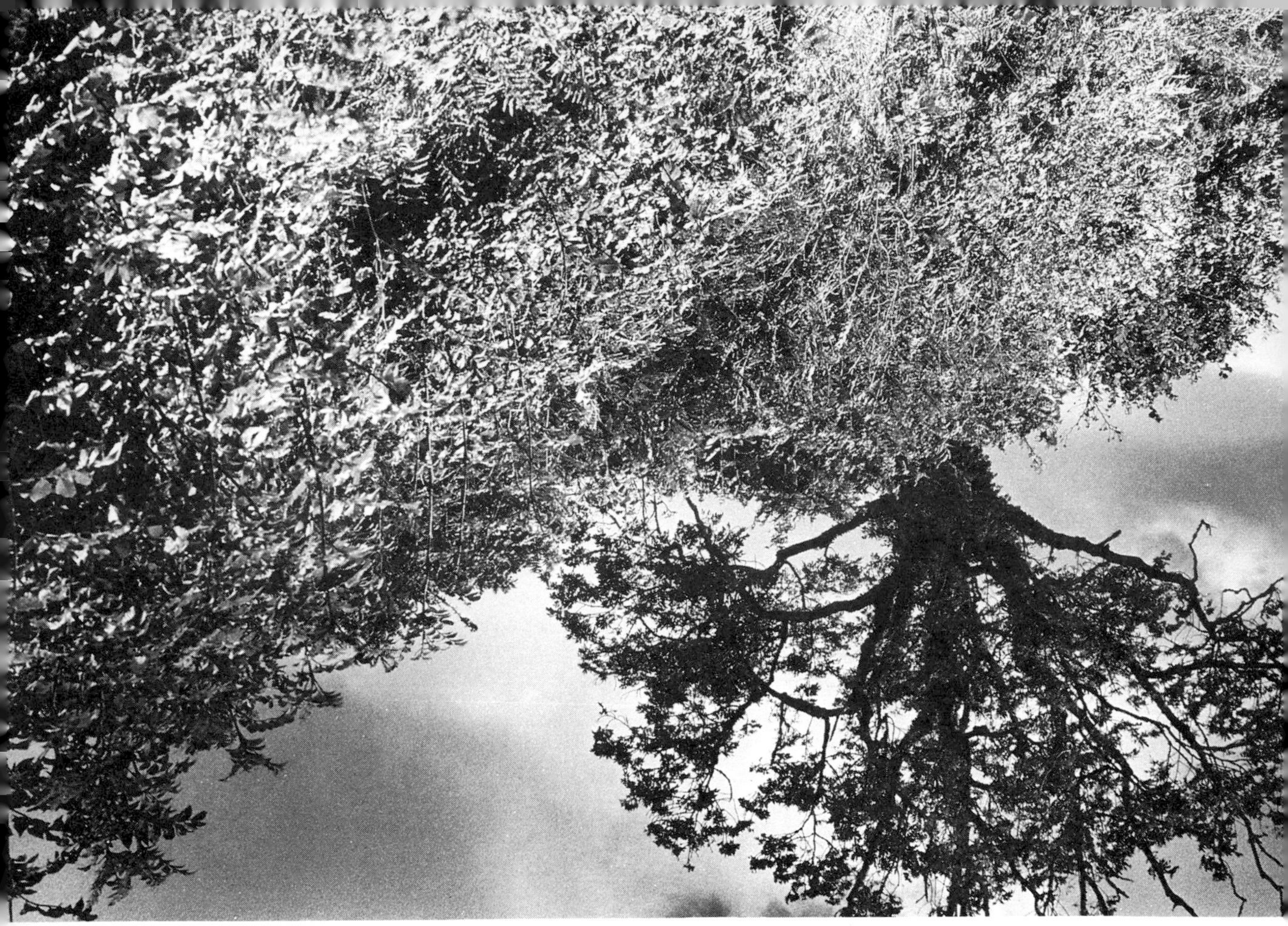

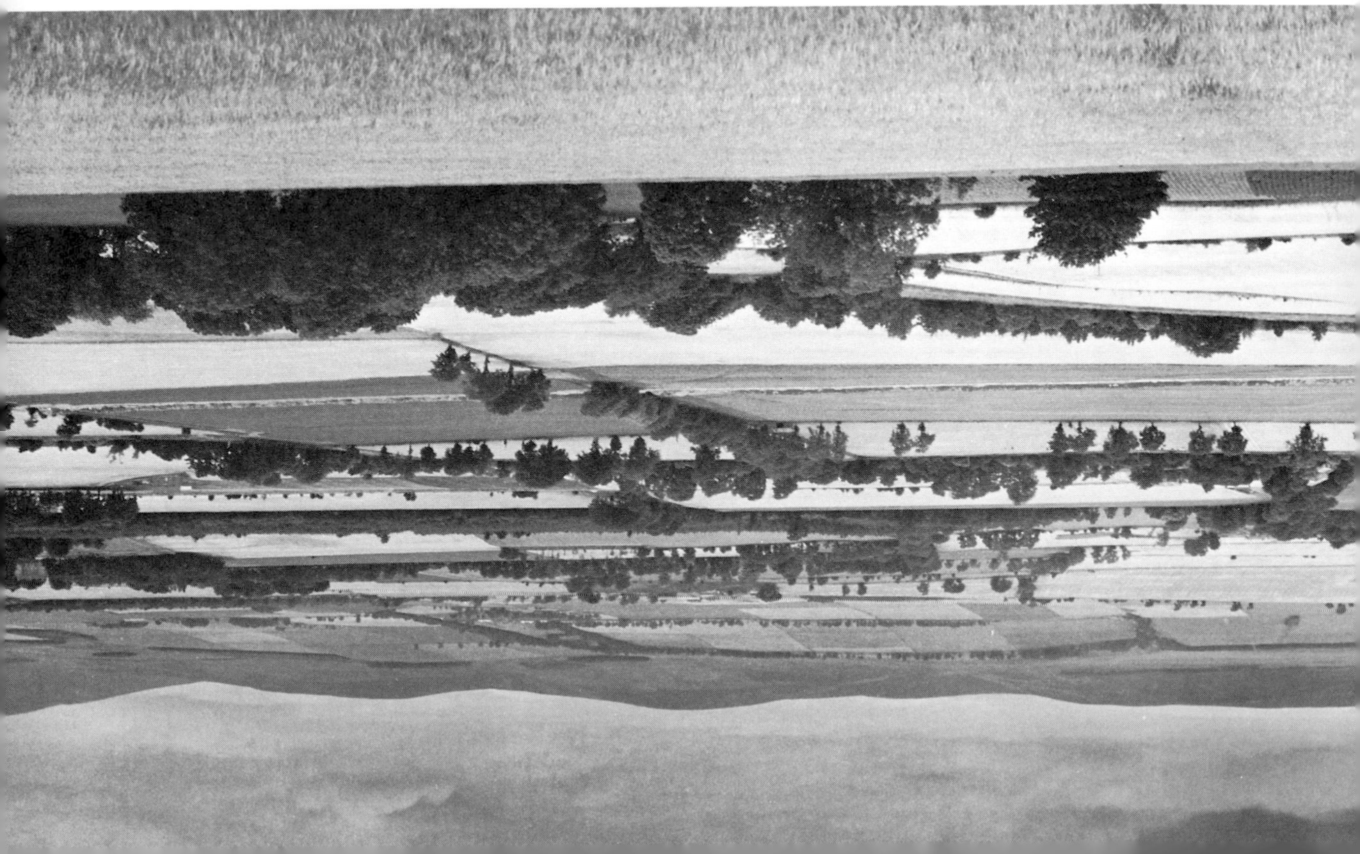

'double-brushed', with bushy ends projecting on both sides of the hedge. This provides a measure of protection to both sides of the newly laid hedge where, as is frequently the case, there is no ditch. Most Welsh hedges have banks rather than ditches, although these banks may be known, confusingly, as 'ditches'. Stakes are not always used, while in some places 'crops', or living stakes are exploited. 'Crooks' are also used: crook-shaped stakes which help to hook and hold down the laid pleachers. In all, about a dozen different Welsh hedging styles have been recognised, varying according to local traditions and conditions and the bulk or athleticism of the sheep they are designed to confine. In the Yorkshire Dales, (where pleachers are known as 'liers') crooks are also used, and were called 'gibs'.

In the English West Country, the hedgebank has ascendancy, the crowning hedge sometimes being little more than a secondary consideration. Many of the westernmost hedges have never been laid and include much briar and brambles. In the east of Devon and the other Wessex counties laying is practised, the aim often being more to provide stock shelter from wind than a daunting barrier, as the traditional lowland sheep varieties here are less agile and adventurous than those of the Welsh uplands. Hedges resemble the 'flying hedges' of South Wales: low hedges laid almost flat upon a substantial bank.

In Devon, particularly, the hedgebanks are a delightful feature of the countryside. Maintenance work begins with the scouring of the ditch, and then the hedgebank is turfed, as necessary. Then the hedge is laid, often in the double-brushing manner, with crooks being used to hold the pleachers or 'steepers' in place. There is good evidence that, while the Cornish walls may not deliberately have been planted, the Devon hedgebanks, once built, were planted with a mixture of shrubs. Pollard, Hooper and Moore quote from the recollections of Charles Vancouver, written around 1800, which describe how banks were built 6 ft (1.8 m) high, faced with turf and planted atop with double rows of oak, ash, beech, alder, hazel and hawthorn. These shrubs were collected from the waste, hedgerows and woods and sold at 1s. 6d. per horse load. Although Vancouver could recall the building of hedgebanks in Devon, the tradition stretched back far beyond his day; and the evidence from Dartmoor, described in Ch. 3, shows that hedged wall banks, planted with ash, hawthorn, holly and blackthorn, were being erected in the fifteenth and sixteenth centuries in association with a rise in sheep farming, while surviving field patterns in parts of Devon might easily date from the Dark Ages or earlier still.

The height of hedgebanks varies enormously; in parts of Wales the bank is just a few inches tall, though in Monmouthshire, Glamorgan and Devon it can be several feet in height. On Exmoor, where the Knight dynasty of Midlands

ABOVE In Scotland 'Improvements' formed the equivalent of the English Agricultural Revolution. Some geometric hedge patterns were created, but frequently stone walls or 'consumption dykes' were favoured. In this picture of an area near Brechin, the Improvements created some hedgerows, but the straight lines of shelterbelts are more obvious. BELOW A typical old Devon hedgebank. Formerly the bank may have been re-turfed in the course of laying; now it is colonised by shrubs, ferns and herbs of the verge.

ironfounders purchased a vast estate in 1818, the fields claimed from the moor were partitioned by gate-high earthbanks which were crowned with beech – a tree which most hedgers regarded as a garden plant finding favour in the south-west. The typical Cornish hedge is really a wall of massive moorstone (granite) boulders, with a tufting of thorn sometimes growing in the earth packing of the wall top. Some of these 'hedges' are solid accumulations of boulders; others consist of an earthbank about 4.5 ft (1.4 m) tall which is faced on both sides with stone and crowned by turf, through which thorn may grow. Some of the oldest fields which are still in use can be seen in the extreme west of Cornwall. They are bounded by 'hedges' formed of granite boulders cleared from the adjacent fields which are topped by stones and earth. Sometimes the 'hedges' wander to include rocks too heavy to shift. Incorporated into these banks and providing evidence of the date of their construction are artefacts of the Bronze Age.

While the Cornish wall is a 'hedge', the Irish hedge is a 'ditch'. On old estate land in Ireland one may see geometrical hedge patterns which date from eighteenth- and nineteenth-century improvements and resemble the Parliamentary Enclosure hedges of Britain. But there are also ditches in the vernacular style, consisting of earthbanks which are faced on their only vertical side with stone. Thorns are sometimes planted in the bank between the stones of the wall base, with gorse and bramble growing atop the bank. The brambles provided fruit and could be split and flattened to produce a useful rope which had many uses, such as lashing together the rolls of straw to make traditional bee hives or skeps. The gorse could be crushed to provide fodder for horses.

While it can be claimed that each old Welsh county had its own distinctive hedging style, this is not true of England. Some subtleties reflect only the preferences of local hedgers, but the most common denominator of English hedges is neglect. For each stretch of well-maintained Midland bullock hedge or Yorkshire sheep hedge encountered, one will find many miles of hedge which have not been laid for decades and at best experience only an annual trimming by a mechanical cutter. Gappy sections are not replanted but crudely bridged by wire or fencing boards and the anonymity of neglect masks whatever signs of regional craftsmanship there may have been.

The main hedging tool is the curved billhook, double-sided with a straight blade on the back or furnished with a notch or 'hedge grip'. Many local variants on the billhook were produced by blacksmiths and workshops, and although the designs must have been influenced by local conditions and preferences it would be easy to exaggerate the romance of regionalism involved. (Within a certain circle of friends any reference to a particular countryside writer whose enthusiasm and whimsy greatly exceed his knowledge is always prefaced by the cry 'Arr wor be my Berkshire billhook?') The Leicestershire-Warwickshire

ABOVE On Dartmoor the Cornish tradition of the stone 'hedge' sometimes takes over from that of the Devon hedgebank. This example is near Widecombe. BELOW A typical Cornish 'hedge', beside the Merry Maidens stone circle. Hawthorn, bramble, rose or bracken may colonise the earthen packing at the top of the 'hedge', but such growth is incidental.

billhook enjoyed popularity far beyond the bounds of these counties, while the heavy, long-handled Yorkshire billhook was sometimes used in Wales, which lay outside the domain of the Leicestershire form. A Cambridgeshire thatcher whom we knew was desperate to replace his old Norfolk billhook, which he considered ideal for working hazel, but the demise of the old blacksmiths and the standardisation of tools by big manufacturers make it hard to obtain many traditional designs.

Garden hedges constitute a very special category and it is notable that most of the plants favoured – even natives like yew, box or juniper – are seldom, if ever, seen in farm hedges. In fact, a number of garden hedging plants are poisonous to browsing livestock: they include yew, rhododendron, box, cherry laurel, broom and the cypresses. Consequently any discovery of hedges with a garden composition in open countryside raises interesting questions. For example, in 1985 Dr Hooper discovered a straggly hedge of yew near Grafham, Cambridge-shire, and an inspection by the archaeologist, Christopher Taylor, confirmed that this was part of a relict lost garden. Most other favoured garden hedging plants lack the vigour, robust constitution or stock-proof qualities demanded of a farm hedge. Beech, hawthorn, hornbeam and the slow-growing holly are exceptions to this rule. Beech is good when mixed with other native shrubs and hornbeam is a good but neglected hedging plant, although it appears to have great difficulty in colonising country hedges. Wild privet is a relatively common shrub in the hedgerows of the English chalklands, though too flimsy to be of much value on its own. With the eruption of urbanisation and industrialisation, privet came into its own as a plant which could withstand atmospheric pollution to form a dense evergreen screen, though the favoured species was Japanese privet rather than our native wild variety, the alien species being less subject to winter leaf fall. If allowed to grow a height of 10 ft (3 m) or more, Japanese privet will form an excellent refuge for garden birds, though it will rob the soil of much of its goodness. However, privet has tended to be superseded in the suburban garden by the *Cupressus* sub-species, which are very quick-growing. This has led to the coining of the phrases 'Leylandii blight' and 'Leylandii pollution', and such hedges or shelterbelts are only attractive when grown to the potentially unneighbourly height of over 20 ft (6 m). The cypress is not quite the newcomer that one might imagine. Italian cypresses were imported in the seventeenth century, but were wiped out in the terrible winter of 1683–4, and those used today are mainly of North American origin. During the excavations of the 'palace' villa at Fishbourne in Sussex, presumed to be the mansion of the native client king, Cogidubnus, the bedding trenches of the garden hedges were recognised. The medieval garden was usually quite small, with lawns, streams, pools, flower beds, arbours or terraces enclosed by lofty walls or hedgerows, while the evidence for the garden in the bailey of Farnham Castle, quoted in Ch. 3, shows that dead thorn hedging was also used in this way.

With the decay of the Middle Ages the private castle was superseded by the stately home, and gardens of greater size and complexity were built to grace the sites of the magnificent mansions. These gardens were formal in nature, hedged and with much lower hedges defining the intricate tracery of their fashionable knot gardens. In 1571 'Didymus Mountain' (Thomas Hill) wrote *The Gardener's Labyrinth*. He thought that 'the most commendable inclosure for everie garden plot, is a quickset hedge, made with brambles and white thorne.' Other hedges which he favoured were made with wild eglantine briars (sweet briar), brambles, gooseberry and berberis and he mentioned one with elders planted three feet (0.9 m) apart and interplanted with bramble. He claimed that the latter type would, within three years, 'grow to such a strength and sureness, that the same will be able inough to defend the injuries both of the theefe and the beast'. In 1599 Thomas Platter of Basel paid a visit to the palace at Hampton Court, where he saw garden hedges of 'hawthorn, bush firs, ivy, roses, juniper, holly, English or common elm, box and other shrubs, very gay and attractive'. John Evelyn was a champion of the garden hedge as well as of the planting of timber trees. He favoured yew: 'I do again name them for hedges, preferable, for beauty and a stiff defence, to any plant I have ever seen.' He claimed to be the first to advocate the use of yew, which was more hardy than the fashionable Italian cypresses, and to have introduced alaternus, a French buckthorn. Hawthorn, phillyrea, tamarisk, American yucca, beech, elm and hornbeam were other hedging plants that he favoured.

In due course the fashions in gardening changed. The landscaped park, devoid of hedges and such visual obstructions, gained ascendancy over the intricacies of the formal garden while ditches; 'sunken fences' or 'ha-has' were used to confine the deer to the lawns and spinneys of the 'naturalised' landscape. In the heyday of 'Capability' Brown and Humphry Repton it was felt that 'Nature' should begin at the wall base of the mansion, and the low box hedges of the parterre gardens were often swept away, along with the straight avenues, and tall hedges of beech, holly or yew, whose formalised geometry was no longer a hallmark of fashion. In due course the garden hedge returned to favour in Victorian and later reconstructions of the old knot and parterre gardens; indeed, Victorian gardening had the same liberal magpie qualities as the architecture, with an emphasis on diversity.

The formal gardens seen in England today are relatively recent re-applications of the old mode, with the closest approach to authenticity being seen at Kirby Hall in Northamptonshire, where the Elizabethan gardens were reconstructed after excavations had revealed the stone slabs which outlined the beds. To obtain the most dramatic impression of the intricate splendour of an original 'French' garden one must travel to the Netherlands, to the gardens of the royal palace of Het Loo, near Deventer, where Prince William III of Orange (1650–1702), who became King of England in 1689, provides the strong link with Britain.

In 1685 work began on a palatial hunting lodge in the Prince's hunting territory, and Het Loo then became the favourite country palace of William and Mary. The site was probably chosen with gardening in mind, for although the land is notoriously sandy a number of brooks on the surrounding higher ground provided the opportunities for fountains and irrigation. Designs solicited from the Academie Royale d'Architecture in Paris, the Dutch architect Jacob Roman, and the French refugee designer Daniel Marot were all influential in determining the form of the gardens and decorative motifs from the stucco

The intricate new box hedges in the magnificent reconstruction of the gardens at Het Loo palace, near Deventer, in the Netherlands.

ceilings of the house were replicated in the intricate patterns of the garden. The integrity of the gardens survived for a century, but then they were plundered and neglected during the Napoleonic wars after the flight of Prince Willem V in 1795. King Louis Napoleon took possession of Het Loo and the original gardens were obliterated and a pattern of geometrical avenues was super-imposed. The Dutch monarchy was restored in 1813, and in the ensuing period various changes were made to the gardens, which reflected the English concept of landscaping and the nineteenth-century passion for collecting exotic trees. In 1970, with the granting of the royal palace to the Dutch nation, the decision was taken to convert it into a national museum, and in 1974 it was decided to restore the palace and gardens to their original appearance (the cool pinkish-grey brickwork of the palace had been rendered and the whitened walls and window shutters had combined to give the aura of a French chateau).

Between 1977 and 1984 a remarkably ambitious scheme to restore the entire garden complex to its original seventeenth-century appearance was pursued. An exact reconstruction was made possible by the survival of numerous prints and descriptions of the old gardens and also by excavations, which revealed features of the lay-out which had been entombed by the earth added during the landscaping at the time of Louis Napoleon. Full-scale plans of the garden lay-outs were made and placed *in situ*, allowing the outlines of the original patterns to be marked on the ground. The water supply was reactivated and thousands of box plants were established to recreate the formal hedge tracery. However, the use of buried synthetic sheeting, which was installed to suppress weed growth, initially resulted in waterlogging and the death of many of the young plants. But now the courage and ambition of the recreation scheme has been amply rewarded, the gardens of Het Loo throng with visitors and they are compared favourably with the gardens of Versailles. There is no better destination for the reader who would like to see the formal box hedge in all its glory.

While Britain has nothing to compare with the grandeur and authenticity of the box hedges at Het Loo, the British Isles lay claim to the largest box hedges. At Birr Castle in Co. Offaly there are some quite recent formal box hedges, but pride of place goes to a 200-year-old box avenue with hedges 35 ft (10.7 m) tall – said to be the tallest hedge of its kind in the world.

In suburbia the garden hedge still reigns supreme. With their characteristic misunderstanding of human life and nature, modern planners have often demanded open-plan housing estates. Yet it is interesting to see how the quest for privacy will nibble away at the designs, and soon after the first boundary hedges have made their furtive appearance then many more will follow. Then the estates become better places for people and wildlife, and only the vandals and planners feel thwarted.

There is much more that might be written about garden hedges, but the hedgerows of the countryside are our main concern. In this respect, however, it is relevant to note how some cultivated plants may exploit niches in adjacent hedgerows. Non-native plums, cherries and elms, naturalised apples, berberis, laburnum, snowberry, gooseberry, raspberry and numerous other plants are much more likely to be found in proximity to village gardens than elsewhere. The majority of ornamental garden hedging plants lack the tough, competitive constitutions needed to establish themselves in field hedges, but in particularly favourable circumstances a few of the less robust species may succeed. The most showy plant which one is very likely to see in a wild hedgerow is the crimson and purple flowering *Fuchsia magellanica*. This is cultivated in garden hedges in Cornwall and the Republic of Ireland, and in the mild, moist south-west of Ireland it has successfully colonised numerous field hedges.

Finally in this chapter mention should be made of a few unusual and specialised types of hedge. Most notable are those which are exploited for their ability to provide boundaries and shelter in the sandy, windy and salty coastal environments. Sea buckthorn is an invasive native and garden shrub which will flourish in such places and it can occasionally be seen in a mixed planting with buckthorn. Tamarisk can survive in shelterbelts in western and southern England and is superior to the poisonous broom. Gorse is employed on some dry, sandy coasts and heaths, but is prone to fire. Willow is not stock-proof in single-species plantings, but is quick to root from cuttings and grows very rapidly. As a result it is occasionally planted in windbreaks in arable areas of East Anglia and managed by a simple coppicing technique while it can form a spontaneous hedge on damp verges. Cherry plum is a freely suckering shrub which was formerly grown for its fruits and which is fast-growing, easily raised from seed and good on heavy ground and seaside locations. Formerly it was recommended as a rival to hawthorn in the planting of farm hedges, but the cheapness of hawthorn, problems encountered in laying cherry plum and, perhaps, the conservatism of country folk seem to have arrested the challenge.

·8·

THE CRAFT OF HEDGING

In the course of a country drive one is likely to see hedgerows in various different conditions. Some will still be effective stock-proof barriers, others gappy and neglected, while one seldom has to look far for evidence of hedgerow removal. Two other kinds of hedge are now uncommon sights – the newly planted and the recently laid. The craft of hedging involves the planting and the maintenance of hedges. Planting demands no specialised skills, and, given the apparent immortality of the well-maintained hedge, it is a much less frequent task than were those of trimming and laying hedges and the associated work of ditching and repairing hedgebanks.

PLANTING HEDGES

As we have seen, in pre-Georgian times the majority of hedges seem to have been created from various kinds of young shrubs which were dug up from woods, roadsides and wastes. Most Parliamentary Enclosures and more recent hedges, in contrast, were of materials purchased in bulk from commercial nurseries. It is clear that in medieval and earlier times hedges were sometimes grown from seed, as described in Ch. 5, and cuttings may also have been used. However, the most useful hedging plants do not produce seeds which germinate freely and 'stratification', involving the decomposition of the berry and the exposure of the seeds to two seasons of winter frost, is usually necessary to produce germination in hawthorn and holly. Moreover, a seed-planted hedge may require some ten years of protection from grazing before a barrier is established. Dogwood and willow are two plants which root readily from cuttings, and can be transplanted to the hedgerow in their third spring. All things considered, it is not surprising that the medieval farmer found it most expedient to dig up suitably sized natural seedlings.

Because of the difficulty of establishing bare-rooted shrubs when growth is active, soils dry and the rate of transpiration high, the hedge-planting season runs from about October to March, with an autumn planting allowing the shrubs to settle gently into their new situation. While garden hedges need a manured hedge trench, native hedgerow shrubs will grow in relatively infertile soil, with drought posing the main threat during the first year or so after planting. In an old hedge it is impossible to deduce the density of the original planting. Most garden hedges should be planted at a density of four shrubs to the yard using plants about 18–24 in (50–60 cm) tall. This may seem quite a close planting, but the recommended rates for field hedges can be even higher. One can sometimes tell that some old hedges were double-planted, with two quite closely spaced rows of shrubs, and this method, though more demanding of labour and materials, will tend to produce a substantial hedge more quickly and facilitate the task of laying. A planting distance of 9 in (23 cm) is advisable in single-row hedges, but in double-row hedges the rows can be 6 in (15.5 cm) apart and the plants in each

A newly planted hawthorn hedge in the Weald. Barbed wire and wire mesh protect the young hedge from browsing and taller saplings have been incorporated as future hedgerow standards. In the modern age this is the most pleasing scene that the English countryside has to offer.

row placed at 10 in (25.5 cm) intervals, producing a density of about nine shrubs to the yard (0.9 m). Although hawthorn plants are still quite cheap, a mile of double-row hedge of plants spaced at 9 in (23 cm) will consume over 14,000 plants, and so it seems very doubtful that such a dense rate of planting was employed in medieval times.

Perhaps the greatest drawback of the hedgerow has been its vulnerability to browsing during its formative years. The main purpose of the hedge has always usually been that of separating horn and corn, as recalled in the old nursery rhyme:

> Little boy blue come blow up your horn,
> The cow's in the meadow, the sheep's in the corn.

(In fact there might be more to this rhyme than meets the eye. Boy Blue could be Thomas Cardinal Wolsey, the son of an Ipswich butcher who tended flocks for his father when a child. But another possible source is Shakespeare's *King Lear*:

> Sleepest or wakest thou, jolly shepherd?
> Thy sheep in the corn
> And for one blast of thy minikin mouth,
> Thy sheep shall take no harm.

In any event, in its early days the hedge has always faced the threat of becoming a meal rather than a dinner monitor. A ditch (sometimes enhanced by a hedgebank) often provided protection on one side of the juvenile hedge, and today a few strands of inexpensive barbed wire can guard one or both sides of a new hedgerow. In former times, however, it was necessary to build either a fence or a dead hedge to protect the vulnerable quick hedge. Occasionally hints of the taking of timber for protective fencing as well as the digging up of living plants occur in the medieval references to hedges, and subsequently the mentions become more specific. In 1330 the accounts of Gamlingay estate in Cambridgeshire note the cost of ditching and planting a quickset hedge at 4*d*. per perch – or about the equivalent of 10p for 115 ft (35 m) in modern measures, disregarding inflation. Oliver Rackham has quoted the accounts of the Earl of Orford for hedging part of the parish boundary at Chippenham in Cambridgeshire in 1718. Some £15 was spent on building the protective fence, while the shrubs and labour proved much cheaper: 280 elms and 36,000 hawthorns cost £5. 18*s*. 8*d*.; 5,000 crab apples cost only £1 and the labour bill was £3. 4*s*. 0*d*.

In a few cases the detailed instructions for hedge planting have survived. Thus on 19 February 1684/5 Lord Wharton, who owned an estate and lead mines in Swaledale, wrote from London to his man, Philip Swale:

> I think I intended a quick hedge from the hedge that comes from the plantation of ashes to be continued through the upper end of the broad closse [close] to forme a fair lane betwixt the broad closse and the new wall of the court garden and orchard. . . If those that have best judgement in quicksetting think it not now to late in the year, I wish it were done this year, but if they think it better to forbear, I wish it were early done next year.

In some parts of Britain hedgebanks were favoured. Such banks enhanced the barrier, gave the shrubs a deep root-run and improved the drainage. On the other hand they demanded more labour in construction and maintenance. The material for the bank came from the digging of an adjacent ditch, and normally shrubs were planted in top soil spread on the crown of the bank, though where strong winds threatened the young shrubs the plants might be set in the side or foot of the protective bank.

Experts appear to disagree about the best way of promoting strong, bushy growth in a newly planted hedge. Some recommend cutting the plants hard back to a height of just a few inches after the first season of growth; others favour a light trimming while allowing leaders to grow to the full height of the finished hedge before trimming.

THE MANAGEMENT OF HEDGEROWS

Work on the maintenance of hedgerows used to be accomplished during the dormant season, and hedging and ditching provided employment on the farm during lulls in the agricultural year. The tasks included the annual ones of trimming, scouring of adjacent ditches and repairs to hedgebanks, and the

A boxy flat-topped form of trimming has been favoured for this Parliamentary Enclosure hawthorn hedge in Nidderdale. This style exposes the maximum surface area to sunlight but could lead to the accumulation of an excessive burden of snow.

periodic task of hedge-laying. We do not know whether much time was generally devoted to the weeding of hedgerows, although it is notable that a number of common hedgerow plants are poisonous to people or animals that are careless enough to eat them. They include both black and white bryony, bittersweet or woody nightshade, black and deadly nightshade, spindle, fox-glove, monkshood, hemlock and stinking hellbore, as well as the marsh marigolds and cowbane which might be found growing in the ditch.

The typical country hedge would be trimmed once or twice each year, but allowed to grow for a couple of years or so preceding the far more drastic operations of laying, which would take place every 8 to 25 years. Trimming and laying are not entirely compatible, for while laying restores and revitalises a hedge, trimming at first encourages the formation of a dense, twiggy hedge, but eventually it results in an outer layer of nobbly twigs covered in scar tissue and poor, gappy growth in the base and centre of the hedge, which can only be remedied by laying. On the other hand, trimming gives a hedge a tidy appearance and reduces the shading of the adjacent crops or pasture.

Different opinions are current concerning the ideal form of trimming: square or triangular cross-sections, and flat, chamfered or rounded tops all have their advocates. The square-cut hedge has a broad, flat top exposed to invigorating sunlight, though the base of the hedge on its northern side is heavily shaded and the flat top is likely to accumulate a heavy blanket of snow which may bear down upon the branches. The triangular hedge seems to provide the best shelter by reducing swirling eddies of wind and it exposes a greater area of the hedge to sunlight, but if the batter of the side is too pronounced then side growth near the top of the hedge will be too closely cropped. Battered sides together with a chamfered or rounded top may combine a number of useful features and reduce the snow problem.

In the past, hedges were trimmed by hand using a long-handled billhook or slasher. The 'switching bill' was also used: a light billhook on a short handle. Since the timber being cut was thin or soft, trimming tools were lighter than those used in laying. The tools were kept razor-sharp and wielded with an upward stroke, though downward cutting was used when it was necessary to encourage growth down towards the foot of the hedge. Today most trimming is done by mechanical trimmers. This can lead to the splintering of twigs and a consequent exposure to fungal attack, and it is less easy to preserve promising saplings for growth into hedgerow standards.

Eventually a trimmed or an overgrown hedge will require a thoroughgoing renovation. The antiquity of the craft of hedge-laying is uncertain, though Caesar's description of the Belgic hedge (see Ch. 1) certainly seems to describe a laid hedge. Medieval documents frequently mention repairs to hedgerows, but without specifying details; and the tenancy agreements of the Georgian and Victorian periods often required this form of periodic management. Even so, the practice does not seem to have been universal and there may be some very old hedges which have never been laid. One can usually recognise a hedge that has experienced laying from the elbow – like forms of the main trunks in the base of the hedge, signs that these stems were once bent over to serve as pleachers. Hedges planted during the last couple of decades or so can be recognised by the absence or paucity of colonists, the small and uniform size of the constituents – almost invariably hawthorn – and, frequently, the survival of the double fence or field-side fence erected to protect young shrubs.

Laying restores a gappy hedge and rejuvenates one which has developed a dense, nobbly and moribund outer layer of twigs as a result of successive trimmings. It is a demanding craft and the skilled hedger must draw upon a great deal of accumulated experience. Sadly, these skills are dying along with the old hedgers and the majority of hedges which one sees in the course of a country ramble will be greatly in need of re-laying. Operations begin by restoring the true line of a hedge by removing colonists and growth from suckers which deviate from the chosen alignment. Then dead or moribund growth is cut out of the hedge and the living wood is reduced, leaving the tall, vigorous stems which will serve as pleachers. Thin stems and very thick old trunks are removed and thornless growth may be cut out in preference to thorn, where such a choice is possible. Undesirable species, notably elder, may be dug out entirely – an awkward and energy-consuming operation. By this stage the hedge will ideally consist of a series of tall, evenly spaced pleachers which have been trimmed to remove entangling growth, but which retain bushy growth at their tops, as this growth will help to protect the newly laid hedge against browsing. However, most hedges will deviate from this ideal, and the skilled hedger will improvise and use all his experience in the selection of pleachers with good root growth and the retention of material needed to bridge awkward gaps.

The pleachers are then cut with a downward-sloping blow at an angle of about 45° to 60°. The cut is made at a height of around 1½ in (4 cm) to around 5 in (13 cm) above ground level and it travels more than three-quarters of the way through the stem of the pleacher, but it must not pass completely through the tissues of the cambium, the layer of wood just beneath the bark. In effect the pleacher is now linked to its roots by a slender living hinge of un-severed cambium, allowing a

Two young conservation volunteers about to lay a pleacher. Note how the side-growth has been trimmed away and the base of the pleacher cut away to leave only a slender bark and cambium hinge.

continuing flow of water and nutrients from the roots. Pleachers which are up to about three fingers in width can be cut with a single blow, though novices must chip away carefully or risk severing the pleacher completely.

The pleacher can now be tipped over and laid in a position which is slightly above the horizontal and at an angle of less than 45°. Each laid pleacher is angled slightly outward from the hedgeline, so that the bushy ends usually all point in the same direction and lie on the far side of the hedge and away from the ditch on the near side, where such a ditch exists. After a few pleachers have been laid

Conservation volunteers engaged in hedging near Easingwold. Laid pleachers and posts are in place on the right of the photograph, though the heathering is still to be added, while on the left the pleachers are placed flat on the ground and the posts have not yet been inserted

in this way stakes are driven in at regular intervals of about 2–3 ft (0.6–0.9 m). The stakes are placed just to the far side of the hedgerow roots and are pushed between the cut pleachers to strengthen and stabilise the barrier.

Heathering completes work on the hedge shown on the previous pages. Hazel was not available, so willow from an adjacent plantation is being employed.

The task of laying a section of hedgerow is completed by the addition of 'heathering' or binding to the top of the hedge. Binders are straight, pliable wands about 3 yds (about 3 m) in length. Hazel is the preferred material, although willow wands or briars can be used if hazel is in short supply. The binders are rolled or woven tightly between the tops of the stakes to create a strong top level to the hedge and to prevent the pleachers from springing up. They are woven between the stakes and over and under each other, and when the binders are tamped down with the handles of the billhook they bind the components of the hedge tightly together. Finally the laid hedge receives a tidy trim, with the tops of the stakes being cut obliquely at an even height.

In some places the hedger is likely to encounter gaps which cannot be bridged by a conveniently adjacent pleacher. Sometimes the gap can be closed by laying a pleacher in the opposite direction to its neighbours and then cutting its upper end and bending it back in the direction of the other pleachers. Gaps can also be filled by a new planting or by encouraging a laid pleacher to root into the gap. The pleacher is laid at a horizontal angle so that it comes into contact with the earth in the gap. A half-buried pleacher may root, and rooting can also be encouraged by cutting a notch in the stem and covering the notched portion with a small mound of earth.

After laying the hedge is rejuvenated. Soft new growth arises from the 'stools' or stumps of the cut timber, from elm or blackthorn suckers, and it grows upwards from buds along the laid pleachers. In due course the dead stakes, binders and any incorporated dead hedging materials will decay, and after an interval of 8 to 25 years the hedge will again be ready to be laid.

ABOVE The top of a Wealden hedge two years after laying. The heathering is still intact and new growth (hazel and dogwood can be recognised) is beginning to envelop it. BELOW A hedge at Barton in Cambridgeshire, photographed two years after laying, with vigorous new growth arising from the base and pleachers.

As we have described in Ch. 7, Britain supports a number of different hedging styles, and even within the domain of the Midlands bullock hedge, some variations will be seen. Occasionally one will see half-hearted attempts at laying where heathering has been omitted. An old Cambridgeshire farm-worker described to us how tree saplings with an upright growth could be planted at close intervals in a hedge to serve as living posts which would substitute for the stakes used in hedge-laying, and how he would take prickly handfuls of living brambles and briars and roll them into the top of the hedge to serve as heathering.

Lambs will find a way through all but the densest hedges, although they are unlikely to stray very far so long as their mothers are confined in the field. With Welsh sheep hedges much more dead material was incorporated into the newly laid hedge to maintain its sheep-proof qualities. Double brushing is frequently practised, the pleachers being laid alternatively to the left and right sides of stakes placed in the centre of the hedge, so that their bushy tips guard both sides of the hedge, and when stakes are used they are usually stout and hammered in at a sloping angle. Living stakes as 'crops' may be employed instead, while 'crooks' or hook-topped stakes are sometimes used to peg down the pleachers (as described in Ch. 7).

OPPORTUNITIES IN HEDGING

An interest in hedgerows can be carried far beyond the bounds of passive observation. The hedge-laying techniques described in this chapter should not be attempted without expert supervision. A first-rate and highly detailed guide to the craft, *Hedging; A Practical Conservation Handbook,* is published by the British Trust for Conservation Volunteers (36 St Mary's Street, Wallingford, Oxfordshire OX10 0EU), and the regional groups of Conservation Volunteers carry out hedge-laying courses and projects which would allow readers to gain experience and tuition in the various aspects of hedging.

Any reader with a garden also has the opportunity to plant a country-style hedgerow, perhaps replacing an old Japanese privet, cupressus or ornamental hedge with one which will prove more robust and which will offer far more interest and numerous niches for wildlife. Fortunately, there are now a number of specialist nurseries which offer young plants of authentic native stock, although the typical local garden centre will offer a minimal range of hedging shrubs and those which are stocked may be of a foreign or cultivar parentage. A mixed planting of native species will provide more interest and visual appeal than a single-species planting of hawthorn, although hawthorn is widely available and surprisingly cheap.

One might choose to recreate a section of a favourite countryside hedge, replicating the exact ordering of shrubs and climbers within the hedgerow. Such a reproduction hedgerow can be seen in the botanical gardens at Cambridge, where a species-rich hedgerow from Hayley Woods, a few miles away, has been recreated. Alternatively, one might choose to incorporate a range of the most visually attractive native hedgerow plants, like guelder rose, honeysuckle or burnet rose. In our own locality in North Yorkshire hedgerows are dominated

Five years after laying, this Wealden hedge is perfectly able to cope with browsing.

by holly, hawthorn, elm and hazel, with wild gooseberry being the most frequently encountered of the unusual components. Instead of reproducing a local country hedge we chose to pack our garden hedge with the lovely plants of the southern downlands: wayfaring tree, spindle, guelder rose and dogwood. These, and a range of other hedgerow shrubs, were planted at a ratio of one non-thorn followed by three hawthorn, thus reducing the planting bill. Costs can also be reduced by propagating plants for inclusion. Goat willow and dogwood will root easily from cuttings; softwood cuttings of honeysuckle will root with a little more care, while splendid wild roses, like the sweet briar and burnet rose, will grow profusely from seed, though perhaps not germinating during the first year of planting.

The only disadvantage of the native as opposed to the Japanese privet or cupressus garden hedge is that of winter leaf fall, which reduces the effectiveness of the screen. Holly provides the densest of all garden hedges; beech retains its dead leaves, and oak may do so to a much lesser extent. In the section of our hedge where screening is most important, we have experimented with wild privet underplanted with slow-growing holly seedlings, hoping that the holly will eventually dominate the screen. Almost all native hedgerow plants will flourish in the more controlled conditions of the garden hedge, even though they may not be found in the country hedges of the area, providing that the problems of shading and atmospheric pollution are not too severe. When planting a mixed hedgerow it is as well to be aware of the preferences of the component plants, placing willow in any damp patches and perhaps incorporating some lime sand into sections where lime-loving plants are placed. When ordering plants it is important to insist on native stock and certain confusions are possible. If you ask for 'buckthorn' you are likely to receive sea buckthorn, commonly grown as a decorative shrub, rather than purging buckthorn; while sweet briar, *Rosa rubiginosa*, may be confused with the non-native *R. rugosa*, a handsome Asian shrub-rose species which is often used in rose hedges.

Bearing in mind the national love of privacy and seclusion, the prime role of the garden hedge is that of the screen. Considered solely as screening plants the *Cupressus* species are probably supreme, though they are about as visually appealing as a plate full of spinach. Country-loving readers with the desire and available space for a tall screen could consider an application of the traditional hedgebank. Such a bank can provide a total screen up to eye-level height and could be crowned with a five-foot mixed hedge of native species. Such a bank should have a pronounced batter, one that is 6 ft (1.8 m) high being built with a base width of six feet and tapering to a width 3–4 ft (1–1.2 m) at the top. Not everyone would be prepared to devote six feet of space at the margin of the garden to accommodate such a hedgebank, though it is worth noting that a *Cupressus* hedge of a height equal to the hedgebank plus its hedge will cover almost as broad a zone at its base. The great joy of the hedgebank is that it then allows one to complete the rural illusion by growing native hedgebank herbs, like foxgloves, cow parsley, cowslips, bluebells, wild daffodils and many others on the bank. Most hedgebanks have a sunny and a shaded side, and the shady side can be used for the cultivation of woodland plants and the lovers of semi-shade, like ramsons, lily of the valley or primroses; while moist soil at the foot of the bank could provide a setting for globe flower, yellow or purple loosestrife or meadowsweet. Nowadays specialist seedsmen can supply a wide range of native wildflower seeds, but the slopes of the hedgebank must be stabilised by grass. Native mixed grass and wildflower seed mixtures are available, and the secret of success is to deprive the hedgebank of grass cuttings and fertilisers, otherwise the grass will grow too strongly and smother the flowers. If low-growing wildflowers, like daisies or tormentil, are sown, the grass of the hedgebank can be mown regularly, with the mower blades set high. Otherwise it can be mown in spring and in late summer or autumn, after annual wildflowers have shed their seeds. Hedgebanks sown with meadowland plants like buttercups, betony, milkmaids and so on can be cut in the manner of the traditional flower-rich hay meadows.

The hedgebank should be constructed with a very slightly concave face, which should gradually become straight after the soil has settled. A straight-faced bank will settle to a convex form, while a convex original bank could 'belly out' and become unstable. The tall hedgebanks of Devon were turfed and

An expertly laid hedge photographed near Longstowe in Cambridgeshire.

Much about the history of management can be learned from a close look at a hedge. Here the ditch of this Yorkshire example, originally encased in stone, has been scoured, but scouring has unfortunately exposed roots and the earth from the ditch has not been deposited on the bank. Traces of laying are obvious in the 'elbows' at the base of the hedge, but laying has not been attempted for many decades, and fencing (far left) has been inserted to plug a gap. Dense, twiggy growth a couple of feet above the 'elbows' is a legacy of repeated trimmings at this height, but recently the hedge has been allowed to grow much taller, to shelter a fruit crop.

occasionally repaired by returfing. Turf is laid to a brickwork pattern, but with the vertical joints all slightly sloping in one direction. The turf used came from the adjacent verge, but commercial turf could be used, while avoiding ryegrass. Such turf will be poor in wildflowers, though seed could be scattered in the turf after a very close mowing. Alternatively, suitable flowers could be pot-grown and then transplanted into the turf.

From the point of view of the farmer, hedges not only form boundaries and farming compartments but they also shelter livestock from cold winds and crops from dry, desiccating breezes. They are less prone to damage than fences and less likely to injure animals than barbed wire. Hedges also produce abundant timber and a range of fruits and are hosts to a remarkable range of wildlife. If properly maintained the hedge will serve as a permanent barrier, in comparison to a barbed-wire fence which will need to be renewed every two decades. Once the inital cost of planting has been borne, the cost of properly maintaining an established hedgerow is only about 20 per cent greater than that of perpetuating a barbed-wire fence, although all the other benefits of hedges over fences continue to be enjoyed. In addition, any future switch of farming subsidies in favour of conservation rather than surplus production could bolster the position of the farmer who has been concerned with the visual and wild amenities of his holding. Grants are already available for hedging work.

SHRUB AND SEED SUPPLIERS

With the recent resurgence of interest in nature gardening with native plants, seeds and shrubs are becoming more readily available from local garden centres. The following firms have a wide selection available by mail order.

SUPPLIERS OF NATIVE SHRUBS

Bamber and Sons Ltd, The Norfolk Nurseries, Elm, Wisbech, Cambridgeshire.
Bernhard's Nurseries Ltd, Bilton Road, Rugby, Warwickshire.
J & W Blackburn Ltd, Pennine Nurseries, Shelly, Huddersfield, Yorkshire.
Goatcher's Nurseries, Washington, Sussex.
Hillier and Son, Winchester, Hampshire.
Mill House Nursery, Mill Lane, Gressenhall, East Dereham, Norfolk.
Oakover Nurseries, Potters Corner, Ashford, Kent.
Seafield Nurseries Ltd, Boyndie, Banff.
Simpsons of Lower Peover, Crown Lane, Lower Peover, Knutsford, Cheshire.
Tacchi's Nurseries, Wyton, Huntingdon, Cambridgeshire.
Tilhill Forestry Nurseries Ltd, Greenhills, Tilford, Farnham, Surrey.
Weasdale Nurseries, Newbiggin on Lune, Kirkby Stephen, Cumbria.
Wyevale Nurseries Ltd, Kings Acre, Hereford.

SUPPLIERS OF WILDFLOWER SEEDS

John Chambers, 15 Westleigh Road, Barton Seagrave, Kettering, Northamptonshire.
Chiltern Seeds, Bortree Stile, Ulverston, Cumbria.
Emorsgate Seeds, Emorsgate, Terrington St Clement, Norfolk.
W. W. Johnson and Son Ltd, Boston, Lincolnshire.
Naturescape, Little Orchard, Main Street, Whatton-in-the-Vale, Nottinghamshire.
The Seed Exchange, 44 Albion Road, Sutton, Surrey.
Suffolk Herbs, Sawyers Farm, Little Cornard, Sudbury, Suffolk.

·9·

MEETING THE MEMBERS OF THE HEDGEROW

If all Britain's hedgerows were examined, we would find that just about every species of native British tree and shrub as well as many introduced species may be found somewhere or other along these lines of greenery. But only a few of these occur sufficiently frequently for them to be thought of as 'hedgerow plants'.

The commoner species appearing in our hedgerows were either the planter's choice or else have gained a foothold through some form of natural colonisation. The most widespread hedgerow tree is hawthorn, the ideal choice for a robust farm hedge. It was particularly favoured during the era of Parliamentary Enclosure and today it is still very common over much of eastern England and eastern and southern Scotland. Other shrubs which can dominate hedgerows include blackthorn in Dorset, parts of Cambridgeshire and Sussex; holly in parts of Leicestershire and Staffordshire; sea buckthorn along parts of the East Lothian coast; broom in East Suffolk; gorse in Pembrokeshire; beech on some enclosures on Exmoor and in the Midland valley of Scotland; and elm in parts of Wales, Shropshire, Devon, Kent, the Weald and parts of East Anglia. Their local dominance must reflect their natural success in the areas concerned, which in turn made them available to the planters of hedges. But whatever the species planted, in due course others are likely to gain a foothold, so that the composition of the hedge will alter, at different rates in different places. A hedge planted with just one species could become quite species-rich, though equally a mixed planting could become much less diverse, particularly when invasive species like elm, blackthorn and holly flourish. Also, the history of the human management can greatly affect the health and composition of a hedge; so too can environmental factors, like Dutch elm disease or hazelnut removal by grey squirrels.

Mixed hedges which have many broadleaved woodland species may be so because diverse and healthy woodland was more abundant when they were planted and becoming established. Young trees or saplings were then readily available to be dug up in the forests, and planted in hedgerows; also seeds in abundant supply could be carried by wind and animals. In fact the processes by which seeds are dispersed could be complicated. One of the richest hedges in our locality is a 'spontaneous' one, created by the colonisation of a railway embankment in the course of just a century. Although it is flanked to the south by riverside oaks and alders and to the north by a mature beech and larch plantation, it includes goat willow, silver birch, crab apple, ash and hazel, none of which are particularly common in the vicinity.

Calcareous soils, formed on chalk or limestone or lime-rich boulder clay, particularly in the warm south, support higher numbers of common and rarer hedgerow plant species such as dogwood and field maple and the less frequent purging buckthorn, guelder rose, wild privet, spindle and wayfaring tree, all of which are to some degree 'calcicolous', and are therefore more likely to be able to establish naturally on such soils. Acid soils, in contrast, support a poorer flora so it follows that there will also be fewer potential colonising hedgerow species; generally speaking, it is the commonest species, such as hawthorn, blackthorn, elder, bramble and the various wild roses, which are tolerant of a broad cross-section of soil types, that are best able to colonise.

It has frequently been said that the conditions in a multi-species hedge are more conducive to 'slow colonisers', such as wayfaring tree, spindle and field maple, which are often absent from hedges with less than six species. If the laws of succession are correct, then one would expect that some species could occur only at certain stages – though, of course, a mixed planting would invalidate such theories. In contrast, the presence of elder is seen to decline in hedges with many species. The nature of the elder enables it easily to colonise loosely overgrown and sparse hedges, but it is said to have difficulty in maintaining itself in a dense mature hedge. However, other forces may be at work, for it was common practice for elder to be dug out of a hedge during laying operations. But whichever way a hedgerow has originated and eventually developed, the way it is managed must also have an effect, for only certain shrubs will tolerate the apparently rough treatment – laying, browsing and now mechanical trimming – to which many boundary hedges are subjected. The suckering shrubs will obviouly be the most resilient and competitive.

Many species of vertebrates and invertebrates have been recorded in our hedgerows and, as we shall see in this and other chapters, a hedge will offer the attractions of sanctuary and food, as well as hibernation, breeding and nesting places. In turn many creatures will help in the distribution and propagation of hedgerow plant species. Many hedgerow inflorescences are insect-pollinated, and if the flowers are not colourful, their scent and nectar will become the attraction. Most flowering shrubs are hermaphrodite: that is, they produce both male and female sexual organs (the stamen being made up of anther and filament; and the pistil, of ovary, style and stigma) in the same flower, enabling either self-fertilisation, when the pollen comes in contact with the female stigma in the same flower, or cross-fertilisation, if the pollen is carried to the stigma of a flower on another plant of the same species. However, certain species will avoid self-pollination in one of several ways: when the flower's male and female parts mature at different times (dichogamous); when each plant produce separate male and female flowers (monoecious); or when a plant in the one species bears all female or all male flowers (dioecism). In these cases, for fertilisation to take place, not only is it important to have another appropriate plant of the species within a suitable range, but the role of insects becomes even more important in spreading the pollen, and during bad weather, when insect-pollinators are scarce, little seed may be set. Birds which feed on the fruit of many hedgerow species are not only effective in dispersing the plant species; for various seeds, such as those of the hawthorn, the effect of being exposed to a bird's digestive process will stimulate earlier germination (up to a year sooner than uneaten haws).

Wind-pollinated flowers have no need for conspicuous petals or sweet-smelling nectar, and usually their tiny flowers consist of little more than the reproductive organs, but set in clusters, they can make very attractive inflor-escences to the human eye. Wind-pollinated flowers are often unisexual, containing either just male or female parts, as with many catkin-bearing trees whose flowers are gathered into either male or female clusters. Wind-borne pollen grains are smaller and lighter than those that are insect-borne, while the female parts are usually larger and feathery, designed to trap pollen grains passing in the wind.

In the sections which follow we examine the characteristics of some of the commoner native broadleaved hedgerow shrubs and trees, in order to assist their identification and appreciation. Their frequency in the hedgerow which is being studied and the form they take may not only tell us something about their success as a locally common species, but possibly something of the nature of the soil and the local availability of seed and stock. We may even learn something of the hedgerow's management and history (particularly if there is corroborative documentary evidence).

Perhaps the easiest way to identify a hedgerow shrub is by its leaves. But when the leaves have fallen, clues to the shrub's identity are provided in the colour of the twigs, particularly the youngest twigs on the ends of branches from the previous summer's growth, and the shape, size, form and arrangement of the buds, which bear the following year's leaves and flowers. For example, some buds are scaled and others are not; flower buds are usually much fatter than leaf buds; buds of superficially similar trees, such as hornbeam and beech, may be distinguished by the way the buds of beech stand away from the twig, while those of hornbeam lie close to it. Berries are another identity tag, distinguished by their shape, size, colour and arrangement. The colours, cracks and fissures of bark form distinctive patterns in each species, but this form of identification is easier on tree trunks than on the mature branches of shrubs. However, the distinctive texture and arrangement of the breathing pores is obvious in some species. Flowers are not always the easiest way to identify shrubs, particularly amongst the wild roses and amongst the wild cherries and plums. However, many flowers are easily recognisable, such as hawthorn, spindle, elder and guelder rose. The only trouble is that not only are they short-lived, but also they depend on the management of the hedge, for on mechanic-ally trimmed hedges they are less prolific.

THE COMMONEST QUICK-GROWING SHRUBS

THE HAWTHORNS

Common hawthorn is one of our two native species of hawthorn. It thrives on all soils, is steadfast in strong winds and shade-tolerant, and before it became widely used in hedgerows it was a characteristic tree of gladed forests and a scrub plant of neglected pastures and wastes. The other species, Midland hawthorn, is much less common, found mostly on the heavy clay soils of central and southern England where it is much more a shrub of shady woodland habitats. Close to its natural range it can be found in hedgerows dominated by or including common hawthorn, where various hybrids between the two are likely to be seen. The two hawthorns can be distinguished by their leaves and also by the fact that even in its ideal woodland setting the Midland hawthorn seems a rather sad, droopy and emaciated tree, in contrast to its robust cousin.

The term hawthorn means 'hedgethorn', since 'haw' is thought to be derived from the Old English *haga* meaning hedge. This confirms that hawthorn has been a hedge plant for a long time. It has long enjoyed a prominent place in folklore, and being in full flower and prettiest during the month, it inevitably also became known as 'may', the blossom which heralded the arrival of summer. It was and still is associated with festivities welcoming the arrival of summer and hawthorn blossom is an essential decoration of the maypole and the May Queen's crown. May Day used to coincide with the flowering of hawthorn, until the changes of calendar in 1752, when it was advanced into the colder season by thirteen days. Quickthorn, quickset and white thorn are other common names for hawthorn (though in the medieval texts quick, quickthorn and quickset do not necessarily denote hawthorn).

ABOVE The blossom of hawthorn, shown here in close-up, is unmistakable, though the colour ranges from white to deep pink. LEFT Hawthorn berries provide an invaluable winter food supply for hedgerow birds, particularly the members of the thrush family.

Variation in hawthorn leaves. Where growing together, common and Midland hawthorn produce a wide spectrum of hybrids. Note the variation from the typical Midland hawthorn leaf, lower left, to the typical common hawthorn leaf, upper right.

From ancient times hawthorn has been regarded as a plant of conflicting magical endowments. On the one hand its blossom has been used to avert evil – 'Creep under the thorn. It will save you from harm' – but on the other there was the superstition that to bring may blossom indoors invited death into the house. This latter reputation may have originated from the observation that after the Black Death, hawthorn – being a rapid coloniser – appeared to spring up in many abandoned hamlets and farmsteads deserted after the plague – though folklore is often more colourful than accurate.

Hawthorn features in early ecclesiasticial carvings and symbolism. It often forms part of the design carved into the roof bosses of churches. It is sometimes seen wreathing or capping 'Green Men', often considered to be fertility symbols, which adorn many of our medieval churches; though frequently the leaves concerned might better be identified as vines, which are more symbolic of rapid, exuberant growth.

The proverb 'Cleave to the crown though it hangs in a bush' is thought to originate in the hawthorn's association with the House of Tudor. After the Battle of Bosworth in 1485, the body of Richard III was stripped of everything, including the crown, which was hurled into a hawthorn bush. Lord Stanley retrieved it and placed it on the head of his son-in-law, Henry Tudor, and thus with the reign of Henry VII the royal Tudor dynasty was born. The Tudor emblem is a crown borne in a berry-laden hawthorn bush.

Traditionally it has been assumed that the Roman soldiers made Christ's crown of thorns from hawthorn. Then there is the 'Christian' hawthorn, the Glastonbury Thorn, which reputedly blooms in December and, before the calendar changes in 1752, was said sometimes to flower on Christmas Day. Actually it is a form of common hawthorn which, while flowering normally in May, could again come into leaf less prolifically and flower for a second time in winter. There seem to be several versions to this legend, which goes along the following lines. When Joseph of Arimathea arrived in Britain on his mission to convert its inhabitants, he struck his staff into the ground at Glastonbury (Avalon), and found that in due course it had both rooted and blossomed. Taking this as a sign from the Almighty, he set up his headquarters at Glastonbury where, so the story goes, the descendants of the original hawthorn bush have bloomed annually around the anniversary of his landing ever since. A lovely story, but nonsense, and the earliest Christian remains excavated at Glastonbury post-date the era of Joseph by several centuries.

When flowering in May hawthorn is covered with clusters of white, five-petalled blossom speckled with pink, and deep pink forms can also be seen. Closely clipped hedges are, in contrast, very sparse-flowering. A familiar sight in autumn is the shrub's crimson haws, which are sometimes so plentiful as to cause the bush to glow red in the autumn sunshine, like a smouldering fire. When allowed to grow unchecked, and if protected against browsing animals which find its leaves and young shoots quite palatable, common hawthorn will attain the stature of a small tree, but it rarely reaches more than 15 ft (4.5 m) in height in a hedgerow. Its sturdy trunk, often gnarled and twisted, bears a dull grey to deep brown bark, which is split into a jigsaw pattern of squares and rectangles. The characteristic of the tree which has made it so valuable as a hedging material is its numerous strong branches, supporting a dense network of thin, dark twigs, which when young will produce small pink buds, many of which will eventually take the form of sharp thorns.

Apart from the distinctive geographical distributions and ecological preferences, there are other differences between common and Midland hawthorn. The easiest ones to recognise are that the latter's leaves are less deeply and less numerously lobed, while its slightly bigger flowers have two or more styles and therefore there are two (or more) stones to its fruit. Also, its flowers appear a week to ten days earlier than the common species and are less prolific. Where the two species come into contact with each other in woods or hedgerows, hybridisation can take place. The subsequent population may then contain specimens of the original parents as well as a range of intermediates, where there are not only first-generation hybrids but also subsequent generations.

Hawthorn is a very long-living species, but after it has reached a height of about 30 ft (9 m) it continues growing only very slowly. There is a now shattered but ancient specimen at Hethel, south of Norwich. When measured a century ago, in its prime, its girth measured nearly 14 ft (4.3 m) and it was then estimated to be around five centuries old.

THE SMALL PLUMS

Blackthorn or sloe is another native, dense, twiggy shrub, which, if allowed to grow, takes the form of a small tree up to 20 ft (6 m) tall, but usually it is seen at only half that height. Like hawthorn, it is tolerant of a wide range of soils, except for extremely acid conditions, and is found in most British counties; in some it is the principal hedge plant.

A close-up view of opening blackthorn blossom.

People often assume blackthorn hedges to be composed of hawthorn – though there is no mistaking the billowing pure-white clouds of blossom which appear a few weeks before hawthorn comes into flower. At its finest, in certain favourable years – like 1984 and 1985 when the blossom was exceptionally profuse – the bare fields seem to be hemmed in white lace. Its flowers open before its alternate leaves, which are small and oval with slightly toothed margins and hairy undersides, and are a brilliant green when in bud. In autumn they can turn beautiful shades of yellow and reddish brown.

However, it is the plant's blackish bark which gives it its common name. In winter the young twigs are grey or black and produce short, lateral shoots which become thorns bearing rounded buds. These details may often be hidden under a growth of lichen, which grows abundantly on blackthorn. When trimmed and polished, blackthorn's straight stems make handsome walking sticks, while the astringent properties of its bark have been exploited for tanning leather and manufacturing ink.

Another distinct feature of the species is its globose, bluish-black fruit, or sloes, which mature in October and have a dull sheen. Although very bitter, with ample sugar added to their pulp they make a tasty preserve; but far more popular is sloe gin, produced in countless cottages by steeping the fruits in the spirit, in which they impart a piquant flavour. Birds will take the sloe's flesh in autumn, dropping its hard, indigestible seed and therefore accomplishing its dispersal, but the plant is also quite free-suckering. Bullace may be mistaken for blackthorn but can best be distinguished by its larger ripe fruit which may be green, yellow or red as well as black. Other members of the domestic plum family may also establish in hedges, especially those close to gardens, as escapees of cultivation.

BRAMBLES

While hawthorn is a common hedgerow shrub very largely because it was deliberately planted, brambles are so frequently found in hedgerows because they are such successful spontaneous colonisers. However, there is good evidence that bramble seeds were once planted in hedges. In the sixteenth century Thomas Tusser, the author of *Five Hundred Points of Good Husbandry*, wrote:

Where speedy quickset for fence ye will draw
To sow in the seed of the bramble and haw.

Perhaps the bramble was planted partly for its fruit, but the long, thorny, pliable stems may have been rolled into the strong, twisting 'heathering' atop the newly laid hedge.

There are several hundred native microspecies of bramble, each aptly adapted to their own distinct local or regional setting and each displaying minute differences, such as the way their stems arch, or the shape and size of the leaves and leaflets, or the size, shape and direction of their thorns all features which are probably best left to the experts. One such was the late W. C. R. Watson who recorded 387 species in the British Isles alone. Experts who have followed him claim that there are many more still.

Bramble is successful because it is such a prolific propagator. Most species are self-fertile, but the flowers are also widely insect-pollinated. Its numerous seeds are also spread in large numbers by mammals. Members of the thrush family can often be seen to eat the berries then wipe their bills on the leaves to get rid of the seeds. The familiar purple stains on clothes hanging out to dry in autumn provide unwelcome reminders of the thrushes' September feast. When dispersed, the seeds are able to remain dormant in the soil for long periods until germinating conditions are suitable. Where soils are inhospitable to the seeds the species is still able to spread, as its main stems, which root at the tips, will establish themselves in the soil and produce new plants. This often seems to be the principal form of propagation, allowing the plant to spread along a hedge line. Since the bramble is armed with such proficiency for spreading, one almost begins to imagine that were it not for rabbits, which are most partial to its tender shoots and seedlings, the countryside would be inundated by these plants.

For many people, their first interest in shrubs and trees was experienced when 'blackberrying' as children, so there is little need to describe the distinctive shrub. During the course of the year, some leaves will be affected by the rust fungus, and curl and turn brown. Leaf miners will also invade the leaves, which when afflicted appear scribbled with white lines, representing the tunnels of small moth caterpillars, beetle and fly grubs which are chewing their way through the leaf. These white tunnels will show up vividly on the brown dying leaf in winter.

Pinky-white five-petalled flowers appear in clusters between May and September, after which the fruit will appear in varying shapes, colours and flavours, depending on the microspecies. In addition to its delicious fruit, the bramble used to be a handy source of twine, the pliable stem being used to tie in thatch, lash bundles of brushwood or wrap into the woven heathering to complete hedge-laying operations. However, in neat garden hedges bramble can be an untidy intruder which is extremely hard to eliminate. The related dewberry occasionally appears in loose hedgerows; it is usually a plant of rough, dry grasslands and scrub on neutral or calcareous soils and is most frequent in the east of Britain. It differs from bramble in its unridged stems with weak prickles and its fruit is covered by a whitish bloom.

THE WILD ROSES

There are numerous species of wild roses; experts say over 100 species have been identified in our woods and hedges. However, out of all these, five are more common and fairly easily recognisable from certain distinguishing features. These are dog rose, field rose, downy rose, burnet rose and sweet briar, but the last is uncommon in hedgerows. In fact, the majority of roses seen in hedgerows are either the dog or the field rose.

The dog rose, a variable plant, is by far the commonest and most abundant wild rose, occurring throughout the British Isles, but less common in Scotland. Long, arching stems bear large, broad-based thorns with pronounced hooks, helping the stems to prop up strongly against supporting shrubs and burst out of the hedge like an exploding rocket. Clusters of flowers, generally a soft pink, open almost flat in June and July, to display the five petals enclosing a group of free styles. Egg-shaped hips begin to form in late summer, and although the shrivelled stamens may persist in the form of a tufty crown, the sepals fall off before the fruit ripens, usually by November. Sometime in its history the rose may have been crossed with the damask rose to produce the White Rose of York, which was cultivated in some medieval gardens.

Flowering marginally later than dog rose, field rose has also been fairly widely distributed throughout England and Wales (and less so in the north), but is now becoming scarcer in parts of west Wales and the fenlands of East Anglia. It has a preference for heavy soils. It is more of a low, rambling plant; its trailing stems are much weaker than those of dog rose and therefore it tends to flop and fall out of hedgerows in a less dramatic manner. Its flowers are nearly always white and are distinguished from other roses by fused styles. As a result, the hips have columnar crowns, the sepals having fallen before the fruit ripens.

The northern and southern halves of Britain each have their own variety of downy rose. *Rosa tomentosa*, which is widespread throughout England and Wales, is becoming scarce in Scotland, while *R. villosa* is a plant of northern Britain, although it can be found as far south as southern Wales. The most distinctive feature of the downy rose is its leaves, which are densely hairy on both sides. *R. tomentosa* has arching stems and slightly curved prickles, while *R. villosa* has erect stems and straight prickles. Both varieties have pink flowers but those of *R. villosa* are smaller and have a deeper colour, almost purple-pink. The rose hips of both are globose, but the sepals of *R. tomentosa* will have fallen off before the fruit ripens, while those of *R. villosa* will persist as a leafy crown. An intermediate species, *R. sherardii*, has also been identified in the downy rose group. It has the stems and prickle characteristics of *R. tomentosa* but the deep pink flower colouring of the latter. It too is a plant of northern Britain and can occur in hedgerows.

Burnet rose, a suckering, clump-forming shrub, prefers calcareous substrates,

ABOVE LEFT Field rose is a pretty white rose, less boisterous than the dog rose and recognisable by its fused styles forming a column in the centre of the flower. ABOVE RIGHT The hips of the dog rose are distinctly egg-shaped. BELOW Dog rose is a variable species with blossom ranging from white to the rich pink which characterised this specimen.

and its most characteristic habitats are the scrubs on shallow dunes and grassy sand hills on Britain's coasts, particularly in the north and west. Inland it can be found on the limestone pavement of northern England and the rough chalk grasslands of the south. This rose is easily distinguished by its small leaves, often flushed with purple, and densely prickled stems on which large numbers of thorns are mingled with long, stiff bristles. Its white flowers are borne singly. Another characteristic, unique among wild roses, is that its fruit are purple-black instead of red and bear a star-shaped crown of unlobed sepals.

Sweet briar is not unlike dog rose, but less tall and vigorous, and although widespread on calcareous soils in lowland Britain is rarely found in hedgerows. Its lovely flowers are deep pink, but the most distinguishing feature is the dense covering of brownish, sticky, gland-bearing hairs on the undersides of its leaves, which when crushed, will produce a characteristic apple fragrance.

ELDER

None of our native trees grows more rapidly in its earliest years than the elder, for any bit of its living wood will readily take root to grow quickly into an irregular, straggling, deciduous bush, with several stems shooting up from a common base. In many newly planted hedges it will become one of the first species to colonise, taking advantage of disturbed ground or any gap that has been formed in the hedge. However, it has a preference for well-drained, fertile soil which is rich in nitrogen and phosphorus, so it will invariably become established around farmyards or where there is an accumulation of droppings, such as near rabbit warrens, badger setts and starling or pigeon roosts, where it will benefit from the organic enrichment.

Elder's buds are unscaled and are set in opposite pairs (that is, each pair of buds is arranged opposite each other and at right angles to the pairs above and below). The leaves may begin to unfold very early in spring and, if the winter has been mild, this will happen sometimes as early as January, so that the leaves may be fully expanded by April. The compound leaves are normally light green, but yellowishness indicates a nitrogen deficiency. The leaves are poisonous to some creatures, such as rabbits, who will consequently avoid them; but although they are not harmful to cattle, they too find them distasteful. On the other hand, many insect larvae feed on them, such as those of the swallow-tailed moth.

The shrub's fawn twigs have raised breathing pores; they are brittle and have a core of thick white pith. As generations of country children know, this pith may easily be hollowed out to make peashooters or whistles. Older stems develop into hard white wood useful for the manufacture of small durable articles such as tool handles, while watchmakers used to make fine prickers out of them for cleaning mechanical parts.

Although the elder is a rather ugly tree in winter, it compensates for this during the rest of the year with its profuse blossom and fruit. Creamy flat-topped clusters of yellow-white flowers are borne on the ends of young shoots.

ABOVE The beautiful burnet rose has small leaves, dense, straight prickles and masses of white flowers. BELOW The distinctive blossom of elder.

These inflorescences can be very large – up to 1 ft (30 cm) across – but are usually only half this size. They have a heavy, sour scent, possibly unpleasant to some. Their stigma and anthers mature simultaneously and pollen is plentiful, favouring self-pollination, but cross-pollination also takes place and anyone examining the flowers will see that they are visited by multitudes of insects. Strangely though, dried elderflowers are said to make good insect repellent; apparently farm carts used to be drawn by horses whose bridles had sprays of withering elderflowers attached to them in order to deter flies. The blossom also makes an exceedingly fine white wine, which could easily be mistaken for a superior French vintage, and a cordial.

By September the branches become heavy with soft, juicy, purplish-black, red-stalked seeded berries. These are very attractive to birds which will aid seed dispersal. Old countryfolk favour them, too, for pies and jellies, and the fruits also make strongly flavoured wines, rich in Vitamin C. Other parts of the shrub had their uses, as we have already seen, while the bark used to be used as a purgative. In addition, dyes were obtained from different parts of the tree: green from the leaves, blue from the flowers and black from the bark.

Despite its numerous virtues, the shrub makes very poor hedging material and was often removed – a task requiring a great deal of digging and effort. Nowadays several alien elders and cultivars are grown in gardens for their considerable ornamental appeal and these occasionally escape into our wild hedgerows, as the cultivar variety *Sambucus laciniata* has done. It resembles elder in many ways but its distinct features are its leaves: its leaflets are cut into very slender lobes and their form resembles fool's parsley.

OTHER COMMON SHRUBS AND TREES

Our hedges contain many species which are members of the shrub layer of broadleaved woods. Some of these were deliberately planted when plant stock was more abundant while others have colonised naturally. Some species are only locally common on lime or chalk soil and here are found the hedges which bear the largest numbers of species.

HAZEL
Common hazel grows throughout Britain, and in the home counties, after hawthorn and blackthorn, it is one of the most commonly planted hedgerow species. Its early flowering habit makes it a distinctive hedgerow shrub and the yellow lamb's tail catkins have graced many a school windowsill. The pliant nature of its twigs and branches has made it valuable for a variety of useful products since ancient times. In the Mesolithic period, before about 5000 BC, hazel nuts were gathered in great numbers to provide winter rations at a time when vegetable food was in short supply.

The name 'hazel' originates from the Anglo-Saxon word *haesl* or *haesel*, appropriately signifying a baton of authority, for its sinuous twigs are said to have been used to drive cattle and slaves. Hazel poles for support and cut hazel rods for heathering (as well as the living bushes) have been much used for

Hazel catkins are evident in the frosts of winter (LEFT) and the opening of the flowers heralds the return of spring to the hedgerow (RIGHT).

creating the layered hedgerow framework. Today the presence of hazel in a mixed hedge may, in some places, suggest that the hedge is quite old; in the East Midlands it seems to be a feature of older rather than newer hedgerows, although in the wetter west it colonises hedgerows more vigorously. Not only was it planted in hedges to provide a source of timber and nuts, but it was also grown as coppiced underwood in countless medieval woods. Hazel provided the most valuable and versatile light timber. It could be used as wattle in walling or in hurdles; and split branches were first twisted and then bent to produce the staple-shaped 'spars' used to peg down roofing thatch. Thicker stems were used for walking sticks.

Although it will grow almost anywhere if planted, hazel prefers fertile, moist soils, where it will flourish. Yet its wood is said to be best when it grows on chalky sub-soil. In woods it is often seen as coppiced bushes, where many stems rise from the 'stool' and in hedges it may be laid or seen as a twiggy bush, the coarse leaves very loosely resembling those of the elm.

In winter, hazel twigs are covered with bristles. The scaled, large, round, green or red-brown buds are set alternately (arising from one side of the shoot and then the other, all the way up the twig). Small grey, scaly, male catkins hang from December to the spring, depending on the season and situation, becoming bright yellow lamb's tails laden with pollen. Female flowers consist of small, less conspicuous, bud-like catkins, which sprout a tuft of crimson styles. Towards the end of pollination, broadly oval, alternate, serrated leaves unfold. Each fertile female flower will develop into clusters of up to four large, round nuts which are enclosed among the leaf-bracts of the flowers (now enlarged) which form a cup shape. By October they are brown, ripe and edible and quickly taken by birds and mammals, the depredations of the grey squirrel threatening the prospects of the shrub in many places.

BEECH

Beech is certainly indigenous in the southern chalklands, although there is some doubt about whether beech was native in Britain before the Iron Age. Because it needs warm summers to ripen its seeds, beech does not normally reproduce naturally north of the Midlands and South Wales, though when it has been planted, as it has been throughout Britain and Ireland, it is a successful hedge plant. For instance, in the village of Meikleour, near Perth, there is a quite spectacular beech hedge which was planted in 1746 and is 580 yds (530 m) long and 85 ft (26 m) tall. In Exmoor, beech was favoured as a shelter hedge planted on high earthen banks; and other shelterbelts of beech are numerous in East Anglia. When clipped at the start of autumn it will retain its dead leaves, losing them only when the fresh leaves unfold. It can be clipped closely and remain dense because it is shade-tolerant, making it a popular choice for garden hedges. It also tolerates high altitudes and exposed situations, and for that reason it can be seen as an upland hedging plant, even though it is not entirely frost-hardy when young. It is not popular with most lowland stock farmers as stock are too partial to it. But beech particularly was planted in the eighteenth and nineteenth centuries in ornamental-cum-pheasant-cover woodland, the heavy canopy suppressing undergrowth and producing vivid amber autumn tones. Small beech and larch plantations were favoured in the north of England. It is grown as a standard or pollard and does not coppice well. While common in plantations, shelterbelts and ornamental screens, beech is not particularly common in old mixed hedges where it seems to have difficulty in gaining a foothold. Beech is shallow-rooting and can therefore survive well on the thin soils of the chalk downs or on steep slopes elsewhere. In fact, it grows well on a wide variety of soils, provided they are well drained.

Beech has alternating winter buds which are pointed and project at an angle from the twig, and have chestnut-brown scales. When the oval leaves unfold they are a fresh, translucent green, unmistakable as they shimmer in the spring sunshine. They will then darken as summer gets under way, turning brown and golden in autumn. The short-lived flowers, seen just before the leaves unfold, are male or female. The male catkins hang tassel-like on a soft stalk and consist of dense bunches of tiny flowers, each consisting of stamens with greenish anthers enclosed in purple bracts. Female flowers are erect, reddish-brown structures of overlapping scales, each enclosing three styles which project at the apex of the bract. The fruit sets in a woody, spiney husk which splits to shed the triangular brown nut. They are readily eaten by many mammals and were once valued as food or 'mast' for pigs.

HORNBEAM

This is by no means a common hedgerow shrub, though it is sometimes seen as a pollard within a hedgerow. It is notable that while both beech and hornbeam are today popular and effective as single-species hedgerow plantings, neither is really frequent in traditional hedges. Although a member of the *Betulaceae* family, along with hazel, hornbeam superficially resembles beech and might be mistaken at a distance for a rather stunted and twisted beech – though on closer acquaintance it can be recognised as a distinctive and attractive tree.

The winter twigs of hornbeam are dark brown, with buds arranged alternately. The buds, very similar to those of beech in that they are also scaled, narrow and pointed, can be differentiated because they are closely appressed to the twig. Hornbeam's leaf differs from beech, in that while both are broadly oval with prominent parallel venation, beech has wavy margins and the base of each leaf is slightly unequal. The leaves of hornbeam are more narrowly veined, more pointed and their margins distinctly toothed. However, it is in the fruit that the most obvious distinction lies. Hornbeam fruit hangs down in clusters and consists of opposite pairs of winged fruit. Each fruit is a single, tiny green, ribbed nutlet enclosed in a papery leaf-bract, which effectively carries the seed away on the wind. Male and female catkins are borne on the same branch. The female flowers are usually near the tip of the twig and are fairly erect; their pink styles emerge from a mass of leafy green bracts. Male catkins are pendulous, their yellow-green bracts sprouting bunches of crimson-anthered stamens.

Hornbeam is native only to south-eastern England, although it also seems quite well established in parts of the West Country and South Wales, preferring the damp, heavy clay soils that beech dislikes. There is evidence that it seems to produce seedlings more successfully in unmanaged hedges, the saplings growing close around the parent tree, so in managed hedges it is more likely to have been planted. Like beech, it makes an excellent shelter or garden single-species hedge, retaining its low-grown leaves throughout winter, but because it, like beech, is slower-growing, it is sadly neglected in favour of the now so prevalent Leyland Cypress, and in many a country garden a native species would be much more in keeping with the surroundings.

The name hornbeam refers to the hardness of the timber, which formerly had many uses, such as the cogs for mill machinery, ox yokes, flails and butchers' chopping blocks. It was also coppiced extensively for its firewood. Pollarded hornbeams can be seen on Enfield Chase and Epping Forest to the north of London, apparently only becoming numerous there in the Middle Ages, when it must have been encouraged as a pollarded timber tree. There they will also sometimes form a component of the hedges on the banks at the edge of the woods.

FIELD MAPLE

Field maple often grows in hedges on calcareous soils in the south and east of Britain and is not uncommon in hedgerows in the north and west. Dr Hooper considers that this is a species marking a mature hedge, as it seems to grow only when there are already four other species in a hedge (though this might only show that it did not tend to be planted in Parliamentary Enclosure hedges and has not yet made its presence felt in them). It is Britain's only native maple species and a most attractive little tree.

The shrub is best recognised by the distinctive pale reddish-brown colour of its young shoots which exude a milky sap. The small, scaled, brown and green buds are set in opposite pairs. The characteristic deeply divided leaves of maples are another of their distinct features. When fresh they are a soft green, prettily tinged with pink, then later in the year they will bring a red-gold glow to the hedgerows. The fairly inconspicuous monoecious flowers develop in the same erect clusters, the female flowers being distinctive in their winged ovaries. Subsequently the fruit develop two broad wings. There are always fewer fruit than flowers because the flowers rarely all fully develop. As the seeds fall from the shrub, they twirl like the blades of a helicopter.

SYCAMORE

Far more common than field maple is the sycamore, a close relative of the maple. It is hard to believe that it was only introduced from the continent in the sixteenth century, for through vigorous colonisaton it is widespread and well established everywhere – too well established for many tastes. Wherever there is a sycamore tree there will almost invariably be a sycamore sprouting in hedges nearby for they not only seed abundantly, but also grow very easily. It has the ability to withstand salty winds so it can be seen growing near the coast. Sycamore has large maple-like leaves with sharp lobes. Its larger fruit are also winged like those of field maple, but while those of the latter hang in a cluster on multi-lengthed stalks so that all the seeds appear to be in an inverted flat-topped cluster, those of sycamore hang down in a long, dense cluster. Sycamore wood is fine grained and can be beautifully veined, particularly if shown up with high polish, so it was formerly very desirable for furniture and decoratively grained pieces. Once regarded as an ornamental tree, sycamore can sometimes be seen growing as a standard in hedgerows.

GOAT WILLOW

Goat willow or great sallow is the commonest of the hedgerow willows, and has the ability to withstand drier conditions better than any other British willows. It is perhaps more familiar in springtime under the name of 'pussy willow' because of the striking, kitten-furred catkins it produces at this time. Shiny winter twigs bear red-brown, single-scaled catkin buds, which start to emerge as silky white forms early in spring. The species is dioecious. Male catkins are grey at first, turning yellow when ripe and tipped with pollen. Female catkins are only marginally less pretty in their greenish-white guise. The early flowers, emerging when few others are available, provide insects with nectar, and on bright sunny days large numbers of early bumble bees can be seen visiting the catkins, thus aiding pollination. The female catkins then set and turn into fruit, which, when ripe, are contained in woolly capsules; these are easily carried away on the wind. The leaves will unfold sooner on male trees than on female ones. These alternate, toothed oval leaves are grey-green on top and downy beneath.

ABOVE Field maple coming into leaf in an old Cambridgeshire hedge. The young leaves and blossom are a very fresh shade of green, while in autumn the tree provides strong tints of red and amber. RIGHT The blossom of sycamore.

Willow can make an effective rough hedge on damp ground but is even more open-growing than hazel, and because of this its soft, pliable wood tends to spring out of position more than most hedging plants when laid. As a result hedgers may cut out willow if they can, although willow rods can substitute for hazel in heathering. However, the British Conservation Volunteers claim that it is useful for filling gaps where the ground is too wet for other species and is therefore more welcome in hedges in parts of Wales and the peaty areas of East Anglia, while it may colonise broad damp verges to form a loose spontaneous hedge.

DOGWOOD

Dogwood has no obvious connection with dogs, for its name is a corruption of 'dagwood', since butchers made 'dags' or skewers from its tough wood; however, a more local name is 'houndberry tree' which is thought to have originated because it was said that the bark of dogwood made an excellent wash for mangy dogs. Its generic name, *Cornus*, means horny, referring to the hardness of its wood, while *sanguinea*, meaning bloody, signifies the blood-red colour of its twigs – the feature also represented in another of its several local names, 'bloody twig'.

Dogwood will grow throughout Britain, but it is most common on chalky soils. Although it is more usually seen as a free-suckering deciduous shrub, as a result of its striking appearance in winter months it is favoured in parks and gardens where it may sometimes form a small round-headed tree up to 20 feet (about 6 m) in height. In this respect alien dogwoods, with even more striking winter coloration, are now often preferred and occasionally become naturalised.

Dogwood's overwintering, unscaled, opposite buds are also red and unfold into long, broadly oval green leaves. A noticeable feature of its leaves is that their lateral veins curve distinctly towards the leaf apex, so that if a leaf is torn in half, the veins hold it together. Their autumn tints can be very attractive reds and purples.

From late May to about July dogwood opens its four-petalled white flowers, which are bunched together in dense inflorescences. They are very successfully pollinated by flies and beetles in particular, for they give out what seems to us an unpleasant smell, but one which renders them very attractive to these insects. By autumn the flowers will have developed into clusters of round, glossy, black berries, each containing one and sometimes two hard stones. They are said to yield an oil which was used for soap manufacture and for burning in lamps. The fruit is exceedingly bitter to taste, but birds gather them quite readily and later deposit the seeds, aiding the species' rampant propagation. It also spreads by suckering and if permitted, it will overgrow and shade out lesser plants. But grazing animals are partial to its young leaves and shoots and help check its invasion, perhaps explaining why the shrub is less common than one might expect.

Hedgerow dogwood in full bloom.

PURGING BUCKTHORN

Clad in its freshly unfolded leaves, purging buckthorn may sometimes be mistaken for dogwood, for it bears a superficial resemblance to it. However, in winter its thorny twigs are pale grey and its brown, pointed buds are not quite opposite. It has two kinds of shoots – the long shoots extend its growth, while the short erect shoots bear the leaves, flowers and fruit. The leaves are of the same shape as those of dogwood, with similar tipward-arching, conspicuous, lateral veins, but they have distinctly toothed margins, while those of dogwood are so slightly toothed that this is barely noticeable. The caterpillars of the brimstone butterfly may often be found amongst the leaves, as this species (along with alder buckthorn) is their main food plant.

The species is dioecious. Tiny yellowish-green flowers, borne at the end of short, ridged stalks, are set in loose clusters emerging from the leaf axils. Female flowers can be distinguished by the globulous ovaries enclosed in the four widely spaced petals. Although inconspicuous, the flowers must yield a heady nectar, for they are insect-pollinated. Flowers are followed by clusters of black berries. In former times this fruit and the shrub's bark were used to concoct a violent purgative, and this is probably how it derived part of its common name.

WILD PRIVET

Wild privet is mainly a shrub of England's southern chalklands, where it is quite common, though it can be seen elsewhere, as in woods on limestone slopes in the north of England. The common garden variety, Japanese or oval-leaved privet, is almost evergreen except in hard winters, but wild privet tends to lose its leaves in winter and therefore form a less dense hedge.

Wild privet has smooth dark stems, the young twigs being downy at first. The opposite leaves are long, narrow and leathery and the pairs are set more widely spaced than those of the garden variety. The small, white, four-petalled, funnel-shaped flowers are borne in tight, conical inflorescences. The flowers are heavily scented and will attract many flying insects which aid pollination. The black, seeded berries will persist throughout winter to supply survival rations for birds, but are very poisonous to humans. However, the herbalist John Gerard, writing in the sixteenth century, contended that a potion of privet leaves could be used to combat swellings, such as abscesses and ulcers of the mouth and throat.

As it loses its leaves in winter, wild privet is not as effective in well-trimmed hedges as the garden variety, but it provides good shelter when mixed with the thorns, although it is too weak to be a welcome member of stock-proof farm hedges. When grown uncut it provides good bird cover, and while it is tolerant of quite heavy shade it flowers and fruits best in the open. It is the primary food plant of the larvae of the privet hawk moth.

HOLLY

The holly is one of the most easily recognised of our native trees. In different hedgerows it may be absent, a minor member of the community or predominant, and in the more acid soils in the Yorkshire Dales it can be seen expanding at the expense of the hawthorn of the original planting. Whether holly was a

ABOVE LEFT A close view of the tiny flowers of purging buckthorn; each cluster is only about the size of a 1p piece. ABOVE RIGHT The blossom of wild privet. BELOW The familiar berries of the holly. When holly is allowed to grow as a hedgerow tree, as it was sometimes to provide a source of winter fodder, only the lower leaves bear thorns.

popular choice with hedge planters is uncertain. On the one hand it is very slow-growing when newly planted and is sometimes said to be poorly stock-proof; on the other hand it can form a good ornamental or windproof barrier and its prickly leaves serve as hard winter rations for hungry stock in winter. As a result it was grown in special woods in medieval times, as 'Hollings' place-names reveal. Old holly standards seen in some hedges may have been encouraged for the same reason.

Holly is quite a remarkable survivor. Not only is it tolerant of regular cutting, for new shoots will sprout from cut stems, but if a fire should kill the tree above the ground (its bark and foliage being quite inflammable) it can regenerate from the base. The tree is also more tolerant than most trees of frost and drought, making physiological adaptations to survive. For instance, the waxy surfaces of its thick leaves enable them to resist water loss when the winter soil is frozen (but it cannot survive arctic conditions indefinitely). To withstand the summer drought, young plants may respond by shedding their leaves to replace them in the following spring. In normal circumstances, the leaves may last on the tree for up to four years.

The tree's two-toned leaves – dark, glossy green above and paler green below – are wavy-edged and protected by spines on the lower parts of the tree. Here we see another of its physiological adaptations: when the tree reaches a height of 10 ft (3 m) or so, many of the leaves on its upper branches, where browsing animals cannot reach, have no spines, so it is generally assumed that the prickly leaves have evolved in self-defence. Holly is very slow-growing, so a tree at this height will be a good many years old.

Normally holly trees will bear either male or female flowers, but hermaphrodite specimens are not uncommon. However, all types of tree will bear small clusters of waxy-white, four-petalled flowers, but the male flowers will contain a functionless ovary. The flowers' nectar is very attractive to bees, and other insects as well, enabling cross-pollination, but the berries borne by female trees only (and the hermaphrodites) will ripen from July onwards. It is often said that a good crop of berries heralds a hard winter, but in fact a bumper crop really indicates a fine summer just past: July temperatures of 12°C and over will encourage a good fruit crop. The clustered berries are glossy and bright red and as winter develops, thrushes, starlings and wood pigeons will soon strip the trees of them, but those fruit that are not eaten generally persist until spring. The shed seed lies dormant for at least 18 to 20 months before it germinates, starting its life with two soft, deciduous seed leaves, but from its third leaf onward it will develop its evergreen prickly foliage. Although holly does not sucker, downward-growing branches will readily root in the leaf mould beside the parent tree. Though disliking cold clay soils, holly can establish quite successfully on soils of shales, peat, sand, gravel and chalk. It is also easily found up to a height of 1800 ft (550 m) and the occasional tree may even be found in spontaneous hedges on river banks. However, being an evergreen, it is unhappy in the smoky conditions of city life.

As it is so slow-growing, holly timber is exceedingly fine-grained, hard and heavy and used to be in demand for decorative furniture-making. It was a cheap substitute for box and, when dyed, for ebony too. A curious use for its twigs was to boil them down to produce a glutinous substance, bird lime, which was smeared on twigs and branches to catch hapless small birds for the pot.

Young holly trees are clad in a fine, silvery-grey bark and that of older trees is more fissured, but a tree's bark is often covered by the growth of the striking mottled grey and black lichen *Graphis elegans*. Holly leaves will also quite often show disfiguration in the form of blotch-shaped mines caused by the larvae of insects, such as the fly *Phytomyza ilicis*. After hatching on the underside of the leaf the larvae tunnel along the midrib as they feed and then move to the inside of the leaf between the upper and lower epidermis, overwintering there until they pupate, emerging as adults in the following spring. A frequent hedgerow butterfly, the holly blue, will lay her first spring brood of eggs on holly's flower buds, as the caterpillars prefer the flower buds of their food plant to the leaves. (The second generation brood, laid in August, prefer the buds of autumn-flowering ivy. The holly blue is unique among British butterflies, its caterpillars having these different preferences for their food depending on what time of the year they hatch.)

Like hawthorn, holly is associated with many pagan superstitions and religious observances, which one imagines would have easily arisen of a tree which shows healthy, shining leaves in the midst of winter. Parts of the tree have magical medicinal powers attributed to them, such as a concoction made from the bark which could be claimed to allay fever, while a rather peculiar cure for chilblains prescribed thrashing them with holly twigs. Inevitably holly became linked with Christmas, evidenced not only in the holly decorations of Christmas but also in its local names 'Christmas', and 'Christian thorn', while the medieval monks called it the 'holy tree'.

THE WILD APPLE

The pinkish-white blossom of our crab apple competes with that of our hawthorns to enliven hedgerows in early May, while later in the year their golden leaves add to the colours of autumn. Hedgerow and woodland crab apples have a mixed parentage, but most experts will probably agree that there are two sub-species. Our wild crab apple, *Malus sylvestris ssp sylvestris*, recolonised Britain after the Ice Age and is therefore regarded as a native tree, while the other, the cultivated apple, *M. sylvestris ssp mitis*, is introduced. The wild variety is found throughout the British Isles, except in the northernmost parts of Scotland, but its distribution has been somewhat obscured by ornamental species and confusion with specimens of the cultivated variety which has naturalised. The two are superficially very similar, but on closer examination the leaves of the cultivated variety have downy undersides and the leaf stalks and young leaves are hairy.

The crab apple has densely branching shoots and crooked branches which spread widely, so that sometimes the diameter of the crown exceeds the height of the tree. Rarely is this more than 25 ft (about 8 m) and the tree will always remain shrubby. The mature twigs of the wild variety will bear spines. The crab apple has a purple-brown bark which becomes so rough with age that it cracks into small square plates and peels off in thin scales.

The red-brown overwintering buds are alternate and downy. It has pointed,

The blossom (ABOVE) and fruit (LEFT) of the crab apple.

oval leaves and the flowers are borne in clusters on separate short stalks, from which miniature, sour yellow or greenish apples, faintly flushed with red, will hang in autumn. Those of the cultivated variety are larger and sweeter, but with sugar added to taste, both make excellent jelly. However, they are a more valuable food source for many insects and birds, particularly the wasps and thrushes, and when fallen, for mammals. In early spring numerous seedlings may be discovered in hedgerows where birds have roosted, developing from the fruit's black pips, but most of these are soon crowded out of existence when established plants come into leaf.

THE WILD CHERRIES

An ancestor of the cultivated cherries and one of two of our native wild cherry species, the gean or wild cherry is the most widely distributed member of this group throughout the British Isles. Its usual habitat is the understorey layer of a mixed oak woodland, but not uncommonly it appears in hedgerows, occasionally as a hybrid with a cultivated species.

It has a preference for base-rich soils, on which a mature tree may attain a height of between 20 to 40 ft (6 to 12 m) with reddish, stout, upward-growing branches forming a well-proportioned tree. The species' ability to sucker sometimes allows it to form clumps in hedgerows where a parent tree has been felled and new plants have suckered from its roots.

Cherries' have their scaled buds clustered on short side shoots. In April some of the buds burst into dainty, white blossoms to transform the bare branches, but this beauty is short-lived, for the clusters of flowers fall within a week. Although their pistils and stamens mature at the same time, the plants are self-sterile. As the flowers fall, the long leaves unfold, revealing lumpy glands at the base of each leaf. When the fruit first begin to set they are yellow and then shiny red when ripe, nearly always hanging in pairs. The scattering of the indigestible stones by birds will aid the plant's propagation, but few seedlings survive.

The gean's smaller relative, the bird cherry, can be quite a prominent member of old hedgerows on acid soils, particularly in sheltered valleys, in northern Britain, where, once it becomes established, it can effectively spread by suckering. It is rarely found south of Wales and Leicestershire, present only in moist woodlands. Bird cherry's winter buds are different from gean, and are not

The blossom of gean.

The bird cherry bears what is perhaps the prettiest blossom of any hedgerow tree.

set in clusters, but singly on very short stalks growing at an angle to the twigs. Its blossom is also different in appearance, for the flowers are borne in long pendant racemes. The species is dichogamous and the plant has a peculiar way of ensuring that its flowers are pollinated, for prior to fertilisation the flowers are erect, after which they will droop, to be out of the way, ensuring that the unfertilised blossom is fully visible to visiting insects. The bird cherry bears black fruit, very bitter to the taste, but which are nevertheless favoured by birds. Another characteristic of this species is the unpleasant scent, reminiscent of bitter almonds, that is given off when its thin grey-black bark is peeled from its warty twigs.

The sour cherry, a native of Asia Minor, has long been cultivated in Europe and has frequently naturalised in hedges. However, it rarely extends further north than Yorkshire. It is also thought to be the parent of the Morello or Brandy Cherry and the Kentish Cherry. Various kinds of alien cherries may occasionally be seen growing as standards in eighteenth-century Enclosure hedges and can provide a special surprise for country-lovers.

THE *SORBUS* SPECIES

The two *Sorbus* species which are most likely to be found in hedgerows are whitebeam and rowan. The first is seen in hedgerows on chalk, limestone and sometimes sandy soils in southern England and Ireland; the second is commoner in upland districts and hilly country.

The Saxons are reputed to have used whitebeam as a boundary marker because of its distinctive appearance with its whitish foliage. A tree will grow fast on suitable soils, its rate of growth slowing down considerably after about ten years, but a mature tree can achieve a height of 80 ft (24 m) to stand erect, bearing upswept branches and a wide-domed crown. A young tree is more conical in outline. Whitebeam will not colonise naturally on acid soils though it will grow on them if planted, but on poor soils the species grows to no more than a small bush. All *Sorbus* species hybridise freely and whitebeam is no exception; therefore there are numerous localised sub-species, some of them very rare.

Alternate, pointed, red-scaled winterbuds are arranged on stout grey twigs. Because of the many sub-species, leaves vary in shape, size and serration. However, typically they are broadly oval with slightly serrated margins and are sometimes shallowly lobed. Their most distinctive feature is their white, downy undersides, and when freshly unfolded they form goblet-shaped clusters, green on the inside and white on the outside. The down remains on the leaves even when they have fallen in autumn, and helps the tree to conserve moisture on dry sites right through its growing season. Creamy-white, bisexual flowers, which appear in May, develop in loose clusters and are followed by yellowish-brown or red berries, which, though too sour to be eaten raw, are said to make a tasty jelly for venison. Birds will eat the flesh and scatter the small seeds contained within. Although its fruit and tough wood may have made an important feature of the countryside in the past, today whitebeam is more desirable for planting in gardens, parks and streets as a decorative tree, and due to its compact shape it can easily be planted in restricted spaces. It is no longer considered a very good hedgerow shrub because of its 'open' nature.

Rowan or mountain ash is another open tree with distinctively ascending branches. Although rapidly growing and regenerating well when cut, it is not a good mixer, quickly succumbing to the shade of denser species, so it is most likely to be found in sparse hedgerows. While it is not uncommon to see several scattered bushes and even trees in hedgerows on light soils in the north, in the richer soils of the south one may walk for many miles without seeing a hedgerow rowan, but in a few regions in the west, such as southern Wales and south Shropshire, it forms a fairly frequent member of the hedgerow communities.

In winter, rowan's large, blunt-pointed, hairy buds are set alternately on dark twigs with distinctive breathing pores. The compound leaves are made up of numerous pairs of stalkless leaflets. They are superficially like those of ash and give the tree its common southern name, mountain ash. Numerous small, creamy-white flowers, similar to those of whitebeam, develop in denser flattened clusters. The berries follow, yellow at first, then becoming orange and finally scarlet; their flesh is bright yellow. Rowan berries are also made into a jelly to accompany game dishes and, being rich in Vitamin C, used to be made into a drink to prevent scurvy. The berries are beloved of birds and were used by bird-catchers as bait to snare hedgerow birds, particularly members of the thrush family. The tree features in various religious superstitions.

A third member of the *Sorbus* family is the handsome wild service tree. It is one of the rarest of our native trees, and is found mainly in Kent and Sussex, where it grows happily in hedgerows. Woodland specimens, which can reach a height of 65 ft (20 m), may have suffered at the hands of charcoal burners, reducing the tree's ability to colonise hedgerows, while the slow-growing tree produces seeds which are often reluctant to germinate. The lobed leaves are alternate, whitish in bud and maple-like in autumn. Small, rounded heads of creamy-white flowers appear in May and June and the rounded, leathery, brown fruit are borne in clusters.

SPINDLE

Spindle has a preference for base-rich substrates and so, although indigenous to Britain, is not generally common. In fact it is a shrub that does not seem to occur in the more recently planted hedges and is regarded as a poor coloniser. In the past, its hard, white, smooth-grained wood, which had the added advantage of not splintering, was used extensively for making items such as knitting needles, pegs, skewers and small turnery, and before the advent of the spinning wheel the wood was used extensively for making spindle-whorls.

Usually a straggling, inconspicuous deciduous shrub, which may very occasionally grow into a small tree, the spindle may well be overlooked until autumn when the tree is definitely at its best, clad in its crimson, purple and gold leaves and pink fruit. However, during the other seasons the shrub is certainly worth seeking out, for it has some interesting features. In winter its twigs will take on a distinct bright green coloration, and in cross-section they are almost square. Small, opposite, pointed buds have green and brown scales. It has thin, serrated leaves, tinted blue underneath. Loose clusters of small greenish-white flowers appear in May or June. In autumn the four-capsuled fruit splits to reveal black seeds cushioned in a bright orange pulp. When bruised or crushed, like all parts of the shrub, the berries give off a most unpleasant smell. They are emetic and poisonous to humans but other uses have been found for them: dried and powdered berries make a powerful insecticide; when boiled they have been used as a hair rinse; the berries' husks lent themselves to the manufacture of a kind of red dye; and a yellow dye was made from their pulp. However, these berries will readily be eaten by birds, which they do not seem to affect, so that seed is distributed.

A close-up view of the minute flowers of the spindle.

WAYFARING TREE

Another shrub with berries which are poisonous to humans is the wayfaring tree, which was given this name by John Gerard, who noticed its occurrence in the hedgerows along the old drove roads over the chalk downs. The shrub is still locally common in that area, favouring dry, chalky soil, and it can be found on similar soils throughout southern England and Wales where it is native. If it is found in the north it will invariably have been planted.

Lost in the mist of time are its other local names, such as 'mealy-tree', 'cotton-tree', 'cottoner' and 'hoarwithy', expressing the hairiness of its twigs, buds and leaves; while 'twist-wood', 'whipcrop' and 'hithy-tree' indicate the supple nature of its fibrous branches, which used to be twisted to form a sort of rope for binding bundles with. Sometimes these were made into temporary hoops with which to fasten gates, or into flexible handles for whips.

Seldom does the plant grow into a tree, attaining its maximum height of about 20 ft (6 m), and even then there is not a trunk in the usual sense of the word, but slender branches stemming from a common point near ground level. The downy branches usually grow in pairs; that is, they fork from a common point on previous growth further down the shrub. In winter these will be covered with large, opposite buds which are devoid of scales, but instead are protected from frost by their hairiness. The alternate leaves are broadly oval, soft and velvety. They have small teeth, and while only slightly downy above, have a dense, almost white, hairy underside, and their wrinkled texture emphasises their venation.

The unmistakable blossom and furrowed fleshy leaves of the wayfaring tree.

The dense clusters of small creamy-white flowers are quite sickly-smelling and will give rise to oval, red berries, borne in a flat head. These will ripen to become like beads of jet later in the season. The berries hold single, flat, ribbed seeds which birds will disperse along hedgerows. The shrub is very hardy and regenerates well after cutting, but as its downy nature easily attracts dust particles, it is not happy in a smoky, polluted atmosphere.

THE GUELDER ROSE

Related to the wayfaring tree, the guelder rose, also aptly called the 'snowball tree', is pretty when its snowy-white, ball-shaped flowering clusters are in bloom, but sensational with its red leaves and fruit in the autumn. Although a native of Britain, it is only locally common, thriving best in damp heavy soils and even in fen peats, though being partial to the moister chalk soils. It is not tolerant of shade and does not flower or fruit well when the light is poor. It is much more numerous in the south, but is also found in the north of England.

In winter, stripped of its leaves, the shrub reveals its open, spreading branches covered in tiny buds which are wrapped in green scales tinged with purple. The paired leaves are maple-like and toothed. Bright green when fresh, they develop into shades of bright crimson, orange and russet, setting off the translucent red berries in autumn.

In June or July umbrella-shaped clusters of two forms of flower blossom. Large five-petalled 'fakes', entirely without stamens or pistils, will frame the inner, tiny, fertile flowers. The function of the outer blossom is therefore solely to attract insect life to the bell-shaped bisexual flowers. Clusters of luscious red berries follow, but for all their tempting beauty they are nauseous to the taste and emit an offensive odour. However, birds seem to find them quite edible and spread the single stones borne within, but only the most favourable conditions will determine whether germination takes place or the seedlings survive. A well-established shrub, guelder rose can survive hedgerow trimming to regenerate quickly, and if cut back to its roots will produce suckers from them.

The lustrous fruit of the guelder rose.

COMMON STANDARDS IN HEDGEROWS

Many hedges, particularly those bordering and enclosing farmland, possess large standard trees. However, these days it is also common to see lines of trees across fields, evidently surviving from hedges that have long since died. Although we may not always know whether it was deliberate policy or natural accident that resulted in the free upward growth of many of the present hedgerow standards, such trees must once have been carefully preserved and managed for they were an important source of heavier constructional timber. Some of the specimens that we see are standards, others were 'beheaded' to grow as pollards, which produced a crop of poles above the reach of browsing livestock. We can assume that desirable timber trees were allowed to grow tall in many medieval hedges, though the planting of such trees in Enclosure hedges seems to have found more favour in the eighteenth century than in the nineteenth. Today some enlightened farmers are tagging suitable hedgerow shrubs at intervals, seeking to protect them from mechanical hedge-cutting and allowing them to grow as new hedgerow standards. Most of the hedgerow trees which yielded heavy constructional timber, like oak, elm and ash, can also be seen growing in mixed hedges at hedgerow height. In the past, pollarded hedgerow trees were much more numerous, and Oliver Rackham has quoted a case of a 187-acre (75-ha) farm at Thorndon in Suffolk which had 6,058 pollard trees standing in its hedgerows in 1742.

Dr Rackham has found that hedgerow trees show regional variation: for example, oak is typical in Norfolk, ash in the north-east Midlands and Northumberland, holly in Staffordshire and elm in Essex. As hedgerow trees are awkward to fell and transport, those that are removed today are often not replaced because, as Jon Tinker sadly points out, 'hedgerow timber now brings in a good price for farmers to fell it for the money, but not enough for it to be worth continuing to grow hedgerow trees as an additional source of income.' However, in times gone by cartwrights were said to prefer hedge-grown timber, finding it tougher than timber from woods.

ASH

The ash is not always considered to be a suitable hedgerow shrub for planting today, for although it is as quick-growing as the thorns, it grows thickly and competes with its neighbours. It is also much tougher than the thorny species, making it harder to cut when large and therefore it must be maintained by frequent laying. However, as a tree it is ubiquitous in hedgerows thoughout the country and the most common tall hedgerow tree in some counties.

The tree has a large spreading crown and shows up best in winter after its leaves have fallen revealing its grey, olive-tinged, lacey-patterned bark and the velvety black buds on its down-curving branches. Ash comes into flower long before its leaves appear and its late-leafing has made ash unpopular as an ornamental parkland tree. Clusters of petal-less flowers sprout from their buds in April: they may be male, female or bisexual, and all types may well appear not only on the same tree, but also on the same branch. The flowers are very simple: male flowers consist of dense bunches of stamens and female flowers on longer stalks consist of a pistil with an extended style and cleft stigma. Compound leaves consist of up to six pairs of oval leaflets with one single leaf at the apex. Ash not only comes into leaf late (possibly because it is susceptible to spring frosts) but also loses its leaves earlier than most trees, while they are still green. By September clusters of delicate paper-thin winged seeds, 'keys', form and are dispersed by the autumn winds. Although numerous seeds are dispersed, they do not germinate until more than a year after they have fallen – though gardeners will testify to the free-seeding qualities of the tree. The seeds can persist on the tree throughout the autumn and well into winter, and they therefore form an important food source for the bullfinch at this harsh time.

Ash wood is tough and does not splinter easily. It was and is therefore popular for the poles and handles of farming and garden implements, such as pickaxes and hammers, to which much force is applied. It used also to be widely used to make the curved pieces of furniture, such as the backs of Windsor chairs, for it bends quite easily after steaming. More recent uses include the construction of frames for sports cars and aircraft.

ELM

The common elms form many hybrids and varieties and their distinction is a matter of some difficulty. They were once frequent trees in the landscape and perhaps formerly the commonest hedgerow and field tree in southern England. In the old farming landscape the English elm dominated the Midlands and southern England; the smooth-leaved elm was common in East Anglia; while the Cornish elm was found in the west and south-west of Britain. But today all species are fast disappearing due to the ravages of the Dutch elm disease which has raged unchecked. As a result, all that remains in many hedges today is a line of stark dead trunks. However, afflicted trees may still sucker and shrubby hedgerow elm is less affected than the standards and can still be very invasive.

The disease is caused by the fungus *Ceratocystis ulmi*, the spores of which are carried by elm-bark beetles, *Scolytus scolytus*, which tunnel beneath the elm bark. The fungus encourages the elm's cells to produce a sticky substance in its defence, but this has the effect of blocking the conducting tissues of the tree, so that parts of it will become short of water and nutrients, the first signs of which are the leaves turning yellow and withering. This is accelerated during hot summers, like that of 1976, when the loss of elm trees was catastrophic. The larvae of the elm bark beetle, which lays its eggs in dying elm, are now thought to feed on the fungus. So when they emerge as adults in search of another elm tree in which to breed, they probably carry spores away with them. This way of transmitting the disease, and the fact that it can spread through the shared root system of this suckering species, has probably hastened the demise of elm from the disease, though new suckering can bring about the regeneration of an afflicted tree.

There are a few pockets where English elm may still survive in the south, as in East Sussex. In the north, where the trees were more widely spaced, the disease was slower to spread, but it has now killed most trees here as well. However, where it is alive the elm appears as a tall, narrow-crowned tree, anything up to about 130 ft (40 m) in height with its complement of sucker shoots at the base.

The distinctive silhouette, so frequent in Constable's landscapes, was a keynote of the old English countryside.

Elm bark is rough, with deep vertical fissures, and the twigs are often corky. The trees flower very early in the year producing numerous clusters of reddish or purple petal-less, bisexual flowers long before the leaves begin to unfold. Elms have broad, oval, toothed leaves of a rather coarse appearance and texture. Oval, winged fruit, produced in vast numbers, set earlier in the year than the fruit of most trees, in about April or May, but they are usually sterile and rarely ripen. As a result, seedlings are uncommon.

Wych elm grows naturally in hedgerows and woods in the south, but like rowan is probably naturally associated with upland glens and waterside vegetation. It rarely forms suckers like the common elm, but instead reproduces by seed and hence has a greater resistance to elm disease. Wych elm has the roughest leaves of all elms, and they are capable of inflicting a sting similar to that of nettle. But they were once highly valued as cattle fodder. In the Middle Ages long-bows were often made from the supple wood of this tree, from which it may have derived its common name – 'wych' meaning supple.

Elm wood was specially favoured by virtue of its resistance to decay and splitting. Because it is so durable it was used for coffins and weather-boarding; and early water engineers used elm for pipes, whole trunks being bored out and driven together to make mains pipes. Village pumps were also of elm wood right down to the moving parts and valves. Wheelwrights used it for the hub or nave of cart wheels.

Elms provide feeding and breeding grounds for large numbers of insects, which in turn attract insect-eating birds. Their high trunk and canopy is much valued by rooks, kestrels and owls for nesting and the loss of these trees has undoubtedly affected all elm-frequenting creatures, perhaps most of all the white-letter hairstreak and large tortoiseshell butterflies, whose main food plant is the elm.

THE OAKS

As we have already seen, the wood of almost every hedgerow tree and shrub has been put to use according to its particular properties, but the most valuable of standard or pollarded trees has been oak, supplying timber for uses from the timber frames of houses and the hulls of ships to charcoal. As it happens, oak is also the most valuable tree to hedgerow fauna. In hedges, oak was mainly a planted species and most frequently maintained by pollarding, and many of the trees seen today are old pollards. Subsequent seedlings that may have colonised naturally, survived and become established are today usually managed like the other hedgerow shrubs.

There are two species of native oak: common or pendunculate, generally found on heavy lowland clays, and durmast or sessile oak, usually found on the poorer hill soils of the north and west. It is the common oak that is most frequent in the hedgerows. However, a third species has also become quite common as it has naturalised in many hedgerows close to parks and gardens: this is the introduced turkey oak, with its distinctive stipules (thin thread-like leafy growth). The following features differentiate the three species.

ABOVE Oak seedlings, destined to become hedgerow standards, were planted at regular intervals in this Yorkshire Parliamentary Enclosure hedge. RIGHT The snowberry, with its pink flowers (left) and globular white berries (right) is one of the commonest garden escapees and hedgerow colonists.

	COMMON	SESSILE	TURKEY
winter buds: clusters at tips of terminal shoot, alternate on twigs	round, brown, hairless	larger, pointed hairy	small, blunt, enclosed in stipule
leaves: lobed	deep, irregular lobes, ear-like extension at base, hairless	shallow, regular lobes, wedge-shaped at leaf base, underside hairy	deep, irregular lobes, stipules at leaf base
flowers	male flowers hang in slim catkins; stalked female flowers at tips of shoots	male flowers hang in catkins; bud-shaped, stalkless female flowers at tips of shoots	male flowers hang in slim catkins; stalked female flowers enclosed in stipules
acorns	often paired on long stalks, striped when mature	stubbier than common species, stalkless	enclosed in bristly cups

As we said at the outset, almost any native and introduced tree can be encountered in a hedge, though many shun hedgerow life. The native, small-leaved lime-dominated expanses of the ancient wildwood can occasionally be found in hedgerows, though it seems too fastidious to enjoy the competitive conditions of this habitat. Alder and long-leafed willows, like crack willow, osier, or white willow, may be seen in damp ditch hedges or riverside hedges. Snowberry was planted in woods as pheasant cover and, if very hungry, birds will take the unpleasant white berries, allowing this North American shrub to establish itself in hedgerows. The barberry, in contrast, is becoming very rare in countryside hedges but has gained popularity as a garden shrub. The discovery that the shrub was host to wheat rust fungus led to vigorous campaigns for removal from commons, woods and hedges. Silver birch may be seen in loose spontaneous hedges on the verges of upland lanes where soils are reasonably light and dry, but this is normally a tree of sandy woods and wastes. Horse chestnut was introduced as a statuesque, ornamental tree when parkland planting was very active in the seventeenth and eighteenth centuries. The horse chestnut can sometimes be seen growing as a massive hedgerow standard, its branches festooned with dead sticks hurled by children seeking to dislodge the autumn crop of conkers.

·10·

CLIMBING AND TWINING IN THE HEDGEROW

The tangled mass of a flourishing hedgerow in riotous bloom and vigorous growth resembles a great anarchic battlefield of plants, each apparently seeking to overpower its fellows in the race for space. In amongst this battle are the roses, which seem to be stealing the march by taking advantage of their neighbours and climbing up them or grasping onto them for support as though they were ladders to the sun. In using other plants for support and not needing to grow strong stems of their own, the climbers are able to convert their energy into rapid growth through the dense hedgerow to reach openings where their leaves can unfold to absorb the sunlight and where their flowers are placed high in an advantageous position for pollination and later for dispersal when seeds are set. It is interesting to note how these plants climb and here we examine some of the common species and the various organs which help them to succeed.

TWINING STEM CLIMBERS

The honeysuckle, of course, gets its common name from the sweet nectar which it holds at the base of each flower. It is a vigorous stem climber, preferring to exploit smooth-barked plants unhampered by numerous branches, such as hazel, though also found embracing others. It climbs by twisting the growing tip of the stem to the left, then hanging over and turning a wide circle to coil again. The grip of the main shoot may be so firm as to constrict the outer tissue of the supporting plant, giving it a corkscrew deformity which may have the effect of destroying saplings: hence it is also known as 'woodbine'. The poet William Cowper describes some of these characteristics:

> As woodbine weds the plant within her reach,
> Rough elm or smooth-grained ash, or glossy beech,
> In spiral rings ascends the trunk, and lays
> Her golden tassels on the leafy sprays;
> But does a mischief while she lends her grace,
> Slackening its growth by such a strict embrace.

THE HEDGEROW
IN BLOSSOM

RIGHT A spray of blossom of the burnet rose. BELOW A spray of blooming dogwood. The unpleasant scent is attractive to insects. BOTTOM RIGHT The flowers of the dog rose.

LEFT The blossom of the guelder rose, with the small, fertile flowers surrounded by a ring of larger, infertile blooms. BELOW The bold yellow flowers of Tutsan can be seen on hedgebanks in the south-west of England during the summer. The leaves of the plant were gathered for their antiseptic properties.

INSECTS AND POLLEN

RIGHT The painted lady is a beautiful migrant butterfly. BELOW The common blue butterfly is likely to be seen visiting flowers on verges in chalky areas.

The elephant hawk moth is our most vividly colourful moth and may be seen taking nectar from various flowers ranging from bramble to honeysuckle. The eggs are laid on the leaves of the willowherbs of ditch and verge, the foodplants of the larvae.

Honeysuckle leaves are among the earliest new leaves to appear in hedgerows; they are quite distinctive oval, short-stalked, two-toned forms, dark green on top and bluish below. Clusters of whitish flowers, tinted pink and yellow, appear throughout summer, with flowering peaks in June and September. The flowers' long corolla tubes are typical of moth-pollinated plants and their fragrance becomes stronger towards dusk when they attract mainly the hawk-moths with long probosces, such as the pine hawk-moth and the almost hand-sized convolvulus hawk-moth; these will hover at the flower rather than land on it and simply jab their tongues into the nectar tubes. There are a few other insects that will seek this deep source of nectar if they can manage to reach it; some larvae may be able to force their way down the tube, and that of the rare white admiral has been known to do so. Bees, however, tend to avoid the flowers because the tubes are too narrow to admit their fat, round bodies and their probosces are not long enough to reach the nectar from the outside.

Found throughout the whole of the British Isles, honeysuckle is a common plant of hedgerows and woods on acid to calcareous soils, but it avoids waterlogged conditions. Being so widespread it is one of the traditional flowers of love and poetry and is associated with many romantic superstitions, one being that if honeysuckle is brought into the house a wedding will follow. Also, herbalists have long used the flowers in their potions, ranging from 'cures' for headaches to lung diseases.

Honeysuckle, the most heavily perfumed of hedgerow plants.

Another strong clockwise climber is the hop. In spring the plant will shoot several thin, rapidly growing, twining, squarish stems which are covered with tiny hooked prickles, enabling the plant not only to spiral round, but also to grasp on to supporting shrubs and trees in the hedgerows. Distinguishing features are its toothed, lobed leaves and cone-like female flower-heads: male and female flowers develop on separate plants. It is the sprays from the female flowers that have been harvested since the Middle Ages to be used to clarify, preserve and flavour beer:

> Hops, reformation, bays and beer
> Came into England all in one year.

The cultivated hop is said to have been introduced in the early sixteenth century in the reign of Henry VIII and since then the species has been cultivated fairly widely in the south-east of Britain, where today it is commonly seen twining up 12 to 14 ft (4 to 4.3 m) poles or strings in Kent, Hampshire, Surrey and Sussex and in the West Midlands, Herefordshire and Worcestershire. Hop has also been introduced in both Scotland and Ireland where it has become naturalised in widely scattered localities. In fact many records throughout the British Isles of wild hops in hedgerows and elsewhere are probably of relics and escapees of cultivation. However, before commercial production, which started in a small way when farmers, innkeepers and country squires kept their own little patches to flavour their homemade brews, the hop was native to the damp woods of southern England.

Hedge bindweed twists its stem in an anticlockwise direction; it is capable of climbing spirally up to 10 ft (3 m) high through hedges. It grows so quickly that its tip may complete a full circle within a couple of hours. At first its stems are so pliable that they can easily be twisted into a knot, but they become woody as they mature, containing strong fibres, so the plant may remain in place for many years. Both its leaves and flowers are large: the leaves are shaped like hearts or arrowheads, and its white blooms are like trumpets. The flowers are largely moth-pollinated, and, though scentless, are luminous in fading light. They are said to remain open all night in moonlight (and through to dawn, hence their West Country name 'Morning Glory').

Black bryony, another unbranching stem-climbing perennial, twines to the left and grows luxuriantly to the top of the hedge. It is primarily a plant of shady hedgerows and wood margins on well-drained, fertile soils, and although it is distributed throughout the whole of England and Wales, it is commonest in the south. One of the attractive features of this plant is its large, shining, heart-shaped leaves that grow densely all the way up the hedge. The species is dioecious, and, with its sprays of tiny greenish-white flowers followed by red berries, it is not immediately obvious why it has been named 'black', although 'bryony' is apt, coming from the Greek word meaning 'to grow luxuriantly'. In fact, 'black' derives from the colour of its fleshy underground tuber, from which fresh stems arise every spring; it is the only British member of the yam family, but unlike the tubers of its tropical relations, those of black bryony are poisonous. The fruits, which may hang in luscious, scarlet garlands in autumn,

LEFT Hedge bindweed can completely cover a hedgerow. RIGHT Black bryony with its greenish blossoms.

are also poisonous, containing the toxic glucoside, saponin, and even birds will ignore them. The berries were once collected and preserved in gin to be used as a remedy for chilblains, and they were also prescribed for removing skin blemishes or healing bruises.

CLIMBING BY TENDRILS

White bryony is botanically unrelated to black bryony. It distribution does not extend far beyond lowland England, but there it is a frequent plant of undisturbed hedgerows and wood margins on well-drained calcareous or base-rich soils. It climbs by means of tendrils arising at the base of the leaf stalks, which are so sensitive that if touched they will soon spring into a coil. The tendril will draw the bryony towards the supporting plant and hook around it. While swaying in the breeze the tendrils are continuously rubbing against their support which stimulates them to grow faster and wrap spirally up the plant. The part of the tendril between the supporting plant and the bryony stem will then shorten by coiling up, enabling a firm, elastic-like grasp so that the bryony is less likely to be dragged away from its support in, say, a strong wind. White bryony is dioecious, and sprays of white flowers spring among the hairy, maple-like leaves.

A member of the gourd family, the common name also refers to the colour of its roots, distinguishing it from black bryony. Medieval charlatans used to sell the swollen and curiously twisted roots of white bryony as the rare mandrake

Mandragora officinalis, the roots of which are reputed, from as long ago as biblical times (viz. Genesis XXX, 14–16), to cure sterility in women. The flower sets into many-seeded, green or white berries which turn red when ripe, and they hang in attractive garlands long after the leaves have withered. Although extracts of the plant have been used by herbalists for various body disorders, such as the treatment of rheumatism and even leprosy and dropsy, white bryony is poisonous, especially its berries. The toxin is a glycoside, bryonin, which acts as a drastic purgative.

A LEAF STALK CLIMBER

'Wild clematis... groweth plentiously between Ware and Barckway [Hertfordshire] in the hedges, which in summer are in many places al whyte wyth the downe of thys vine,' wrote William Turner in 1548. In fact, *Clematis vitalba* is quite widely spread, being a familiar sight in the hedgerows on the chalky downs and limestone hills of England and Wales (though rare elsewhere). The English botanist, John Gerard, named it 'traveller's joy', as he saw how it was found 'decking and adorning ways and hedges where other people travell'.

After it has sprouted from the ground as a two-leafed seedling, *Clematis* soon develops a rope-like stem bearing toothed leaves on long stalks, composed of five leaflets – a terminal and two pairs. If a leaf stalk touches a supporting stem, it will twist, tendril-like, around the support and grasp it. In this way the main stem will be carried to the top of the hedgerow, becoming thick and woody as it matures.

The flowers do not have true petals, but instead the well-developed sepals open like petals to reveal a dense cluster of long stamens. The flower heads will then develop their autumn plumes, a long feathery style flowing from each seed, collectively resembling tufts of curly white hair, hence the plant's other popular name, 'old man's beard'. In this form the seeds will be carried far on the wind. Nurserymen still sometimes use wild clematis seedlings as stock for choice garden varieties of clematis and even the showy deep blues and pinks of the garden varieties provide their displays with coloured sepals.

CLIMBING WITH ADHESIVE ROOTS

The ivy clings to its support by means of a number of tiny outgrowths which sprout only from the shaded sides of its branches. On a young twig these are apparent only opposite the leaf stalks and then they spread to develop all along the stem. There are two distinct phases in the life of ivy, most obvious in the appearance of its leaves. In the juvenile stage, when it is creeping along the bottom of the hedge or just beginning its way up what will become its support, the leaves are broad and lobed; these branches do not bear flowering shoots. As it works its way up its support, the stem of ivy clings firmly with its tiny roots

'Old man's beard' *(Clematis)* derives its name from the masses of feathery seeds produced in autumn.

which adhere it to the supporting plant. These roots draw no nourishment from the support, nor does ivy strangle it, but ivy's underground roots compete with those of its support for nutrients, and if ivy clambers all over the supporting plant it certainly reduces the light reaching the latter. As ivy becomes firmly established and continues to grow upwards it begins to bear upright, rootless stems, with oval or pointed unlobed leaves. These stems also bear the flowers and berries.

In reverse of the normal plant seasons, ivy flowers in autumn or winter and bears berries in spring. It bears yellowish-green flowers arranged in globular heads. These are largely pollinated by wasps and flies, and by any moths and butterflies still on wing seeking food on one of the last flowers of nature's year. The holly blue butterfly's second brood is raised on ivy where the caterpillars feed on the flower buds. Another butterfly associated with ivy is the sulphur-coloured brimstone which hibernates in the plant. The veins of its wings are unusually pronounced and when folded the wings resemble ivy leaves, successfully camouflaging the insect as it hibernates. Night-flying insects which also feed on ivy's flowers provide food for bats emerging from their roost in ivy cover.

Ivy, like holly, clad in glossy, evergreen leaves in the midst of winter, inevitably became a winter and Christmas decoration. Formerly it was also endowed with magical powers, such as its ability to keep homes safe from witches and demons when it was growing up walls, green and fresh, but heralding disaster if it withered. It has even been used as a love oracle: a girl would place a twig of leaves in her pocket and go for a walk with the conviction that the first man who thereafter spoke to her would become her husband. Decoctions made from various parts of the plant have been used for remedies for all sorts of disorders, from jaundice and whooping cough to preventing drunkenness and falling hair.

Ivy is most unusual in flowering during the winter months. Here the leaves and flowers are outlined in frost.

THE SCRAMBLERS

Scrambling plants do not spiral, coil or adhere to their supporting plants but are either armed with spines or thorns for grasping with, or have plant stems enabling them to thread their way up the hedge.

Some of the shrubs mentioned in Ch. 9 such as bramble and the wild roses, with their prickly thorns, are obvious examples of grapplers and graspers; a less obvious example is the annual, cleavers or goosegrass. This apparently frail plant with a stem which is very soft and brittle is, in fact, remarkably vigorous. Its square stems, lance-shaped leaves which grow in rings, and fruit are all equipped with backward-arching prickles enabling cleavers to catch readily on to other plants and sprawl up a hedge, and by the middle of summer it can seem to have smothered the hedge in places. But were it not for the support from other plants, cleavers would stand a poor chance of success. Its tiny, green globular fruit are very effectively spread by clinging to the fur and feathers of any creature brushing against the plant effectively scattering in all directions (and it is with fond memories that we recall our late adventurous spaniel, Bramble, returning from country walks thoroughly decorated with the wretched seeds).

A scrambler of another sort is the woody nightshade. This plant does not possess any obvious mechanism with which to clutch supporting stems, but climbs by threading its pliant stalks in and out of other plants for support. If it lacks support, as it does on sand-dunes and shingle beaches where it forms an early coloniser, it looks very different, sprawling on the ground. The species is widespread throughout England and most of Wales, but it is becoming rare northwards (though there are still plenty of specimens in many of our less disturbed hedges in Nidderdale), and in fact it is almost absent from central and northern Scotland. In Ireland, though localised, it is scattered throughout.

Woody nightshade is a very decorative member of the hedgerow. It first puts on a brilliant display of clusters of purple-blue flowers with a central core of bright yellow anthers from early summer. The flowers are then followed by shiny yellow and red berries in autumn. The berries, though not as poisonous as those of the unrelated deadly nightshade (for woody nightshade is a member of the potato family), can cause sickness if eaten. The species' scientific name *S. dulcamara* is derived from the Latin words meaning 'sweet and bitter'; hence the plant's other common name, 'bittersweet'. All parts of the plant contain a toxic alkaloid, solanine, and if tasted, against better judgement, they will seem bitter at first, then sweet.

The presence and nature of these climbers will also depend on the management of the hedge. Cleavers and hedge bindweed are so persistent that they can survive even if most of the plant is ripped out and if undisturbed they will readily form dense patches. Honeysuckle, ivy and hop are quite tolerant of mechanical trimming but clematis, the bryonies and woody nightshade prefer less disturbed hedges.

·11·

A CASE FOR THE
ROADSIDE VERGE

Bordering one or both sides of the strip of shrubbery, climbers and trees that form the hedge are the herbaceous layers in which the grasses usually predominate. Sometimes the hedge may be fashioned on a bank (see Ch. 7) which may slope down via a ditch to a roadside verge. The roadside verge forms a buffer zone of infinite length and variable but modest width between the hedge and the highway. Where the hedgerow has been uprooted and replaced by barbed wire or a wooden fence, and in areas of intense arable agriculture, verges may be the only strips of land offering refuge and the only distribution pathways for the much reduced and more adaptable wildlife that still exists in such places. Some of our roadside verges have ancient origins: there are routes we travel today which have been used since prehistoric times, while others follow Roman roads or medieval droveways. Today many of our grasslands have been ploughed and drained to grow crops or rye grass fodder and have been treated with damaging fertilisers and herbicides. As a result the verges of these old roads may be found to accommodate the relict plant communities of the old grasslands they once traversed. Although verges created as a result of more recent road schemes do not have a historic link with natural vegetation one cannot fail to notice how they have become colonised with plant species such as poppies, charlock, or even corn marigold and chicory, eliminated from agricultural land as a result of chemical sprays, but which flourish on bare, disturbed soil.

The Royal Society for Nature Conservation (RSNC), which in 1986 launched the 'British Wildlife Week', made it one of its main objectives to focus attention on the importance of roadside verges for plants and animals. They reported that about thirty of Britain's rarest plants are now found on roadside verges and in hedges. Two of them, the downy woundwort – known only in Oxfordshire – and Plymouth pear, are now not found in any other habitats. The Tenby daffodil can very occasionally be seen in the banks and verges in the regions of Narberth, Meidrym and Crymych in Pembrokeshire. This distinctive brilliant yellow dwarf specimen has virtually disappeared in the wild due to the plundering of Victorian gardeners, who removed them by the thousand. Tenby Museum has a record of half a million bulbs being dispatched to London in a two-year period.

A survey of roadside verges by J. M. Way of the Institute of Terrestrial Ecology reveals a total verge area of 524,396 acres (212,220 ha) for the mainland United Kingdom, traversing most of the main geological strata and soil types, and associated with all the varying climatic, latitudinal and longitudinal regions. Verges reflect the way in which they have been managed and may also reveal something about the history and use of the adjacent road. Before mechanisation, many verges had decades of traditional management, similar to that applied to some other grasslands. 'Lengthmen' were employed to maintain the road verges. They worked through the seasons cutting back invading shrubs and keeping the grass down with their scythes and as they worked along the same lengths of the country roads year after year they became familiar with those features worth preserving. Hay crops were taken from verges in some parts of the country, and along drove roads, as in the Yorkshire Dales, they were grazed by cattle and sheep as the animals were driven to market. Even today, grazing animals like goats or ponies are sometimes tethered on the verges.

The list of plant species associated with roadside verges is a long one: Dr Way and his colleagues have assembled a list of 870 native species from the British total of 2000 and claim that 'about half of our list might be found at any time by reasonable searching of roadsides in an area, say, of an average English county . . . [but] a relatively narrow range of species and typical communites is found most often' – reflecting local seed stock, climate and soil type. Seeds may

The verge in high summer, with nettles and grasses growing up towards the top of the hedge.

have been carried to the verge by mammals and birds or have been blown by the wind along the highway corridors, carried by the slipstream of cars and wagons, or even transported on their undersides and tyres. Verges are also teeming with animal life: throughout the country 20 of our 50 species of native mammals, all 6 reptiles, 5 of the 6 species of amphibians, 40 of the 200 nesting birds, and 60 or so native butterflies have been recorded in roadside verges and hedges.

The management policies of the various highway authorities are gradually changing from intensive management where 'tidiness' is an important aim, to programmes involving the sparse use of herbicides (in exceptional cases to deal with the statutorily defined 'injurious weeds' – see below) and graded mowing. With the more enlightened authorities the conservation of wildlife is often the main concern. The RSNC's roadside management code points out that graded verges produce herb-rich communities ('herb-rich communities' are essentially composed of long-established perennial species in contrast to short-lived weedy species). For roadside safety considerations, the first few feet of verge from the road should be mown regularly to about a foot in height and the next few feet should be mown no more than twice a year to create a short meadow sward of wildflowers. The area beside the boundary (hedge, ditch, wall or fence) should be cut once every two years to encourage tall perennials and biennials to seed. In areas like this roadside verges can take on the characteristics of 'edge habitats' where, within a small space, there is a combination of the typical species of individual communities (that is, arable, hedge, pasture, meadow, woodland, aquatic – where a ditch also exists) together with the specialised species that are present where one habitat overlaps another. Unfortunately, through reasons of economy, some verges are no longer mown at all and there the unchecked growth of the coarser shrub species have swamped the herbaceous ones.

On most roadsides trampling is restricted to the first few feet nearest the road. This disturbed zone will also suffer the worst effects of salt sprayed from the highway in winter. Many roadsides also have a history of recent disturbance such as digging for services. The flora found in these disturbed zones will be akin to the short-lived species of cultivated or disturbed land.

It is not surprising that hedgebanks and verges are blamed for the dispersal of weeds into arable fields, particularly with the newer policies of generally minimum intervention. But what must also be realised is that many of the 'weeds of cultivation', that is, those that grow in direct competition with the crop, are species which need bare surface on which to grow and will quickly colonise disturbed ground. However, as they cannot stand much competition from other plants, they are less likely to establish in little-disturbed hedgebanks and verges, unless they are persistent creeping perennials.

Ephemeral annual species that complete their life cycles in a few weeks are a problem because they produce vast amounts of seed which quickly germinate and grow, and examples include members of the daisy family such as groundsel, scentless mayweed, spear thistle, as well as others like hairy bitter cress, shepherd's purse, petty spurge, common chickweed, corn spurrey, fumitory and scarlet pimpernel. A single plant of scarlet pimpernel is able to produce up

In early summer the cow parsley completely smothers many verges.

ABOVE LEFT Cowslips, one of the most familiar flowers of old pastures, now find a refuge on the hedgebank and verge. ABOVE Giant bellflower with its pale-blue flowers is the most stately plant of the northern hedgebanks and verges. LEFT Yellow loosestrife making a spectacular show in a Yorkshire ditch.

OPPOSITE PAGE TOP This painted lady butterfly has completed its migration early and is taking nectar from fallen blackthorn blossom. CENTRE The frog has proved very vulnerable to the drainage of farm ponds and ditches and the spread of farm chemicals. As a consequence it has vanished from many of its old haunts and is rare in others. BOTTOM Paired toads swimming in a hedge-foot ditch. Toads will emerge from hibernation in spring to migrate to their birth-places in ponds and ditches. These breeding grounds are often places where many generations have spawned and sometimes toads will assemble from over a considerable area forming large migratory groups. Where roads now cross the traditional migration routes there are many casualties.

to 12,000 seeds, and if it flowers early enough to produce seeds, it is self-pollinating, and a second generation of plants may appear later in the same year. Fat hen shows another remarkable adaptation to an unstable environment. Its seeds have varying dormant periods so that germination may be spread over a number of weeks, increasing the chances of at least some seeds germinating in favourable conditions. Many of the perennials have persistent or creeping roots which, once established, are very resilient. Even if their roots are broken up by digging, they are still capable of producing new plants. Such species include coltsfoot, creeping buttercup, creeping thistle and common bindweed.

Some of these species, such as dock, are scheduled as 'injurious' weeds under the Weed Act of 1959 and can be eliminated with the use of herbicides. But while such treatment is not selective and very unsightly, the greatest loss is the impoverishment of hedgebank and verge fauna, for many of the plant species provide food and breeding grounds for invertebrates which will in turn affect the abundance of predatory fauna.

Certainly botanically, the richest verges and hedgebanks are invariably those that have been relatively undisturbed and have received

ABOVE The slow worm resembles a snake but is more closely related to lizards. In spite of its name it is able to retreat at a fair speed if approached, but when hunting it is quite likely to lose its prey because of its habit of 'contemplating' its prey before seizing it. Its stare is not hypnotic like that of a snake's because it blinks. RIGHT The bank vole, the hedgerow equivalent of a quick snack, lives in constant danger from predators.

the same management treatment over a long period. Those bordering ancient highways where there is still a good supply of seed may approach the composition of traditional hay meadows, while the presence of a variety of woodland herbs and mixture of native shrubs in the adjacent hedge may indicate this habitat is all that remains of a long-lost woodland.

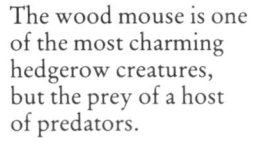

The wood mouse is one of the most charming hedgerow creatures, but the prey of a host of predators.

·12·

CONNECTIONS

From Nature's chain, whatever link you strike,
Tenth, or tenth thousandth, breaks the chain alike.
Alexander Pope in *An Essay on Man*

A hedgerow environment of rich and varied plant communities and of
overlapping characteristics of other habitats can offer a multitude of micro-
habitats for animal life within which the purposeful innate activities carried out
by each – defending territory, seeking a mate, courting, breeding, nesting and
food gathering – intermesh into complicated relationships. Here we examine
the behaviour of some hedgerow fauna through their network of feeding
relationships.

There are the plant-eating creatures which feed on the trees, shrubs, grasses
and herbs. They in turn become food for the invertebrate predators and flesh-
eaters – and so 'food chains' develop. But these chains are not straightforward,
for at each stage each creature is competing for its life requirements with
members of its own and other species, and will in turn itself be food to several
different animals. Those animals that are easily adaptable to changes in their
environment are most successful. Many birds and mammals show this characteristic, for in spite of the fact that their normal diet is that of vegetation or flesh
– their bills and teeth are important indicators of both diet and method of
feeding – they can turn to other foods to supplement their main diet. Hence the
interconnecting food chains in fact form a 'food web'.

Birds and mammals are active creatures and use up energy quickly, and many
need to eat as much as one third of their own body weight daily. During periods
of pregnancy, egg production and bringing up young the need for food
increases. The nature and composition of the food will, of course, influence the
amount eaten. For instance, it takes many invertebrates to keep, say, one blue tit
alive, but it takes relatively fewer titmice to feed one sparrowhawk. This
demonstrates the 'pyramid of numbers': as the number of animals available on
the food ladder decreases their size increases. There can never be more
consumers than there is food, so if there is proportionally more plant food than

there are plant-eaters and these are more numerous than their predators, then the 'pyramid' is in balance. However, due to man's manipulation of the environment and the unpredictability of nature (such as the effect of the weather and parasites), populations will fluctuate and adapt. But when the entire habitat is destroyed, as with the removal of the hedgerow, then the complete food web is destroyed and only the more mobile creatures have the opportunity of seeking food elsewhere; others certainly die.

A VARIETY OF VEGETARIANS

Many invertebrates, amphibians, mammals and birds number among the hedgerow vegetation-eaters, but it is the first group that forms the largest variety and population. Among the myriad invertebrates found in the hedge only a few groups have developed the ability to feed on the leaves of shrubs and trees, and even then the leaves of some species seem more palatable than others: oak, willow, and hawthorn, bramble and other members of the rose family are among the most favoured species, while hazel and hornbeam with their hairy leaves, and holly with its thick waxy foliage, are less sought after. It is perhaps appropriate that the commonest hedge tree and hedge shrub – oak and hawthorn respectively – support among the largest number of species. Many more invertebrates feed on the softer foliage of the grasses and plants of the herb layers, some creatures being associated only with particular food plants or a few closely related species. Then there are the sap-suckers and fruit-eaters, and many which feed on pollen and nectar.

Most butterflies and moths seek the nectar in flowers, the length of their probosces determining the type of flower they approach. However, their caterpillars spend almost all their time eating, the energy from the food being stored in the body to take them through the chrysalis stage and the final conversion to adulthood. The adult insect lays its eggs only on its caterpillar's appropriate food plant. Some 284 invertebrate species are associated with oak, of which at least 100 are species of moth. Moth populations are also prolific on hawthorn, for the caterpillars of at least 80 species of the larger moths have been recorded on this plant, the easiest of which to find are those that live in groups, in a silk web spun across several leaves and twigs, such as the young of the brown-tailed tussock, the small lackey and the small ermine (also found on blackthorn). Butterfly larvae associated with hawthorn are said to include the black-veined white and the now rare brown hairstreak (also found on blackthorn).

By far the largest numbers of caterpillars of butterfly species found in hedges are in the herb-layer plants and, according to Dr Moore, only three species feed on the shrubs and two on the trees. Among the commonest caterpillars in the herbaceous layers are invariably those of certain species of the 'white' butter-flies. 'Cabbage white' is a popular name given to the small and large white butterflies, whose caterpillars, although pests to the cultivated cabbage, have also been recorded on sixty wild members of the cabbage family. Before the use of organic insecticides, their caterpillars reached plague proportions, and it is

said that cabbage fields were covered by a fluttering haze of adult insects. Only the wild relatives in the cabbage family, about thirty or so species, are the food plants of the caterpillars of the orange tip. These include cuckoo flower, large bittercress, creeping yellow-cress, wild turnip and garlic mustard, also sought after by the green-veined white butterfly.

Caterpillars which feed on the grasses, wild members of the pea family and stinging nettle are also common because these plants are so widespread. The grass-eating caterpillars of the meadow brown and small heath butterflies are found throughout Britain, while more common in England and Wales are those of the wall, gatekeeper or hedge brown and the large and small skippers. Bird's foot trefoil is favoured by the caterpillars of the common blue and the migrant clouded yellow butterflies

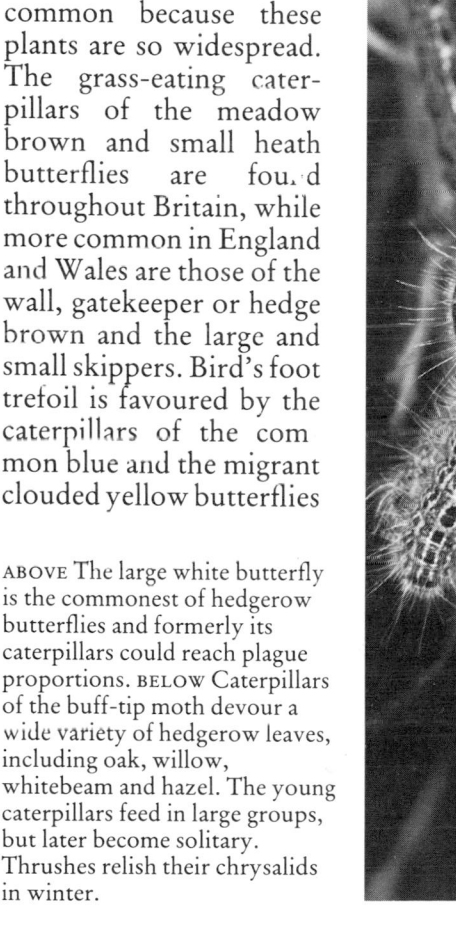

ABOVE The large white butterfly is the commonest of hedgerow butterflies and formerly its caterpillars could reach plague proportions. BELOW Caterpillars of the buff-tip moth devour a wide variety of hedgerow leaves, including oak, willow, whitebeam and hazel. The young caterpillars feed in large groups, but later become solitary. Thrushes relish their chrysalids in winter.

The bizarre caterpillar of the vapourer moth feeds on blackthorn, hawthorn, hazel and rose. The old name of the moth signifies a loud-mouth, deriving perhaps from the boisterous flight of the male moth as it follows the crest of a hedgerow.

The cockchafer or May bug is one of our largest beetles. The adult feeds on hedgerow shrubs while larvae devour the roots of growing crops and are a favoured prey of the rook.

The scorpion fly is a common insect of shady hedges, feeding on dead insects and fruit. During mating the female would kill the male if he did not distract her with a gift of edible saliva. It takes its name from the scorpion-like tip to the abdomen.

as well as the poisonous larvae of five-spot and six-spot burnet moths; all except the migrant are quite common. But according to B. N. K. Davis, the stinging nettle feeds an apparent army of vegetarian invertebrates – his painstaking research has revealed that in Britain twenty-seven species are almost entirely dependent on it and a further seventeen use it as a food source. All parts of the plant are eaten and nettle fauna includes larvae and adult forms, but each exploit the plant differently, by subtle variations in feeding habits and lifestyles. For instance, the larvae of weevils (four species are restricted to nettle) feed on and hibernate in the rhizomes and stems; adult weevils and the larvae of butterflies and moths use the leaves; crawling among the male flowers are pollen-chewing beetles; while the bugs, with their ability to pierce and suck, exploit the fruit and sap from the stem and leaves. When closely related species all feed on the same part of the plant, as do the three species of leafhoppers of the genus *Eupteryx*, they are able to do so because their life-cycles are staggered and they also prefer different habitats: *E. urticae* is least selective and therefore most abundant, *E. urticae* prefers open habitats and *E. cyclops* prefers nettles on peaty and sandy soils.

Beetles and bugs are another major group of hedgerow plant feeders. Vegetarian beetles are the leaf beetles, such as the spectacular cockchafer, and the weevils, while those of the true bugs include the aphids, hoppers and scale insects. The weevils, like all beetles, have 'jaws', but these are carried at the tip of an elongated, pointed snout or 'rostrum' which enables them to 'drill' through plant tissue. Although many bugs resemble beetles, unlike beetles, 'true bugs' (in this case the term has a precise meaning in insect classification) pass through incomplete metamorphosis; that is, they do not pass through a pupal stage, but their young resemble adults. Bugs too have beak-like mouthparts, but theirs is a sucking 'beak', and it is usually carried under the head when not in use, and erected for feeding. One of the most familiar bugs is the common frog hopper, not because the mottled brown adult can quite easily be found between May and September, but because of the little patches of foam, known as 'cuckoo-spit', that appear on a whole host of hedgerow plants in summer. It is the larvae of these creatures which exude the foam while it sits in the middle feeding on the plant sap, generally protected from predators and desiccation.

The bug family of aphids (usually referred to as 'greenfly' and 'blackfly') is also well known for the damage they do to our roses and beans. There are in fact 500 species of aphid in Britain. Many have complicated life histories, of which the history of the black bean aphid is typical. The dense summer populations are a result of parthenogenetic reproduction – no males are involved. In spring, wingless females hatch from eggs laid in trees and shrubs (usually spindle or sterile guelder rose) to reproduce live young females without mating. They mature quickly, themselves reproducing winged forms, which migrate to the summer herbaceous food plants where reproduction continues and the colony, mainly of wingless females, builds up. In autumn, winged offspring are born, and a proportion of these are male. These creatures fly to trees and shrubs where the females give birth to wingless females, which are fertilised by the males and then lay overwintering eggs – and the life-cycle is started again. With this peculiar form of reproduction the descendants of a

The hedgerow bug *Liocoris tripustulatus* feeds
on plant foods and lays its eggs on nettles.

single aphid would number millions
each year if they all survived, but as
we shall see, they not only form abundant prey for many hedgerow animals, but also a varied food source,
for they exude a sugary substance
called 'honeydew' used as food by
insects including ants – which are
said to 'milk' aphids by stroking
them – moths and butterflies.

Slugs and snails also feature among the more conspicuous hedgerow vegetarians, though to avoid predators and desiccation they are generally creatures
of the night. However, damp weather brings them out in search of food during
the day, when they seek fungi and rotting leaves in preference to fresh foliage.
They then run the risk of being found by predators – and the song thrush is
particularly partial to snails. The birds smash open their shells by hammering
them on a stone. Piles of shells found scattered around a favoured stone have
been studied, and, as one might expect, those snails with more conspicuous
shells (the least camouflage-efficient) are more likely to become casualties.

There are many invertebrates feeding on hedgerow foliage and we have
examined just a few of the most conspicuous representatives, but it is usually
the activity of the flower-visiting invertebrates to which one's attention will
first be drawn when studying a hedge in spring and summer. Adult bees, wasps,
flies, butterflies, moths and even some spiders (such as the red velvet mite)
obtain nectar and pollen, while at the same time fertilising the flowers (see p.
194). Nectar provides the fuel source for immediate energy requirements, while
pollen is the body-building, protein-rich food.

By far the most frequent of the insect visitors are, of course, the bees. Most
people are familiar with the industrious honey bee and the bumble bee, but
there are in fact about 250 different kinds of bee in the British Isles. This
includes about eighteen species of bumble bee, one species of honey bee and the
great majority of the rest are solitary bees; that is, they do not live in organised
colonies, but instead the female usually makes small nests where she lays only a
few eggs at a time.

Bee larvae also feed on honey and pollen. In a colony it is usually the worker
bees, sterile females, which do the collecting of honey and pollen, but with
solitary bees, which have no worker caste, the female performs these tasks. As
the bee visits a succession of flowers, surplus honey is stored in her 'honey
stomach', while at the same time the hair covering her body sweeps up pollen
from the flowers' stamens. At intervals the bee brushes and scrapes pollen from
her hairs, using her antennae and all six legs, and together with the regurgitated
nectar she transforms it into a sticky mass which she stuffs into a 'pollen basket',
formed in the hollow joint of her hindleg, held together by curved bristles. She
then carries the contents of these baskets back to the hive or nest.

Not all bees are able to collect the pollen, which is so necessary for larvae, because they are hairless, so these bees resort to laying their eggs in the nests of other bees; hence they are called 'cuckoo bees' The genus *Nomada* consists of twenty-seven British species of wasp-like bees which usually invade the nests of the 'mining bees' (bees which excavate burrows in the soil) while the bumble bees also have their cuckoos, large bees of the genus *Psithyrus*, which closely resemble their hosts. Hibernating female *Psithyrus* emerge after *Bombus* females, to allow the latter to produce the worker caste. The cuckoo female then enters the nest of a bumble bee, and, if she survives her confrontation with the defending workers, she lays her eggs. The workers then bring up her young – for once established she kills the bumble bee queen and eats her eggs. Wasps also have their 'cuckoos'.

The feeding preferences of wasps are different from those of bees, in that while adult wasps are vegetarian, existing on a sweet saliva their larvae produce, and a diet of nectar and fruit juice, they feed their young on animal material, paralysed by their sting and left at their nest. Parasitic wasps do not build nests for their offspring, but instead inject their eggs into the bodies of live invertebrates. On hatching, the grubs, rather gruesomely, eat their way out of the host. Examples are the wasp *Apanteles glomeratus*, a parasite of butterfly caterpillars – and in some years they may be responsible for an 80 per cent death-rate of the caterpillars – and the *Aphidius* larvae, which feed on the body tissue of aphids; if one thinks about it, wasp larvae are really quite useful creatures, probably consuming a huge number of 'pests'.

Although bees and wasps are so conspicuous in sporting bold patterns, few are eaten, unless perilously snapped up by young birds testing new foods – but these juveniles soon learn to avoid the stinging creatures. A number of other insects have adapted to make use of this reaction and have mimicked the black-and-yellow-striped guise of bees and wasps. Such mimicry is effective only if the model is more common than the mimic, otherwise the young birds would find enough edible bee- and wasp-like creatures to associate these bold patterns with good food, so it is safer for the mimic adults to emerge after the period of testing is over. Hoverflies are one of the most successful creatures in the mimicry strategy, not only because they are able to mimic a wide range of bees and wasps, but some single species exist in more than one form, such as the hoverfly *Volucella bombylans*, which imitates several species of bumble bee. This is another way of ensuring that the mimic can increase its population without exceeding the total numbers of its model. The mimic must also live in the same habitat for the disguise to be effective, so a hoverfly mimic may often feed alongside its model; the adults feed on nectar and pollen, while their larvae usually feed on an invertebrate diet.

The seeds and berries of the hedgerow are another rich source of food. As blackberry fruit ripen in autumn, wasps abound. The now dwindling population of workers from wasp colonies, such as those of the common wasp, are no longer supplied with the larvae saliva, for their charges have now joined them on wing as new queens and drones in search of mates. They are now independent of each other for food, seeking their own sweet food sources, as fuel to power their flight and, in the case of the queens, to build up energy to take them through hibernation. Wasps are able to pierce the skin of succulent blackberries to get at the flesh (as are other sap suckers, such as aphids). Then, as the blackberries become more mushy, numerous flies and butterflies, such as the red admiral butterfly, come to sip the juices with their probosces. But it is many of the birds and mammals of the hedgerow that harvest most of the seeds and fruit.

Several factors influence the choice of food taken by birds. To begin with, each group in a particular family has pre-adapted diet and food-seeking techniques, based on their physical features. For example, bills are very important: a short, stout bill encourages a vegetarian diet, while a thin, curved bill facilitates probing in cracks and crevices to extract animal food. But within the family groups each species has special habits and preferences enabling it to share its habitat with other closely related species. Not many hedgerow birds are entirely vegetarian, for each species has what ornithologist Dr Eric Simms has termed a 'food spectrum . . . with wide bands for its best-liked foods and narrow ones for the less readily taken'. In this way different food resources can be exploited as each season unfolds. For instance, the dunnock consumes a lot of insects in summer, but in winter it turns almost entirely to seeds. Many mainly vegetarian birds, such as the finches and buntings, seasonally take insects themselves, but regularly feed them to their young, so that their offspring can be raised on a high-protein diet. To illustrate how even close-related species show variation in their food preferences we can examine the finches and thrushes found in hedgerows.

The finches have stout, conical bills and strong jaw muscles, which enable them to deal with seed husks and shells. Early in the year, when seed is scarce, these birds supplement their diet with flowering buds and even insects; the nestlings are fed on a diet of invertebrates crushed with seed husks in the parents' crops and regurgitated into the mouths of their young. A wide variety of seed, which forms the main part of their diet, is taken. To reduce competition for food, each species specialises in seeds of a particular size, these preferences being largely related to the marginal differences in bill shape and size.

One would almost be forgiven for imagining the chaffinch to be omnivorous, for it is such a common sight in the countryside and often bold enough to solicit food from picnickers and at the garden bird table. But such food sources are more likely to be oases of unusual and improbable food for the more opportunistic creatures, for the chaffinch is mainly a seed-eater, with the habit of feeding off the ground on weed and wildflower seeds and fallen beech mast and, in winter, on grain and berries. The short, broad bill of the greenfinch enables it to tackle tree fruits and seeds; when the trees were common, they were partial to elm seeds. These birds also take the grain from cultivated cereals, such as wheat and oats, as well as the seeds of a large number of weeds and wildflowers – preferring chickweed, groundsel and dandelion and, during

TOP RIGHT The sturdy bill of the boisterous greenfinch allows it to tackle tough seeds and fruits. RIGHT The chaffinch is mainly a ground-feeding bird which seeks fallen seeds and berries in the foot of the hedge.

ABOVE The blackbird – this is the female with its slightly speckled dark brown plumage – takes a range of hedgerow fruits. BELOW This song thrush is searching for food at the foot of the hedge, scrabbling through the snow to stir-up the leaf litter.

winter, charlock and persicaria – picking both from the plant and fallen seed. The bullfinch has a short, rounded bill with sharp edges enabling it to tackle the tree seeds of wych elm, sycamore, birch and ash as well as berries, such as those of privet. In spring it feeds mainly on buds, particularly those of fruit trees. In fruit-growing areas it visits commercial orchards where it is considered a serious pest. Bullfinches usually feed direct from the plant. Seeds and buds are nipped off, crushed and then rotated on the tongue against the lower jaw, thus peeling away the husk or skin from the flesh. This feeding action also enables the bird to remove snails from its shell; they are the only finches to feed on these invertebrates. The smallest of the finches, the goldfinch, has a long, thinner bill which enables it to extract deeply embedded seeds, not easily available to other finches. It can be seen clinging with great agility to the plant stems or hanging on the flower heads while deftly extracting seeds from plant species of the thistle family, which can amount to a third of its diet. It also takes seeds of dandelion, groundsel, ragwort and burdock. When flower seeds are scarce the goldfinch can turn to the cone seeds of trees, such as the birches and alder. The linnet favours hedges in open country, for it specialises in the weeds of cultivated land, mainly from the cabbage, daisy, dock and goosefoot families. The populations of the finches are said to be declining, particularly those of the linnets, which are almost exclusively seed-eaters, because of the increased use of weedkillers and toxic seed dressings, which has considerably depleted their food supplies. Even the chaffinch, though still one of our most widespread and common birds, has been decreasing in population since the 1950s.

The common members of the thrush family are voracious harvesters of hedgerow fruit, but they also readily eat seeds, invertebrates and other animal food. Although they do not have specialised bills like the finches, they are able to manipulate their beaks very effectively, especially in the search and collection of animal food. The different species avoid severe competition by exploiting different parts of a shared habitat. In hedges they not only generally nest and feed at different levels, but also their body and bill sizes vary; marginal though these variations are, they do influence the foods favoured. For instance, different species can show a preference for different hedgerow fruits. The blackbird and mistle thrush can take larger fruits, and commonly feed on those of gean, crab apple, plum, damson, hawthorn, rose and wild service tree. The slightly smaller song thrush can cope better with smaller fruits, like those of bird cherry, bramble, currants, yew and holly. The flocks of winter-visiting redwing and fieldfare arrive in time for the autumn hedgerow fruit harvest, but these large flocks move about the countryside and also seek fields and pastures for the rotting remnants of root crops and grain, and for fallen grass seed. Blackbirds, the most common thrush of a suburban garden, also eat the berries of some alien ornamental hedgerow shrubs, such as snowberry, cotoneaster and barberry.

Other hedgerow birds which are mainly vegetarian include wood pigeons, collared doves and the buntings – yellowhammer and corn bunting – which are typical of open farmland, both nesting amongst the dense ground vegetation of the hedge and feeding chiefly on cultivated grains and the seeds of weeds of cultivation. Not many birds eat leaves, but wood pigeons pick at the freshest

Young pheasant seeking refuge in the bottom of the hedge.

leaves and shoots of trees such as elm and elder. Game birds, such as the pheasant and grey partridge, also eat a variety of vegetable matter, including roots, nuts, acorns, berries, grass seeds and weeds, but they are really quite omnivorous, for they also eat a lot of animal food.

Like many birds feeding in the hedgerow habitat, no hedgerow mammal is exclusively vegetarian, for even rabbits occasionally eat snails and earthworms, but this animal and the rodent inhabitants have a strong tendency towards plant food.

The rabbit will eat a pound or more of fresh green food every day. Feeding is by refection: food is eaten, then excreted in semi-digested form as soft moist pellets. These pellets are then available to be eaten and, when passed through the intestine again, they are more thoroughly digested. Rabbits are quite choosy about what they eat, preferring the seedings and young plants of grasses, clover and other perennials; but if superior food is available, such as arable crops, they will be sure to take advantage. Where these creatures are abundant they can alter the composition of the vegetation, destroying the perennial stock and enabling annuals to colonise the bare area. They avoid prickly, poisonous and tough plants, so species such as thistles, nettles and ragwort flourish near warrens. Unless starving they also avoid hawthorn and elder, but devour spindle. Some animals benefit from the activities of rabbits. For instance, ants do well in open, rabbit-grazed areas, and this in turn sustains insectivorous birds and mammals. The death of millions of rabbits from myxomatosis – estimated at 100 million in some reports – will have had severe short-term effects on animal communities. A whole range of predators will have suffered from the loss of this food source for young or adult rabbits are favoured prey of weasels, stoats, owls, buzzards, ravens, crows and hawks; foxes and even badgers dig out young. Stoats (and buzzards) are known to have suffered especially, for rabbits formed the main part of the diets of these creatures. There must also have been immediate effects on the populations of alternative prey, such as voles and mice, but being such rapid breeders these will have recovered fairly quickly. Voles, mice and other hedgerow inhabitants may eventually have benefited from the decline of the rabbit, as the vegetation was allowed to develop so that new vegetarian food supplies and nesting sites became available. The rabbit population is now recovering from the epidemic but periodic outbreaks keep numbers fluctuating. Nowadays many infected rabbits do not necessarily die directly from the disease, but probably still fall prey to predators while incapacitated.

Harsh winters, like those we have experienced recently, must also take their toll, when starving rabbits even turn to gnawing bark of well-grown trees. However, if they can avoid it, they do not venture out of their burrows in inclement weather, for not only are their movements hampered and they dislike having wet fur, but they are more likely to be spotted by predators. They sustain themselves on their own faecal pellets – but there is a limit to this process, for eventually the results of refection are hard, dry pellets. (Rabbit pellets are also fed to the larvae of 'dung' beetles, an example of which is the minotaur beetle, usually found on sandy soils. The male beetle collects rabbit droppings and delivers them to the female by rolling them along with his 'horns'. She then deposits them in her burrow and lays an egg on each dropping. When the larvae hatch they eat the dung.)

The rabbit can devour a pound or more of green plant food in a day, leaving its hedgerow burrow to graze the adjacent fields.

Rodents are the most abundant mammalian hedgerow vegetarians, and the three commonest are the wood mouse, bank vole and field vole. Their jaws are ideally suited to coping with vegetation, seeds and nuts. They have two large incisor teeth in each jaw, which operate as chisels for slicing bite-sized pieces of food or for gnawing through hard seed shells and bark to reach the softer tissue inside. These teeth grow continuously, so the animal is provided with an ever-ready cutting edge. At the rear of the incisors are the strong molars for grinding.

The wood or long-tailed field mouse is a creature of dawn or dusk. Although a seed-eater by preference – and it often gnaws right through to the kernel of berry stones – it also eats grains, seedlings, buds, nuts and other fruits, such as rose hips; it is also known to take birds' eggs, and invertebrates such as snails, biting into their shells. The presence of this and other mammals is often more easily inferred by evidence of their food remains. For instance, a close look at discarded hazelnuts, which are a favourite food of

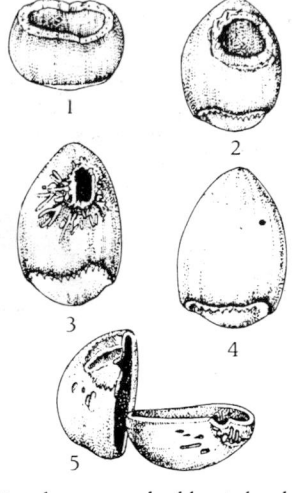

Hazelnuts attacked by 1. bank vole, 2. wood mouse, 3. bird, 4. weevil, 5. squirrel. (Reproduced from *Discovering Hedgerows* by David Streeter and Rosamund Richardson with the permission of BBC Enterprises Ltd.)

many hedgerow creatures, can sometimes reveal which animal has eaten the nut. Squirrels are able to split the nut in two with their powerful incisors, while mice and voles have the habit of sitting up on their haunches and holding the nut in their forepaws with the base of the nut standing firmly on the ground. They thus gnaw a small hole near the top of the nut. A corrugated pattern round the hole indicates mouse tooth marks: the imprinted action of their lower incisor working while the nut was rotated. Birds, which hammer at the nut with their strong, sharp beaks to pierce through to the kernel, leave jagged holes.

The bank vole also has a catholic diet, including fruits, seeds, especially cereals, nuts, berries, roots, bulbs, fungi and green herbage. Like the wood mouse it is a good climber: in spring it may climb rose and hawthorn bushes to nibble new leaves, while in autumn it ascends to the tips of twigs for hips and haws. The much smaller field or short-tailed vole is more typical of animals of rough pasture, and therefore does not compete with the bank vole. It feeds mainly on the stems and leaves of grasses, rushes and sedges, and in winter on roots, rhizomes and bark.

The grey squirrel prefers to inhabit deciduous woodland, but manages quite well in well-established hedgerows with mature trees; food is sought at all levels by these adaptable and bold creatures. They are largely vegetarian, acorns being one of their most important foods, but their diet also includes nuts, beech mast, fungi, tree seeds and newly emergent buds and shoots – gathering these is destructive in woodland plantations – catkins and bark. They strip bark to extract the nutritious inner layers, and if a tree is ring-barked, then it dies above the scar – much to the annoyance of foresters. The grey squirrel is also blamed

This grey squirrel is busy in autumn burying a cache of hazel nuts – which are just as likely to be found by another squirrel.

for the widespread shortage of young hazel trees: the animals are such efficient gatherers of nuts that the seed stock has declined. Squirrels also take a small amount of animal food, such as insect larvae – oak galls are torn open for the animal food within – and certain rogues are known to have plundered birds' eggs and nestlings. Although many people enjoy their acrobatics, chattering and scolding, like other alien creatures rashly introduced to the British Isles the grey squirrel has achieved enormous 'pest' populations and is now unwelcome to foresters, and to farmers whose cereals, fruit and vegetables they plunder. But attempts to reduce their population have failed. The truly wild populations do fluctuate in severe winters when food is scarce.

INTRIGUING INSECT-EATERS

Among the vast hedgerow invertebrate populations are many that are predatory – though some, as we have seen, only feed the victims to their young – and their numbers and activity increase proportionally as summer progresses, sustained and strengthened by the growing numbers of prey. Predatory invertebrates are very useful, for they not only seek out and destroy vast numbers of minute, invertebrate plant-eating pests, but they in turn convert food (or energy) into a more useful form for their own predators, which need to eat fewer of these larger creatures.

The most familiar predatory invertebrates are the spiders, and most are stimulated only by moving and living prey. But, as they cannot injest solid food, digestive juices are introduced to prey immobilised by their venom and the digested food is sucked out, leaving the husk and inedible parts undamaged.

All spiders are able to produce silk, formed in the abdominal glands and extruded through 'spinnerets' near the tip of the abdomen. Several kinds of silk with strands of sticky and dry qualities are produced for different purposes, such as for carrying sperm, for wrapping up eggs or constructing nurseries, for approaching prey, for use as a lifeline, for moulting and, of course, for web-making. Only spiders – and certain caddis fly larvae – share man's ability to

make traps of any kind. Each species has its own pattern of web; the most attractive, especially when highlighted with glistening dewdrops shining in the morning sun, are the polygonal orb webs made by the garden spider and about ten other related species, designed principally to catch insects in flight. And when one studies the stages involved in the design and construction of these webs (also described in helpful detail in numerous books) it seems incredible that they can be created within the space of an hour, with nothing more than instinct for the blueprint.

The web of the garden spider, which is common in hedges.

Another very common type of hedgerow web is the horizontally spread sheet or hammock creation characteristic of the small money spiders, their large family consisting of 250 of the 600 species of British spiders. Their webs are not sticky, but are such an intermeshed tangle of threads that if a luckless invertebrate should fall into it, struggling to get free would only enmesh it further; the spiders themselves only pull the prey through the web from beneath.

Spiders are able to identify what falls into the web from the different vibrations received by the sensory hairs on their bodies and limbs, and these inform them of the presence and nature (via chemosensitive hairs) of nearby prey. Plant debris or dead invertebrates that get blown into these traps are ignored until they can be cut away and removed. An acceptable morsel is seized upon and made immobile by being bundled up in silk and then bitten with venom for good measure, before the digestive juices are introduced. So when a male spider, often smaller than the female, approaches her web, he must do so with an innate signal tapped in high-pitched vibrations via the threads, so she can distinguish him from her prey. However, she may not recognise this signal immediately and, if she attempts to attack, he is able to swing out of reach on a silken lifeline which is prudently trailing behind him as he approaches her. But if several approaches are needed before mating, this will soon sap his energy; and by now he will also be weakening from lack of food, for away from his own web he cannot catch his prey. If he is no longer alert, and his function in mating is over, he may well end up as an extra meal for the female, for she now needs extra food energy to form her eggs.

Many spiders make no webs at all but actively hunt their prey or are able to rely on their camouflage to the extent that unsuspecting victims come so close that they are able to be seized easily. The hunters are divided into night shift and day workers. Diurnal species tend to have good eyesight, while creatures of the night sense the presence and nature of the prey via the sensory hairs, and their lightning reflexes enable them to hunt just as effectively by this method as by sight. Most hunters attack prey which is smaller than they are and run from larger insects. As spiders are cannabilistic it is advantageous if the smaller juveniles are able to occupy marginally different niches from the larger adult stages or they risk becoming prey. The problem of size also arises in courtship when the male is smaller than the female. In some species there is a good deal of 'dancing' in front of the female to display his distinguishing markings, which has the effect of reducing the female's predatory tendencies. But the male wolf spider has 'learnt' to woo his female with a gift of a silk-wrapped morsel of food, and while she is occupied with consuming this, he mates with her – or else she may well make a meal of him. The less active, fat-bodied, crab spiders use the art of camouflage to catch their prey, by matching the colours of the flowers, usually of the daisy family, on which they live. They wait here in ambush with legs splayed at the ready to spring on unsuspecting prey.

Closely related to spiders are the harvestmen, of which Britain has twenty-six species. Insect food is also included in their diet, which they seize in their pincer-like jaws, and some species use sticky hairs on their mouthparts to ensnare and hold their prey. They themselves are prey to large spiders and may sometimes get away minus a leg, which continues to wriggle and hold the attention of the predator. A harvestman suffering such an injury cannot regrow the lost limb, but this seems to have little effect on its movement.

Beetles, with their hardened bodies and extraordinary mouthparts (mandibles), look the part of predatory insects, but while among the 3,700 British species, which come in an immense variety of shapes and sizes, there are many that are predatory, there are also other groups such as the plant feeders (as we have seen), the destructive bark beetles adapted for boring into wood and generally feeding on fungi, and the scavenging species.

Ladybirds are one of the most familiar predatory beetles, and probably the only ones most people will be prepared to handle. There are over 40 British species but only about 12 are easily recognised, because of their brightly coloured, shiny, spotted bodies. The most well-known species is the 7-spot ladybird, found almost anywhere with vegetation, while the yellow and black 22-spot ladybird is fairly common in hedgerows in southern Britain, where it can often be found on nettles. Ladybirds have a voracious appetite for scale insects, mealy bugs and mites, but most of all for aphids, which are eaten by both the adults and larvae. A fully grown grub can eat up to fifty aphids a day. Aphids will attempt to fight back by 'ganging up' on the predator in large numbers in the attempt to dislodge it, while some aphid species are able to extrude a waxy secretion which causes temporary paralysis.

Another group of predatory beetles are also easily spotted because they are so common on umbelliferous flowers, such as hogweed, in late summer. These are the soldier and sailor beetles, long, narrow insects with brown or black wing cases and red or black heads. Both the larvae and adults feed on small nectar-feeding insects, but they are also cannibalistic. These beetles and the ladybirds are unpalatable to birds, for they exude a foul-tasting fluid when attacked, and like other conspicuous insects their bright colours signal as a warning. But while this deters birds, some spiders, such as the orb weavers, have poor eyesight and with the advantages of immobilising their prey in silk and feeding on the internal body fluids, their diet commonly consists of bees, wasps and beetles.

A careful search in damp hedges and verges is more likely to reveal the common toad than any other of the five amphibians that have been recorded in these habitats – the others being the common frog, and the smooth, palmate, and great crested or warty newts. Toads are most active at dusk, when they emerge from their resting places, which may be holes created by other burrowing creatures, to search for invertebrate food. A toad catches its prey by lashing out the free end of its long sticky tongue; the other end is hinged to the floor of the jaw, at the front of the mouth. Hence it does not need its forefeet to hold its prey. Instead the victim is wedged between the toad's jaw by compressing from the eyeballs which are drawn down into the cavity of the mouth.

In spite of the toad's various defence mechanisms, many juveniles will fall victim to different hedgerow predators, including birds of prey, stoats and snakes as well as the omnivorous creatures such as rats, hedgehogs and crows. The toad's most effective form of defence is to keep very still, relying on the camouflage of its yellowish or khaki skin. Mature toads stand a better chance of survival, for they are able to increase their size by 50 per cent by filling their lungs with air and inflating their bodies. This deceives their enemies into thinking that they will be unable to swallow so large a mouthful. Another deterrent is the toad's ability to emit a sour, milky liquid from the glands on its warty skin, causing it to be hastily dropped.

Among the seven species of British mammalian insectivores, four species are common hedgerow inhabitants: the hedgehog, the mole and the common and pygmy shrews. Insectivores have teeth suited to seizing, holding and chewing insects, the most characteristic feature being the small points on the upper surfaces of their cheek teeth (the molars and premolars). They are primitive animals which have not evolved much in the last 50 million years, simply because their design and instinct must work very well and have enabled them to adapt to the changes in their environment, for these creatures have certainly stood the test of time.

Most people who have them in their gardens will know that the hedgehog begins to become active at dusk, when it comes out of its daytime rest place to hunt for food. It makes up for its poor eyesight with excellent hearing and a well-developed sense of smell – easily tested by tempting a curled-up hedgehog with a saucer of milk, which it cannot resist once its nose starts twitching.

Hedgehogs find their food by random foraging, searching leaf litter, and turning over stones and bits of wood with their snouts in search of earthworms and other invertebrate food. But they also take amphibians, reptiles, mammals and birds. They are able to use their front paws to dig in search of mouse nests to eat the young. Creatures which are usually left alone by other predators are often tackled by the hedgehog without ill effect – such as bees and wasps. Even a viper can become its victim. It is not that the hedgehog is immune to the snake's venom, but that the creature's dense coat of spines prevents the viper's fangs from piercing the skin. While flesh-eaters by preference, hedgehogs will take plant food, including fruit, berries and nuts, and as the widely reported case of the North Ronaldsay (Orkney) hedgehog population demonstrated, birds' eggs can provide a major source of food, for they bite into the shells with their canine teeth and lick out the yolk. This versatility somewhat questions a seemingly harsh comment made by Desmond Morris that 'insectivores are incapable of grasping anything awkward, either physically or mentally'. Hedgehogs certainly have a primitive brain, but they have shown a capacity to adapt and, dare we say it, learn – though the lesson of the motor car still eludes them!

While the mole may not generally be regarded as a hedgerow animal, an experienced mole-catcher tells us that these solitary, aggressively territorial animals have runs located beneath hedgerows. Occasionally mole hills can be spotted on roadside verges. Although worms are their main and preferred diet, in time of drought, when worms are relatively inactive, moles seek insect grubs, snails and other ground-living invertebrates. In winter, they may have to dig deep down in search of worms which have migrated downwards to avoid freezing. Moles are active right through the twenty-four-hour period, alternating four hours of activity with three hours of rest. Much of their feeding is done when the earthworms burrow through the walls of mole tunnels. Moles can die of starvation without food for a few hours, so when earthworms are abundant they bite their heads off and store them alive. Experiments have shown that a decapitated worm will not escape in the dark until it has grown a head. But if there is time enough for a worm to do so, because the mole has not returned to the store for some time, the worm will regenerate this missing part and burrow away. When eating an earthworm, the mole holds it in its forepaws and pulls with its jaws, its hindpaws set wide bracing the body. By working the worm through its forepaws, the mole cleans the soil off as it eats its prey.

Shrews are closely related to moles, and during their short, hyperactive lives, consume an enormous amount of invertebrate food, mainly ground-living types, including earthworms, beetles, woodlice, larvae, spiders, flies, crickets and grasshoppers. They are quite able to leap and catch the latter in mid-air. They also take fresh carrion. Shrews have acute senses of hearing, smell and touch, which are more important in their search for food than is their sight. They must constantly keep finding food to stoke up, alternating periods of activity with periods of relaxation, throughout the twenty-four hours, for they need to eat three-quarters of their body weight each day – and one-and-a-half times if a pregnant female. Because of their high metabolism shrews are short-lived and drop dead of old age – living not much more than a year – even with plenty of food available.

Shrew flesh is distasteful to many mammals. The creatures possess scent glands which are thought to be used in marking territory and mating, and explain the shrew's unpalatability; but owls will eat them quite readily.

Their adaptation to flight has enabled bats to exploit a source of food not available to the land-bound insectivores – night-flying insects. They do not compete with insect-eating birds because they fly at dusk and at night when few birds are active. Although insects on wing, such as moths and beetles, are their principal prey, bats are also able, some species more than others, to pick invertebrates off vegetation. The proverbial blindness of bats is erroneous, for they are not blind, although they do not hunt by sight, but by sound. The creatures emit immensely high-pitched ultrasonic sounds when in flight, which are bounced back in echoes from their prey. The nature, distance and direction of the echo tells the bat how far away it is from its prey and also from other obstacles, so, in fact, providing what has been called a 'sound picture' of its surroundings.

Old trees in hedgerows may offer roosting places for bats, but being very versatile and great opportunists, bats will exploit any good feeding site where there are large concentrations of insects, such as roadside verges warmed by tarmac and hedges creating wind eddies. Although Britain has fifteen species of bat, and some are more common than others, their presence depends on the nature of the surrounding countryside. Common species which share hunting grounds seek prey in different places, and the shape and span of their wings will, to some extent, affect their flight and hunting technique. Generally, their manner of flight is roughly straight lines or swooping half circles, with sudden turns to one side or another, up or down to grasp their prey, which is caught in the mouth. The most likely species feeding a little above head height near or over hedgerows and verges are members of the three smaller bat types which are also fairly widespread and common: the pipistrelle, the natterer's bat, and the whiskered bat (now rare in East Anglia). The pipistrelle, the smallest of all British bats, is by far the most ubiquitous, and has the habit of patrolling a regular stretch. It has a small wing-span and a rapid-beating flight, so it darts and dives in erratic, short, straight lines. The slightly larger whiskered and natterer's bats have broader wings and relatively larger wing-spans. They tend to flutter with slower wing beats in the manner of a swooping flight. They can therefore hunt quite effectively in open woodland and at the edge, winding their way through the tree trunks.

Many of the birds feeding at the hedgerows take a wide range of the potential food items available when food is scarce. When food is abundant their choice is narrowed to those that suit them best and many birds are predisposed to invertebrate food. Those that may be seen feeding on insect food at the hedgerow include many woodland species, such as the woodpeckers, some of the warblers, tits, tree creeper, cuckoo and spotted flycatcher, as well as the more adaptable birds that originated from the woodland stock, but now show a preference for hedgerows, such as members of the thrush family, whitethroats and the dunnock or hedge sparrow. But the extent to which some species are found in any single hedge and not in another depends on the differences in requirements of different birds and on the characteristics and management of the hedge where they can establish a territory.

The blue tit is an insect-eater which will turn to other foods in winter. In gardens it has shown remarkable ingenuity in obtaining nuts from elaborate devices designed to measure its learning powers – though perhaps it only applies innate patterns of feeding acquired for life in the wild.

The principal function of the territorial system is to spread individuals, pairs and even large groups over a habitat, making the maximum possible use of all that a habitat may offer, so that as many young birds as possible may survive. Bird territories, claims Dr Eric Simms, 'have been likened to rubber discs, since the more you compress them the greater is their resistance to further compression so that bird populations can be limited by the territorial behaviour of individuals that compose them'. By holding a territory a bird may avoid competition for food, as the presence of settled birds in territories generally deters competing would-be settlers from establishing themselves. Once established, a bird acquaints itself intimately with the full range of food sources for the duration of the period it holds its territory. Although many small species abandon their territories after nesting, as it is more advantageous to gather in flocks (see p. 91), those such as robins and wrens which hold their territories throughout the year are able to exploit the best food sources as each season unfolds.

Although the birds that can be seen at the hedgerow show a range of physical adaptations to exploit the various foods offered in the different parts of this habitat, the best indicators, as we have seen with the vegetarian birds, are their bills. All birds whose diets consist largely of invertebrates have thin, pointed bills. Those such as the warblers and spotted flycatcher that mainly catch airborne insects have bills with a broad base, so that they can open their mouths wide: they perch still and upright on branches watching for insects, dart to catch them on wing and then return to the same watch-point. These birds also hover at the trees and tall shrubs, gleaning prey off the foliage. The blue and

The harmless grass snake can stage a disconcerting display of aggression. Its diet consists of many hedgerow vegetarians and amphibians and in turn it becomes the prey of the mammalian carnivores, but displays a few defence mechanisms such as emitting a mass of foul-smelling excrement, or shamming a strike as if it were venomous, while at the same time inflating its body to appear fierce. When all else fails it may resort to feigning death by coiling on its back, belly upward, its head flopped back, mouth open and tongue hanging out.

coal tits are so light that they are able to perch at the very ends of small twigs, which will not bear heavier birds, and feed on the invertebrates living on the growing tips of plants. Tits energetically explore cracks and crevices in trees and shrubs and puncture plant galls, and it is thought that this inquisitive tendency may have led them to discovering the food resource under milk bottle tops!

All woodpeckers have strong, sharp bills to bore deep into dead or infected wood for invertebrates. Their tongues, linked to a flexible system of bones and elastic tissue, can be extended far beyond the end of their beaks – up to six inches (16cm) in the case of the green woodpecker. The tree creeper has a thin, curved bill enabling it to reach small prey which are elusive to other birds in cracks in the bark. The bird searches for its food most systematically, starting at the base of the tree and climbing up spirally. Because it cannot descend in the same way, it flies from the top of the trunk down to the base of another tree to begin the process again.

Birds feeding on the defoliating invertebrates, nectar- and pollen eaters and ground-living creatures at shrub, herb and ground level include the dunnock, warblers, wren, titmice and the versatile starling and thrushes. The thrushes are said to have good sight, but are also thought to be able to locate some of their prey by sound, for they are known to extract invertebrates from just under the soil surface. The birds use their bills to turn over leaves and other debris, while the song thrush can cope most effectively with snails (see p. 166). Most gardeners will be familiar with the endearing behaviour of robins in winter as they perch close by waiting for invertebrates to be dug up, which they promptly snap up; they watch wild animals, such as moles, at work in the same way. The starling's feeding technique is to push its closed bill into the soil and then open it and seize the prey, dragging it out of the soil. Many birds that eat soil-covered invertebrates are able to clean their bills by rubbing them sideways on the ground or on vegetation, and in the same way they can remove the slime from slugs before they consume them. Ground feeders also include the green woodpecker and the game birds. The woodpecker, besides relishing the larvae of wood-boring invertebrates, is particularly partial to ants and their grubs. It has also been seen to probe and excavate the nest of mining bees and wasps as well as the hives of the colonising species, in search of its grubs. The omnivorous game birds will take much invertebrate food in the summer months, usually snails, beetles, ants, crickets, grasshoppers and larvae, but the pheasant is known to have taken larger creatures such as lizards, slow worms and grass snakes. These birds have frequently choked swallowing field mice.

CANNY CARNIVORES AND CARRION-EATERS

The populations of the invertebrates, mammals and bird species already mentioned, while achieving some balance in their interactions with each other, are also controlled by the animals whose diets consist largely of flesh: the carnivores and the birds of prey, at the top of the food pyramid.

The four main hedgerow mammalian carnivores are the fox, the badger, the stoat and the weasel. The special adaptations of carnivores are their dentition, for tearing flesh, and their speed and agility, for running down prey; and while this latter characteristic can hardly be applied to the badger, it is certainly true of the other three mammals. In winter, when the bounty of vegetarian and insect foods is diminished, rodent and bird populations are correspondingly low, so predators either have to alter their diet (and now a lot of carrion is taken), or move further afield, to adjacent woodlands and fields in search of food. Hedges act as convenient corridors during this time, making it safer for animals to move under cover.

At the hedgerow, essentially hunting at dusk and at night, the fox searches for rabbits, mice, voles, hedgehogs and game birds. Foxes have perfectly good eyesight, but it is their hearing and sense of smell which are most important when tracking prey. However, as the mammal does not actually seek any particular species especially, it will automatically pounce on anything it sees or hears moving. It uses different techniques to catch rabbits as opposed to mice and voles. As rabbits feed in groups, it is less easy for the fox to approach unseen. Therefore it stalks as close as possible, then sprints into the group, creating sudden alarm and confusion, enabling it to grab an unlucky, slower individual – probably a senile or sick creature, or a young, inexperienced one. The fox pounces upon solitary prey from a rearing leap, nose and forepaws bearing down on the victim at the same time. It also springs upon birds, but usually catches them on their nests. The fox takes insect food in summer, when it is so abundant and can be found with little effort, while in late summer or autumn the fox appreciates fruits and berries; foxes have been seen to reach up on their hindlegs and pluck the berries from the shrubs. Foxes have a reputation for being wasteful killers, said to be killing for the pleasure of it. But as they are predatory by instinct it is their nature to kill if an opportunity arises. So if a marauding fox is faced with easy prey of dozens of moving chicken, or birds in a colony, it kills more than it can eat. Normally, however, foxes kill only to satisfy their hunger, and store suitable surplus, such as eggs from a bird's nest.

Badgers, though carnivores by definition, are essentially omnivorous, opportunistic feeders, with a diet dependent on availability. Given a chance they will take lizards, mice, voles, amphibians, rabbits and even moles, while young birds fallen from their nests are certainly not ignored. But it seems that their favourite food is earthworms; and they will also dig for larvae, leatherjackets, beetles and slugs. Wasp nests are frequently raided and in the excitement the badger's hair stands on end, effectively deterring the angry wasps from getting to its skin to sting. Both the badger and the fox have become aware of the relatively recent food source of victims of traffic accidents, but if they do not collect the carrion and take it away to feed on, they invariably become victims themselves. A large variety of vegetable food also features in the badger's diet, including acorns, beechmast and other seeds, fruits, grass, clover and roots. Like the fox, the badger has been accused of killing poultry, but this is unusual and likely to have been an act done in hard times.

Weasels and stoats are truly carnivorous, rejecting little that is flesh. They are specialists in that most of their diet consists of rodent prey. Both kill their prey by a bite to the back of the neck. They are active by day and night, hunting mainly by scent. These mammals usually hunt alone, or in pairs, but they may hunt in family parties if they have young. Both species have a high metabolism,

The weasel is a tiny predatory with remarkable aggression and speed. It often falls victim to gamekeepers because after gaining cover its inquisitive nature lures it back to have a second look at its enemy.

and therefore need to feed at frequent intervals, alternating spells of activity with periods of rest. If there is an abundance of rodent food they kill much more than they need and store the rest. Juveniles are apt to play with dead rodents, practising their hunting skills.

Although there is some overlap in the feeding and hunting habits of these related creatures, they do differ somewhat. Weasels, being much smaller, naturally prey on smaller rodents. They are able to pursue their prey into the burrows and through the underground runs of the latter. They are also able to work their way quite easily through the most tangled branches of hedgerow shrubbery in search of nestlings and eggs; indeed, weasels are known to have been able to slip through the minute holes of artificial tit nest boxes. Stoats are able to hunt larger mammals, and rabbits used to feature largely in their diet before the 1954 myxomatosis epidemic, which was a severe blow to the stoat population. In many parts of the country stoat populations are only now returning to their pre-1954 numbers, unless man has since then further affected their prospects by removing hedgerows and other cover and destroyed options for breeding habitats. Rabbits appear to be terrified by the approach of a stoat, and instead of running away are paralysed with panic, enabling the stoat to make easy victims of the creatures. Though widespread and common the weasel is confined to mainland Britain. Stoats, however, are present on many offshore islands, and, to confuse the issue, stoats are known as weasels in Ireland!

Although fox, owls and hawks take stoats and weasels as their prey, man is the main enemy of the fox and badger. But all these carnivores are widely persecuted in the interests of 'sport'; badger baiting – which is illegal – fox hunting – which soon should be – and game preservation.

BIRDS OF PREY

Kestrels, sparrowhawks and the tawny, barn and little owls visit hedgerows in search of prey, where they take birds, small mammals and insects. The barn owl is now quite a rare British bird: a consequence of the use of pesticides and the demolition or conversion of so many barns. It may be seen as a ghostly and silent whitish bird flying low over hedgerows in search of prey. The much commoner tawny owl, in contrast, is essentially a pouncing hunter with little stamina for long flights, and is often to be seen at dusk in a hedgerow tree, which serves as a look-out post. The little owl is a successful introduced bird, and though its main diet is of beetles and other invertebrates, it is cruelly persecuted by gamekeepers. Hedgerows may also provide tree nesting sites for tawny and little owls (see p. 203).

Often the only clue to the presence of animal life in a hedgerow is the spectacular sight of a kestrel hovering, or a sparrowhawk sweeping over the hedge like an arrow. A sudden dive and a swoop, and a small hapless creature is carried away in its talons. The birds are able to hunt flying prey or seize animals from the ground because their body shape and wing design enables fast, silent flight.

The forward-looking eyes of birds of prey give them excellent binocular vision, and so they judge distance accurately and pinpoint prey exactly. Their hooked beaks are used for tearing flesh and for plucking feathers. Birds of prey also use their feet together with their bills while actually feeding. The food is usually held down by one foot, or both, while the bill tears the flesh and, in the case of the sparrowhawk, plucks the feathers before consumption. Owls swallow their small victims whole. The ingestible fur, feathers and bones are later coughed up and ejected via the beak in the form of pellets, which one can dissect to identify the chosen prey.

While these birds of prey do not usually take carrion, they certainly take sick or injured birds and mammals, and owls are known to pick the badly injured and freshly killed road casualties. However, a group very characteristic of scavenging are the members of the crow family, the common hedgerow inhabitants being the magpie, whose diet frequently consists of carrion, and the rook and jay, which do not ignore carrion if hungry. Their more usual diet is that of soil invertebrates, fruit, nuts, acorns and cereals, but in spring and early summer the jay and magpie commonly prey on eggs and nestlings of small birds. The magpie is also known to kill small mammals caught unawares.

With so many species competing and interacting with each other, quite small changes in the hedgerow habitat can trigger off a chain reaction. The constant growth and regular cutting means that the habitat is continually changing, and while this encourages diversity, much depends on when the hedge is cut – a difference of a few weeks can greatly alter the composition of the dependent flora and fauna – and how this is done. As spring and summer are the principal

Unlike the hovering kestrel ABOVE the sparrowhawk BELOW swoops swiftly over the hedgerow, seizing frightened small birds as they break cover. Those who have seen the flame-eyed sparrowhawk at close quarters will appreciate that, pound for pound, it is our most wild-looking bird of prey.

breeding seasons for most hedgerow fauna, management is best kept to a minimum and this is, in fact, the case in many parts of Britain. But the brown hairstreak butterfly is an autumn species which lays her eggs on the projecting shoots of hawthorn and blackthorn, where they can remain dormant through the winter. However, in autumn and early spring when the hedges are mechanically trimmed, it is found that 80 per cent of the eggs are lost. As a result this species is now rare, confined mainly to the West Country and parts of Wales and Ireland where hedges are still laid, and in East Anglia it has become extinct. Nature also takes its toll, but this illustrates how important this species is to its predators, for of the 20 per cent of eggs that do hatch, 90 per cent of the caterpillars and chrysalides are eaten. Hedge cutting by modern tractor-drawn machines is changing the nature of hedgerows. These machines are cheap to use, but not selective, and therefore destroy the strong saplings of species such as oak, which may grow into trees and support a host of wildlife, as well as any interesting new colonising tree species that may have been introduced by a bird or mammal. Also, these machines do not deal effectively with the coarse vegetation that establishes at the bottom of the hedge, which eventually has the effect of suppressing the more delicate and interesting flora which support a more varied wildlife.

But by far the most destructive of man's deliberate or accidental actions have been the use of insecticides and weedkillers and the complete destruction of hedges, by fire, where stubble burning has got out of hand, and deliberate uprooting. Amphibians have proved vulnerable to the drainage of farm ditches and the spread of farm chemicals. Some of the pesticides, such as the organo-chlorines, have high toxicity and persistence, so that lethal amounts can grow cumulatively through the food chain right to the predators at the end. DDT, Aldrin, Dieldrin and Heptachlor, largely used in arable areas of eastern England, have proved to have far-reaching effects. They have severely reduced the populations of many grain- and seed-eaters and their predators. The poisons are stored in the tissues and body fat, which is absorbed in times of shortage. This weakens the animal, making it vulnerable to prey, or eventually kills it. Predators eating infected animals in turn concentrate these substances into their own bodies. There are also side effects, as have been shown in birds which have become infertile, laid eggs with thinner shells or produced less fertile eggs that do not produce offspring. The survival of young birds has been further affected because they have been fed with infected prey. Many of the chemicals have been banned or brought under control in the last few years, and already the barn owl, tawny owl, sparrowhawk, and kestrel have started an increase in numbers after a serious decline, which came about when the poisons began to build up in their bodies. New chemicals continue to be introduced, but these have still to stand the test of time and Dr Simms quotes a case when in 1975 the Ministry of Agriculture, Fisheries and Food had to re-examine a seed-dressing passed as safe following the death of 700 geese after feeding close to fields of winter-sown wheat dressed with a substance called Trithion, a recommended replacement for Dieldrin.

Many creatures living by the roadside lose their lives or become badly maimed, leaving the injured at a disadvantage in the harsh and competitive world of nature. During the limited survey for the Hawk Trust in 1983, Colin Shawyer found five owls dead in one night on a single mile of motorway (two of our own tawny owls are maimed for life as a result of a road accident and will never be able to be released like the others). Many hundreds of badgers and toads are killed every year when they persist in following traditional routes, established before the roads were built. On busy roads the solution may be to build a special underpass. Where these have been built or where drainage culverts have been modified, or where strong fences have been erected to direct badgers to safer crossing places, the eventual reduction in mor-

The beautiful barn owl hunts along hedgerows like a silent white ghost.

talities has been encouraging. The Wellington (in Somerset) badger pass took three years to take effect, although it was purpose-built and bait was used to attract them – including such ingenious methods as a man with a badger's scent on his coat crawling through the narrow tunnel! The feeding grounds across the highway began to be ignored but for a few stalwarts who attempted to cross overground and usually came to a tragic end. However, nature took its course when the badger population increased and larger food supplies had to be sought. It was then that the badgers finally 'opened' the pass and in due course claimed it as part of their territory by placing latrines at either end.

Hedgerow flora and fauna also suffer many natural hazards. Some are drastic like the Dutch elm disease, but most have the effect of keeping the population levels in some sort of a balance. Apart from predation, deaths are caused by food shortages and disease. But provided there are some strong survivors the reduction in population in this way enables the survivors to make more effective use of the smaller resources and eventually produce healthy offspring. The natural maintenance of balanced populations depends on the production of more young than are necessary to replace adults that die. Some of the young will soon become prey to predators, and others may not reach maturity through failure in the competition for limited food resources and the effects of disease before the surviving offspring will in turn breed.

·13·

FACETS OF THE HEDGEROW YEAR

Plants and animals respond to the changes in daylight and temperature. These factors regulate their life-cycles and behaviour, preparing them for the abundance of summer and the hardships of winter. Lengthening daylight and the increasing warmth of spring triggers plant growth and stimulates the opening of flowers, prompting insect eggs to hatch and hibernating adults to emerge as food sources become available. These then become food supplies for birds and mammals, encouraging them to breed. When this cycle begins to approach the end of its course, shorter days and colder weather herald the rigours of winter, and for some birds and insects it is time to migrate. For many of those remaining behind, life may be near to the close; for others that means of survival, the autumn bounty, supplies a signal that they should begin accumulating food stores or fat.

THE SUCCESS OF SPRING FLOWERS

The earliest flowering plants are those which can be wind-pollinated or which reproduce vegetatively. In most annuals the whole life-cycle is from seed to seed, frequently accomplished in a single season, so it is to their advantage for their seeds to lie dormant until growing conditions are just right. Many of the earliest flowering plants are perennials that do not have to rely on seed for reproduction. The exposed parts of perennial plants die back in the seasons of the year unfavourable for growth, while the plants retain their food reserves in their root stock. Some of the root structures, such as tubers, bulbs and creeping roots, multiply vegetatively and produce new plants. It is this characteristic, and the fact that some flowers can be fertilised by their own pollen, when insect pollinators are scarce, that enable many of the early-flowering plants to expose their flowers to the rigours of inclement weather. In addition, some species can temporarily generate marginally higher temperatures than the surrounding air by growing their plant tissues rapidly. But the duration of this ability depends on their food reserves, and prolonged frost would inevitably cause starvation and collapse. Many of the spring-flowering plants are low-growing and must bloom before they are shaded by the taller plants of the verge in summer.

One of the most welcoming signs of spring is the blooming of the snowdrop. There is some speculation as to whether it is truly native anywhere in Britain, for it so frequently becomes naturalised as an escapee of cultivation. The snowdrop is so hardy that it can freeze solid and then recover in the thaw. The bulb 'seals' itself to protect its food preserves and reproductive parts and the water within is withdrawn from the cell tissue to be stored in minute intervening air spaces. Here it can safely crystallise and thaw without causing the cell structures to collapse. While the bulb effectively produces small new bulbs or offsets, the snowdrop provides an early feast for bees, which in turn pollinate the flowers.

Another spring example of reproduction without the aid of insects is that of the lesser celandine, which even if insect-pollinated produces little seed. The plants are propagated mainly by tuberous roots which, being a source of food to rodents and game birds, rely on these creatures for the dispersal of root tissue. The wild and barren strawberries, rather similar in appearance, and our earliest and only fragrant violet, the sweet violet, are all able to reproduce because their runners or 'stolons' root at intervals to form new plants. Although both germander speedwell and greater stitchwort produce plenty of viable seeds as a result of attracting a host of insects, each has its own fail-safe mechanism for reproduction: the horizontally spreading stems of speedwell will take root at intervals and produce upright flowering stems. If cross-pollination has not taken place by the end of the flowering period, the anthers of stitchwort droop towards the stigma to enable it to pick up the pollen and thus the flower fertilises itself. (Greater stitchwort is nevertheless disappearing from many hedgebanks and verges because it is intolerant of pollution from heavy traffic.)

These 'do-it-yourself' methods, while ensuring the production of offspring, reproduce plants identical to the parents. Although the new generation is well enough suited to the exact habitat in which the parent is growing, it may not succeed if the habitat should change. Another disadvantage of self-fertilisation is that undesirable characteristics may be passed on to the offspring, and self-fertilisation over a few generations intensifies these characteristics. Cross-fertilisation, aided by wind or invertebrates, ensures a combination of characteristics. The resulting variations produce plants with an adaptability for survival should the habitat alter.

The lesser celandine relies mainly on its spreading tuberous roots for propagation.

The greater stitchwort will achieve self-pollination if cross-pollination fails. It must complete its flowering cycle early, for soon the plant will be overwhelmed by the shooting nettles and cleavers of the verge.

Many dioecious early-flowering shrubs and grasses are wind-pollinated. Dog's mercury with its inconspicuous yellow-green flowers can bloom as early as February because its flowers are borne on long, slender, upright spikes which facilitate wind pollination.

The primrose's flower is peculiarly designed to rely on cross-fertilisation. Two types of plant occur: one bears 'pin eyed' flowers and the other version is 'thrum-eyed'. The pin-eyed flower has a long style reaching the top of the flower tube revealing the stigma like a pin-head in the middle of the flower. In the thrum-eyed version it is the pollen-bearing anthers that show at the top of the tube. This arrangement prevents self-fertilisation as well as the chances of a flower being pollinated by pollen from another flower of the same plant. In addition, the two different kinds of flower have pollen of different sizes and surface sculptures that are only compatible with the stigma of the other kind. The name *Primula* derives from the Latin words meaning 'first rose', apt for primroses which may flower as early as February. But when few insects are about the flowers remain unpollinated – or more picturesquely expressed in Shakespeare's *The Winter's Tale:* 'pale primroses that die unmarried'.

LEFT The hazel relies on wind pollination and produces great clouds of yellow pollen. In this close-up picture of the catkins one can see the stamens exposed to the breeze. The female flowers are tiny reddish 'tufts' on the stem and are easily overlooked. RIGHT The ash produces its flowers in April before the leaves have appeared and loses its leaves early, while they are still green, but the 'keys' or seeds, shown here, may remain on the tree through winter. Some trees produce mainly male flowers, others mainly female flowers, or flowers of both sexes and hermaphrodite flowers.

ATTRACTING INSECT POLLINATORS

A community of any hedgerow plants has representatives that rely on insect pollination. These flowers have evolved solely for the purpose of attracting their pollinators to carry the pollen from their anthers for transfer to the stigma of another flower. The male cell emerges from the stigma and grows down the style, through the ovary where it fuses with the female cell in fertilisation. The flower's colour, patterns on the petals and scent initially attract the insect. Once the creature has landed, the food sources of nectar and pollen provide the inducement for it to stay long enough to ensure that some pollen is transferred to its body. Those flowers (such as the poppy) that have no nectar must entice insects with their pollen alone, producing it in such abundance that while most of it is eaten there is some spare for reproductive purposes.

Butterflies are among the few exceptions in the animal kingdom that have a broad visible spectrum ranging from the ultra violet at one end to yellow-orange and red at the other; most other insects have a much narrower spectrum. And so they are attracted to patterns of lines and dots on the petals which act as guidemarks for leading the insects to the nectar via contact with the flower's reproductive organs. Many of these guidemarks are visible to the human eye, such as the yellow centre surrounded by blue in forget-me-not and speedwell, the darker-toned lines of eyebrights, cranesbills and violets, and the spotted patterns on the spurs of many tubular flowers. Scent is also graded, becoming stronger towards the base of the petals. Some flowers, such as some kinds of

The guide lines on the flowers of the meadow cranesbill (exaggerated in the photograph by high-contrast printing) are not conspicuous to the human eye, but when seen in the ultra-violet spectrum by insects they are vivid guides to the nectar.

The flower tube of the foxglove is designed to accommodate its bumble-bee pollinator. Hairs on the flower impede smaller insects, but the patterns on the flowers' interior attracts the bees.

comfrey, change in colour towards maturity from pink in bud, to blue when mature for reproduction, and become rich in nectar. This encourages their pollination by bees, which are more sensitive to blue than pink, and which therefore visit those flowers that are ready to be pollinated.

In a flourishing hedgerow with a variety of flowers it may seem that the insect is spoilt for choice, and indeed there are many flowers that are indiscriminate about the numbers and types of insects that they attract, such as the open-flowering roses, bramble, buttercups, poppies and cranesbills, and those with flowers arranged in flat-topped clusters, such as the umbels. In these the nectar lies readily available in shallow pools and is greatly welcomed, particularly by those insects with short to medium-long tongues. But the pollen of such flowers is largely wasted, for the insects they attract may visit all kinds of different flowers. In order to ensure the chances of at least some pollen reaching the stigma of the same species these flowers have numerous stigmas to produce large quantities of pollen.

However, flowers in which the petals have fused together into a corolla tube can protect their pollen and nectar from all but the effective pollinators from a select group of insects. Hence they can afford to be more economical in the production of their pollen (some, such as certain orchid species, bearing only one stigma). The foxglove's chief pollinator is the bumble bee which has to crawl right up the tube to reach the nectar reservoir at the base of the flower. It is therefore sure to brush under both the four anthers and the stigma, situated under the upper part of the flower tube. As the stamens ripen before the stigma, cross-pollination is assured. The large, rounded body of the bumble bee fits neatly in the flower tube and is certain to make contact with the reproductive parts, but any smaller insects, which would be ineffective pollinators, are prevented from entering the flower and stealing the nectar by the sticky hairs growing inside the corolla tube in which they would get tangled.

The arum, a very common hedgebank plant, traps its pollinators temporarily at the base of its spadix to ensure pollination, having attracted them with a scent like rotting meat.

The exotic-looking *Arum maculatum* has a complicated mechanism to ensure cross-pollination. The male and female flowers grow at the foot of the projecting club-like structure, the spadix, which is enclosed within a broad sheathing hood, a modified leaf, called the spathe. When the spathe opens fully towards the afternoon, it emits a scent likened to rotting meat. This attracts midges and small flies which follow the scent to the base of the spathe, crawling past a fringe of backward-pointing hairs growing below the projecting purple head. Trapped under these hairs they crawl around the receptive female flowers spreading the pollen they may be carrying. After pollination the male flowers of that particular plant open to release their pollen. The spathe hairs then wither, allowing the insect to escape carrying the pollen from this plant to another. The process is a lengthy one and may take more than a few days to complete. If pollination is successful, a cluster of flame-red berries are produced in autumn.

HEDGEROW SERENADES

A walk along any hedgerow is certain to be enlivened by bird song and the chirruping of grasshoppers and crickets from spring to early autumn, and even in winter there is enchantment in the melancholy winter song of a robin. But while to our ears these serenades are a part of nature's charm, they are very important signals for the singers and their audiences, and are interlocked with other aspects in the lifestyles of these creatures.

The vocal signals of birds – composed of calls and song – are very complex, and Eric Simms describes how each call carries 'information associated with different activities in a bird's life – territorial behaviour, pairing, mating, coping with danger, reassuring young birds and also acting as a kind of identity card for other birds'. Some birds are able to make brief but effective sounds using wing beats or their bills, and these have the same effect on their audience as would vocal ones. (Our young tawny owls, now released, would click or snap their bills to express irritation or provide a warning if they were caught unaware and recognition was not immediate. They would also clap their wings in aggressive display.) Passerine birds have the most elaborate and varied calls and songs and the blue tit, for example, whose vocabulary has been particularly well studied, is

The robin is one of the most aggressively territorial of hedgerow birds and sings on a number of points around its territory.

capable of forming at least forty distinguishable sounds. There are territorial calls which reflect in sequence the change in the bird from mild uncertainty to furious and sustained attack. There is also a graded series of alarm calls to include distress or warnings of a predator. Single long notes which are high in pitch and pure in tone make the birds difficult to pinpoint. There are calls and songs associated with mating, while from the young there are calls of begging for food and informing the parents of their location after they have left the nest and before becoming independent.

Bird calls are used by both sexes in everyday situations, but the melodious phrases which are considered to be true bird song emerge mainly from the male birds – and call notes may be included in the development of their song phrases – to reveal that they are in breeding condition, they are asserting territorial rights or they are advertising for a partner. Therefore, spring and summer are the best times to hear these repertoires, and particularly at dawn when the birds are making their presence known after a period of inactivity. Bird song, though innate, is developed with learning and experience and those birds with the largest repertoire have held their territories longest; so females are able to recognise age and experience by a male's song. To ensure the full effect of display and advertisement many birds select high song perches, and these are used to mark and define their territories. Female bird song is unusual, though hen robins which hold territories in autumn and winter will make their presence felt in song. Song thrushes, blackbirds, wrens and starlings also utter fitful notes in autumn; tawny owls are particularly vocal in early autumn when adults defend their territories against their young. Also characteristic in autumn is 'subsong' or brief, undeveloped phrases regarded as a practice exercised by young birds with a low but growing sex-hormone level, a factor which is said to regulate the nature of the song.

It takes a lot of observation of corresponding behaviour to understand the complexities of bird song and although it is difficult to describe in words, and is in fact now widely available on records and cassettes, attempts have been made to translate these sounds into 'words' such as 'tsee, pee' ('social call of great tit') and 'zzzz' ('aggressive call of chaffinch'). Others are more memorable such as the song of the yellowhammer which has been described as 'little-bit-of-bread-and-no-cheese'!

The chirping sounds of our crickets and grasshoppers are certainly no easier to describe, although some admirably patient records have been translated into song-diagrams composed of 'pulses', representing distinct bursts of sound. The song is a vibration produced by the rapid to-and-fro movement of the hindleg of grasshoppers or the forewing in crickets and bush crickets. Bush cricket songs are usually high-pitched and it takes a keen ear to pick up the sounds in their frequency range. Bush crickets also show a leaning towards the nocturnal way of life, and though they might be active during the day their main activities begin towards dusk and after dark. In both grasshoppers and crickets it is the males that have the fully developed stridulatory apparatus, so the purpose of the song is apparently for territorial assertion and courtship. In bush crickets the hearing organ that picks up the vibrations is in the forelimb, while in the grasshoppers it is on the base of the abdomen.

NESTING BIRDS

The activities associated with nesting occupy half the hedgerow year. During the bitter weeks of February, long before the return of the migrant hedgrow birds, several types of bird, like some finches, are seeking to establish and guard their intended nesting territories. Some hedgerow birds have completed their nests and begun to incubate a brood long before buds have burst and leaves help to shelter the nest. The female mistle thrush begins nest-building in February and both blackbirds and song thrushes can be found sitting on eggs in March in the southern counties. Most other birds defer laying until late April, when the food supply for their fledglings is more reliable. This is the time when migrants are returning from their winter retreats. Some, like the spotted flycatcher, begin their breeding activities directly on arrival. The song of the blackcap, however, can be heard as early as March and by late summer the birds have all completed their moult and are ready to migrate to tropical Africa. The garden warbler is a migrant with a very brief infancy. The birds arrive in April, the eggs hatch within twelve days of laying and within ten days of hatching the young are fledged and ready to leave the nest.

The eggs of most hedgerow birds hatch within twelve to thirteen days of laying and youngsters usually spend about a fortnight in the nest. The

The collared dove may raise five broods in the course of the nesting season and sometimes the fledglings leave the nest too soon. This one was rescued just in time from a lawn patrolled by cats and hand-fed until safely released. However, unless one is experienced in bird-rescue work fledglings should never be handled. It is a near certainty that their parents will take care of them until they are independent.

vulnerability of fledglings and juveniles to predators, the need to raise additional broods to exploit the summer food reserves in full and the need to be in good condition to face the migration flight or the rigours of a British winter all argue for rapid growth rates. The rapidity of growth and the abundance of summer food supplies encourage many hedgerow birds to produce a second brood, the males frequently tending to the youngsters of the first brood while the female incubates the second. Some birds, like the dunnock, raise a third brood in favourable years, though others, like the chiffchaff, attempt only one brood. The collared dove is exceptional: its nesting may begin in March and by September no less than five two-egg broods may have been completed.

Most of the birds which the rambler can expect to see in a hedgerow are woodland birds. Hedges are features of the man-made rather than natural environment, but they replicate woodland conditions of shelter and food supply, and are therefore attractive to these birds. Most of the birds which are common in hedges – the thrushes, dunnock, chaffinch, greenfinch, wren and titmice – are also frequently seen in gardens, which similarly provide an attractive juxtaposition of trees and shrubs and more open areas. Some kinds of hedge are much more attractive to nesting birds than others, while different types of birds have different ideas about what constitutes the ideal hedgerow abode. This allows different birds to exploit all the different niches and storeys in the hedgerow habitat and reduces inter-species competition for nesting sites. For example, the ecologist G. W. Arnold has described how, while blackbirds and song thrushes favoured similar hedges – bushy ones which are at least 4½ ft (1.4 m) tall to provide cover above a nest built at a height of about 3 ft (1 m) – the more bulky, ground-nesting and -living pheasant and partridge preferred sparser hedges which did not impede their movements.

A wide range of factors governs the attractions of a hedgerow to birds in general and certain birds in particular. The local traditions of hedgerow planting and management and modern maintenance practices affect the abundance and quality of hedges; the composition of hedges also determines the quality of the cover and the nature of the food supply. The general setting of a hedgerow has a considerable effect: if there is an abundance of woodland nearby some birds prefer to exploit the alternative woodland nesting sites; if there are gardens close at hand then these supplement the critical winter food supply, though proximity of towns and popular footpaths cause greater human disturbance. The quality of concealment can be crucial. In both low, close-trimmed hedges and tall but lank and open hedges, nests are visible and threatened both by human interference and, usually more seriously, by predation from stoats, weasels and members of the crow family. The interplay of various hedgerow variables produces quite complicated results, as we have already seen in Ch. 12; and for example here, Dr Arnold found that

whilst numbers of blackbirds, tits and dunnocks increased with hedge height those of skylarks decreased. Increasing numbers of species of shrubs and herbaceous plants favoured game birds, finches and dunnocks, but had an adverse effect on numbers of doves, song thrushes, blackbirds, starlings and house sparrows... The number of song thrush and blackbird

Rooks may colonise hedgerow trees after the felling of their traditional home.

territories . . . was more strongly influenced by ditch volume and cover than by other characteristics. When it came to nesting, numbers of thrush nests increased with hedge cover, but declined in the presence of trees.

The range of birds seen in a hedge will be much broader if the hedgerow is punctuated by mature standard trees. Rooks normally prefer to establish their communal rookeries in woods and spinneys but often nest above hedgerows, particularly if their 'traditional' home is felled – a common occurrence today. The familiar nest, a seemingly untidy bundle of twigs, is actually bound with soil and lined with roots, leaves and moss, the female doing the building and her mate providing the materials. Though a useful consumer of insect pests, like leatherjackets, wireworms and cockchafers, the rook is needlessly persecuted by some farmers who wrongly believe that the birds attack new-born lambs – and thus confuse the rook with its cousin, the carrion crow. Another cousin is the jackdaw, smaller, neater and with a distinctive grey nape. Jackdaws may be seen nesting in holes in hedgerow trees, though they exploit a wide range of other niches, from chimney-pots to rabbit burrows. Like the rook, the magpie has been the victim of needless persecution. The nest, a large domed structure, may be built high in an overgrown thorn hedge or hedgerow standard and the birds become furtive in the nesting season. Even so, groups of magpies can be seen in the spring; they congregate to 'beat' a hedgerow for prey, and take eggs as well as fledglings.

ABOVE LEFT Young tawny owls, like this one whose down is passing to its adult plumage, are vulnerable to capture by children. They should never be treated as pets – it is illegal and the owl requires fur and feathers with its meat. This one, confiscated from its captor, was passed to the authors for rearing, and is now safely established in the wild. ABOVE RIGHT The dunnock nests near the base of the hedge and its turquoise blue eggs are familiar to most country children. BELOW The great tit is a hole-nesting bird which exploits slightly larger crannies than those favoured by the blue tit.

Tawny owls nest in shallow scrapes at the base of tree holes, or occasionally in the discarded nests of other birds. During evening rambles one may hear the monotonously repetitive 'sheevick' call of the young rising from a hedgerow tree, making the owls vulnerable to capture by thoughtless humans. Barn owls also nest in tree holes, which sometimes allow a few pairs of these beautiful predators to survive in a locality after the demolition or conversion of their favoured farm buildings. The kitten-sized little-owl is more common than most people realise and is another tree-hole nester. It may even take to bringing up its offspring in disused rabbit burrows in secluded hedgebanks.

The size of a potential tree-hole nesting site governs the type of tenant; many birds seek a hole which is just large enough to admit them, while preventing their eviction by larger birds and predation. The blue tit, very common in tall hedges and nesting in mature hedgerow trees, exploits the smallest openings, building a nest of leaves, grass, moss and wool lined with down and hairs at the base of the cranny. Slightly larger holes are occupied by the great tit, while tree creepers nest either in tree trunk cracks or in the crevice behind a loose flake of bark. The spotted flycatcher nests in smallish tree holes following its return from African winter quarters. This inconspicuous bird is most frequently glimpsed as a flickering burst of light grey feathers, seen when the bird loops out from a perching point to take an insect in flight. Whereas starlings and spotted woodpeckers compete for the occupation of nest boxes with larger-than-tit-sized holes, the woodpeckers have the advantage of being able to drill their own nest holes.

Large shrubs in overgrown hedges are likely to provide supports for the seemingly flimsy and 'amateurish' nest of the wood pigeon. Tree sites as well as buildings are favoured by the smaller, sleeker collared dove, which began to expand westwards into Europe in the 1930s, nested in Britain in the 1950s and is now one of our commonest birds. Generally less evident, the presence of the lovely turtle dove is usually announced by its restful purring coo. These migrants which winter in Africa generally choose lower nesting sites than other doves, sometimes gravitating down to the bramble level.

In the hedgerow proper the most obvious nests are normally those of the song thrush and blackbird; the nests of the former are neatly lined with mud and those of the latter have a layer of dried grass over mud. In contrast, the mistle thrush prefers to nest above the hedgerow, in the fork of a high tree. Two broods are often laid, the male feeding the young birds of the first brood while the female incubates the second. Away from the nest site, the mistle thrush can be distinguished from the slightly smaller song thrush by its slightly whitish cast.

The dunnock or hedge accentor is commonly if misleadingly known as the 'hedge sparrow'. A shy and drab bird whose delicate mottling can be appreciated only by close inspection, the dunnock nests in the lower levels of the hedge and the fledglings leave the nest before they are a fortnight old. Sometimes a derelict nest is adopted as the foundation for a dunnock nest. The wren is the most common British bird with a piercing call which belies its lack of stature. The success of the wren is partly due to its versatility in choice of habitats and nesting sites, and in hedges its distinctively domed nest with its small entrance hole may be found tightly wedged between the trunk and branches of a shrub. Despite the rather elaborate construction of the nest, the male builds several alternative abodes, from which the female makes her choice. The robin is also versatile in its choice of a nesting place, exploiting discarded containers, roots and hedgebank undergrowth, while particularly favouring places where ivy around a trunk or branch offers a firm, shady anchorage. In the case of the robin the female is entirely responsible for nest-building, though the male cares for the first brood while the second brood is incubating. One of the most variable nests is that of the house sparrow – a rather untidy and amorphous structure when built in a roof or wall, but a 'homely' domed construction when built in a hedge.

The most common hedge-nesting member of the finch family is the chaffinch, though the vast population of chaffinches has declined recently, partly as a result of hedgerow destruction. While chaffinch nests can be found in hedges of modest proportions, greenfinches favour tall hedges and bushes, seldom building at a height of less than three feet (1 m) and sometimes nesting at a height of 16 ft (5 m). While chaffinches tend to flock in winter, around February the birds become intensely territorial, even though nest-building does not normally begin until April. Though the chaffinch and greenfinch are both attractive birds, the bullfinch, which nests in the three to 7 ft (1–2 m) height range, is more striking still, with its pink breast, white rump and black head. But even this gaudy customer must yield to the brilliance of the little goldfinch, which nests in trees and tall, neglected hedgerows in the 13–33 ft (4–10 m) height range. Spiders' webs are used to bind the trim nest of moss, roots and lichen and the cup is lined with thistledown.

In the spring one often sees hedgerow birds carrying nesting materials, but the whitethroat with its pale bib always seems deceptively to be carrying a white feather in its beak. The sub-Saharan droughts have severely affected the whitethroat and it is now a less common migrant. The nest is frequently sited on a clump of nettles and, like the wren, the male whitethroat provides his mate with a selection of abodes. The lesser whitethroat is visually very similar, though its sparse nest tends to be built a little higher and in much denser cover. Two other warblers are even more difficult to distinguish: the willow warbler and the chiffchaff. However, the domed nest of the willow warbler is built at ground level, while that of the chiffchaff is normally in dense brambles or nettles a few inches above the ground. The garden warbler lacks the yellowish cast of the willow warbler and chiffchaff; it is not really a garden bird, but nests in dense bushes and brambles in the lower levels of the hedge. Its close relative, the blackcap, is easily recognised by the black cap of the male and the brown bonnet of the female, and again nest sites in brambles and dense bushes are favoured. This warbler may be beginning to develop a resident as well as a migrant strain.

The most familiar of the hedgerow buntings is the yellowhammer, which flourishes in areas of open hedgerow country. The female builds her nest low down or at ground level in the deep shelter of the hedge base. The larger and less colourful corn bunting usually nests in dense grass and thistle cover but sometimes adopts a site low in a hedge; though the cirl bunting, which lacks the hardiness to flourish north of the Thames, is more adaptable and may choose a ground, hedge or tree situation.

One of the largest of the birds found nesting on the ground in the base of the hedge is the grey partridge. Its decline in many arable counties must be largely attributed to hedgerow destruction and that of the hedge-foot brome grass and nettles where it seeks shelter. In some places the dubious pleasure of partridge shooting provides the only incentive for conservation which landowners can comprehend. N. Gray, of the Ely Game Advisory Station, has written that 'If the present rate of hedgerow destruction continues we can foresee serious consequences. The steady decline of the grey partridge may accelerate to a disastrous landslide.' Usually seen bumbling noisily around, like an accident in search of a venue, the pheasant seems to match its hunters in matters of intelligence and subtlety, and the wild population is vastly augmented by birds bred and released for slaughter. More adaptable than the partridge, the pheasant is equally at home in woodland, though where woodland nesting sites are not available hedgerow cover is essential to this non-native bird.

This young cuckoo, with its distinctively barred immature plumage, was probably raised in a hedgerow nest and was photographed on a cliff-top fence post as it prepares for its first migration flight to Africa.

Finally there is one hedgerow bird which is distinguished by its lack of a nest. As a result of the male's famous song the cuckoo is much more frequently heard than seen. In flight the grey cuckoo can be mistaken for a small hawk, and cuckoos are most easily seen around cliff tops in late summer, when the young, with their immature barred plumage, may seem to be summoning the courage for their long maiden flights to Africa. The female lays a single egg in the nest of up to a dozen different hosts. One egg is removed from the nest. In twelve days' time the young cuckoo hatches and begins to evict its bedfellows, by squirming and shuffling around the nest so that eggs or fledglings are moved to the brink of the nest and fall or are tipped out. The stimulus to pop food into the gaudy gape of the young cuckoo overcomes any inhibitions that the host may have regarding their enormous and insatiable youngster. A particular cuckoo may specialise in exploiting a single host species, and it is claimed that cuckoos are able roughly to replicate the general appearance of the eggs of the selected hosts. Bird species used as hosts generally have features in common: their nests are not too deeply cupped to enable easy eviction of eggs and nestlings; they breed at the same time of the year as the cuckoo and their diet is mainly that of insects, which is the most suitable food for the young cuckoo. Hosts must also be tolerant of disturbance and egg mimicry and therefore the dunnock, robin and garden warbler are strongly favoured in hedgerows.

WATCHING BUTTERFLIES

The first butterflies to appear in spring are likely to be members of one of the species which hibernate in the adult stage. They venture out on the first warm day, which can be very early in the year if it is sufficiently mild. Emerging early as adults, or fresh from the chrysalis stage enables some species to lay their eggs in time for a second generation of butterflies to emerge later in the year. In some species, such as the holly blue, there is considerable variation between individuals in different broods. The small tortoiseshell is another butterfly that has two broods a year and a chart noting its flight periods can be interpreted as follows:

J	F	M	A	M	J	J	A	S	O	N	D
−	−	+	+	−	−	+	−	+	−	−	−

summer brood

second generation
winter brood

---------→   ---------→
hibernating   − adult absent   hibernating
adult   + adult on wing   adult

Being a cold-blooded creature, a butterfly's body temperature fluctuates according to the surrounding temperature. Sunny days find the creatures far more active and they can be seen perched early in the day sunning themselves, wings spread, the darker pigments of their scales absorbing more heat to generate energy for flight, and once airborne they will maintain this by muscular activity. In the heat of the day, when they are perched in the shade, they may be attempting to lose body heat, with their wings angled or spread out to control heat loss.

With their preferences for particular plants or plant associations the species of butterfly found in any hedgerow generally depends on the locality of the habitat, its general setting in relation to the surrounding countryside and the nature of the hedge. Butterflies seen at the hedgerow are also seen in other habitats and the habitat preference for any particular species is generally similar over the whole of its distribution. Comma and peacock are woodland-edge

The silver-washed fritillary is a rare butterfly of southern wood margins and hedgebanks and is unique in laying its eggs on tree trunks, the caterpillars descending to feed on violet leaves. The butterflies roost in tree tops and flutter down to take nectar from bramble and thistles.

species; the whites, painted lady, clouded yellow, meadow brown and small heath are open-ground species; and the small tortoiseshell, gatekeeper, red admiral and orange tip are open-scrub species. Hedgerows in the chalk downlands attract the blues and skippers, while those adjacent to deciduous woods and coppices in England and Wales may be within range of some of the fritillaries. The caterpillars of the six British fritillaries are said to be dependent almost exclusively on violet plants for food, but the adults will visit many wildflowers to drink nectar. But, as entomologist Dr Paul Whalley has observed: 'Sometimes an apparently suitable habitat with the right food for the caterpillars and nectar for the adults will not have the butterflies one might expect. The answers here might be related to the recent history of the habitat.' For instance, fire may have led to the local extinction of a species whose recovery is slow. Insecticides also destroy populations, whereas the effects of herbicides and verge trimming are far more obvious, for they may kill the food plants. Severe winters cause warm-blooded creatures to seek out whatever food thay can and so far more than usual quantities of overwintering insects may be eaten. However, snow cover may actually protect the eggs and chrysalides.

Migrant species may turn up anywhere, for red admiral and painted lady are widespread in Britain. The clouded yellow is more frequent near the south and east coasts, but fewer than 500 individuals are recorded in Britain each year. Butterfly migrants arrive to breed and some of their progeny reverse migrate. Although tag-marked butterflies have been shown to fly long distances it has been suggested that there may also be breeding *en route*, with the progeny flying on.

Butterflies flap their wings at a relatively slower rate compared to many other insects, to prevent rapid energy consumption. The gatekeeper has a very weak, fluttering flight, rarely moving more than a hundred yards or so from where it emerges to adulthood. In their flight period between July and August they can be seen abundantly at the hedgerows where they are locally common in England and Wales, gracefully competing for patches of flowering bramble.

Hedge verges are likely to attract the small, brownish members of the skipper family of butterflies. With their fluffy bodies and stubby wings they might be mistaken for moths.

However, in migrant species, and others such as the small tortoiseshell which has a fast, rather wild flight, it has been calculated that when using their powerful wing muscles these fragile-looking creatures are consuming energy approaching twenty times the rate of a man working flat out. It is hardly surprising, therefore, that they are able to reach speeds of 25 m.p.h.!

Many male butterflies have territories, and it is thought that these are marked by scent emitted from special scales on the wings. Territorial battles are brief, vigorous affairs: two males fluttering vertically, spiral-like, for a moment or two, before the intruder usually retreats gracefully from the encounter without damage. Longer flight displays of a pair of butterflies are usually part of a complicated courtship procedure which includes specialised displays, such as the figure-of-eight dance of the peacock, and the release of chemicals called 'pheromones' to stimulate the ritual behaviour of the opposite sex. But as mating, back to back, cannot take place until the female settles, courtship may be a lengthy affair, involving a lot of fluttering, perching, jerky body movements and wing stroking, depending on the species.

The fertile female then responds to the stimulus of seeking a host plant on which to lay her eggs. The detection of the correct food plant is by its chemical nature, for experiments have shown how a female can be persuaded to lay her eggs on the wrong plant treated with the appropriate chemical stimulant.

AUTUMN LEAVES

When in full leaf the shrubs and trees of the hedgerow lose a great deal of water by evaporation through the leaves. But this loss is replaced as the roots take up the water from the soil. When the ground is frozen, the roots are unable to draw up water, so deciduous trees shed their leaves in autumn to prevent water loss in winter. (Evergreen conifers are hardly ever seen in hedgerows and gardens, and although they do shed their leaves throughout the year, they are never bare-branched because their narrow needle-like leaves have a thick outer skin and a small number of pores. In winter, species such as pine are able to reduce this loss even further by rolling their leaves inwards along their length and conserving what little water is available.)

Just before the trees and shrubs shed their leaves, the hedgerow is a cascade of colours. Leaves are turning shades of yellow, orange, red and brown, their intensity varying not only from one species to another, but also among the trees and individual leaves of the same species. The colours emerge when the leaves cease to produce chlorophyll – which gives them their green colours – in response to the decreasing daylight hours of autumn. Now the leaf pigments that were previously masked show through. A combination of warm autumn days and very cold nights seems to produce the best colours, but the apparent brilliance may well be the effect of bright light from above and shade from below. Among the most brilliant of the autumn hedgerow hues are the amber of the field maple and crimson of the guelder rose; the scarlet berries of hawthorn, rose and guelder rose add to the cacophony of colours. The red fruits of the rowan are more prominent in late summer when the tree is still in leaf.

HEDGEROW BIRDS IN WINTER

In winter cold increases energy requirements, but food becomes hard to find and can no longer support the density of the bird population that has built up to a peak at the end of summer. Migration is essential for the survival of some species of birds breeding in the hedgerow, including the cuckoo, spotted flycatcher and warblers which make long-distance journeys southward to Africa for winter, and return in spring to the same area where they were reared. For these populations migration is part of the yearly pattern of their lives. Flight has to be timed with great accuracy, for lingering too long in autumn or returning too early in spring may be a risk to survival. Night journeys are favoured by many small migrants, which use the stars and the earth's magnetic field to guide them. Prior to departure the birds feed avidly to build up reserves of up to twice their normal body weight, accumulating subcutaneous layers of fat to fuel their flights. The effects of drought, while having devastating effects on the African peoples, is also beginning to affect some of our migratory bird populations. For example, the numbers of common whitethroat have dropped considerably since their wintering area in the savannah region of the Sahel has been severely affected. To fuel their return journey to Britain saltbush (*Salvadora*) fruits are very important, but this shrub cannot survive prolonged drought.

It may seem extraordinary how migratory birds return in spring to the same site where they previously bred or were reared. Chris Mead, of the British Trust for Ornithology, has found birds returning to the same nest where they were ringed the previous year. Such accuracy, he claims, is achieved by memorising landmarks, and for young birds the period in autumn between reaching independence and flying south is the crucial learning period when the birds explore the area to which they will return to breed.

The migratory arrivals in autumn find the British winter more tolerable than those of their breeding grounds further north. In the hedgerows and fields near the shores of Britain hungry and exhausted redwings, fieldfares, bramblings and goldcrests can be seen feeding greedily to replace the energy consumed in their flights across the sea.

The recent severe winters in Britain have certainly taken their toll on our resident birds, which attempt to cope with the perils of the season in various ways. Most birds manage to maintain a fat reserve, which can be drawn upon as well as insulating their bodies from the cold. The shorter daylight hours reduce the time that can be spent searching for food, so birds spend most of the day feeding; for instance, blue tits feed for 85 per cent of the daylight hours. A heavy snowfall makes it impossible for ground-feedings birds to feed, so instead of wasting energy in a fruitless search they may not even attempt to do so, but instead continue roosting with their feathers fluffed up for extra insulation. Usually solitary birds, such as the wren, change their behaviour remarkably in winter, congregating in flocks and roosting communally to keep themselves warm. Last winter (1985–6) there was a report of seventy-five wrens seen entering one small nestbox to huddle together. Many hedgerow birds leave their summer territories to congregate in autumn and winter flocks. Flocking enables young birds to learn from others where the best food sources are to be found in winter, although older birds dominate and steal from them. Also, many pairs of eyes are able to keep a better watch on approaching predators, who are also hungry at this time of the year.

Coal tits, jays and rooks have learnt to store their food; coal tits hide aphids, beechmast and slugs, and jays and rooks bury acorns. Great tits and blue tits, however, save themselves the effort of storing but instead search out and rob the stores of other birds.

HIBERNATION

The response of many animals to the cold weather and scarcity of food in winter is to hibernate. All hedgerow mammals become lethargic and spend long periods in the shelter of their nests and burrows, but the hedgehog, bat and dormouse slip into a torpid state, so that heart and pulse and breathing rates are so low that they require only a minimal amount of energy to be maintained. The body temperature then drops to match that of the surroundings, while fat, fur, warm nesting material or huddling together serve as insulation.

Before an animal goes into hibernation it has to eat plenty of food to accumulate fat to be drawn on during the long months it is at rest. Its body weight may be increased by one third in autumn. Only the dormouse truly hibernates; its state of torpidity usually lasts uninterrupted from October to April, so this creature may emerge from hibernation with only half its normal body weight. Bats and hedgehogs may interrupt their sleep with short periods of activity. They may wake up when it gets too cold simply to look for a better place to settle, though 'partial arousal' itself increases the temperature of the nest as the creature's body heat is raised with relative activity. But they are more likely to leave their nests and roosts in search of food. While the omnivorous hedgehogs may be able to balance the food they are able to find with the body fuel burned in their expedition, bats have little hope of catching insects to replace the energy they waste, possibly reducing their resources to an inadequate level for survival.

Amphibians and reptiles bury themselves away from the effects of the winter

THE HEDGEROW
HUNTING
GROUND

RIGHT The hedgehog is
omnivorous and its spines offer
it some protection against larger
predators. BELOW The bank vole
must be constantly alert for
predators for it is a favourite
prey of owls, hawks and foxes
whose numbers will increase
when voles are plentiful.

ABOVE The caterpillars of the yellow-tail tussock moth can be found in such numbers as to damage the hedgerow shrubs on which they feed. The caterpillars hibernate through winter when still young and are brightly coloured and covered with hairs which are irritants to predators.

BELOW Puss moth larvae can be found on the leaves of hedgerow willows. When threatened by predators they adopt a menacing posture, raising their forked tails and displaying their red collars.

AUTUMN AND WINTER IN THE HEDGEROW

ABOVE The brilliant berries of the woody nightshade help to colour the hedgerow in autumn. TOP RIGHT The bramble continues flowering into the autumn, while rose hips are already ripening. CENTRE RIGHT The white bryony displays its attractive but poisonous red and white berries in autumn. BOTTOM RIGHT The berries of the rowan are displayed in late summer, attracting large numbers of thrushes.

LEFT The robin defends its territory in winter and proclaims its ownership loudly in spring. BELOW A Nidderdale hedgerow in winter.

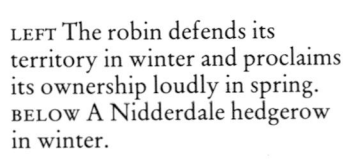

The hedgehog seeks a cosy hibernation place in the foot of the hedge or a disused rabbit burrow.

frost, their metabolisms only just working, but they do not freeze, for as a protection against the cold, some sugar in their blood is converted to glycerol which works rather like an antifreeze in car radiators. Invertebrates that live for more than a few months in their adult stage also produce this antifreeze, such as the peacock, tortoiseshell, comma and brimstone butterflies; some moths; bees; wasps; and the ladybirds, among others. During their inactive state, cold-blooded creatures consume minimal energy, so they can survive without further food. The majority of invertebrate adults, however, have short life spans and are more likely to have experienced winter earlier in their life spans in the inactive egg or chrysalis stages. Snow can be a good insulator for animals tucked in underground. Air is trapped beneath the snow, raising the temperature of the ground below the snow by a few degrees and keeping out the extra chilling effect of the wind.

TRACKS AND SIGNS

In winter, when the hedgerow is bare of foliage, it is certainly easier to spot any moving wildlife. However at a hedgerow bereft of any visible movement there may still be all sorts of tracks and signs of life and following prints in fresh snow may reveal something of the animals' activity. Some signs are very simple, such as worm casts, mole hills, rabbit burrows, droppings, feathers or tufts of fur. Others may be less common, but are also unmistakable, such as a badger's earthworks and slides, a thrush's anvil, nibbled nut shells, stripped pine cones, and in an abandoned bird's nest, which is now very easy to spot, there may be a little mammal curled up asleep, or even a cache of food. Meal remains disclosing the presence of birds of prey may enable identification, such as pellets disgorged by a roosting owl or feathers plucked by a sparrowhawk before the prey bird has been eaten.

A fresh moderate snowfall touched by frost reveals all sorts of tracks. Many mammals have regular trails, and those using hedgerows as sheltered highways may now be revealed by their footprints. Following the trail of a rabbit may reveal where it has stopped to nibble at bark, and a fox's trail may reveal where it has made a kill. A fox pounces on its victim and the place where it smacked down on the creature may be shown up in the snow. Bird tracks are also familiar. A pigeon walks with its toes turned in. Small birds hop along and leave a trail of parallel footprints. Where birds have landed or become airborne, wing tip and tail prints also show up. As many hedgerow animals are difficult to observe, a lot of information can be gleaned from their tracks and signs, which builds up a picture of activities and life in the hedgerow in winter.

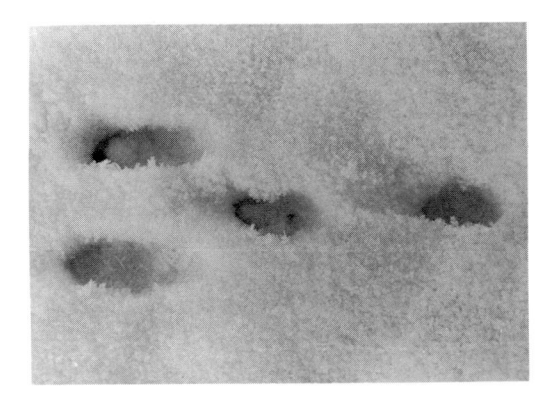

The hedge-foot tracks of the rabbit are unmistakable, with the small, staggered prints of the front paws and the larger depressions made by the hind legs.

THE LAST LINK

Life and death are the inseparable features of the hedgerow year. We may marvel at the beauty of the butterfly and become absorbed in the behaviour and antics of the hedgerow creatures above ground; but beneath the soil there is a vast army of 'decomposers', which convert the amorphous organic residue of rotting plant material and animal carcasses to nutrients available for plant growth. While representing an essential connection in the hedgerow food web above the ground, these creatures form a complex food web in the soil; one group consumes plant litter, another group consumes the by-products of the first (and third) group, while a third group preys on the first two and scavenges on animal matter (and is in turn preyed upon by ground-feeding creatures above the soil). The first group includes creatures such as earthworms, slugs, snails, woodlice, millipede and springtails, while microscopic bacteria (and fungi) feed on their by-products. (A small spoonful of dry soil from a hedgerow habitat may contain twice as many soil bacteria as there are people in the world.) But the most gruesomely fascinating creatures are members of the predator and scavenger group and include the ground-feeding spiders (p. 177) false scorpion, common centipede and many beetle species.

The black and orange sexton beetles are more aptly also known as grave-digging beetles, because of their habit of burying dead animals as a foodstore for their offspring. These beetles fly well and can pick up the scent of a decaying carcass up to 2 miles (3 km) away if the wind is in the right direction. The carcass tackled is usually that of a small mammal or bird, and is buried where it lies. The mating pair dig a shaft below the dead mammal or bird and drag it down. The skin and feathers are rolled off the body as it is pulled into the shaft. The female then lays her eggs in a chamber in the shaft and remains with them to protect them against predators and parasites until they hatch. Any parasitic or other creatures, such as maggots, that are already on the carcass, are eaten by the parent beetle. The mother first feeds her offspring when they hatch on partially digested pieces of carcass. The rapidly developing larvae are then helped into the rotting flesh by the female, which bites an entry hole. She will finally leave them when they can cope independently.

While fungus mycelium is present in soil throughout the year, this becomes obvious only when the fruiting bodies form, and temperature and moisture to create the right humid conditions are important determining factors. It is the saprophytic species (that is, those utilising dead or decaying organic matter) that play a vital role in decomposition and those that can commonly be found in the leaf litter in hedgerow habitats include the spectacular St George's mushroom in spring, the shaggy inkcap from late spring to autumn and the common puff ball from July onwards. Parasitic species which fruit on living trees and shrubs may also be present, such as the massive caps of the bracket fungus on the trunks of mature trees and the honey fungus on trees and shrubs. There may also be an array of parasitic rusts and moulds.

The shaggy ink cap fungus can often be seen on hedgerow verges on chalky soils, where it 'feeds' on decaying plant matter.

·14·

EXPLORING A HEDGEROW

Each hedge has its own particular history and natural history, and each is a worthwhile subject for study. There is no such thing as a 'typical' hedge – a fact ensured by all the variations in origin, planting, management and environment that we have described. In this chapter we explore a hedgerow that has provided us with plenty of interest. We do not pretend that it is exemplary of hedges in other parts of the country, but the study does suggest some of the possibilities, problems, surprises and interest which could emerge if – and, we hope, when – the reader explores one of his or her favourite local hedgerows in more detail.

Let us first look at the hedge in its historical and environmental context, for these factors are sure to be proclaimed in its content and character. In fact, technically, we are exploring four hedgerows, those on either side of two old lanes. Having already rejected the theory of hedgerow-dating, we cannot therefore say how old our hedges are, and are obliged to assume that they might be as old as the lanes that they border. The two lanes form a 'V'-shape and join on the outskirts of the medieval wood and deer park of Ripley, North Yorkshire. The flanks of Nidderdale, North Yorkshire, are patterned with old lanes, several of which are probably prehistoric in origin. One lane runs westwards from the deer park to Clint, a linear hamlet of mainly modern houses which occupies the site of a deserted medieval village (whose cross and stocks are still preserved). Clint is first mentioned in 1315 and is likely to have been founded by the de Clint family, who moved here from Swaledale late in the previous century. This lane must be at least of medieval date, though it could be much older.

The second lane, running south-westwards from the deer park, has a more tantalising history. It forms part of the Nidderdale Way, though this is a modern concoction. If we mentally project the alignment of the lane across the Nidd valley south-westwards for a distance of about 4 miles (6.4 km), then we see that it lines up with an arrow-straight section of 'living' Roman road, part of the route from Ilkley to Aldborough. There is no doubt that this road originally crossed the Nidd at or near Hampsthwaite bridge, about ¼ mile (0.4 m) from the end of our lane, and as the Roman road proceeded towards Aldborough it must have approximated to the line of the lane. Moreover, the track which runs from the terminus of our lane, through the wood and deer park, is paved with stone slabs and is thought by many to be the Roman road. The lane is not straight, though this would not disqualify it from being Roman. We suspect, however, that in Dark Age times the real section of Roman road here became neglected and overgrown and that our lane only roughly preserves its alignment. In one place, and for no apparent reason, the lane makes a sharp dogleg. The only sensible explanation is that here it was diverting around something – perhaps a homestead or the corner of a field – that is no longer visible. In any event this modest little lane had considerable importance during at least one phase of history, for on one of John Ogilby's famous route maps of 1675 it is shown to be forming part of the main road between York and Lancaster. This is hard to believe today for you almost feel that with arms outstretched the fingertips would touch the hedges on either side of the well-worn track. In summer they actually can. All this is written to suggest that the best hope of dating a hedgerow comes from studying the history of the countryside of which it is a part. Our lanes are at least of medieval dates and could be much older. Their hedges might be as old as they are.

Our hedges are at heights of about 225–325 feet (70–100 m) above sea level; the bedrock is of carboniferous gritstone covered with a smearing of locally derived glacial boulder clay. Given the somewhat acid soils and northerly location we cannot expect to find any of the jewels of the southern hedgerows, like guelder rose, wayfaring tree, clematis or wild service tree. Hedges in the surrounding fields are plainly younger, and generally in a poorer state of health.

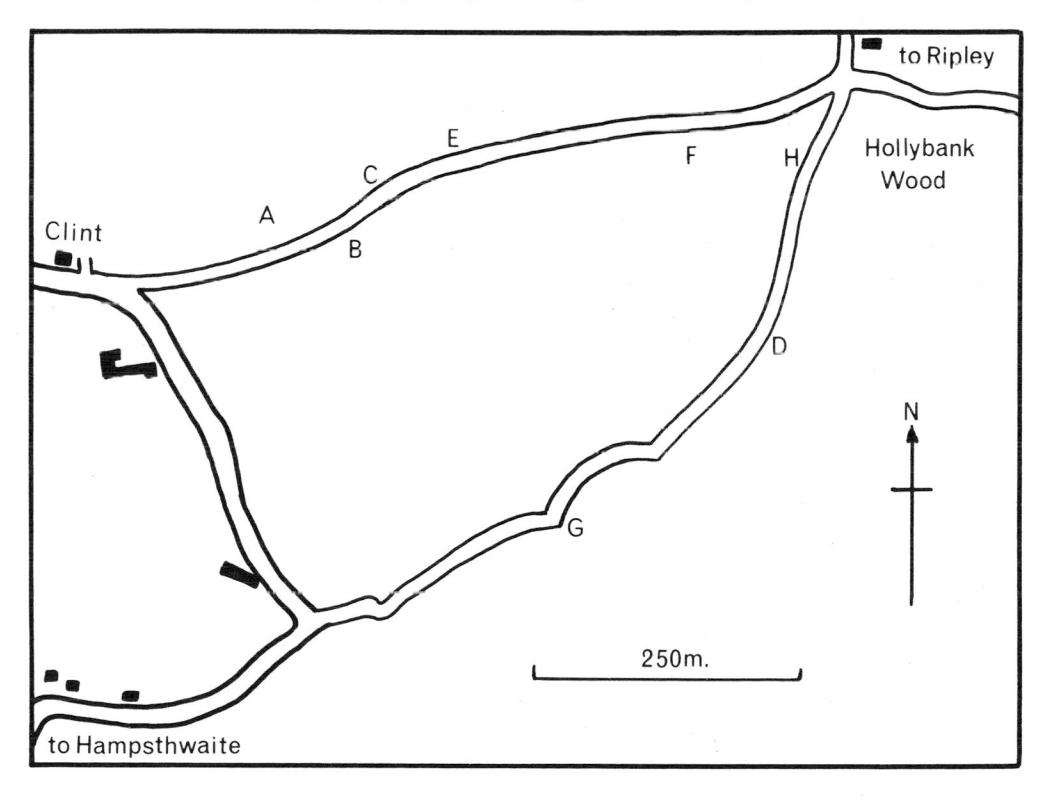

They are hawthorn Parliamentary Enclosure hedges and date from the 1770s. The fields that they bound are pastures grazed by Friesian cattle, and the re-seeding of the grazings with rye grass has removed the old plant communities and given a special value to those surviving on the hedgerow verges.

Joining our first lane at Clint the first feature of note is a tiny, open wood with a few hawthorn and dead elms and some fine field maples which stand about 40 ft (12 m) tall and so must be flourishing here. Surely then our hedges will be packed with field maple like the grand old hedges of southern England? In fact, although we explore more than three miles of hedgerow there is not a single hedge field maple to be found, in spite of the excellent opportunities for colonisation provided by this grove at point A. It is interesting and puzzling that of the trees which grow as standard timber trees hereabouts only elm – the standards now all diseased – have had much success in colonising the hedges. Oak, ash and elm stand as old hedgerow trees, beech grows in directly adjacent plantations and there are a few hornbeams providing an available source of seed in nearby Ripley wood. But like the field maple, the beech and hornbeam have completely failed to enter the hedges and both oak and ash are poorly represented, though they have had ample time to do so. Indeed, there are plenty of less venerable hedges that are packed with field maple, oak and ash.

The complete survey shows that the hedges have a fairly consistent character and that the essential framework of species consists of hawthorn, blackthorn, holly and elm with moderate amounts of hazel, crab apple, dog and field rose, honeysuckle, bittersweet and bramble, and elder exploits various gaps that have appeared.

Our second point of interest comes at B, where a section of old hedgerow has been removed to accommodate a narrow little lane-side plantation of beech and ash. The plantation is bounded by a hedge which is plainly of a younger and different character. Judging by the sizes of the trees in the plantation the feature

One of our hedged lanes approaching Ripley Wood; the second lane runs off to the right beside the gate.

will be about 40 to 70 years old and its hawthorn hedge has so far only been lightly colonised by elder, sycamore and bramble. Further down the lane there is a similar plantation with beech and a horse chestnut, its young hedge harbouring just the odd rose and elder.

Our first surprise, apart from the absence of field maple in the hedges, appeared at C. The first survey was done during the May of the very late spring of 1986 and here we were puzzled by a 'strange' shrub with bursting buds. It provides a warning of the danger of preconceptions – I had been hoping and half expecting to find dogwood and thought that I had. Nina said 'no' – and comparison with our garden hedge specimen proved her right. In fact the source of the controversy was bird cherry, normally a woodland-edge shrub of the northern woods. Further along our way, at D, a low and well-watered stretch of hedgerow is actually dominated by bird cherry, with goat willow, hazel and blackthorn as neighbours, demonstrating the way that subtle environmental differences are reflected in an old hedgerow. Here the bird cherry is actively invading both hedge and lane, spreading by the rooting of the tips of downward-growing branches.

Although there is little excuse for the wrong identification of shrubs in full leaf or in blossom, surveys done in springtime can produce mistakes unless each shrub is carefully inspected. Here are examples of some pitfalls: with catkins gone and leaves opening, hazel can easily be confused with elm; the shiny young leaves of crab apple can be mistaken for blackthorn, for in the closely trimmed hedge there may be no distinctive blossom to ease identification; ash and oak are relatively late in coming into leaf and may be overlooked if neighbouring plants are in leaf.

Next to our first bird cherry specimen is a 19-yd (17 m) stretch of pure elm hedge; then we find a solitary goat willow and then 24 yds (22 m) of pure elm. This does not reflect the original planting of the hedge but the common phenomenon of elm invasion, all other shrubs in the hedge community having been evicted by the slow but relentless advance of the elm. Our hedges also contain other invasive species: bird cherry already mentioned has excluded other shrubs from two 8-yd (7 m) and one 6-yd (5.5 m) long stretches; holly absolutely dominates several stretches of hedge including pure holly stretches of 12, 16 and 23 yds (11, 15 and 21 m), while blackthorn has also achieved total mastery of a few lengths, including ones of 13 and 30 yds (12 and 27 m).

All this is bad news for the hedgerow-dating enthusiast. More bad news is provided by the clear evidence of replanting. Different stretches of the hedges – two of about 30 yds (27 m) in length, one of 50 yds (46 m) and one of 90 yds (82 m) – have plainly been replanted, using hawthorn, relatively recently. This is easily seen by the absence of other shrubs, the youthful appearance of the hawthorn and the survival of the protective field-side fencing which was erected to protect the young thorns against grazing. This replanting must have taken place in post-war times – but how could we have recognised replanting from previous centuries and how much of our hedges, if any part, has escaped replanting at one time or another?

When studying a hedge it is vital to continue the work through different seasons. In late spring and summer the presence of blossom and leaves greatly

The old York to Lancaster road in spring (ABOVE) and (RIGHT) the same stretch of lane seen from the opposite direction in midsummer, now almost completely overgrown.

aid identification, but other things can be missed. Because we were able to study our hedges before their bases were masked by herbage we were able to see that a long stretch of hedgerow running eastwards from G was actually growing upon a partly buried wall and one 90-yard (82 m) section of hawthorn had actually been replanted atop the buried wall. Some of the wall-top hedge was old, so how old was the wall that it has so completely colonised – and had the wall itself been built to replace a still older hedge?

The lack of field maple and bird cherry provided our first surprises; the next was met at F with the discovery of a hedgerow rowan, and a second specimen was found at G. A further surprise came at H, where a number of gooseberry plants had secured a niche in the hedgerow. These seem to be true wild gooseberry plants rather than garden escapees; there is just one habitation nearby, and that is about 100 yards (91 m) away.

To summarise, our survey shows that in this particular location the mature hedge contains holly, elm, hawthorn and blackthorn in abundance. Rose, bramble and hazel are well represented and crab apple, goat willow, bird cherry, rowan, gooseberry, honeysuckle and bittersweet occur in places. Oak and ash are much less frequent than one would expect, while beech, field maple, hornbeam and horse chestnut all exist as potential colonists but have proved quite impotent in this role; and gean, which would have seemed a much more likely constituent than bird cherry, is absent. Although the hedges generally are

quite rich in species, if one bears in mind the unavailability of more southerly hedgerow species – spindle, wayfaring tree and so on – they contain numerous single-species stretches. These are in some cases the products of invasion by elm, blackthorn, holly and bird cherry and in others the result of recent replanting with hawthorn.

Given the rather poor conditions of the adjacent Parliamentary Enclosure hedges, the lane-side hedges provide the dense cover essential to hedgerow-nesting birds. Starlings, blue tits, great tits and tawny owls utilise the hedgerow standards and song thrush, robin, blackbird, chaffinch, dunnock, wren and yellowhammer nest in the hedges. Although rye-grass monoculture prevails in the surrounding fields, curlew are still nesting there and the hedgerow verges provide a refuge for the traditional flora. Species surviving here include dog's mercury, dandelion, cow parsley, sweet cicely, greater stitchwort, celandine, ground ivy, wood avens, bluebell, hedge woundwort, red and white clover, crosswort, stinging nettle, red and white dead nettle, foxglove, hardheads, cotton and creeping thistle, bush vetch, meadow vetchling, red campion, arum, bracken, dock, and in the damper patches – for there are stretches of ditch, one with permanent water – meadowsweet, common sedge and great and rosebay willow herb.

To get an impression of how the somewhat acidic nature of the soils was affecting the composition of our hedge we travelled just four miles to look at a mile of hedges on the sweeter soils of Magnesian limestone, near Burton Leonard. Here the hedges contain field maple (in abundance), hawthorn, blackthorn, elm, elder, sycamore, holly, crab apple, hazel, dog rose, field rose and burnet rose, honeysuckle, black bryony, goat willow, crab apple, ash, bramble and snowberry. Although the hedges studied here are probably slightly younger than those already described, the lime-rich soil does seem to support a more varied community of shrubs. Sycamore and elder are much more in evidence, perhaps because at some previous stage gaps had been allowed to develop. Although purging buckthorn was not found and is rare even in the limestone area, it does occur in a nearby quarry and in two other hedges close by. The snowberry could well have been artificially introduced as game cover, while the burnet rose is a treasure of the northern limestone hedgerows.

Our hedges have some surprises but a shrub and flora content which reflects their northerly setting. In the previous year one of the authors explored three old hedges at the other end of England, in Chiddingstone parish, Kent. The list of shrubs in these hedges presents a useful comparison: field maple, dogwood, hazel, Midland, common and hybrid hawthorn, ivy, honeysuckle, broom, spindle, ash, dog rose, gean, field rose, bird cherry, blackthorn, wild service tree, yew, holly, bullace, oak, elm and goat willow. These hedges were growing on neutral soils, while hedges studied on Cambridgeshire chalk included both hawthorns, blackthorn, spindle, dogwood, wayfaring tree, guelder rose, clematis, white and black bryony, wild privet, bramble, dog and field rose, ash and elm. Some hedgebanks we examined on the sweet red soils of Devon were found to be dominated by elm, probably both planted and invading, and to be rich in species, with field maple and hawthorn quite well represented along with all of the commoner hedgerow trees, plus a little beech.

·15·

FAREWELL TO HEDGEROWS?

The hedgerow network of Britain developed over thousands of years, along with the man-made landscapes of which hedges were often such a vital component. The countryside patterns were always in a state of evolution. Sometimes the transformations were minimal, at other times, in places, they could be quite revolutionary. There were periods where the hedgerow patterns formed an intricate tracery, so that, when seen from treetop height, the scenery from horizon to horizon would seem to be sectioned by an interminable sequence of twining green barriers. But there were also other periods when the local farming settings were reorganised and when folk with spades and mattocks hacked out more open vistas. Hedgerows came and hedgerows went, but it seems likely that most parts of Britain were quite heavily hedged from at least Iron Age times onwards. Today, however, the hedgerow web has become broken and tattered, and we must wonder whether the damage will ever be made good, and wonder too whether we belong to the last generation which will ever be able to enjoy the most characteristic of English scenes.

In times gone by, the patterns of farming were determined by need and the current notions of good husbandry. Almost invariably these simple stimuli resulted in the creation or perpetuation of lovely, vibrant and finely detailed countrysides. Today, the real needs of the populace seem to have little influence over agriculture, and good husbandry is sacrificed on the altar of quick profit. Let us not romanticise the past; at times when the countryside looked its best the social conditions in the land were loathsome. The English landscape came to its glorious maturity in Victorian times, when children were being worked to death on farms and in factories. During the heyday of the Enclosure era a youth could be executed for stealing a pie from a cottage windowsill, and lovely woods concealed mantraps which would maim the starving poacher or kill a wandering infant. Even so, we would argue that the best commentary on our shabby, unprincipled modern society will not be found in the pages of an erudite journal but can be seen written large across the face of the land in the course of a typical country walk. If this society allows its heritage of scenery and wildlife to be pillaged by the city slicker, the money-grubbing barley baron, the bent councillor, the self-seeking politician, the idiot planner and the half-

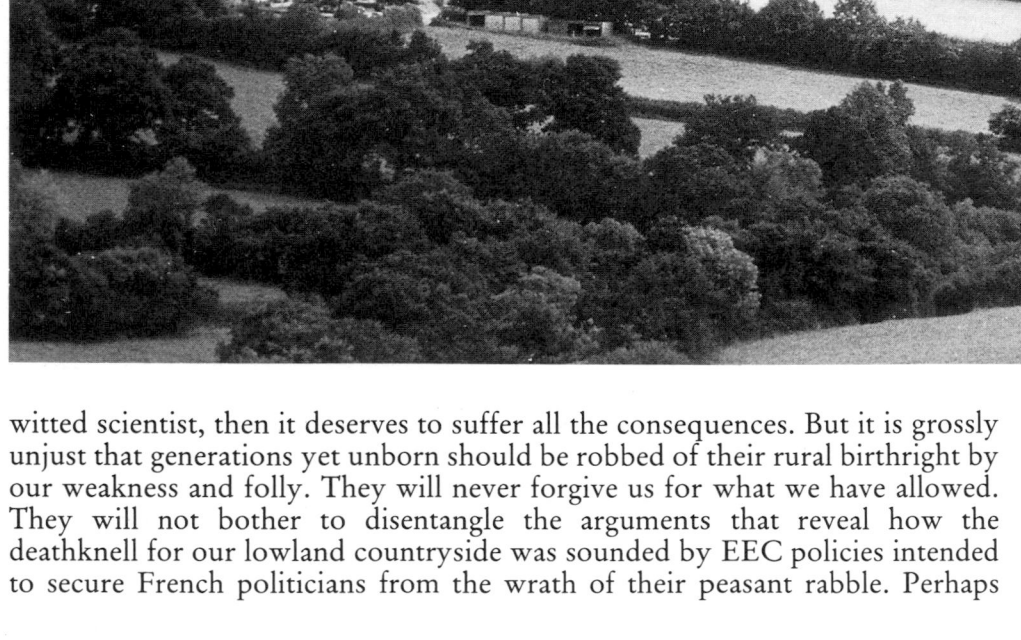

witted scientist, then it deserves to suffer all the consequences. But it is grossly unjust that generations yet unborn should be robbed of their rural birthright by our weakness and folly. They will never forgive us for what we have allowed. They will not bother to disentangle the arguments that reveal how the deathknell for our lowland countryside was sounded by EEC policies intended to secure French politicians from the wrath of their peasant rabble. Perhaps

Is not hedged countryside like this surviving expanse below Dumpdon hillfort in Devon more worthy of preservation than any finance-gobbling stately home?

they will recognise us only as a pawnshop society, selling off the heirlooms for ready silver, too selfish and demoralised to contemplate the future and too corrupted to consider the common good.

Road building, mining, airfield construction and urban expansion have been responsible for some hedgerow losses, but these losses are small in comparison to the devastation wrought by modern farming. The deliberate destruction of hedges is substantially, though not entirely, a phenomenon of the post-1945 era. However, in the arable eastern counties, where the gaunt and lifeless prairie fields provide a more universal vision of the future, a considerable amount of hedgerow destruction took place in the inter-war period and can be recognised on early air photographs. In Britain generally, the decades before the 1939–45 war witnessed a quite severe agricultural depression. As a result hedges were often neglected. A benefit of this neglect was the fact that many trees grew up freely from the hedgerows, so that the post-war countryside seems to have contained many more hedgerow trees than did the Victorian setting. But a penalty of the neglect of laying and general hedgerow maintenance was the deterioration in the condition and stock-proof qualities of so many hedges. Now, when one peers into the base of a typical hedge it is plain from the gnarled and gross appearance of the angular timbers that laying has not been attempted for perhaps seven decades.

Until very recently estimates of hedgerow losses were uncertain and debatable, but in the course of the 1980s information which is much more precise and

In the Vale of Taunton Deane large rents in the hedgerow mesh show where farmers have adopted a prairie field policy.

reliable has become available. In 1984 a House of Lords committee was told that Britain has lost a quarter of its hedgerows, amounting to 126,000 miles (202,778 km) of hedges since 1945. If this 'guesstimate' is correct, then the removal of hedgerows in the post-war period has been proceeding on average at a rate more than 50 per cent greater than the planting of hedges during the Parliamentary Enclosure era. However, any national average rate of hedgerow destruction masks the considerable local inequalities. In Norfolk, for example, a county as yet less despoiled than its neighbours, about half of the hedges had gone by 1970, and now four-fifths of Norfolk's old hedges are said to have been lost.

The destruction of hedgerows was thought to have been at its peak in the 1960s, when there were still plenty of hedges to be removed. Between 1963 and 1966 the British Trust for Ornithology, during its Common Bird Census, examined 29 sample areas, each about 200 acres (80 ha) in extent. It was deduced that the average rate of hedgerow removal then was 1.1 yds (1 m) per acre per year. In Huntingdonshire, however, M. D. Hooper and his associates found a 1963–5 average of 5.1 yds (4.7 m) per acres per year, which lay within a 1946–68 average of 1.08 yds (0.99 m) per acre per year. This average was much lower than its peak component because the 1946–68 level was a less drastic 0.55 yds (0.5 m) per acre per year rate of hedgerow destruction. At the end of 1968 Dr Hooper reported to a symposium on hedges and hedgerow trees that his figures implied 'that hedges are being removed from the country as a whole at a rate somewhere between 7,000 and 14,000 miles (11,265 and 22,530 km) each year. Even if the lower rate was assumed, should the process be maintained the last hedge in England would be grubbed up in the winter of 2049 AD.' In the following year the Nature Conservancy looked at a small range of samples and guessed that the rate of removal in 1962–66 may only have been 3,500 miles (5,633 km) per year. Also, it was found that government grants were being paid for the removal of 750 miles (1,207 km) of hedgerow each year – scenic carnage paid for by the unwitting taxpayer. If the 1984 estimate, quoted above, is correct then the average rate of hedgerow destruction since 1945 would be 3,150 miles (5,069 km) per year, suggesting that the peak 1960s rate of removal was closer to Dr Hooper's minimum figure; but more recent information suggests a rate of hedgerow destruction which has accelerated to a rate of 4,000 miles per year in the 1980s.

In 1984 the Nature Conservancy Council, in its report *Nature Conservation in Great Britain*, explained that: 'By using air photographs, it has been estimated that, of around 500,000 miles of hedge existing in England and Wales in 1946–7, some 140,000 miles had been removed by 1974; and all but 20,000 miles of this loss was attributable to farming.' The most up-to-date information available at the time of writing derives from research on 'Monitoring Landscape Change' produced by the Countryside Commission and Hunting Technical Services. This estimates that the absolute length of hedgerows in England and Wales was reduced by about 190,000 miles, or 22 per cent, during the survey period 1947–85. This new research reveals an actual acceleration in the rate of hedgerow loss from about 2,600 miles per year during the early part of the survey period to about 4,000 miles per year in the 1980s, with the greatest recent losses in East Anglia and the East Midlands. The absolute lengths of hedgerows in England and Wales were estimated as follows:

1947	1969	1980	1985
495,000 miles	437,000 miles	406,000 miles	386,000 miles

In 1974 the Countryside Commission presented the results of investigations into seven widely scattered study areas. In the Leighton Bromswold area of the former county of Huntingdonshire it was found that 39 per cent of hedges and 80 per cent of hedgerow trees had been lost in the periods 1945–72 and 1947–72 respectively. At Preston-on-Wye in Herefordshire the figures for losses of hedgerows and hedgerow trees were 9 and 18 per cent – though the rates of destruction would seem to have increased considerably in Herefordshire in more recent times. In Myton-on-Swale in Yorkshire the area had lost 14 per cent of its hedges and 35 per cent of hedgerow trees, but most of the surviving hedges were too severely trimmed to be of much interest to man, bird or beast. Grandborough in Warwickshire seemed to present a more comforting picture, with only a 7 per cent loss of hedgerows, though here Dutch elm disease and the introduction of wire-fenced paddock grazings were anticipated. The sixth study area was that of Prickwillow in the Cambridgeshire Fenland, an area where trees and hedges have been rare through historical times. Crewkerne in Somerset completed the sample. Here 14 per cent of hedges and 70 per cent of hedgerow trees had been lost during the period studied, and the consultants predicted that coming years would see the loss of all the remaining hedgerow trees and a considerable further loss of hedges.

Crewkerne is an interesting study area, for a decade after the hedgerow study was made there was another investigation here, this time of soil erosion, which was conducted by two researchers of the Soil Survey of England and Wales. Some forty fields between Crewkerne and Yeovil were chosen randomly and monitored for soil erosion. The average soil loss from fields under winter cereal crops was 4.2 tonnes per hectare, though two of the fields monitored lost a staggering 11 and 21 tonnes of soil from every hectare. Doubtless the farmers whose fields were shedding soil at these stupendous rates had followed all the advice proferred by modern agricultural scientists – perhaps the very same scientists who have claimed that hedgerows have no value in the reduction of soil erosion. With talents which are no doubt comparable to those of the scientists who designed the nuclear masterpieces at Sellafield (Windscale) and Chernobyl, perhaps the agricultural scientists will explain the remarkable coincidence of hedgelines and massive lynchets of stabilised soil. What can the answer be? When these peculiarly gifted boffins have solved this riddle, perhaps their brainpower can be directed to explaining why cattle apparently seem often to be seen sheltering from cold winds beside hedgerows – a tantalising question since the experts have already disparaged the hedge as an effective shelter for stock.

In 1983 Richard Westmacott and Tom Worthington returned to the seven study areas and compiled a report of their 'second look'. Although it was found that the pace of destruction had slowed, a continuing deterioration of the

In this featureless area near Cambridge, suburban expansion and motorways have devoured farmland, but the worst scenic destruction has been wrought by hedgerow removal.

landscape was worrying. There has been a severe further removal of hedgerows in Warwickshire, where the devastation of hedgerow trees by elm disease and the removal of the dead elms had been accompanied by the grubbing-up of hedgerows. In the Huntingdonshire area 20 per cent of the hedges surviving in 1972 had been removed, with roadside hedges being particularly vulnerable. Here repeated severe trimming, the use of herbicides and stubble-burning had caused more destruction than the actual grubbing-up of hedges. Dorset, Somerset and Herefordshire also showed a deterioration in the quality of the surviving hedges. The authors reported that:

In many arable areas, hedges are given a close trim annually, starting with accessible roadside hedges from early July, continuing with internal hedges from mid-July after the rape harvest, finishing in mid-September before corn drilling makes them inaccessible. As any horticulturalist knows, summer pruning of bushes generally reduces vigour. . . It could be that current maintenance may be gradually sapping hedges' vigour, which over a period will inevitably lead to plant losses.

HEDGES (IMPERIAL)

STUDY AREA	CAMBS. P'WILLOW	HUNTS. L. BROMSWOLD	DORSET P'HINTON	SOMT. CREWKERNE	HEREFS. P-ON-WYE	YORKS. M-ON-SWALE	WARKS. G'BOROUGH
Farming enterprises	intensive arable (vegs, roots, cereals)	extensive arable (cereals, rape)	extensive arable (cereals) & dairying & mixed	dairying, some cereals	general cropping, mixed & dairying	general cropping	cereals & mixed farming
Average field size,							
1945 (acres)	14	19	18	9	11	15	12
1972** (acres)	33	46	21	14	16	19.5	15.5
1983 (acres)	33.5	53.5	25	16	16	21.5	19
Increase in field size, 1972–83 (%)	1.5	16.5	19	14.5	0	10	22.5
Length of hedges* removed:							
1945–72 (feet/acre)	47	37	9	20	19	15	13
1972–83 (feet/acre)	0.5	12	7	6	1	3.5	14
Length of hedges* remaining:							
1972 (feet/acre)	75	58	84.5	125.5	197.5	94.5	166
1983 (feet/acre)	74.5	46	77	119	196	90	152
Length of hedge removed as a % of length of hedge remaining in 1972:	0.5	20.5	8.5	5	0.5	4	8.5
Quality of remaining hedges (% of total on 1–4 scale)		'72 '83	'72 '83	'72 '83	'72 '83	'72 '83	'72 '83
1	n/a	8 4	18 8	28 13	16 13	8 6	5 16
2	n/a	30 30	35 28	47 32	40 26	9 21	23 31
3	n/a	34 46	37 47	16 41	39 52	54 50	45 39
4	n/a	28 20	10 17	9 14	5 9	29 23	27 14

* figures refer to dykes in Cambridgeshire study area
** The 1972 figures differ slightly from those published in *NAL*, since the effect of averaging and then rounding both the 1972 and 1983 field sizes distorts the calculated percentage increase in field size in several study areas.

(*Agricultural Landscapes: A Second Look*, 1984. Reproduced by kind permission of the Countryside Commission.)

The report also found that 'In most study areas the hedgerow tree is gradually disappearing and is not being replaced.'

Why are hedges being destroyed? For countless centuries peasants and farmers, who lived close to the earth and survived or perished according to the wholesomeness and productivity of their lands, devoted considerable time to the quite demanding tasks of ditching and planting and maintaining hedgerows. Were they all fools indulging in a worthless pastime? Two factors have been largely responsible for the demise of the hedgerow: mechanisation and subsidy. Mechanisation has spawned an attitude of mind which has no time for skilled crafts, like hedge laying, which cannot be done by lumbering gadgets; and subsidies have created environments in which crops can be grown irrespective of any real need or real competitive economic justification for growing them.

With the advent of the monstrous machines of modern farming (and the consequent departure of most of the rural labour force) operators have demanded clear straight runs of at least 1,640 feet (500 m) – and hedgerows have been removed to create the vast, empty arenas of mechanised farming. Farm subsidies created artificial economic environments, so that farmers do not have to perservere with the forms of farming which are best suited to their holdings, but can exploit the most lucrative items on the Common Agricultural Policy menu. Thus old mixed farming land has become an exclusive preserve for wheat, barley, beet and oilseed rape. The loss of hedgerows has been greatest on the mixed farming land which has become arable country, in counties like Cambridgeshire, Bedfordshire and Lincolnshire. The traditional pastoral counties of the damper west tended to preserve their hedgerows, but now, just as planted rye grass extinguishes the old herb and wildflower meadows, so there is

These sheep are sheltering from a March gale beside a Yorkshire sheep hedge. Nobody can have told them that 'experts' have decided that hedgerows have no value as windbreaks.

a switch to paddock grazings. Hedgerows are grubbed up to produce vast fields which are subdivided into equally sized paddocks by wire fences. Other factors also affect the patterns of destruction. Old, winding hedges seem to be more vulnerable than straight Parliamentary Enclosure hedges, because they are less amenable to the straight runs demanded by unwieldy modern machines. Owners who are interested in wildlife or partridge shooting are less likely to destroy their hedges, but heaven help the hedgerows on land obtained by a pension fund corporation or development partnership company.

The question of farm subsidies arose before Britain's entry into the EEC, and in 1969 it was estimated that, with subsidies running at the rate of £400 million a year, public money was providing two-thirds of farming's net income. After 1973 there was a meteoric rise in subsidies, and at the time of writing, two-thirds of the EEC budget, or a sum of *£13 billion*, is being consumed each year by the Common Agricultural Policy. Not surprisingly, agriculture has often directed its efforts towards the harvesting of subsidies at any cost to the consumer or the rural setting, resulting in the accumulation of the well-known food mountains. In 1985 over half the UK harvest, amounting to 12 million tonnes of unwanted grain, was taken into EEC stores. The cost of storing the surplus alone amounted to £100 million. Forgetting the incalculable cost of countryside destroyed, it has been estimated that as a direct result of the Common Agricultural Policy, consumers of farm produce pay 15 per cent more for their food than they would if they were free to buy it at prevailing world market prices.

A Lincolnshire soil-blow. The hedgerow has stabilised some of the drifting soil, but the surviving hedges are now too few, too closely cropped and too poorly maintained to do very much good. The picture encapsulates the triumph of modern 'scientific' farming.

By the mid-1980s it had become plain that the cost of agricultural subsidies was unbearable and British politicians were attempting, with scant success, to introduce some sanity into the situation. Over the years, however, agriculture had developed an unusually cosy relationship with successive governments. Although Labour governments had only the smallest levels of voter support in the farming community, successive Labour agriculture ministers were wined and dined, wooed and won by the stupendous National Farmers' Union public relations operation. To the Conservative hierarchy, however, the landowners are 'our kind of people'; farmers provide enormous support for Conservatives in the shire constituencies, often dominating party branches, parish and district councils as well as the committees which select Conservative parliamentary candidates. The contradictions between Conservative policies to state subsidy in general and to state subsidy of affluent farmers were noted by Christopher Hall in *The Countryman* in 1983: 'Paying farmers to do nothing is an odd policy for a government devoted to the work ethic . . .' Even with the adoption of monetarism with the restrictions on public-sector wages, the selling-off of nationalised operations and the denigrating of state subsidies, British farming continued to attract public funds amounting to a total that was greater than the support given to all nationalised industries together. As rail services crumble, shipyards close, universities contract and the health and education services decay, the sums spent on storing *just one year's* grain surplus could be used to build ten new regional hospitals.

As a consequence of agriculture's very special relationship with the political parties an unattractive arrogance has been reinforced within the farming community. In 1984, for example, a spokesman for the National Farmers' Union warned the public in general and conservationists in particular of what would happen if criticisms of farming methods continued: 'Push farmers into a corner with nowhere else to go and they will go for your throat. Rest assured that a significant proportion will get their tractors out and rip up perhaps a grove of orchids, meadowland and hedgerows out of sheer frustration and annoyance.' This threat did not achieve much popular press coverage – though what fun the tabloids would have had if a spokesman of the Football Association had announced that if criticism of football hooligans did not cease then soccer fans would be forced to break more windows and vandalise more telephone kiosks!

By the 1980s it was clear that public opposition to both the level of subsidies and the effects of the agri-business movement on the British countryside had reached a high level. Fears for the future of the countryside permeated all levels of society, and in April 1985 Prince Charles, speaking as the Duke of Cornwall and one of Britain's largest landowners, told a land-use conference in Devon that: 'Food surpluses have gained but the countryside and the nation have been the losers . . . Fascinating places, wetlands, moorlands and hedgerows, have been lost, often in response to greed.'

Given the strength of public opposition to the destruction it may seem surprising that the political action has been so inept and that platitudes have been regarded as adequate substitutes for forceful policies. The answer is that at election times issues like employment, armaments, extremist fringe groups and foreign policy have tended to monopolise the political agenda. Unlike some European countries or American federal states, 'green' parties and pressure groups have not yet made a great impact on British politics and are denied a presence in Parliament by the unusual British electoral system. The message of experience seems to be that politicians will not attempt seriously to protect the landscape heritage until it is apparent that substantial numbers of votes are at stake. Despite the platitudes and sham legislation the horrors have continued. the *Guardian* reports that in 1981 a Kent farmer bought 39 acres of ancient woodland at under £300 an acre. Because the trees were protected by the Preservation Orders they might have seemed safe. In June 1986 however, the Lands Tribunal ruled that Canterbury District Council – in other words the local community – should pay the farmer concerned £46,000 to allow the trees to survive. The woods lay within the Kent Downs Area of Outstanding Natural Beauty and the North Downs Special Landscape area. Impressive titles; empty words. And so other stalwart Kentish farmers have queued up for more of this easy ransom money; but Canterbury, it was reported, cannot gain compensation for protecting the communal heritage and may have to abandon the enforcement of tree preservation orders.

If farmers have been the targets of criticism this is not surprising given the public funds and scenic carnage involved. However, it must be remembered that hedgerows are not natural features, but part of a working field environment. It should also be remembered that there are many conscientious farmers, some who regret their blind faith in Ministry of Agriculture advice and some whose love for the countryside and its wildlife is just as great as that of the conservationists. Plenty of readers will be familiar with the type of barley baron who suddenly arrives to tell you that the footpath you are on has been 'removed'. He usually has a waxed cotton jacket, a flat tweed cap and shares his Range Rover with a dopey labrador called 'Dog'. His hands are soft, his work consists of sessions with his accountant and ordering machine drivers around on a walkie-talkie. He spends his ample spare time shooting pheasants with his identical friends. He is very rich and very nasty.

And there are many other farmers, not all of them welcoming to ramblers, but who are not rich, work hard and do what they can to preserve the look and life of the countryside. Sadly they are a disappearing breed. The rich farmers cream off the subsidies while the poorer tenants find it hard to meet their rising rents or to raise the capital and loans needed to compete with the barley barons. Small family farms are disappearing at an alarming rate, and as they go so too do men with a feeling for the land and a knowledge of country crafts.

Meanwhile a new breed of man emerges. He promises landowners handsome rewards for entering into a partnership agreement designed to cream off the

A historic Cambridgeshire 'drift' or drove photographed just before (TOP LEFT) and just after (TOP RIGHT) the destruction of the bordering hedges in 1984. Before its sudden descent into prairie field anonymity Cuckoo Drift was a place of considerable historic interest. Probably a prehistoric trackway, in the Middle Ages it existed as a hedged road between two sets of open fields, a part of the King's Highway to the Isle of Ely. RIGHT After decades of neglect this Northamptonshire hawthorn row has ceased to function as a hedgerow.

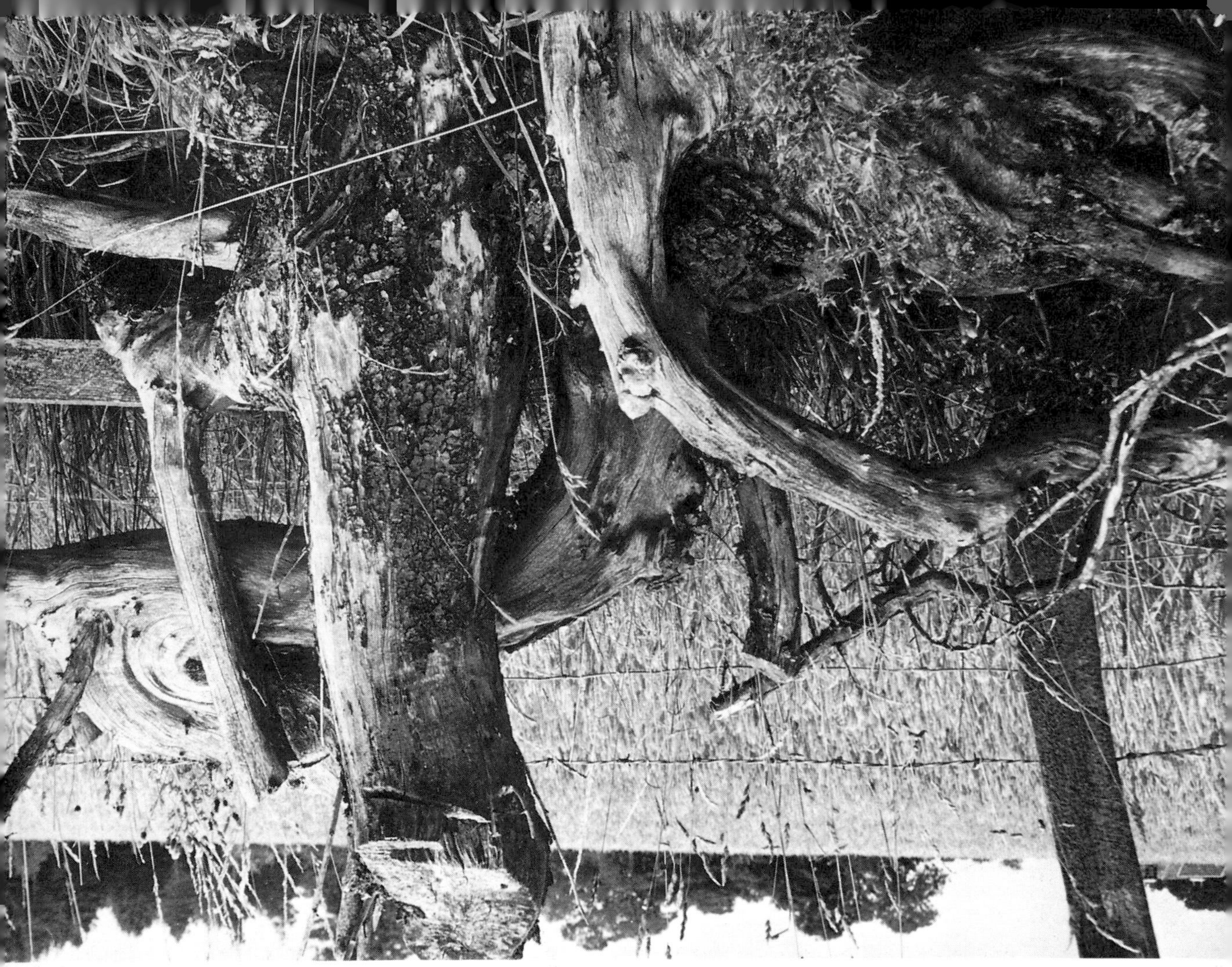

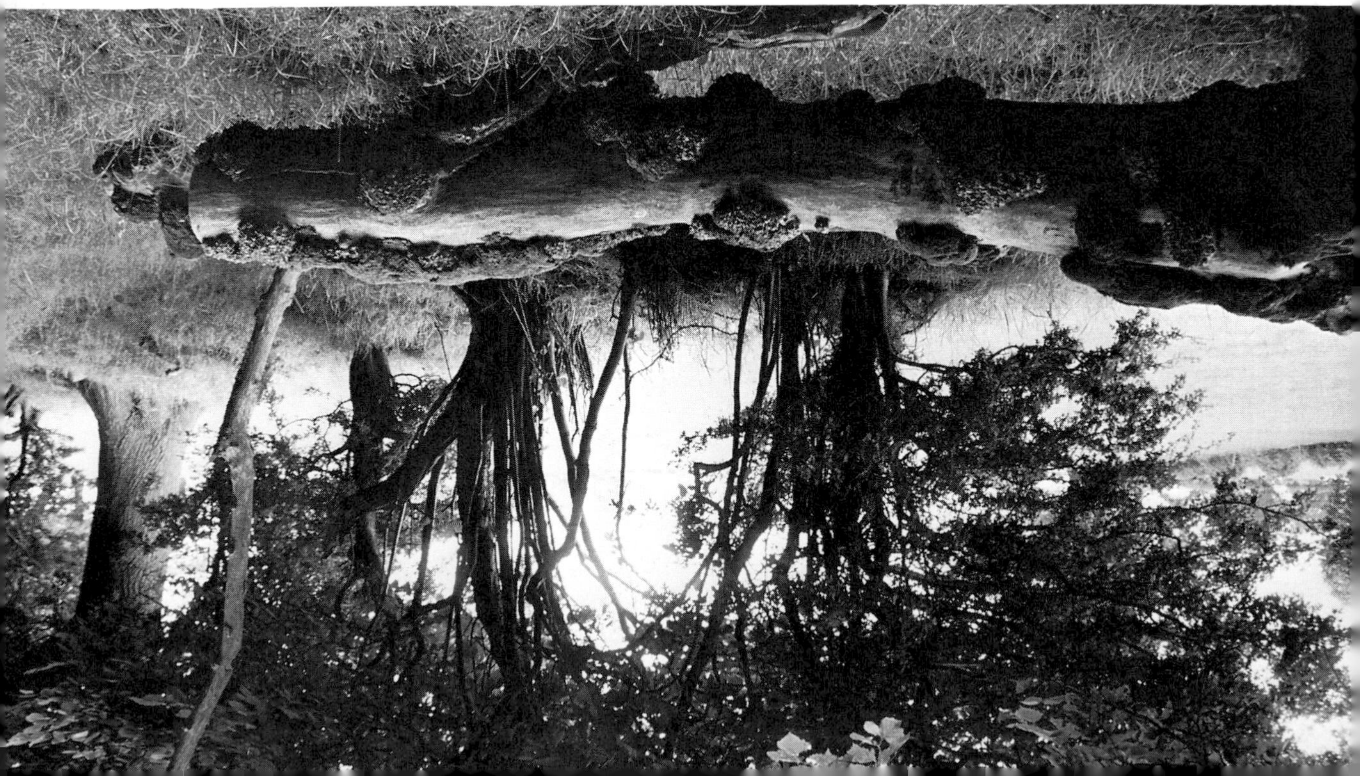

greatest possible subsidies. Arriving on the lands concerned, he fires all the employees except the tractor drivers, has the livestock slaughtered, drains the wetlands, grubs up orchards and hedgerows and shoots, traps or poisons the wildlife. He may then make a profit of up to £200 per acre (£500 per hectare), growing grain which nobody wants in barren prairie fields.

The English countryside is being recast in his image.

While a rambler can, quite rightly, be prosecuted for disturbing roosting bats, the devastator of life and loveliness across a chain of parishes is likely to end up a millionaire with a string of honours after his name. Indeed, any sizable gathering of county councillors and rural Justices of the Peace is likely to include some of the greatest vandals that our nation has ever spawned.

The grubbing-up of hedgerows has been the subject of much public criticism, but very little is said or done about the hedges which are slowly dying from neglect or killed by stubble-burning. Even in areas where hedges are still expected to perform their role as stock proof barriers, gaps are seldom repaired by laying or replanting. Normally a few fenceboards or strands of wire are slung across the breach. Repeated trimming without laying creates a scarred,

Stages in the death of Nidderdale hedgerow: TOP LEFT With the withdrawal of maintenance, gaps widen and standards fall, decay and are not replaced. BOTTOM LEFT Hedgerow trees die from neglect and the effects of stubble-burning. Strands of barbed wire replace the hedgerow. BELOW The dead relics of the hedge are bulldozed together to form a bonfire.

twiggy 'crust' to a hedge and gradually saps its vitality. Where the skills of laying have been lost or where the costs are too high, arable field hedges could be rejuvenated by coppicing every ten or fifteen years, as happens on the better-tended farms in some south-eastern counties, like Essex.

Once gaps appear in a neglected hedge they are likely to be widened by any livestock in adjacent fields. Gradually, the gaps exceed the hedgerow and eventually the position of a hedge may only be marked by a line of standard trees, the last survivors of the hedgerow. When the trees die, providing that the lost hedgeline is not ploughed, the final indication of a former hedgerow maybe the lynchet bank of soil which was stabilised by the hedge. In the course of a typical county outing the reader can expect to see hedges trimmed down to a worthless height of much less than three feet, hedges which are overgrown and gappy and in desperate need of laying, and lots of hedges with a twiggy crust. But evidence of planting or laying will be rare and special sights.

What of the future of hedgerows? The specialist literature seems to present a very gloomy picture. In an article in the *New Scientist* on 'The End of the English Landscape', Jon Tinker wrote that 'hedges are useless', and this outlook seems to have coloured later debate (though, of course, if you are a song bird, small animal or country-lover, then they are far from being useless). Conservationists have floated the idea that certain especially rich or historic hedges might be preserved through the system of Tree Preservation Orders, but in general the emphasis has fallen on appeals that ribbons or pockets of scrub or wetland might be allowed to flourish on poor ground between the prairie fields. Even the main conservational institutions seem to have signed the obituary of the hedgerow. It is argued that even if hedges were 'protected' the disconsolate farmers would deliberately neglect to maintain them and work for their 'accidental' destruction.

However, all this glum resignation takes no account of the maxim that 'he who pays the piper should call the tune.' Any government which dispenses agricultural subsidies on the profligate modern scale could pass legislation which would instantly outlaw the further destruction of hedges and make the receipt of farming hand-outs conditional on the proper maintenance of hedge-rows – and this could be achieved without calling upon public funds. Moreover, if the sums spent on storing unwanted grain were redirected instead to the more worthwhile task of restoring grubbed-out hedgerows considerable rural employment would be created, and we calculate that over 17,000 miles of new hedgerow could be planted each year, which would probably restore the post-war losses within a decade. How easy; how sensible; how far-sighted! How unlikely!

This will not happen, much as country-lovers may wish that it would. There is a faint possibility that future years will see a significant switch of subsidies towards farming activities which foster rather than undermine conservation. Hedge-planting grants are now available, but even if this policy were to be further developed it is likely that the grants would be siphoned off by the bigger, richer farmers, with no guarantee that, once hedges were planted and grants paid, the new hedgerows would be maintained. Conservational organisations, like the British Trust for Conservation Volunteers, are doing wonderful work in planting and laying hedges at the invitation of concerned landowners, yet nobody could sensibly argue that such efforts represent much more than a drop of altruism in a sea of greed.

One cannot help but reflect that when American tourists, on whom our economy so much depends, visit our countryside, they will now see only reminders of the bland monotony of rural Nebraska or Illinois; they would be entitled to feel conned by the tourism brochures which give no hint of the devastation caused by the removal of woodland and hedgerows.

Neither will our European visitors understand the British governmental contempt for genuine conservation. (I have just returned from a landscape lecture tour in the Netherlands and it is plain to me that the Dutch, still visitors to Britain in amazing numbers, are horrified and perplexed by the way that we tolerate the vandalism of what is regarded abroad as a common European heritage of scenery.) Why should they or other tourists invest in holidays amongst the wastelands of British agri-business?

For far too long the British have liked to imagine themselves as the standard-bearers of civilisation, perpetuating an image which may have been valid forty years ago but which is baseless and pathetic today. Filth from our power stations destroys forests from the Rhineland to Finland. We are the inept nuclear garbage collectors of the world. We flout agreed standards of water purity, we accept pesticides banned in the civilised world, and in almost every field of communal and environmental protection our standards are far below those of the continent.

Greed and deception have become sanctified in the fabric of the state.

Britain has become the dirty old man of Europe.

A nation once admired walks abroad in shame.

A nation weaned on a love of its countryside has stood by mute and inept and watched its heritage vanish.

Our disgrace is now proclaimed across a thousand countrysides.

Against the wishes of millions and for no insurmountable reason our hedgerows are disappearing. They will be sadly missed.

There still remains a slight possibility of salvation at the eleventh hour. In August 1986 the opposition Labour Party, with a conservational record which had hitherto been unencouraging, discussed a package of environmental policies which included a shift of subsidies from the barley barons to the smaller and more conscientious farmer and the protection of hedgerows through the application of planning controls. The summer of 1986 has been said to have witnessed the 'greening' of the main political parties although doubtless this greening is partly or largely based on the recognition that large numbers of conservation votes can be gained in post-Chernobyl Britain. But unless there is a substantial change in governmental attitude towards the land, it is certain that the future for hedgerows and our countryside is bleak indeed.

BIBLIOGRAPHY

Many of the books that are out of print and xerox copies of the articles are generally available for a small fee through the inter-library loan services offered by local and county libraries.

REFERENCES, AND A SELECTION OF BOOKS AND ARTICLES OF INTEREST

Addington, S., 'The Hedgerows of Tasburgh', *Norfolk Archaeology, 37*, 70–83. Chatto and Windus, 1978.

Andrews, Sir Christopher, *The Lives of Wasps and Bees*, 1969.

Arnold, G. W., 'The Influence of Ditch and Hedgerow Structure, Length of Hedgerows, and Area of Woodland and Garden on Bird Numbers on Farmland,' *Journal of Applied Ecology, 20*, 1983, 731–750.

Aston, M., 'Interpreting the Landscape', *Landscape Archaeology in Local Studies*, Batsford, 1985.

Bailey, A. J., *Hedges in Durham County*, A report from Durham County Conservation Trust, 1979.

Baird, W. W. and Tarrant, J. R., 'Vanishing Hedgerows', *Geographical Magazine, 44*, 1972, 545–51.

Baker, A. R. H. and Butlin, B. A., *Studies of Field Systems in the British Isles*, Cambridge University Press, 1973.

Bates, G. H., 'The vegetation of wayside and hedgerows', *Journal of Ecology, 25*, 1937, 469–81.

Beckett, K. and G., *Planting Native Trees and Shrubs*, Botanical Society of British Isles/NCC, 1979.

Beresford, M. W., *The Lost Villages of England*, Lutterworth Press, 1954.

Boatman, D. J., 'Mixed Hedges of the Former East Riding of Yorkshire', *Naturalist, 105*, 1980, 41–44.

Bowden, J. and Dean, G. J. W., 'The distribution of flying insects in and near a tall hedgerow', *Journal of Applied Ecology, 14*, 1977, 343–354.

Boyd, W. E., 'Prehistoric Hedges: Roman Iron Age Hedges from Bar Hill', *Scottish Archaeological Review*, Part I, 1984; 32–4.

British Trust for Conservation Volunteers, *Hedging: A Practical Conservation Handbook*, British Trust for Conservation Volunteers, 1984.

Caborn, J. A., *Shelterbelts and Windbreaks*, Faber and Faber, 1965.

Cameron, R. A. D., 'The Biology and History of Hedges: Exploring the Connections', *Biologist*, *31*(4), 1984, 203–208.

Cameron, R. A. D. and Pannett, D. J., 'Hedgerow Shrubs and Landscape History: Some Shropshire Examples', *Field Studies*, *5*, 1980, 177–194.

Cameron, R. A. D. and Pannett, D. J., 'Hedgerow Shrubs and Landscape History in the West Midlands', *Arboricultural Journal*, *4*, 1980, 147–152.

Clay, C. T., (ed.), *Yorkshire Deeds VII*, Yorkshire Archaeological Society Records Service, 83, *98*, 1932, p. 37.

Coppock, J. T., 'Changes in Farm and Field Boundaries in the Nineteenth Century', *Amateur Historian*, *3*, 1958, 292–8.

Countryside Commission, *New Agricultural Landscapes*, 1974.

Countryside Commission, *Agricultural Landscapes – A Second Look*, 1984.

Coward, T. A., *Life of the Wayside and Woodland*, Frederic Warne & Co., 1923.

Davies, E. T. and Dunford, W. J., 'Some physical and economic considerations of field enlargement,' *University of Exeter, Department of Agricultural Economics, Report, 133*, 1962.

Davis, B. N. K., 'The Hemiptera and Coleoptera of stinging nettle (*Urtica Dioica*) in East Anglia', *Journal of Applied Ecology*, *10*, 1973, 213–238.

Derry, T. K. and Jarman, T. L., *The Making of Modern Britain: Life and Works from George III to Elizabeth II*, John Murray, 1970 (repr., revised).

Eaton, H. J., 'Shelterbelts and Hedges', *Agriculture*, *5*, 1971, 185–9.

Elton, C. S., *The Pattern of Animal Communities*, Methuen, 1966.

Faull, M. L. and Moorhouse, S. A. (eds), *West Yorkshire: an Archaeological Survey to AD 1500*, Vols *1–3*. West Yorkshire Metropolitan County Council, 1981.

Faull, M. L. (ed.), *Studies in Late Anglo-Saxon Settlement*, Oxford University Department of External Studies, 1984.

Forestry Commission, 1955, 'Report of the Committee of Hedgerow and Farm Timber. *Merthyr Report*, HMSO, 1955.

Fowler, P. J., *The Farming of Prehistoric Britain*, Cambridge University Press, 1983.

Gonner, E. C. K., *Common land and Enclosure*, Frank Cass and Co, 1966 (2nd edn).

Harvey J., *Early Nurserymen*, Phillimore and Co., 1974.

Helliwell, D. R., 'The distribution of woodland plant species in some Shropshire hedgerows', *Biological Conservation*, *7*, 1975, 61–72.

Hewlett, G., 'Reconstructing a Historical Landscape from Field and Documentary Evidence: Otford in Kent', *Agricultural History Review*, *21* (2), 1973, 94–110.

Hewlett, G., 'Stages in the settlement of a downland parish: a study of hedges of Chelsham', *Surrey Ant. Collections*, 71, 1980, 91–6.

Hooper, M. D. and Holdgate, M. W. (eds), 'Hedges and Hedgerow Trees', *Proceedings of Monkswood Symposium 4*, Nature Conservancy Council, 1968.

Hooper, M. D., 'Dating Hedges', *Area*, *4*, 1970, 63–5.

Hooper, M. D., 'Hedges and history', *New Scientist, 48*, 1970, 598–600.

Hooper, M. D., 'The botanical importance of our hedgerows', in 'The flora of a changing Britain', *Botanical Soc. British Isles Report 11*, 1970, 58–62.

Hooper, M. D., 'Hedges and birds', *Birds, 3,*, 1970, 114–17.

Hooper, M. D., 'Hedgerow Removal,' *Biologist, 21* (2), 1974, 81–6.

Hoskins, W. G., *The Making of the English Landscape*, Hodder and Stoughton, 1955 and Penguin, 1970.

Hoskins, W. G., *Fieldwork in local history*, Faber and Faber, 1982, 2nd edn.

Howard, E., 'Essex Hedgerows as a Landmark of History', *Essex Review, 20*, 1911, 57–74.

Hunter, J. M., Hedges, J. D., Roberts, C. C. S. and Ranson, C. E. (eds), *Essex Landscape: the Historic Features*, Essex County Council, 1974.

James, N. D. G., *The Arboriculturalist's Companion*, Blackwell, 1972.

Johnson, C. J., 'The Statistical Limitation of Hedge Dating', *Local Historian, 14*, 1980, 28–33.

Johnson, W., 'Hedges – a Review of Some Early Literature', *Local Historian, 13*, 1978, 195–205.

Lee, B., *British Naturalists' Association Guide to Fields, Farms and Hedgerows*, Crowood Press, 1985.

Lewis, T., 'The Distribution of Flying Insects near a Low Hedgerow', *Journal of Applied Ecology, 6*, 1969, 443–452.

Lewis, T., 'The Diversity of the Insect Fauna in a Hedgerow and Neighbouring Fields', *Journal of Applied Ecology, 6*, 1969, 453–458

Mead, C., 'Where Have All the Migrants Gone?', *Natural World, 11*, 1984, 13–14.

Mills, D. R. (ed.), *English Rural Communities. The Impact of a Specialised Economy*, Macmillan, 1973.

Moore, N. W., Hooper, M. D. and Davis, B. N. K., 'Hedges. 1. Introduction and Reconnaissance Studies', *Journal of Applied Ecology, 7*, 1967, 549–57.

Nau, B. S. and Rands, E. B. 1975., 'A Comparative Study of Hedges on the Boulder Clay and Lower Greensand in the Maulden area', *Bedfordshire Naturalist, 30*, 1975, 39–52.

Pollard, E. and Relton, J., 'Hedges V: A Study of Small Mammals in Hedges and Cultivated Fields', *Journal of Applied Ecology, 7*, 1970, 549–57.

Pollard, E., 'Hedges VII, Woodland Relic Hedges in Huntingdon and Peterborough', *Journal of Ecology, 61*, 1973, 343–52.

Pollard, E., Hooper, M. D. and Moore, N. W., *Hedges*, Collins New Naturalist Series, 1974.

Presst, I., *British Birds: Lifestyles and Habits*, Batsford, 1982.

Price, M. J. S. (ed.), 1955, 'Yorkshire Deeds X', *Yorkshire Archaeological Society Records Service, 83, 306*, 1955, 110.

Prime, C. T., *Plant Life*, Collins Countryside Series, 1977.

Rackham, O., *Trees and Woodlands in the British Landscape*, J. M. Dent and Sons, 1976.

Rackham, O., *The History of the Countryside*, J. M. Dent and Sons, 1986.

Reece, R., 'Continuity on the Cotswolds: Some Problems of Ownership Settlement and Hedge Survey between Roman Britain and the Middle Ages', in *Landscape History 5*, 1983, 11–19.

Salter, B., *Beech Hedgerow Study*, Exmoor National Park Committee, 1973.

Sheppard, J. A., 'The Origins and Evolution of Field and Settlement Patterns in the Herefordshire Manor of Marden', in *Occasional Papers, 15*, Department of Geography, Queen Mary College, University of London, 1980.

Simms, E., *A Natural History of British Birds*, J. M. Dent and Sons, 1983.

Standing Conference for Local History, *Hedges and Local History*, National Council of Social Service, 1971.

Streeter, D. and Richardson, R., *Discovering Hedgerows*, BBC Publications, 1982.

Sturrock, F. and Cathie, J., *Farm Modernisation and the Countryside*, University of Cambridge, Department of Land Economy, 1980.

Taylor, C. C., *Fields in the English Landscape*, J. M. Dent and Sons, 1975.

Taylor, C. C., *The Archaeology of Gardens*, Shire Archaeology Series, 1983.

Terrasson, F. and Tendron, G., *Evolution and Conservation of Hedgerow Landscape in Europe*, Council of Europe, 1975.

Thorpe, H., 'The Lord and the Landscape', *Transactions, Birmingham Archaeological Society, 80*, 1965, 38–77.

Tillyard, R., 'Hedge Dating in North Norfolk: the Hooper Method Examined', *Norfolk Archaeology*, 1976, 272–279.

Tinker, J., 'The End of the English Landscape', *New Scientist, 64*, 1974, 722–27.

Way, J. M., 'Roadside verges and conservation in Britain: a review', *Biological Conservation, 12*, 1977, 65–74.

Whalley, P., *Butterfly Watching*, Severn House, 1980.

Williamson, K., 'The Bird Community of Farmland', *Bird Study 14*, 1967, 210–26.

Williamson, T. M., 'Roman and Medieval Settlement in N.W. Essex', University of Cambridge unpublished Ph.D. thesis, 1984.

Williamson, T. M., 'The Roman Countryside: Settlement and Agriculture in N. W. Essex', *Britannia, 15*, 1984, 225–230.

Williamson, T. M., 'Sites in the Landscape: Approaches to the Post-Roman Settlement of South-eastern England', *Archaeological Review from Cambridge, 4* (1), 1985.

Williamson, T., 'Parish Boundaries and Early Fields: Continuity and Discontinuity', *Journal of Historical Geography, 12* (3), 1986, 241–248.

Willmot, A., 'The Woody Species of Hedges with Special Reference to Age in Church Broughton Parish, Derbyshire', *Journal of Ecology, 68*, 1980, 269–285.

Woodell, S. R. J. (ed), *The English Landscape: Past, Present and Future*, Oxford University Press, 1985.

LEAFLETS, BOOKLETS, USEFUL IDENTIFICATION GUIDES

Clapham, A. R., Tutin, T. G. and Warburg, E. F., *Excursion Flora of the British Isles*, Cambridge University Press, 1959.

Countryside Commission leaflet No. 7, *Hedge Management*, 1980.

Countryside Commission for Scotland Information Sheet No. 1.3.2 CCS, *Shrubs for every site*.

Fairhurst, A., and Soothill, E., *The Blandford Guide to Trees of the British Countryside*, Blandford, 1981.

Farming and Wildlife Advisory Group, *Trees and Shrubs for Wildlife and the Landscape*, FWAG, 1982.

Farming and Wildlife Advisory Group, *A Hedgerow Code of Practice*, FWAG, 1983.

Gooders, J., *Field Guide to the Birds of Britain and Ireland*, Kingfisher Books, 1986.

Jones, D., *The Country Life Guide to Spiders of Britain and Northern Europe*, Country Life Books, 1983.

Keble-Martin, W., *The Concise British Flora in Colour*, Ebury, 1965 (recently reprinted).

Lawrence, M. J. and Brown, R. W., *Mammals of Britain. Their tracks, trails and signs*, Blandford, 1973.

Lyneborg, L., *Butterflies in Colour*, Blandford, 1975.

Lyneborg, L., *Moths in Colour*, Blandford, 1976.

Ministry of Agriculture, Fisheries and Food leaflets: No. 762, *Managing Farm Hedges*; No 763, *Planting Farm Hedges*; No. CCP 91, *Grants for Amenity Tree Planting*.

Nature Conservancy Council, *Hedges and Shelterbelts*, 1979

Nichols, D. O., Cooke, J. and Whiteley, D., *The Oxford Book of Invertebrates*, Oxford University Press, 1971.

Pollard, R. S. W., *Trees and the Law.* Leaflet No 6, Arboriculture Association, 1975.

Reader's Digest, *Field Guide to the Butterflies and Other Insects of Britain*, 1984.

Rose, F., *The Wild Flower Key*, Frederick Warne, 1981.

Young, G. and Jackman, B., *The Sunday Times Countryside Companion*, WATCH Trust for Environmental Education/Country Life Books, 1985.

INDEXES

Numbers in Italics refer to Illustrations

1 SCIENTIFIC NAMES OF FAUNA MENTIONED IN TEXT

·243·

2 SCIENTIFIC NAMES OF FLORA MENTIONED IN THE TEXT

GENERAL INDEX